Collected Short Stories

D. H. Lawrence

Collected Short Stories

Copyright © 2019 Indo-European Publishing

ISBN: 978-1-64439-032-0

CONTENTS

A MODERN LOVER

I

The road was heavy with mud. It was labour to move along it. The old, wide way, forsaken and grown over with grass, used not to be so bad. The farm traffic from Coney Grey must have cut it up. The young man crossed carefully again to the strip of grass on the other side.

It was a dreary, out-of-doors track, saved only by low fragments of fence and occasional bushes from the desolation of the large spaces of arable and of grassland on either side, where only the unopposed wind and the great clouds mattered, where even the little grasses bent to one another indifferent of any traveller. The abandoned road used to seem clean and firm. Cyril Mersham stopped to look round and to bring back old winters to the scene, over the ribbed red land and the purple wood. The surface of the field seemed suddenly to lift and break. Something had startled the peewits, and the fallow flickered over with pink gleams of birds white-breasting the sunset. Then the plovers turned, and were gone in the dusk behind.

Darkness was issuing out of the earth, and clinging to the trunks of the elms which rose like weird statues, lessening down the wayside. Mersham laboured forwards, the earth sucking and smacking at his feet. In front the Coney Grey farm was piled in shadow on the road. He came near to it, and saw the turnips heaped in a fabulous heap up the side of the barn, a buttress that rose almost to the eaves, and stretched out towards the cart-ruts in the road. Also, the pale breasts of the turnips got the sunset, and they were innumerable orange glimmers piled in the dusk. The two labourers who were pulping at the foot of the mound stood shadow-like to watch as he passed, breathing the sharp scent of turnips.

It was all very wonderful and glamorous here, in the old places that had seemed so ordinary. Three-quarters of the scarlet sun was settling among the branches of the elm in front, right ahead where he would come soon. But when he arrived at the brow where the hill swooped downwards, where the broad road ended suddenly, the sun had vanished from the space before him, and the evening star was white where the night urged up against the retreating, rose-coloured billow of day. Mersham passed through the stile and sat upon the remnant of the thorn tree on the brink of the valley. All the wide space before him was full of a mist of rose, nearly to his feet. The large ponds were hidden, the farms, the fields, the far-off coal-mine, under the rosy outpouring of twilight. Between him and the spaces of Leicestershire and the hills of Derbyshire, between him and all the South Country which he had fled, was the splendid rose-red strand of sunset, and the white star keeping guard.

Here, on the lee-shore of day, was the only purple showing of the woods and the great hedge below him; and the roof of the farm below him, with a

1

film of smoke rising up. Unreal, like a dream which wastes a sleep with unrest, was the South and its hurrying to and fro. Here, on the farther shore of the sunset, with the flushed tide at his feet, and the large star flashing with strange laughter, did he himself naked walk with lifted arms into the quiet flood of life.

What was it he wanted, sought in the slowly-lapsing tide of days? Two years he had been in the large city in the south. There always his soul had moved among the faces that swayed on the thousand currents in that node of tides, hovering and wheeling and flying low over the faces of the multitude like a sea-gull over the waters, stopping now and again, and taking a fragment of life-a look, a contour, a movement-to feed upon. Of many people, his friends, he had asked that they would kindle again the smouldering embers of their experience; he had blown the low fires gently with his breath, and had leaned his face towards their glow, and had breathed in the words that rose like fumes from the revived embers, till he was sick with the strong drug of sufferings and ecstasies and sensations, and the dreams that ensued. But most folk had choked out the fires of their fiercer experience with rubble of sentimentality and stupid fear, and rarely could he feel the hot destruction of Life fighting out its way.

Surely, surely somebody could give him enough of the philtre of life to stop the craving which tortured him hither and thither, enough to satisfy for a while, to intoxicate him till he could laugh the crystalline laughter of the star, and bathe in the retreating flood of twilight like a naked boy in the surf, clasping the waves and beating them and answering their wild clawings with laughter sometimes, and sometimes gasps of pain.

He rose and stretched himself. The mist was lying in the valley like a flock of folded sheep; Orion had strode into the sky, and the Twins were playing towards the West. He shivered, stumbled down the path, and crossed the orchard, passing among the dark trees as if among people he knew.

II

He came into the yard. It was exceedingly, painfully muddy. He felt a disgust of his own feet, which were cold, and numbed, and heavy.

The window of the house was uncurtained, and shone like a yellow moon, with only a large leaf or two of ivy, and a cord of honeysuckle hanging across it. There seemed a throng of figures moving about the fire. Another light gleamed mysteriously among the out-buildings. He heard a voice in the cow-shed, and the impatient movement of a cow, and the rhythm of milk in the bucket.

He hesitated in the darkness of the porch; then he entered without knocking. A girl was opposite him, coming out of the dairy doorway with a loaf of bread. She started, and they stood a moment looking at each other

2

across the room. They advanced to each other; he took her hand, plunged overhead, as it were, for a moment in her great brown eyes. Then he let her go, and looked aside, saying some words of greeting. He had not kissed her; he realised that when he heard her voice:

"When did you come?"

She was bent over the table, cutting bread-and-butter. What was it in her bowed, submissive pose, in the dark, small head with its black hair twining and hiding her face, that made him wince and shrink and close over his soul that had been open like a foolhardy flower to the night? Perhaps it was her very submission, which trammelled him, throwing the responsibility of her wholly on him, making him shrink from the burden of her.

Her brothers were home from the pit. They were two well-built lads of twenty and twenty-one. The coal-dust over their faces was like a mask, making them inscrutable, hiding any glow of greeting, making them strangers. He could only see their eyes wake with a sudden smile, which sank almost immediately, and they turned aside. The mother was kneeling at a big brown stew-jar in front of the open oven. She did not rise, but gave him her hand, saying: "Cyril! How are you?" Her large dark eyes wavered and left him. She continued with the spoon in the jar.

His disappointment rose as water suddenly heaves up the side of a ship. A sense of dreariness revived, a feeling, too, of the cold wet mud that he had struggled through.

These were the people who, a few months before, would look up in one fine broad glow of welcome whenever he entered the door, even if he came daily. Three years before, their lives would draw together into one flame, and whole evenings long would flare with magnificent mirth, and with play. They had known each other's lightest and deepest feelings. Now, when he came back to them after a long absence, they withdrew, turned aside. He sat down on the sofa under the window, deeply chagrined. His heart closed tight like a fir-cone, which had been open and full of naked seeds when he came to them.

They asked him questions of the South. They were starved for news, they said, in that God-forsaken hole.

"It is such a treat to hear a bit of news from outside," said the mother.

News! He smiled, and talked, plucking for them the leaves from off his tree: leaves of easy speech. He smiled, rather bitterly, as he slowly reeled off his news, almost mechanically. Yet he knew-and that was the irony of it-that they did not want his "records"; they wanted the timorous buds of his hopes, and the unknown fruits of his experience, full of the taste of tears and what sunshine of gladness had gone to their ripening. But they asked for his "news", and, because of some subtle perversity, he gave them what they begged, not what they wanted, not what he desired most sincerely to give them.

Gradually he exhausted his store of talk, that he had thought was limitless. Muriel moved about all the time, laying the table and listening, only looking now and again across the barren garden of his talk into his windows. But he hardened his heart and turned his head from her. The

3

boys had stripped to their waists, and had knelt on the hearth-rug and washed themselves in a large tin bowl, the mother sponging and drying their backs. Now they stood wiping themselves, the firelight bright and rosy on their fine torsos, their heavy arms swelling and sinking with life. They seemed to cherish the firelight on their bodies. Benjamin, the younger, leaned his breast to the warmth, and threw back his head, showing his teeth in a voluptuous little smile. Mersham watched them, as he had watched the peewits and the sunset.

Then they sat down to their dinners, and the room was dim with the steam of food. Presently the father and the eldest brother were in from the cow-sheds, and all assembled at table. The conversation went haltingly; a little badinage on Mersham's part, a few questions on politics from the father. Then there grew an acute, fine feeling of discord. Mersham, particularly sensitive, reacted. He became extremely attentive to the others at table, and to his own manner of eating. He used English that was exquisitely accurate, pronounced with the Southern accent, very different from the heavily-sounded speech of the home folk. His nicety contrasted the more with their rough, country habit. They became shy and awkward, fumbling for something to say. The boys ate their dinners hastily, shovelling up the mass as a man shovels gravel. The eldest son clambered roughly with a great hand at the plate of bread-and-butter. Mersham tried to shut his eyes. He kept up all the time a brilliant tea-talk that they failed to appreciate in that atmosphere. It was evident to him; without forming the idea, he felt how irrevocably he was removing them from him, though he had loved them. The irony of the situation appealed to him, and added brightness and subtlety to his wit. Muriel, who had studied him so thoroughly, confusedly understood. She hung her head over her plate, and ate little. Now and again she would look up at him, toying all the time with her knife-though it was a family for ugly hands-and would address him some barren question. He always answered the question, but he invariably disregarded her look of earnestness, lapped in his unbreakable armour of light irony. He acknowledged, however, her power in the flicker of irritation that accompanied his reply. She quickly hid her face again.

They did not linger at tea, as in the old days. The men rose, with an "Ah well!" and went about their farm-work. One of the lads lay sprawling for sleep on the sofa; the other lighted a cigarette and sat with his arms on his knees, blinking into the fire. Neither of them ever wore a coat in the house, and their shirt-sleeves and their thick bare necks irritated the stranger still further by accentuating his strangeness. The men came tramping in and out to the boiler. The kitchen was full of bustle, of the carrying of steaming water, and of draughts. It seemed like a place out of doors. Mersham shrank up in his corner, and pretended to read the Daily News. He was ignored, like an owl sitting in the stalls of cattle.

"Go in the parlour, Cyril. Why don't you? It's comfortable there."

Muriel turned to him with this reproach, this remonstrance, almost chiding him. She was keenly aware of his discomfort, and of his painful discord with his surroundings. He rose without a word and obeyed her.

4

III

The parlour was a long, low room with red colourings. A bunch of mistletoe hung from the beam, and thickly-berried holly was over the pictures-over the little gilt-blazed water-colours that he hated so much because he had done them in his 'teens, and nothing is so hateful as the self one has left. He dropped in the tapestried chair called the Countess, and thought of the changes which this room had seen in him. There, by that hearth, they had threshed the harvest of their youth's experience, gradually burning the chaff of sentimentality and false romance that covered the real grain of life. How infinitely far away, now, seemed Jane Eyre and George Eliot. These had marked the beginning. He smiled as he traced the graph onwards, plotting the points with Carlyle and Ruskin, Schopenhauer and Darwin and Huxley, Omar Khayyam, the Russians, Ibsen and Balzac; then Guy de Maupassant and Madame Bovary. They had parted in the midst of Madame Bovary. Since then had come only Nietzsche and William James. They had not done so badly, he thought, during those years which now he was apt to despise a little, because of their dreadful strenuousness, and because of their later deadly, unrelieved seriousness. He wanted her to come in and talk about the old times. He crossed to the other side of the fire and lay in the big horse-hair chair, which pricked the back of his head. He looked about, and stuffed behind him the limp green cushions that were always sweating down.

It was a week after Christmas. He guessed they had kept up the holly and mistletoe for him. The two photographs of himself still occupied the post of honour on the mantelpiece; but between them was a stranger. He wondered who the fellow could be; good-looking he seemed to be; but a bit of a clown beside the radiant, subtle photos of himself. He smiled broadly at his own arrogance. Then he remembered that Muriel and her people were leaving the farm come Lady-day. Immediately, in valediction, he began to call up the old days, when they had romped and played so boisterously, dances, and wild charades, and all mad games. He was just telling himself that those were the days, the days of unconscious, ecstatic fun, and he was smiling at himself over his information, when she entered.

She came in, hesitating. Seeing him sprawling in his old abandonment, she closed the door softly. For a moment or two she sat, her elbows on her knees, her chin in her hands, sucking her little finger, and withdrawing it from her lips with a little pop, looking all the while in the fire. She was waiting for him, knowing all the time he would not begin. She was trying to feel him, as it were. She wanted to assure herself of him after so many months. She dared not look at him directly. Like all brooding, constitutionally earnest souls, she gave herself away unwisely, and was defenceless when she found herself pushed back, rejected so often with contempt.

"Why didn't you tell me you were coming?" she asked at last.

"I wanted to have exactly one of the old tea-times, and evenings."

5

"Ay!" she answered with hopeless bitterness. She was a dreadful pessimist. People had handled her so brutally, and had cheaply thrown away her most sacred intimacies.

He laughed, and looked at her kindly.

"Ah, well, if I'd thought about it I should have known this was what to expect. It's my own fault."

"Nay," she answered, still bitterly; "it's not your fault. It's ours. You bring us to a certain point, and when you go away, we lose it all again, and receive you like creatures who have never known you."

"Never mind," he said easily. "If it is so, it is! How are you?"

She turned and looked full at him. She was very handsome; heavily moulded, coloured richly. He looked back smiling into her big, brown, serious eyes.

"Oh, I'm very well," she answered, with puzzled irony. "How are you?"

"Me? You tell me. What do you think of me?"

"What do I think?" She laughed a little nervous laugh and shook her head. "I don't know. Why-you look well-and very much of a gentleman."

"Ah-and you are sorry?"

"No-No, I am not! No! Only you're different, you see."

"Ah, the pity! I shall never be as nice as I was at twenty-one, shall I?" He glanced at his photo on the mantelpiece, and smiled, gently chaffing her.

"Well-you're different-it isn't that you're not so nice, but different. I always think you're like that, really."

She too glanced at the photo, which had been called the portrait of an intellectual prig, but which was really that of a sensitive, alert, exquisite boy. The subject of the portrait lay smiling at her. Then it turned voluptuously, like a cat spread out in the chair.

"And this is the last of it all-!"

She looked up at him, startled and pitiful.

"Of this phase, I mean," he continued, indicating with his eyes the room, the surroundings. "Of Crossleigh Bank, I mean, and this part of our lives."

"Ay!" she said, bowing her head, and putting into the exclamation all her depth of sadness and regret. He laughed.

"Aren't you glad?" he asked.

She looked up, startled, a little shocked.

"Good-bye's a fine word," he explained. "It means you're going to have a change, and a change is what you, of all people, want."

Her expression altered as she listened.

"It's true," she said. "I do."

"So you ought to say to yourself, 'What a treat! I'm going to say good-bye directly to the most painful phase of my life.' You make up your mind it shall be the most painful, by refusing to be hurt so much in the future. There you are! 'Men at most times are masters of their fates,' etcetera."

She pondered his method of reasoning, and turned to him with a little laughter that was full of pleading and yearning.

6

"Well," he said, lying, amiably smiling, "isn't that so?-and aren't you glad?"

"Yes!" she nodded. "I am-very glad."

He twinkled playfully at her, and asked, in a soft voice:

"Then what do you want?"

"Yes," she replied, a little breathlessly. "What do I?" She looked at him with a rash challenge that pricked him.

"Nay," he said, evading her, "do you even ask me that?"

She veiled her eyes, and said, meekly in excuse:

"It's a long time since I asked you anything, isn't it?"

"Ay! I never thought of it. Whom have you asked in the interim?"

"Whom have I asked?"-she arched her brows and laughed a monosyllable of scorn.

"No one, of course!" he said, smiling. "The world asks questions of you, you ask questions of me, and I go to some oracle in the dark, don't I?"

She laughed with him.

"No!" he said, suddenly serious. "Supposing you must answer me a big question-something I can never find out by myself?"

He lay out indolently in the chair and began smiling again. She turned to look with intensity at him, her hair's fine foliage all loose round her face, her dark eyes haunted with doubt, her finger at her lips. A slight perplexity flickered over his eyes.

"At any rate," he said, "you have something to give me."

She continued to look at him with dark, absorbing eyes. He probed her with his regard. Then he seemed to withdraw, and his pupils dilated with thought.

"You see," he said, "life's no good but to live-and you can't live your life by yourself. You must have a flint and a steel, both, to make the spark fly. Supposing you be my flint, my white flint, to spurt out red fire for me?"

"But how do you mean?" she asked breathlessly.

"You see," he continued, thinking aloud as usual: "thought-that's not life. It's like washing and combing and carding and weaving the fleece that the year of life has produced. Now I think-we've carded and woven to the end of our bundle-nearly. We've got to begin again-you and me-living together, see? Not speculating and poetising together-see?"

She did not cease to gaze absorbedly at him.

"Yes?" she whispered, urging him on.

"You see-I'll come back to you-to you-" He waited for her.

"But," she said huskily, "I don't understand."

He looked at her with aggressive frankness, putting aside all her confusions.

"Fibber!" he said gently.

"But-" she turned in her chair from him-"but not clearly."

He frowned slightly:

"Nay, you should be able by now to use the algebra of speech. Must I count up on your fingers for you what I mean, unit by unit, in bald arithmetic?"

7

"No-no!" she cried, justifying herself; "but how can I understand-the change in you? You used to say-you couldn't.-Quite opposite."

He lifted his head as if taking in her meaning.

"Ah, yes, I have changed. I forget. I suppose I must have changed in myself. I'm older-I'm twenty-six. I used to shrink from the thought of having to kiss you, didn't I?" He smiled very brightly, and added, in a soft voice: "Well-I don't, now."

She flushed darkly and hid her face from him.

"Not," he continued, with slow, brutal candour-"not that I know any more than I did then-what love is-as you know it-but-I think you're beautiful-and we know each other so well-as we know nobody else, don't we? And so we . . ."

His voice died away, and they sat in a tense silence, listening to the noise outside, for the dog was barking loudly. They heard a voice speaking and quieting him. Cyril Mersham listened. He heard the clatter of the barn door latch, and a slurring ring of a bicycle-bell brushing the wall.

"Who is it?" he asked, unsuspecting.

She looked at him, and confessed with her eyes, guiltily, beseeching. He understood immediately.

"Good Lord!-Him?" He looked at the photo on the mantelpiece. She nodded with her usual despair, her finger between her lips again. Mersham took some moments to adjust himself to the new situation.

"Well!-so he's in my place! Why didn't you tell me?"

"How could I?-he's not. Besides-you never would have a place." She hid her face.

"No," he drawled, thinking deeply. "I wouldn't. It's my fault altogether." Then he smiled, and said whimsically: "But I thought you kept an old pair of my gloves in the chair beside you."

"So I did, so I did!" she justified herself again with extreme bitterness, "till you asked me for them. You told me to-to take another man-and I did as you told me-as usual."

"Did I tell you?-did I tell you? I suppose I must. I suppose I am a fool. And do you like him?"

She laughed aloud, with scorn and bitterness.

"He's very good-and he's very fond of me."

"Naturally!" said Mersham, smiling and becoming ironical. "And how firmly is he fixed?"

IV

She was mortified, and would not answer him. The question for him now was how much did this intruder count. He looked, and saw she wore no ring-but perhaps she had taken it off for his coming. He began diligently to calculate what attitude he might take. He had looked for many women to wake his love, but he had been always disappointed. So he had kept himself virtuous, and waited. Now he would wait no longer. No woman and he could ever understand each other so well as he and Muriel whom he had fiercely educated into womanhood along with his own struggling towards a manhood of independent outlook. They had breathed the same air of thought, they had been beaten with the same storms of doubt and disillusionment, they had expanded together in days of pure poetry. They had grown so; spiritually, or rather psychically, as he preferred to say, they were married; and now he found himself thinking of the way she moved about the house.

The outer door had opened and a man had entered the kitchen, greeting the family cordially, and without any formality. He had the throaty, penetrating voice of a tenor singer, and it came distinctly over the vibrating rumble of the men's talking. He spoke good, easy English. The boys asked him about the "iron-men" and the electric haulage, and he answered them with rough technicalities, so Mersham concluded he was a working electrician in the mine. They continued to talk casually for some time, though there was a false note of secondary interest in it all. Then Benjamin came forward and broke the check, saying, with a dash of braggart taunting:

"Muriel's in th' parlour, Tom, if you want her."

"Oh, is she? I saw a light in; I thought she might be." He affected indifference, as if he were kept thus at every visit. Then he added, with a touch of impatience, and of the proprietor's interest: "What is she doing?"

"She's talking. Cyril Mersham's come from London."

"What!-is he here?"

Mersham sat listening, smiling. Muriel saw his eyelids lift. She had run up her flag of challenge taut, but continually she slackened towards him with tenderness. Now her flag flew out bravely. She rose, and went to the door.

"Hello!" she said, greeting the stranger with a little song of welcome in one word, such as girls use when they become aware of the presence of their sweetheart.

"You've got a visitor, I hear," he answered.

"Yes. Come along, come in!"

She spoke softly, with much gentle caressing.

He was a handsome man, well set-up, rather shorter than Mersham. The latter rose indolently, and held out his hand, smiling curiously into the beautiful, generous blue eyes of the other.

"Cyril-Mr. Vickers."

Tom Vickers crushed Mersham's hand, and answered his steady, smiling regard with a warm expansion of feeling, then bent his head, slightly confused.

"Sit here, will you?" said Mersham, languidly indicating the armchair.

"No, no, thanks, I won't. I shall do here, thanks." Tom Vickers took a chair and placed it in front of the fire. He was confusedly charmed with Mersham's natural frankness and courtesy.

"If I'm not intruding," he added, as he sat down.

9

"No, of course not!" said Muriel, in her wonderfully soft, fond tones-the indulgent tone of a woman who will sacrifice anything to love.

"Couldn't!" added Mersham lazily. "We're always a public meeting, Muriel and I. Aren't we, Miel? We're discussing affinities, that ancient topic. You'll do for an audience. We agree so beastly well, we two. We always did. It's her fault. Does she treat you so badly?"

The other was rather bewildered. Out of it all he dimly gathered that he was suggested as the present lover of Muriel, while Mersham referred to himself as the one discarded. So he smiled, reassured.

"How-badly?" he asked.

"Agreeing with you on every point?"

"No, I can't say she does that," said Vickers, smiling, and looking with little warm glances at her.

"Why, we never disagree, you know!" she remonstrated, in the same deep indulgent tone.

"I see," Mersham said languidly, and yet keeping his wits keenly to the point. "You agree with everything she says. Lord, how interesting!"

Muriel arched her eyelids with a fine flare of intelligence across at him, and laughed.

"Something like that," answered the other man, also indulgently, as became a healthy male towards one who lay limply in a chair and said clever nothings in a lazy drawl. Mersham noted the fine limbs, the solid, large thighs, and the thick wrists. He was classifying his rival among the men of handsome, healthy animalism, and good intelligence, who are children in simplicity, who can add two and two, but never xy and yx. His contours, his movements, his repose were, strictly, lovable. "But," said Mersham to himself, "if I were blind, or sorrowful, or very tired, I should not want him. He is one of the men, as George Moore says, whom his wife would hate after a few years for the very way he walked across the floor. I can imagine him with a family of children, a fine father. But unless he had a domestic wife-"

Muriel had begun to make talk to him.

"Did you cycle?" she asked, in that irritating private tone so common to lovers, a tone that makes a third person an impertinence.

"Yes-I was rather late," he replied, in the same caressing manner. The sense did not matter, the caress was everything.

"Didn't you find it very muddy?"

"Well, I did-but not any worse than yesterday."

Mersham sprawled his length in the chair, his eyelids almost shut, his fine white hands hanging over the arms of the chair like dead-white stoats from a bough. He was wondering how long Muriel would endure to indulge her sweetheart thus. Soon she began to talk second-hand to Mersham. They were speaking of Tom's landlady.

"You don't care for her, do you?" she asked, laughing insinuatingly, since the shadow of his dislike for other women heightened the radiance of his affection for her.

"Well, I can't say that I love her."

10

"How is it you always fall out with your landladies after six months? You must be a wretch to live with."

"Nay, I don't know that I am. But they're all alike; they're jam and cakes at first, but after a bit they're dry bread."

He spoke with solemnity, as if he uttered a universal truth. Mersham's eyelids flickered now and again. Muriel turned to him:

"Mr. Vickers doesn't like lodgings," she said.

Mersham understood that Vickers therefore wanted to marry her; he also understood that as the pretendant tired of his landladies, so his wife and he would probably weary one another. He looked this intelligence at Muriel, and drawled:

"Doesn't he? Lodgings are ideal. A good lodger can always boss the show, and have his own way. It's the time of his life."

"I don't think!" laughed Vickers.

"It's true," drawled Mersham torpidly, giving his words the effect of droll irony. "You're evidently not a good lodger. You only need to sympathise with a landlady-against her husband generally-and she'll move heaven and earth for you."

"Ah!" laughed Muriel, glancing at Mersham. "Tom doesn't believe in sympathising with women-especially married women."

"I don't!" said Tom emphatically, "-it's dangerous."

"You leave it to the husband," said Mersham.

"I do that! I don't want 'em coming to me with their troubles. I should never know the end."

"Wise of you. Poor woman! So you'll broach your barrel of sympathy for your wife, eh, and for nobody else?"

"That's it. Isn't that right?"

"Oh, quite. Your wife will be a privileged person. Sort of homebrewed beer to drink ad infinitum? Quite all right, that!"

"There's nothing better," said Tom, laughing.

"Except a change," said Mersham. "Now, I'm like a cup of tea to a woman."

Muriel laughed aloud at this preposterous cynicism, and knitted her brows to bid him cease playing ball with bombs.

"A fresh cup each time. Women never weary of tea. Muriel, I can see you having a rich time. Sort of long after-supper drowse with a good husband."

"Very delightful!" said Muriel sarcastically.

"If she's got a good husband, what more can she want?" asked Tom, keeping the tone of banter, but really serious and somewhat resentful.

"A lodger-to make things interesting."

"Why," said Muriel, intervening, "do women like you so?"

Mersham looked up at her, quietly, smiling into her eyes. She was really perplexed. She wanted to know what he put in the pan to make the balance go down so heavily on his side. He had, as usual, to answer her seriously and truthfully, so he said: "Because I can make them believe that black is green or purple-which it is, in reality." Then, smiling broadly as she

11

wakened again with admiration for him, he added: "But you're trying to make me conceited, Miel-to stain my virgin modesty."

Muriel glanced up at him with softness and understanding, and laughed low. Tom gave a guffaw at the notion of Mersham's virgin modesty. Muriel's brow wrinkled with irritation, and she turned from her sweetheart to look in the fire.

V

Mersham, all unconsciously, had now developed the situation to the climax he desired. He was sure that Vickers would not count seriously in Muriel's movement towards himself. So he turned away, uninterested.

The talk drifted for some time, after which he suddenly bethought himself:

"I say, Mr. Vickers, will you sing for us? You do sing, don't you?"

"Well-nothing to speak of," replied the other modestly, wondering at Mersham's sudden change of interest. He looked at Muriel.

"Very well," she answered him, indulging him now like a child. "But-" she turned to Mersham-"but do you, really?"

"Yes, of course. Play some of the old songs. Do you play any better?"

She began "Honour and Arms".

"No, not that!" cried Mersham. "Something quiet-'Sois triste et sois belle'." He smiled gently at her, suggestively. "Try 'Du bist wie eine Blume' or 'Pur dicesti'."

Vickers sang well, though without much imagination. But the songs they sang were the old songs that Mersham had taught Muriel years before, and she played with one of his memories in her heart. At the end of the first song, she turned and found him looking at her, and they met again in the poetry of the past.

"Daffodils," he said softly, his eyes full of memories.

She dilated, quivered with emotion, in response. They had sat on the rim of the hill, where the wild daffodils stood up to the sky, and there he had taught her, singing line by line: "Du bist wie eine Blume." He had no voice, but a very accurate ear.

The evening wore on to ten o'clock. The lads came through the room on their way to bed. The house was asleep save the father, who sat alone in the kitchen, reading The Octopus. They went in to supper.

Mersham had roused himself and was talking well. Muriel stimulated him, always, and turned him to talk of art and philosophy-abstract things that she loved, of which only he had ever spoken to her, of which only he could speak, she believed, with such beauty. He used quaint turns of speech, contradicted himself waywardly, then said something sad and whimsical, all in a wistful, irresponsible manner so that even the men leaned indulgent and deferential to him.

"Life," he said, and he was always urging this on Muriel in one form or another, "life is beautiful, so long as it is consuming you. When it is rushing through you, destroying you, life is glorious. It is best to roar away, like a fire with a great draught, white-hot to the last bit. It's when you burn a slow fire and save fuel that life's not worth having."

"You believe in a short life and a merry," said the father.

"Needn't be either short or merry. Grief is part of the fire of life-and suffering-they're the root of the flame of joy, as they say. No! With life, we're like the man who was so anxious to provide for his old age that he died at thirty from inanition."

"That's what we're not likely to do," laughed Tom.

"Oh, I don't know. You live most intensely in human contact-and that's what we shrink from, poor timid creatures, from giving our souls to somebody to touch; for they, bungling fools, will generally paw it with dirty hands."

Muriel looked at him with dark eyes of grateful understanding. She herself had been much pawed, brutally, by her brothers. But, then, she had been foolish in offering herself.

"And," concluded Mersham, "you are washed with the whitest fire of life-when you take a woman you love-and understand."

Perhaps Mersham did not know what he was doing. Yet his whole talk lifted Muriel as in a net, like a sea-maiden out of the waters, and placed her in his arms, to breathe his thin, rare atmosphere. She looked at him, and was certain of his pure earnestness, and believed implicitly he could not do wrong.

Vickers believed otherwise. He would have expressed his opinion, whatever it might be, in an: "Oh, ay, he's got plenty to say, and he'll keep on saying it-but, hang it all . . .!"

For Vickers was an old-fashioned, inarticulate lover; such as has been found the brief joy and the unending disappointment of a woman's life. At last he found he must go, as Mersham would not precede him. Muriel did not kiss him good-bye, nor did she offer to go out with him to his bicycle. He was angry at this, but more angry with the girl than with the man. He felt that she was fooling about, "showing off" before the stranger. Mersham was a stranger to him, and so, in his idea, to Muriel. Both young men went out of the house together, and down the rough brick track to the barn. Mersham made whimsical little jokes: "I wish my feet weren't so fastidious. They dither when they go in a soft spot like a girl who's touched a toad. Hark at that poor old wretch-she sounds as if she'd got whooping-cough."

"A cow is not coughing when she makes that row," said Vickers.

"Pretending, is she?-to get some Owbridge's? Don't blame her. I guess she's got chilblains, at any rate. Do cows have chilblains, poor devils?"

Vickers laughed and felt he must take this man into his protection. "Mind," he said, as they entered the barn, which was very dark. "Mind your forehead against this beam." He put one hand on the beam, and stretched out the other to feel for Mersham. "Thanks," said the latter gratefully. He knew the position of the beam to an inch, however dark the barn, but he allowed Vickers to guide him past it. He rather enjoyed being taken into Tom's protection.

13

Vickers carefully struck a match, bowing over the ruddy core of light and illuminating himself like some beautiful lantern in the midst of the high darkness of the barn. For some moments he bent over his bicycle-lamp, trimming and adjusting the wick, and his face, gathering all the light on its ruddy beauty, seemed luminous and wonderful. Mersham could see the down on his cheeks above the razor-line, and the full lips in shadow beneath the moustache, and the brush of the eyebrows between the light.

"After all," said Mersham, "he's very beautiful; she's a fool to give him up."

Tom shut the lamp with a snap, and carefully crushed the match under his foot. Then he took the pump from the bicycle, and crouched on his heels in the dimness, inflating the tyre. The swift, unerring, untiring stroke of the pump, the light balance and the fine elastic adjustment of the man's body to his movements pleased Mersham.

"She could have," he was saying to himself, "some glorious hours with this man-yet she'd rather have me, because I can make her sad and set her wondering."

But to the man he was saying:

"You know, love isn't the twin-soul business. With you, for instance, women are like apples on a tree. You can have one that you can reach. Those that look best are overhead, but it's no good bothering with them. So you stretch up, perhaps you pull down a bough and just get your fingers round a good one. Then it swings back and you feel wild and you say your heart's broken. But there are plenty of apples as good for you no higher than your chest."

Vickers smiled, and thought there was something in it-generally; but for himself, it was nothing.

They went out of the barn to the yard gate. He watched the young man swing over his saddle and vanish, calling "Good-night."

"Sic transit," he murmured-meaning Tom Vickers, and beautiful lustihood that is unconscious like a blossom.

Mersham went slowly in the house. Muriel was clearing away the supper things, and laying the table again for the men's breakfasts. But she was waiting for him as clearly as if she had stood watching in the doorway. She looked up at him, and instinctively he lifted his face towards her as if to kiss her. They smiled, and she went on with her work.

The father rose, stretching his burly form, and yawning. Mersham put on his overcoat.

"You will come a little way with me?" he said. She answered him with her eyes. The father stood, large and silent, on the hearth-rug. His sleepy, mazed disapproval had no more effect than a little breeze which might blow against them. She smiled brightly at her lover, like a child, as she pinned on her hat.

It was very dark outside in the starlight. He groaned heavily, and swore with extravagance as he went ankle-deep in mud.

"See, you should follow me. Come here," she commanded, delighted to have him in charge.

"Give me your hand," he said, and they went hand-in-hand over the

14

rough places. The fields were open, and the night went up to the magnificent stars. The wood was very dark, and wet; they leaned forward and stepped stealthily, and gripped each other's hands fast with a delightful sense of adventure. When they stood and looked up a moment, they did not know how the stars were scattered among the tree-tops till he found the three jewels of Orion right in front.

There was a strangeness everywhere, as if all things had ventured out alive to play in the night, as they do in fairy-tales; the trees, the many stars, the dark spaces, and the mysterious waters below uniting in some magnificent game.

They emerged from the wood on to the bare hillside. She came down from the wood-fence into his arms, and he kissed her, and they laughed low together. Then they went on across the wild meadows where there was no path.

"Why don't you like him?" he asked playfully.

"Need you ask?" she said simply.

"Yes. Because he's heaps nicer than I am."

She laughed a full laugh of amusement.

"He is! Look! He's like summer, brown and full of warmth. Think how splendid and fierce he'd be-"

"Why do you talk about him?" she said.

"Because I want you to know what you're losing-and you won't till you see him in my terms. He is very desirable-I should choose him in preference to me-for myself."

"Should you?" she laughed. "But," she added with soft certainty, "you don't understand."

"No-I don't. I suppose it's love; your sort, which is beyond me. I shall never be blindly in love, shall I?"

"I begin to think you never will," she answered, not very sadly. "You won't be blindly anything."

"The voice of love!" he laughed; and then: "No, if you pull your flowers to pieces, and find how they pollinate, and where are the ovaries, you don't go in blind ecstasies over them. But they mean more to you; they are intimate, like friends of your heart, not like wonderful, dazing fairies."

"Ay!" she assented, musing over it with the gladness of understanding him. "And then?"

Softly, almost without words, she urged him to the point.

"Well," he said, "you think I'm a wonderful, magical person, don't you?-and I'm not-I'm not as good, in the long run, as your Tom, who thinks you are a wonderful, magical person."

She laughed and clung to him as they walked. He continued, very carefully and gently: "Now, I don't imagine for a moment that you are princessy or angelic or wonderful. You often make me thundering mad because you're an ass . . ."

She laughed low with shame and humiliation.

"Nevertheless-I come from the south to you-because-well, with you I can be just as I feel, conceited or idiotic, without being afraid to be myself .

15

. ." He broke off suddenly. "I don't think I've tried to make myself out to you-any bigger or better than I am?" he asked her wistfully.

"No," she answered, in beautiful, deep assurance. "No! That's where it is. You have always been so honest. You are more honest than anybody ever-" She did not finish, being deeply moved. He was silent for some time, then he continued, as if he must see the question to the end with her:

"But, you know-I do like you not to wear corsets. I like to see you move inside your dress."

She laughed, half shame, half pleasure.

"I wondered if you'd notice," she said.

"I did-directly." There was a space of silence, after which he resumed: "You see-we would marry tomorrow-but I can't keep myself. I am in debt-"

She came close to him, and took his arm.

"-And what's the good of letting the years go, and the beauty of one's youth-?"

"No," she admitted, very slowly and softly, shaking her head.

"So-well!-you understand, don't you? And if you're willing-you'll come to me, won't you?-just naturally, as you used to come and go to church with me?-and it won't be-it won't be me coaxing you-reluctant? Will it?"

They had halted in front of a stile which they would have to climb. She turned to him in silence, and put up her face to him. He took her in his arms, and kissed her, and felt the night mist with which his moustache was drenched, and he bent his head and rubbed his face on her shoulder, and then pressed his lips on her neck. For a while they stood in silence, clasped together. Then he heard her voice, muffled in his shoulder, saying:

"But-but, you know-it's much harder for the woman-it means something so different for a woman."

"One can be wise," he answered, slowly and gently. "One need not blunder into calamities."

She was silent for a time. Then she spoke again.

"Yes, but-if it should be-you see-I couldn't bear it."

He let her go, and they drew apart, and the embrace no longer choked them from speaking. He recognised the woman defensive, playing the coward against her own inclinations, and even against her knowledge.

"If-if!" he exclaimed sharply, so that she shrank with a little fear. "There need be no ifs-need there?"

"I don't know," she replied, reproachfully, very quietly.

"If I say so-" he said, angry with her mistrust. Then he climbed the stile, and she followed.

"But you do know," he exclaimed. "I have given you books-"

"Yes, but-"

"But what?" He was getting really angry.

"It's so different for a woman-you don't know."

He did not answer this. They stumbled together over the mole-hills, under the oak trees.

"And look-how we should have to be-creeping together in the dark-"

This stung him; at once, it was as if the glamour went out of life. It was as if she had tipped over the fine vessel that held the wine of his desire, and

16

had emptied him of all his vitality. He had played a difficult, deeply-moving part all night, and now the lights suddenly switched out, and there was left only weariness. He was silent, tired, very tired, bodily and spiritually. They walked across the wide, dark meadow with sunken heads. Suddenly she caught his arm.

"Don't be cold with me!" she cried.

He bent and kissed in acknowledgment the lips she offered him for love.

"No," he said drearily; "no, it is not coldness-only-I have lost hold-for to-night." He spoke with difficulty. It was hard to find a word to say. They stood together, apart, under the old thorn tree for some minutes, neither speaking. Then he climbed the fence, and stood on the highway above the meadow.

At parting also he had not kissed her. He stood a moment and looked at her. The water in a little brook under the hedge was running, chuckling with extraordinary loudness: away on Nethermere they heard the sad, haunting cry of the wild-fowl from the North. The stars still twinkled intensely. He was too spent to think of anything to say; she was too overcome with grief and fear and a little resentment. He looked down at the pale blotch of her face upturned from the low meadow beyond the fence. The thorn boughs tangled above her, drooping behind her like the roof of a hut. Beyond was the great width of the darkness. He felt unable to gather his energy to say anything vital.

"Good-bye," he said. "I'm going back-on Saturday. But-you'll write to me. Good-bye."

He turned to go. He saw her white uplifted face vanish, and her dark form bend under the boughs of the tree, and go out into the great darkness. She did not say good-bye.

HER TURN

She was his second wife, and so there was between them that truce which is never held between a man and his first woman.

He was one for the women, and as such, an exception among the colliers. In spite of their prudery, the neighbour women liked him; he was big, naïve, and very courteous with them; he was so, even to his second wife.

Being a large man of considerable strength and perfect health, he earned good money in the pit. His natural courtesy saved him from enemies, while his fresh interest in life made his presence always agreeable. So he went his own way, had always plenty of friends, always a good job down pit.

He gave his wife thirty-five shillings a week. He had two grown-up sons at home, and they paid twelve shillings each. There was only one child by the second marriage, so Radford considered his wife did well.

Eighteen months ago, Bryan and Wentworth's men were out on strike for eleven weeks. During that time, Mrs. Radford could neither cajole nor entreat nor nag the ten shillings strike-pay from her husband. So that when the second strike came on, she was prepared for action.

Radford was going, quite inconspicuously, to the publican's wife at the "Golden Horn". She is a large, easy-going lady of forty, and her husband is sixty-three, moreover crippled with rheumatism. She sits in the little bar-parlour of the wayside public-house, knitting for dear life, and sipping a very moderate glass of Scotch. When a decent man arrives at the three-foot width of bar, she rises, serves him, surveys him over, and, if she likes his looks, says:

"Won't you step inside, sir?"

If he steps inside, he will find not more than one or two men present. The room is warm, quite small. The landlady knits. She gives a few polite words to the stranger, then resumes her conversation with the man who interests her most. She is straight, highly-coloured, with indifferent brown eyes.

"What was that you asked me, Mr. Radford?"

"What is the difference between a donkey's tail and a rainbow?" asked Radford, who had a consuming passion for conundrums.

"All the difference in the world," replied the landlady.

"Yes, but what special difference?"

"I s'll have to give it up again. You'll think me a donkey's head, I'm afraid."

"Not likely. But just you consider now, wheer . . ."

The conundrum was still under weigh, when a girl entered. She was swarthy, a fine animal. After she had gone out:

"Do you know who that is?" asked the landlady.

"I can't say as I do," replied Radford.

"She's Frederick Pinnock's daughter, from Stony Ford. She's courting our Willy."

"And a fine lass, too."

"Yes, fine enough, as far as that goes. What sort of a wife'll she make him, think you?"

"You just let me consider a bit," said the man. He took out a pocket-book and a pencil. The landlady continued to talk to the other guests.

Radford was a big fellow, black-haired, with a brown moustache, and darkish blue eyes. His voice, naturally deep, was pitched in his throat, and had a peculiar, tenor quality, rather husky, and disturbing. He modulated it a good deal as he spoke, as men do who talk much with women. Always, there was a certain indolence in his carriage.

"Our mester's lazy," his wife said. "There's many a bit of a jab wants doin', but get him to do it if you can."

But she knew he was merely indifferent to the little jobs, and not lazy.

He sat writing for about ten minutes, at the end of which time, he read:

"I see a fine girl full of life.
I see her just ready for wedlock,
But there's jealousy between her eyebrows
And jealousy on her mouth.
I see trouble ahead.
Willy is delicate.
She would do him no good.
She would never see when he wasn't well,
She would only see what she wanted-"

So, in phrases, he got down his thoughts. He had to fumble for expression, and therefore anything serious he wanted to say he wrote in "poetry", as he called it.

Presently, the landlady rose, saying:

"Well, I s'll have to be looking after our mester. I s'll be in again before we close."

Radford sat quite comfortably on. In a while, he too bade the company good-night.

When he got home, at a quarter-past eleven, his sons were in bed, and his wife sat awaiting him. She was a woman of medium height, fat and sleek, a dumpling. Her black hair was parted smooth, her narrow-opened eyes were sly and satirical, she had a peculiar twang in her rather sleering voice.

"Our missis is a puss-puss," he said easily, of her. Her extraordinarily smooth, sleek face was remarkable. She was very healthy.

He never came in drunk. Having taken off his coat and his cap, he sat down to supper in his shirt-sleeves. Do as he might, she was fascinated by him. He had a strong neck, with the crisp hair growing low. Let her be angry as she would yet she had a passion for that neck of his, particularly when she saw the great vein rib under the skin.

"I think, missis," he said, "I'd rather ha'e a smite o' cheese than this meat."

"Well, can't you get it yourself?"

19

"Yi, surely I can," he said, and went out to the pantry.

"I think, if yer comin' in at this time of night, you can wait on yourself," she justified herself.

She moved uneasily in her chair. There were several jam-tarts alongside the cheese on the dish he brought.

"Yi, Missis, them tan-tafflins'll go down very nicely," he said.

"Oh, will they! Then you'd better help to pay for them," she said, amiably, but determined.

"Now what art after?"

"What am I after? Why, can't you think?" she said sarcastically.

"I'm not for thinkin', missis."

"No, I know you're not. But wheer's my money? You've been paid the Union to-day. Wheer do I come in?"

"Tha's got money, an' tha mun use it."

"Thank yer. An' 'aven't you none, as well?"

"I hadna, not till we was paid, not a ha'p'ny."

"Then you ought to be ashamed of yourself to say so."

"'Appen so."

"We'll go shares wi' th' Union money," she said. "That's nothing but what's right."

"We shonna. Tha's got plenty o' money as tha can use."

"Oh, all right," she said. "I will do."

She went to bed. It made her feel sharp that she could not get at him.

The next day, she was just as usual. But at eleven o'clock she took her purse and went up town. Trade was very slack. Men stood about in gangs, men were playing marbles everywhere in the streets. It was a sunny morning. Mrs. Radford went into the furnisher-and-upholsterer's shop.

"There's a few things," she said to Mr. Allcock, "as I'm wantin' for the house, and I might as well get them now, while the men's at home, and can shift me the furniture."

She put her fat purse on to the counter with a click. The man should know she was not wanting "strap". She bought linoleum for the kitchen, a new wringer, a breakfast-service, a spring mattress, and various other things, keeping a mere thirty shillings, which she tied in a corner of her handkerchief. In her purse was some loose silver.

Her husband was gardening in a desultory fashion when she got back home. The daffodils were out. The colts in the field at the end of the garden were tossing their velvety brown necks.

"Sithee here, missis," called Radford, from the shed which stood halfway down the path. Two doves in a cage were cooing.

"What have you got?" asked the woman, as she approached. He held out to her in his big, earthy hand a tortoise. The reptile was very, very slowly issuing its head again to the warmth.

"He's wakkened up betimes," said Radford.

"He's like th' men, wakened up for a holiday," said the wife. Radford scratched the little beast's scaly head.

"We pleased to see him out," he said.

They had just finished dinner, when a man knocked at the door.

"From Allcock's!" he said.

The plump woman took up the clothes-basket containing the crockery she had bought.

"Whativer hast got theer?" asked her husband.

"We've been wantin' some breakfast-cups for ages, so I went up town an' got 'em this mornin'," she replied.

He watched her taking out the crockery.

"Hm!" he said. "Tha's been on th' spend, seemly."

Again there was a thud at the door. The man had put down a roll of linoleum. Mr. Radford went to look at it.

"They come rolling in!" he exclaimed.

"Who's grumbled more than you about the raggy oilcloth of this kitchen?" said the insidious, cat-like voice of the wife.

"It's all right, it's all right," said Radford.

The carter came up the entry with another roll, which he deposited with a grunt at the door.

"An' how much do you reckon this lot is?" he asked.

"Oh, they're all paid for, don't worry," replied the wife.

"Shall yer gi'e me a hand, mester?" asked the carter.

Radford followed him down the entry, in his easy, slouching way. His wife went after. His waistcoat was hanging loose over his shirt. She watched his easy movement of well-being as she followed him, and she laughed to herself.

The carter took hold of one end of the wire mattress, dragged it forth.

"Well, this is a corker!" said Radford, as he received the burden.

"Now the mangle!" said the carter.

"What dost reckon tha's been up to, missis?" asked the husband.

"I said to myself last wash-day, if I had to turn that mangle again, tha'd ha'e ter wash the clothes thyself."

Radford followed the carter down the entry again. In the street, women were standing watching, and dozens of men were lounging round the cart. One officiously helped with the wringer.

"Gi'e him thrippence," said Mrs. Radford.

"Gi'e him thysen," replied her husband.

"I've no change under half a crown."

Radford tipped the carter, and returned indoors. He surveyed the array of crockery, linoleum, mattress, mangle, and other goods crowding the house and the yard.

"Well, this is a winder!" he repeated.

"We stood in need of 'em enough," she replied.

"I hope tha's got plenty more from wheer they came from," he replied dangerously.

"That's just what I haven't." She opened her purse. "Two half-crowns, that's every copper I've got i' th' world."

He stood very still as he looked.

"It's right," she said.

There was a certain smug sense of satisfaction about her. A wave of anger came over him, blinding him. But he waited and waited. Suddenly

21

his arm leapt up, the fist clenched, and his eyes blazed at her. She shrank away, pale and frightened. But he dropped his fist to his side, turned, and went out, muttering. He went down to the shed that stood in the middle of the garden. There he picked up the tortoise, and stood with bent head, rubbing its horny head.

She stood hesitating, watching him. Her heart was heavy, and yet there was a curious, cat-like look of satisfaction round her eyes. Then she went indoors and gazed at her new cups, admiringly.

The next week he handed her his half-sovereign without a word.

"You'll want some for yourself," she said, and she gave him a shilling. He accepted it.

LOVE AMONG THE HAYSTACKS

I

The two large fields lay on a hillside facing south. Being newly cleared of hay, they were golden green, and they shone almost blindingly in the sunlight. Across the hill, half-way up, ran a high hedge, that flung its black shadow finely across the molten glow of the sward. The stack was being built just above the hedge. It was of great size, massive, but so silvery and delicately bright in tone that it seemed not to have weight. It rose dishevelled and radiant among the steady, golden-green glare of the field. A little farther back was another, finished stack.

The empty wagon was just passing through the gap in the hedge. From the far-off corner of the bottom field, where the sward was still striped grey with winrows, the loaded wagon launched forward, to climb the hill to the stack. The white dots of the hay-makers showed distinctly among the hay.

The two brothers were having a moment's rest, waiting for the load to come up. They stood wiping their brows with their arms, sighing from the heat and the labour of placing the last load. The stack they rode was high, lifting them up above the hedge-tops, and very broad, a great slightly-hollowed vessel into which the sunlight poured, in which the hot, sweet scent of hay was suffocating. Small and inefficacious the brothers looked, half-submerged in the loose, great trough, lifted high up as if on an altar reared to the sun.

Maurice, the younger brother, was a handsome young fellow of twenty-one, careless and debonair, and full of vigour. His grey eyes, as he taunted his brother, were bright and baffled with a strong emotion. His swarthy face had the same peculiar smile, expectant and glad and nervous, of a young man roused for the first time in passion.

"Tha sees," he said, as he leaned on the pommel of his fork, "tha thowt as tha'd done me one, didna ter?" He smiled as he spoke, then fell again into his pleasant torment of musing.

"I thought nowt-tha knows so much," retorted Geoffrey, with the touch of a sneer. His brother had the better of him. Geoffrey was a very heavy, hulking fellow, a year older than Maurice. His blue eyes were unsteady, they glanced away quickly; his mouth was morbidly sensitive. One felt him wince away, through the whole of his great body. His inflamed self-consciousness was a disease in him.

"Ah but though, I know tha did," mocked Maurice. "Tha went slinkin' off"-Geoffrey winced convulsively-"thinking as that wor the last night as any of us'ud ha'e ter stop here, an' so tha'd leave me to sleep out, though it wor thy turn-"

He smiled to himself, thinking of the result of Geoffrey's ruse.

"I didna go slinkin' off neither," retorted Geoffrey, in his heavy, clumsy manner, wincing at the phrase. "Didna my feyther send me to fetch some coal-"

"Oh yes, oh yes-we know all about it. But tha sees what tha missed, my lad."

Maurice, chuckling, threw himself on his back in the bed of hay. There was absolutely nothing in his world, then, except the shallow ramparts of the stack, and the blazing sky. He clenched his fists tight, threw his arms across his face, and braced his muscles again. He was evidently very much moved, so acutely that it was hardly pleasant, though he still smiled. Geoffrey, standing behind him, could just see his red mouth, with the young moustache like black fur, curling back and showing the teeth in a smile. The elder brother leaned his chin on the pommel of his fork, looking out across the country.

Far away was the faint blue heap of Nottingham. Between, the country lay under a haze of heat, with here and there a flag of colliery smoke waving. But near at hand, at the foot of the hill, across the deep-hedged high road, was only the silence of the old church and the castle farm, among their trees. The large view only made Geoffrey more sick. He looked away, to the wagons crossing the field below him, the empty cart like a big insect moving down hill, the load coming up, rocking like a ship, the brown head of the horse ducking, the brown knees lifted and planted strenuously. Geoffrey wished it would be quick.

"Tha didna think-"

Geoffrey started, coiled within himself, and looked down at the handsome lips moving in speech below the brown arms of his brother.

"Tha didna think 'er'd be thur wi' me-or tha wouldna ha' left me to it," Maurice said, ending with a little laugh of excited memory. Geoffrey flushed with hate, and had an impulse to set his foot on that moving, taunting mouth, which was there below him. There was silence for a time, then, in a peculiar tone of delight, Maurice's voice came again, spelling out the words, as it were:

> "Ich bin klein, mein Herz ist rein,
> Ist niemand d'rin als Christ allein."

Maurice chuckled, then, convulsed at a twinge of recollection, keen as pain, he twisted over, pressed himself into the hay.

"Can thee say thy prayers in German?" came his muffled voice.

"I non want," growled Geoffrey.

Maurice chuckled. His face was quite hidden, and in the dark he was going over again his last night's experiences.

"What about kissing 'er under th' ear, Sonny," he said, in a curious, uneasy tone. He writhed, still startled and inflamed by his first contact with love.

Geoffrey's heart swelled within him, and things went dark. He could not see the landscape.

"An' there's just a nice two-handful of her bosom," came the low, provocative tones of Maurice, who seemed to be talking to himself.

The two brothers were both fiercely shy of women, and until this hay harvest, the whole feminine sex had been represented by their mother and in presence of any other women they were dumb louts. Moreover, brought up by a proud mother, a stranger in the country, they held the common girls as beneath them, because beneath their mother, who spoke pure English, and was very quiet. Loud-mouthed and broad-tongued the common girls were. So these two young men had grown up virgin but tormented.

Now again Maurice had the start of Geoffrey, and the elder brother was deeply mortified. There was a danger of his sinking into a morbid state, from sheer lack of living, lack of interest. The foreign governess at the Vicarage, whose garden lay beside the top field, had talked to the lads through the hedge, and had fascinated them. There was a great elder bush, with its broad creamy flowers crumbling on to the garden path, and into the field. Geoffrey never smelled elder-flower without starting and wincing, thinking of the strange foreign voice that had so startled him as he mowed out with the scythe in the hedge bottom. A baby had run through the gap, and the Fräulein, calling in German, had come brushing down the flowers in pursuit. She had started so on seeing a man standing there in the shade, that for a moment she could not move: and then she had blundered into the rake which was lying by his side. Geoffrey, forgetting she was a woman when he saw her pitch forward, had picked her up carefully, asking: "Have you hurt you?"

Then she had broken into a laugh, and answered in German, showing him her arms, and knitting her brows. She was nettled rather badly.

"You want a dock leaf," he said. She frowned in a puzzled fashion.

"A dock leaf?" she repeated. He had rubbed her arms with the green leaf.

And now, she had taken to Maurice. She had seemed to prefer himself at first. Now she had sat with Maurice in the moonlight, and had let him kiss her. Geoffrey sullenly suffered, making no fight.

Unconsciously, he was looking at the Vicarage garden. There she was, in a golden-brown dress. He took off his hat, and held up his right hand in greeting to her. She, a small, golden figure, waved her hand negligently from among the potato rows. He remained, arrested, in the same posture, his hat in his left hand, his right arm upraised, thinking. He could tell by the negligence of her greeting that she was waiting for Maurice. What did she think of himself? Why wouldn't she have him?

Hearing the voice of the wagoner leading the load, Maurice rose. Geoffrey still stood in the same way, but his face was sullen, and his upraised hand was slack with brooding. Maurice faced up-hill. His eyes lit up and he laughed. Geoffrey dropped his own arm, watching.

"Lad!" chuckled Maurice. "I non knowed 'er wor there." He waved his hand clumsily. In these matters Geoffrey did better. The elder brother watched the girl. She ran to the end of the path, behind the bushes, so that she was screened from the house. Then she waved her handkerchief wildly. Maurice did not notice the manoeuvre. There was the cry of a child. The girl's figure vanished, reappeared holding up a white childish bundle, and

25

came down the path. There she put down her charge, sped up-hill to a great ash-tree, climbed quickly to a large horizontal bar that formed the fence there, and, standing poised, blew kisses with both her hands, in a foreign fashion that excited the brothers. Maurice laughed aloud, as he waved his red handkerchief.

"Well, what's the danger?" shouted a mocking voice from below. Maurice collapsed, blushing furiously.

"Nowt!" he called.

There was a hearty laugh from below.

The load rode up, sheered with a hiss against the stack, then sank back again upon the scotches. The brothers ploughed across the mass of hay, taking the forks. Presently a big, burly man, red and glistening, climbed to the top of the load. Then he turned round, scrutinized the hillside from under his shaggy brows. He caught sight of the girl under the ash-tree.

"Oh, that's who it is," he laughed. "I thought it was some such bird, but I couldn't see her."

The father laughed in a hearty, chaffing way, then began to teem the load. Geoffrey, on the stack above, received his great forkfuls, and swung them over to Maurice, who took them, placed them, building the stack. In the intense sunlight, the three worked in silence, knit together in a brief passion of work. The father stirred slowly for a moment, getting the hay from under his feet. Geoffrey waited, the blue tines of his fork glittering in expectation: the mass rose, his fork swung beneath it, there was a light clash of blades, then the hay was swept on to the stack, caught by Maurice, who placed it judiciously. One after another, the shoulders of the three men bowed and braced themselves. All wore light blue, bleached shirts, that stuck close to their backs. The father moved mechanically, his thick, rounded shoulders bending and lifting dully: he worked monotonously. Geoffrey flung away his strength. His massive shoulders swept and flung the hay extravagantly.

"Dost want to knock me ower?" asked Maurice angrily. He had to brace himself against the impact. The three men worked intensely, as if some will urged them. Maurice was light and swift at the work, but he had to use his judgement. Also, when he had to place the hay along the far ends, he had some distance to carry it. So he was too slow for Geoffrey. Ordinarily, the elder would have placed the hay as far as possible where his brother wanted it. Now, however, he pitched his forkfuls into the middle of the stack. Maurice strode swiftly and handsomely across the bed, but the work was too much for him. The other two men, clenched in their receive and deliver, kept up a high pitch of labour. Geoffrey still flung the hay at random. Maurice was perspiring heavily with heat and exertion, and was getting worried. Now and again, Geoffrey wiped his arm across his brow, mechanically, like an animal. Then he glanced with satisfaction at Maurice's moiled condition, and caught the next forkful.

"Wheer dost think thou'rt hollin' it, fool!" panted Maurice, as his brother flung a forkful out of reach.

"Wheer I've a mind," answered Geoffrey.

Maurice toiled on, now very angry. He felt the sweat trickling down his

26

body: drops fell into his long black lashes, blinding him, so that he had to stop and angrily dash his eyes clear. The veins stood out in his swarthy neck. He felt he would burst, or drop, if the work did not soon slacken off. He heard his father's fork dully scrape the cart bottom.

"There, the last," the father panted. Geoffrey tossed the last light lot at random, took off his hat, and, steaming in the sunshine as he wiped himself, stood complacently watching Maurice struggle with clearing the bed.

"Don't you think you've got your bottom corner a bit far out?" came the father's voice from below. "You'd better be drawing in now, hadn't you?"

"I thought you said next load," Maurice called, sulkily.

"Aye! All right. But isn't this bottom corner-?"

Maurice, impatient, took no notice.

Geoffrey strode over the stack, and stuck his fork in the offending corner. "What-here?" he bawled in his great voice.

"Aye-isn't it a bit loose?" came the irritating voice.

Geoffrey pushed his fork in the jutting corner, and, leaning his weight on the handle, shoved. He thought it shook. He thrust again with all his power. The mass swayed.

"What art up to, tha fool!" cried Maurice, in a high voice.

"Mind who tha'rt callin' a fool," said Geoffrey, and he prepared to push again. Maurice sprang across, and elbowed his brother aside. On the yielding, swaying bed of hay, Geoffrey lost his foothold, and fell grovelling. Maurice tried the corner.

"It's solid enough," he shouted angrily.

"Aye-all right," came the conciliatory voice of the father; "you do get a bit of rest now there's such a long way to cart it," he added reflectively.

Geoffrey had got to his feet.

"Tha'll mind who tha'rt nudging, I can tell thee," he threatened heavily; adding, as Maurice continued to work, "an' tha non ca's him a fool again, dost hear?"

"Not till next time," sneered Maurice.

As he worked silently round the stack, he neared where his brother stood like a sullen statue, leaning on his fork-handle, looking out over the countryside. Maurice's heart quickened in its beat. He worked forward, until a point of his fork caught in the leather of Geoffrey's boot, and the metal rang sharply.

"Are ter going ta shift thysen?" asked Maurice threateningly. There was no reply from the great block. Maurice lifted his upper lip like a dog. Then he put out his elbow, and tried to push his brother into the stack, clear of his way.

"Who are ter shovin'?" came the deep, dangerous voice.

"Thaïgh," replied Maurice, with a sneer, and straightway the two brothers set themselves against each other, like opposing bulls, Maurice trying his hardest to shift Geoffrey from his footing, Geoffrey leaning all his weight in resistance. Maurice, insecure in his footing, staggered a little, and Geoffrey's weight followed him. He went slithering over the edge of the stack.

27

Geoffrey turned white to the lips, and remained standing, listening. He heard the fall. Then a flush of darkness came over him, and he remained standing only because he was planted. He had not strength to move. He could hear no sound from below, was only faintly aware of a sharp shriek from a long way off. He listened again. Then he filled with sudden panic.

"Feyther!" he roared, in his tremendous voice: "Feyther! Feyther!"

The valley re-echoed with the sound. Small cattle on the hill-side looked up. Men's figures came running from the bottom field, and much nearer a woman's figure was racing across the upper field. Geoffrey waited in terrible suspense.

"Ah-h!" he heard the strange, wild voice of the girl cry out. "Ah-h!"-and then some foreign wailing speech. Then: "Ah-h! Are you dea-ed!"

He stood sullenly erect on the stack, not daring to go down, longing to hide in the hay, but too sullen to stoop out of sight. He heard his eldest brother come up, panting:

"Whatever's amiss!" and then the labourer, and then his father.

"Whatever have you been doing?" he heard his father ask, while yet he had not come round the corner of the stack. And then, in a low, bitter tone:

"Eh, he's done for! I'd no business to ha' put it all on that stack."

There was a moment or two of silence, then the voice of Henry, the eldest brother, said crisply:

"He's not dead-he's coming round."

Geoffrey heard, but was not glad. He had as lief Maurice were dead. At least that would be final: better than meeting his brother's charges, and of seeing his mother pass to the sick-room. If Maurice was killed, he himself would not explain, no, not a word, and they could hang him if they liked. If Maurice were only hurt, then everybody would know, and Geoffrey could never lift his face again. What added torture, to pass along, everybody knowing. He wanted something that he could stand back to, something definite, if it were only the knowledge that he had killed his brother. He must have something firm to back up to, or he would go mad. He was so lonely, he who above all needed the support of sympathy.

"No, he's commin' to; I tell you he is," said the labourer.

"He's not dea-ed, he's not dea-ed," came the passionate, strange sing-song of the foreign girl. "He's not dead-no-o."

"He wants some brandy-look at the colour of his lips," said the crisp, cold voice of Henry. "Can you fetch some?"

"Wha-at? Fetch?" Fräulein did not understand.

"Brandy," said Henry, very distinct.

"Brrandy!" she re-echoed.

"You go, Bill," groaned the father.

"Aye, I'll go," replied Bill, and he ran across the field.

Maurice was not dead, nor going to die. This Geoffrey now realized. He was glad after all that the extreme penalty was revoked. But he hated to think of himself going on. He would always shrink now. He had hoped and hoped for the time when he would be careless, bold as Maurice, when he would not wince and shrink. Now he would always be the same, coiling up in himself like a tortoise with no shell.

28

"Ah-h! He's getting better!" came the wild voice of the Fräulein, and she began to cry, a strange sound, that startled the men, made the animal bristle within them. Geoffrey shuddered as he heard, between her sobbing, the impatient moaning of his brother as the breath came back.

The labourer returned at a run, followed by the Vicar. After the brandy, Maurice made more moaning, hiccuping noise. Geoffrey listened in torture. He heard the Vicar asking for explanations. All the united, anxious voices replied in brief phrases.

"It was that other," cried the Fräulein. "He knocked him over-Ha!"

She was shrill and vindictive.

"I don't think so," said the father to the Vicar, in a quite audible but private tone, speaking as if the Fräulein did not understand his English.

The Vicar addressed his children's governess in bad German. She replied in a torrent which he would not confess was too much for him. Maurice was making little moaning, sighing noises.

"Where's your pain, boy, eh?" the father asked, pathetically.

"Leave him alone a bit," came the cool voice of Henry. "He's winded, if no more."

"You'd better see that no bones are broken," said the anxious Vicar.

"It wor a blessing as he should a dropped on that heap of hay just there," said the labourer. "If he'd happened to ha' catched hisself on this nog o' wood 'e wouldna ha' stood much chance."

Geoffrey wondered when he would have courage to venture down. He had wild notions of pitching himself head foremost from the stack: if he could only extinguish himself, he would be safe. Quite frantically, he longed not to be. The idea of going through life thus coiled up within himself in morbid self-consciousness, always lonely, surly, and a misery, was enough to make him cry out. What would they all think when they knew he had knocked Maurice off that high stack?

They were talking to Maurice down below. The lad had recovered in great measure, and was able to answer faintly.

"Whatever was you doin'?" the father asked gently. "Was you playing about with our Geoffrey?-Aye, and where is he?"

Geoffrey's heart stood still.

"I dunno," said Henry, in a curious, ironic tone.

"Go an' have a look," pleaded the father, infinitely relieved over one son, anxious now concerning the other. Geoffrey could not bear that his eldest brother should climb up and question him in his high-pitched drawl of curiosity. The culprit doggedly set his feet on the ladder. His nailed boots slipped a rung.

"Mind yourself," shouted the overwrought father.

Geoffrey stood like a criminal at the foot of the ladder, glancing furtively at the group. Maurice was lying, pale and slightly convulsed, upon a heap of hay. The Fräulein was kneeling beside his head. The Vicar had the lad's shirt full open down the breast, and was feeling for broken ribs. The father knelt on the other side, the labourer and Henry stood aside.

"I can't find anything broken," said the Vicar, and he sounded slightly disappointed.

"There's nowt broken to find," murmured Maurice, smiling.

The father started. "Eh?" he said. "Eh?" and he bent over the invalid.

"I say it's not hurt me," repeated Maurice.

"What were you doing?" asked the cold, ironic voice of Henry. Geoffrey turned his head away: he had not yet raised his face.

"Nowt as I know on," he muttered in a surly tone.

"Why!" cried Fräulein in a reproachful tone. "I see him-knock him over!" She made a fierce gesture with her elbow. Henry curled his long moustache sardonically.

"Nay lass, niver," smiled the wan Maurice. "He was fur enough away from me when I slipped."

"Oh, ah!" cried the Fräulein, not understanding.

"Yi," smiled Maurice indulgently.

"I think you're mistaken," said the father, rather pathetically, smiling at the girl as if she were "wanting".

"Oh no," she cried. "I see him."

"Nay, lass," smiled Maurice quietly.

She was a Pole, named Paula Jablonowsky: young, only twenty years old, swift and light as a wild cat, with a strange, wild-cat way of grinning. Her hair was blonde and full of life, all crisped into many tendrils with vitality, shaking round her face. Her fine blue eyes were peculiarly lidded, and she seemed to look piercingly, then languorously, like a wild cat. She had somewhat Slavonic cheekbones, and was very much freckled. It was evident that the Vicar, a pale, rather cold man, hated her.

Maurice lay pale and smiling in her lap, whilst she cleaved to him like a mate. One felt instinctively that they were mated. She was ready at any minute to fight with ferocity in his defence, now he was hurt. Her looks at Geoffrey were full of fierceness. She bowed over Maurice and caressed him with her foreign-sounding English.

"You say what you lai-ike," she laughed, giving him lordship over her.

"Hadn't you better be going and looking what has become of Margery?" asked the Vicar in tones of reprimand.

"She is with her mother-I heared her. I will go in a whai-ile," smiled the girl, coolly.

"Do you feel as if you could stand?" asked the father, still anxiously.

"Aye, in a bit," smiled Maurice.

"You want to get up?" caressed the girl, bowing over him, till her face was not far from his.

"I'm in no hurry," he replied, smiling brilliantly.

This accident had given him quite a strange new ease, an authority. He felt extraordinarily glad. New power had come to him all at once.

"You in no hurry," she repeated, gathering his meaning. She smiled tenderly: she was in his service.

"She leaves us in another month-Mrs Inwood could stand no more of her," apologized the Vicar quietly to the father.

"Why, is she-?"

"Like a wild thing-disobedient, and insolent."

"Ha!"

The father sounded abstract.

"No more foreign governesses for me."

Maurice stirred, and looked up at the girl.

"You stand up?" she asked brightly. "You well?"

He laughed again, showing his teeth winsomely. She lifted his head, sprung to her feet, her hands still holding his head, then she took him under the armpits and had him on his feet before anyone could help. He was much taller than she. He grasped her strong shoulders heavily, leaned against her, and, feeling her round, firm breast doubled up against his side, he smiled, catching his breath.

"You see I'm all right," he gasped. "I was only winded."

"You all raïght?" she cried, in great glee.

"Yes, I am."

He walked a few steps after a moment.

"There's nowt ails me, Father," he laughed.

"Quite well, you?" she cried in a pleading tone. He laughed outright, looked down at her, touching her cheek with his fingers.

"That's it-if tha likes."

"If I lai-ike!" she repeated, radiant.

"She's going at the end of three weeks," said the Vicar consolingly to the farmer.

II

While they were talking, they heard the far-off hooting of a pit.

"There goes th' loose a'," said Henry, coldly. "We're not going to get that corner up to-day."

The father looked round anxiously.

"Now, Maurice, are you sure you're all right?" he asked.

"Yes, I'm all right. Haven't I told you?"

"Then you sit down there, and in a bit you can be getting dinner out. Henry, you go on the stack. Wheer's Jim? Oh, he's minding the hosses. Bill, and you, Geoffrey, you can pick while Jim loads."

Maurice sat down under the wych elm to recover. The Fräulein had fled back. He made up his mind to ask her to marry him. He had got fifty pounds of his own, and his mother would help him. For a long time he sat musing, thinking what he would do. Then, from the float he fetched a big basket covered with a cloth, and spread the dinner. There was an immense rabbit pie, a dish of cold potatoes, much bread, a great piece of cheese, and a solid rice pudding.

These two fields were four miles from the home farm. But they had been in the hands of the Wookeys for several generations, therefore the father kept them on, and everyone looked forward to the hay harvest at Greasley: it was a kind of picnic. They brought dinner and tea in the milk-float, which the father drove over in the morning. The lads and the

31

labourers cycled. Off and on, the harvest lasted a fortnight. As the high road from Alfreton to Nottingham ran at the foot of the fields, someone usually slept in the hay under the shed to guard the tools. The sons took it in turns. They did not care for it much, and were for that reason anxious to finish the harvest on this day. But work went slack and disjointed after Maurice's accident.

When the load was teemed, they gathered round the white cloth, which was spread under a tree between the hedge and the stack, and, sitting on the ground, ate their meal. Mrs Wookey sent always a clean cloth, and knives and forks and plates for everybody. Mr Wookey was always rather proud of this spread: everything was so proper.

"There now," he said, sitting down jovially. "Doesn't this look nice now-eh?"

They all sat round the white spread, in the shadow of the tree and the stack, and looked out up the fields as they ate. From their shady coolness, the gold sward seemed liquid, molten with heat. The horse with the empty wagon wandered a few yards, then stood feeding. Everything was still as a trance. Now and again, the horse between the shafts of the load that stood propped beside the stack, jingled his loose bit as he ate. The men ate and drank in silence, the father reading the newspaper, Maurice leaning back on a saddle, Henry reading the Nation, the others eating busily.

Presently "Helloa! 'Er's 'ere again!" exclaimed Bill. All looked up. Paula was coming across the field carrying a plate.

"She's bringing something to tempt your appetite, Maurice," said the eldest brother ironically. Maurice was midway through a large wedge of rabbit pie, and some cold potatoes.

"Aye, bless me if she's not," laughed the father. "Put that away, Maurice, it's a shame to disappoint her."

Maurice looked round very shamefaced, not knowing what to do with his plate.

"Give it over here," said Bill. "I'll polish him off."

"Bringing something for the invalid?" laughed the father to the Fräulein. "He's looking up nicely."

"I bring him some chicken, him!" She nodded her head at Maurice childishly. He flushed and smiled.

"Tha doesna mean ter bust 'im," said Bill.

Everybody laughed aloud. The girl did not understand, so she laughed also. Maurice ate his portion very sheepishly.

The father pitied his son's shyness.

"Come here and sit by me," he said. "Eh, Fräulein! Is that what they call you?"

"I sit by you, Father," she said innocently.

Henry threw his head back and laughed long and noiselessly.

She settled near to the big, handsome man.

"My name," she said, "is Paula Jablonowsky."

"Is what?" said the father, and the other men went into roars of laughter.

"Tell me again," said the father. "Your name-?"

"Paula."

"Paula? Oh-well, it's a rum sort of name, eh? His name-" he nodded at his son.

"Maurice-I know." She pronounced it sweetly, then laughed into the father's eyes. Maurice blushed to the roots of his hair.

They questioned her concerning her history, and made out that she came from Hanover, that her father was a shop-keeper, and that she had run away from home because she did not like her father. She had gone to Paris.

"Oh," said the father, now dubious. "And what did you do there?"

"In school-in a young ladies' school."

"Did you like it?"

"Oh no-no laïfe-no life!"

"What?"

"When we go out-two and two-all together-no more. Ah, no life, no life."

"Well, that's a winder!" exclaimed the father. "No life in Paris! And have you found much life in England?"

"No-ah no. I don't like it." She made a grimace at the Vicarage.

"How long have you been in England?"

"Chreestmas-so."

"And what will you do?"

"I will go to London, or to Paris. Ah, Paris!-Or get married!" She laughed into the father's eyes.

The father laughed heartily.

"Get married, eh? And who to?"

"I don't know. I am going away."

"The country's too quiet for you?" asked the father.

"Too quiet-hm!" she nodded in assent.

"You wouldn't care for making butter and cheese?"

"Making butter-hm!" She turned to him with a glad, bright gesture. "I like it."

"Oh," laughed the father. "You would, would you?"

She nodded vehemently, with glowing eyes.

"She'd like anything in the shape of a change," said Henry judicially.

"I think she would," agreed the father. It did not occur to them that she fully understood what they said. She looked at them closely, then thought with bowed head.

"Hullo!" exclaimed Henry, the alert. A tramp was slouching towards them through the gap. He was a very seedy, slinking fellow, with a tang of horsey braggadocio about him. Small, thin, and ferrety, with a week's red beard bristling on his pointed chin, he came slouching forward.

"Have yer got a bit of a job goin'?" he asked.

"A bit of a job," repeated the father. "Why, can't you see as we've a'most done?"

"Aye-but I noticed you was a hand short, an' I thowt as 'appen you'd gie me half a day."

"What, are you any good in a hay close?" asked Henry, with a sneer.

The man stood slouching against the haystack. All the others were seated on the floor. He had an advantage.

"I could work aside any on yer," he bragged.

"Tha looks it," laughed Bill.

"And what's your regular trade?" asked the father.

"I'm a jockey by rights. But I did a bit o' dirty work for a boss o' mine, an' I was landed. "E got the benefit, I got kicked out. "E axed me-an' then 'e looked as if 'e'd never seed me."

"Did he, though!" exclaimed the father sympathetically.

"'E did that!" asserted the man.

"But we've got nothing for you," said Henry coldly.

"What does the boss say?" asked the man, impudent.

"No, we've no work you can do," said the father. "You can have a bit o' something to eat, if you like."

"I should be glad of it," said the man.

He was given the chunk of rabbit pie that remained. This he ate greedily. There was something debased, parasitic, about him, which disgusted Henry. The others regarded him as a curiosity.

"That was nice and tasty," said the tramp, with gusto.

"Do you want a piece of bread 'n' cheese?" asked the father.

"It'll help to fill up," was the reply.

The man ate this more slowly. The company was embarrassed by his presence, and could not talk. All the men lit their pipes, the meal over.

"So you dunna want any help?" said the tramp at last.

"No-we can manage what bit there is to do."

"You don't happen to have a fill of bacca to spare, do you?"

The father gave him a good pinch.

"You're all right here," he said, looking round. They resented this familiarity. However, he filled his clay pipe and smoked with the rest.

As they were sitting silent, another figure came through the gap in the hedge, and noiselessly approached. It was a woman. She was rather small and finely made. Her face was small, very ruddy, and comely, save for the look of bitterness and aloofness that it wore. Her hair was drawn tightly back under a sailor hat. She gave an impression of cleanness, of precision and directness.

"Have you got some work?" she asked of her man. She ignored the rest. He tucked his tail between his legs.

"No, they haven't got no work for me. They've just gave me a draw of bacca."

He was a mean crawl of a man.

"An' am I goin' to wait for you out there on the lane all day?"

"You needn't if you don't like. You could go on."

"Well, are you coming?" she asked contemptuously. He rose to his feet in a rickety fashion.

"You needn't be in such a mighty hurry," he said. "If you'd wait a bit you might get summat."

She glanced for the first time over the men. She was quite young, and would have been pretty, were she not so hard and callous-looking.

"Have you had your dinner?" asked the father.

She looked at him with a kind of anger, and turned away. Her face was so childish in its contours, contrasting strangely with her expression.

"Are you coming?" she said to the man.

"He's had his tuck-in. Have a bit, if you want it," coaxed the father.

"What have you had?" she flashed to the man.

"He's had all what was left o' th' rabbit pie," said Geoffrey, in an indignant, mocking tone, "and a great hunk o' bread an' cheese."

"Well, it was gave me," said the man.

The young woman looked at Geoffrey, and he at her. There was a sort of kinship between them. Both were at odds with the world. Geoffrey smiled satirically. She was too grave, too deeply incensed even to smile.

"There's a cake here, though-you can have a bit o' that," said Maurice blithely.

She eyed him with scorn.

Again she looked at Geoffrey. He seemed to understand her. She turned, and in silence departed. The man remained obstinately sucking at his pipe. Everybody looked at him with hostility.

"We'll be getting to work," said Henry, rising, pulling off his coat. Paula got to her feet. She was a little bit confused by the presence of the tramp.

"I go," she said, smiling brilliantly. Maurice rose and followed her sheepishly.

"A good grind, eh?" said the tramp, nodding after the Fräulein. The men only half-understood him, but they hated him.

"Hadn't you better be getting off?" said Henry.

The man rose obediently. He was all slouching, parasitic insolence. Geoffrey loathed him, longed to exterminate him. He was exactly the worst foe of the hyper-sensitive: insolence without sensibility, preying on sensibility.

"Aren't you goin' to give me summat for her? It's nowt she's had all day, to my knowin'. She'll 'appen eat it if I take it 'er-though she gets more than I've any knowledge of"-this with a lewd wink of jealous spite. "And then tries to keep a tight hand on me," he sneered, taking the bread and cheese, and stuffing it in his pocket.

III

Geoffrey worked sullenly all the afternoon, and Maurice did the horse-raking. It was exceedingly hot. So the day wore on, the atmosphere thickened, and the sunlight grew blurred. Geoffrey was picking with Bill-helping to load the wagons from the winrows. He was sulky, though extraordinarily relieved: Maurice would not tell. Since the quarrel neither brother had spoken to the other. But their silence was entirely amicable, almost affectionate. They had both been deeply moved, so much so that their ordinary intercourse was interrupted: but underneath, each felt a strong regard for the other. Maurice was peculiarly happy, his feeling of affection swimming over everything. But Geoffrey was still sullenly hostile to the most part of the world. He felt isolated. The free and easy intercommunication between the other workers left him distinctly alone. And he was a man who could not bear to stand alone, he was too much afraid of the vast confusion of life surrounding him, in which he was helpless. Geoffrey mistrusted himself with everybody.

The work went on slowly. It was unbearably hot, and everyone was disheartened.

"We s'll have getting-on-for another day of it," said the father at tea-time, as they sat under the tree.

"Quite a day," said Henry.

"Somebody'll have to stop, then," said Geoffrey. "It 'ud better be me."

"Nay, lad, I'll stop," said Maurice, and he hid his head in confusion.

"Stop again to-night!" exclaimed the father. "I'd rather you went home."

"Nay, I'm stoppin'," protested Maurice.

"He wants to do his courting," Henry enlightened them.

The father thought seriously about it.

"I don't know . . ." he mused, rather perturbed.

But Maurice stayed. Towards eight o'clock, after sundown, the men mounted their bicycles, the father put the horse in the float, and all departed. Maurice stood in the gap of the hedge and watched them go, the cart rolling and swinging downhill, over the grass stubble, the cyclists dipping swiftly like shadows in front. All passed through the gate, there was a quick clatter of hoofs on the roadway under the lime trees, and they were gone. The young man was very much excited, almost afraid, at finding himself alone.

Darkness was rising from the valley. Already, up the steep hill the cart-lamps crept indecisively, and the cottage windows were lit. Everything looked strange to Maurice, as if he had not seen it before. Down the hedge a large lime-tree teemed with scent that seemed almost like a voice speaking. It startled him. He caught a breath of the over-sweet fragrance, then stood still, listening expectantly.

Up hill, a horse whinneyed. It was the young mare. The heavy horses went thundering across to the far hedge.

Maurice wondered what to do. He wandered round the deserted stacks restlessly. Heat came in wafts, in thick strands. The evening was a long time cooling. He thought he would go and wash himself. There was a trough of pure water in the hedge bottom. It was filled by a tiny spring that filtered over the brim of the trough down the lush hedge bottom of the lower field. All round the trough, in the upper field, the land was marshy, and there the meadow-sweet stood like clots of mist, very sickly-smelling in the twilight. The night did not darken, for the moon was in the sky, so that as the tawny colour drew off the heavens they remained pallid with a dimmed moon. The purple bell-flowers in the hedge went black, the ragged robin turned its pink to a faded white, the meadow-sweet gathered light as if it were phosphorescent, and it made the air ache with scent.

Maurice kneeled on the slab of stone bathing his hands and arms, then his face. The water was deliriously cool. He had still an hour before Paula would come: she was not due till nine. So he decided to take his bath at night instead of waiting till morning. Was he not sticky, and was not Paula coming to talk to him? He was delighted the thought had occurred to him. As he soused his head in the trough, he wondered what the little creatures that lived in the velvety silt at the bottom would think of the taste of soap. Laughing to himself, he squeezed his cloth into the water. He washed himself from head to foot, standing in the fresh, forsaken corner of the field, where no one could see him by daylight, so that now, in the veiled grey tinge of moonlight, he was no more noticeable than the crowded flowers. The night had on a new look: he never remembered to have seen the lustrous grey sheen of it before, nor to have noticed how vital the lights looked, like live folk inhabiting the silvery spaces. And the tall trees, wrapped obscurely in their mantles, would not have surprised him had they begun to move in converse. As he dried himself, he discovered little wanderings in the air, felt on his sides soft touches and caresses that were peculiarly delicious: sometimes they startled him, and he laughed as if he were not alone. The flowers, the meadow-sweet particularly, haunted him. He reached to put his hand over their fleeciness. They touched his thighs. Laughing, he gathered them and dusted himself all over with their cream dust and fragrance. For a moment he hesitated in wonder at himself: but the subtle glow in the hoary and black night reassured him. Things never had looked so personal and full of beauty, he had never known the wonder in himself before.

At nine o'clock he was waiting under the elder-bush, in a state of high trepidation, but feeling that he was worthy, having a sense of his own wonder. She was late. At a quarter-past nine she came, flitting swiftly, in her own eager way.

"No, she would not go to sleep," said Paula, with a world of wrath in her tone. He laughed bashfully. They wandered out into the dim, hillside field.

"I have sat-in that bedroom-for an hour, for hours," she cried indignantly. She took a deep breath: "Ah, breathe!" she smiled.

She was very intense, and full of energy.

"I want"-she was clumsy with the language-"I want-I should laike-to run-there!" She pointed across the field.

"Let's run, then," he said, curiously.

"Yes!"

And in an instant she was gone. He raced after her. For all he was so young and limber, he had difficulty in catching her. At first he could scarcely see her, though he could hear the rustle of her dress. She sped with astonishing fleetness. He overtook her, caught her by the arm, and they stood panting, facing one another with laughter.

"I could win," she asserted blithely.

"Tha couldna," he replied, with a peculiar, excited laugh. They walked on, rather breathless. In front of them suddenly appeared the dark shapes of the three feeding horses.

"We ride a horse?" she said.

"What, bareback?" he asked.

"You say?" She did not understand.

"With no saddle?"

"No saddle-yes-no saddle."

"Coop, lass!" he said to the mare, and in a minute he had her by the forelock, and was leading her down to the stacks, where he put a halter on her. She was a big, strong mare. Maurice seated the Fräulein, clambered himself in front of the girl, using the wheel of the wagon as a mount, and together they trotted uphill, she holding lightly round his waist. From the crest of the hill they looked round.

The sky was darkening with an awning of cloud. On the left the hill rose black and wooded, made cosy by a few lights from cottages along the highway. The hill spread to the right, and tufts of trees shut round. But in front was a great vista of night, a sprinkle of cottage candles, a twinkling cluster of lights, like an elfish fair in full swing, at the colliery, an encampment of light at a village, a red flare on the sky far off, above an iron-foundry, and in the farthest distance the dim breathing of town lights. As they watched the night stretch far out, her arms tightened round his waist, and he pressed his elbows to his side, pressing her arms closer still. The horse moved restlessly. They clung to each other.

"Tha doesna want to go right away?" he asked the girl behind him.

"I stay with you," she answered softly, and he felt her crouching close against him. He laughed curiously. He was afraid to kiss her, though he was urged to do so. They remained still, on the restless horse, watching the small lights lead deep into the night, an infinite distance.

"I don't want to go," he said, in a tone half pleading.

She did not answer. The horse stirred restlessly.

"Let him run," cried Paula, "fast!"

She broke the spell, startled him into a little fury. He kicked the mare, hit her, and away she plunged downhill. The girl clung tightly to the young man. They were riding bareback down a rough, steep hill. Maurice clung hard with hands and knees. Paula held him fast round the waist, leaning her head on his shoulders, and thrilling with excitement.

"We shall be off, we shall be off," he cried, laughing with excitement; but she only crouched behind and pressed tight to him. The mare tore across the field. Maurice expected every moment to be flung on to the grass. He gripped with all the strength of his knees. Paula tucked herself behind him, and often wrenched him almost from his hold. Man and girl were taut with effort.

At last the mare came to a standstill, blowing. Paula slid off, and in an instant Maurice was beside her. They were both highly excited. Before he knew what he was doing, he had her in his arms, fast, and was kissing her, and laughing. They did not move for some time. Then, in silence, they walked towards the stacks.

It had grown quite dark, the night was thick with cloud. He walked with his arm round Paula's waist, she with her arm round him. They were near the stacks when Maurice felt a spot of rain.

"It's going to rain," he said.

"Rain!" she echoed, as if it were trivial.

38

"I s'll have to put the stack-cloth on," he said gravely. She did not understand.

When they got to the stacks, he went round to the shed, to return staggering in the darkness under the burden of the immense and heavy cloth. It had not been used once during the hay harvest.

"What are you going to do?" asked Paula, coming close to him in the darkness.

"Cover the top of the stack with it," he replied. "Put it over the stack, to keep the rain out."

"Ah!" she cried, "up there!" He dropped his burden. "Yes," he answered.

Fumblingly he reared the long ladder up the side of the stack. He could not see the top.

"I hope it's solid," he said, softly.

A few smart drops of rain sounded drumming on the cloth. They seemed like another presence. It was very dark indeed between the great buildings of hay. She looked up the black wall, and shrank to him.

"You carry it up there?" she asked.

"Yes," he answered.

"I help you?" she said.

And she did. They opened the cloth. He clambered first up the steep ladder, bearing the upper part, she followed closely, carrying her full share. They mounted the shaky ladder in silence, stealthily.

IV

As they climbed the stacks a light stopped at the gate on the high road. It was Geoffrey, come to help his brother with the cloth. Afraid of his own intrusion, he wheeled his bicycle silently towards the shed. This was a corrugated iron erection, on the opposite side of the hedge from the stacks. Geoffrey let his light go in front of him, but there was no sign from the lovers. He thought he saw a shadow slinking away. The light of the bicycle lamp sheered yellowly across the dark, catching a glint of raindrops, a mist of darkness, shadow of leaves and strokes of long grass. Geoffrey entered the shed-no one was there. He walked slowly and doggedly round to the stacks. He had passed the wagon, when he heard something sheering down upon him. Starting back under the wall of hay, he saw the long ladder slither across the side of the stack, and fall with a bruising ring.

"What wor that?" he heard Maurice, aloft, ask cautiously.

"Something fall," came the curious, almost pleased voice of the Fräulein.

"It wor niver th' ladder," said Maurice. He peered over the side of the stack. He lay down, looking.

"It is an' a'!" he exclaimed. "We knocked it down with the cloth, dragging it over."

"We fast up here?" she exclaimed with a thrill.

"We are that-without I shout and make 'em hear at the Vicarage."

"Oh no," she said quickly.

"I don't want to," he replied, with a short laugh. There came a swift clatter of raindrops on the cloth. Geoffrey crouched under the wall of the other stack.

"Mind where you tread-here, let me straighten this end," said Maurice, with a peculiar intimate tone-a command and an embrace. "We s'll have to sit under it. At any rate, we shan't get wet."

"Not get wet!" echoed the girl, pleased, but agitated.

Geoffrey heard the slide and rustle of the cloth over the top of the stack, heard Maurice telling her to "Mind!"

"Mind!" she repeated. "Mind! you say 'Mind!'"

"Well, what if I do?" he laughed. "I don't want you to fall over th' side, do I?" His tone was masterful, but he was not quite sure of himself.

There was silence a moment or two.

"Maurice!" she said, plaintively.

"I'm here," he answered, tenderly, his voice shaky with excitement that was near to distress. "There, I've done. Now should we-we'll sit under this corner."

"Maurice!" she was rather pitiful.

"What? You'll be all right," he remonstrated, tenderly indignant.

"I be all raïght," she repeated, "I be all raïght, Maurice?"

"Tha knows tha will-I canna ca' thee Powla. Should I ca' thee Minnie?"

It was the name of a dead sister.

"Minnie?" she exclaimed in surprise.

"Aye, should I?"

She answered in full-throated German. He laughed shakily.

"Come on-come on under. But do yer wish you was safe in th' Vicarage? Should I shout for somebody?" he asked.

"I don't wish, no!" She was vehement.

"Art sure?" he insisted, almost indignantly.

"Sure-I quite sure." She laughed.

Geoffrey turned away at the last words. Then the rain beat heavily. The lonely brother slouched miserably to the hut, where the rain played a mad tattoo. He felt very miserable, and jealous of Maurice.

His bicycle lamp, downcast, shone a yellow light on the stark floor of the shed or hut with one wall open. It lit up the trodden earth, the shafts of tools lying piled under the beam, beside the dreary grey metal of the building. He took off the lamp, shone it round the hut. There were piles of harness, tools, a big sugar box, a deep bed of hay-then the beams across the corrugated iron, all very dreary and stark. He shone the lamp into the night: nothing but the furtive glitter of raindrops through the mist of darkness, and black shapes hovering round.

Geoffrey blew out the light and flung himself on to the hay. He would put the ladder up for them in a while, when they would be wanting it. Meanwhile he sat and gloated over Maurice's felicity. He was imaginative, and now he had something concrete to work upon. Nothing in the whole of life stirred him so profoundly, and so utterly, as the thought of this woman.

40

For Paula was strange, foreign, different from the ordinary girls: the rousing, feminine quality seemed in her concentrated, brighter, more fascinating than in anyone he had known, so that he felt most like a moth near a candle. He would have loved her wildly-but Maurice had got her. His thoughts beat the same course, round and round. What was it like when you kissed her, when she held you tight round the waist, how did she feel towards Maurice, did she love to touch him, was he fine and attractive to her; what did she think of himself-she merely disregarded him, as she would disregard a horse in a field; why should she do so, why couldn't he make her regard himself, instead of Maurice: he would never command a woman's regard like that, he always gave in to her too soon; if only some woman would come and take him for what he was worth, though he was such a stumbler and showed to such disadvantage, ah, what a grand thing it would be; how he would kiss her. Then round he went again in the same course, brooding almost like a madman. Meanwhile the rain drummed deep on the shed, then grew lighter and softer. There came the drip, drip of the drops falling outside.

Geoffrey's heart leaped up his chest, and he clenched himself, as a black shape crept round the post of the shed and, bowing, entered silently. The young man's heart beat so heavily in plunges, he could not get his breath to speak. It was shock, rather than fear. The form felt towards him. He sprang up, gripped it with his great hands, panting "Now, then!"

There was no resistance, only a little whimper of despair.

"Let me go," said a woman's voice.

"What are you after?" he asked, in deep, gruff tones.

"I thought 'e was 'ere," she wept despairingly, with little, stubborn sobs.

"An' you've found what you didn't expect, have you?"

At the sound of his bullying she tried to get away from him.

"Let me go," she said.

"Who did you expect to find here?" he asked, but more his natural self.

"I expected my husband-him as you saw at dinner. Let me go."

"Why, is it you?" exclaimed Geoffrey. "Has he left you?"

"Let me go," said the woman sullenly, trying to draw away. He realized that her sleeve was very wet, her arm slender under his grasp. Suddenly he grew ashamed of himself: he had no doubt hurt her, gripping her so hard. He relaxed, but did not let her go.

"An' are you searching round after that snipe as was here at dinner?" he asked. She did not answer.

"Where did he leave you?"

"I left him-here. I've seen nothing of him since."

"I s'd think it's good riddance," he said. She did not answer. He gave a short laugh, saying:

"I should ha' thought you wouldn't ha' wanted to clap eyes on him again."

"He's my husband-an' he's not goin' to run off if I can stop him."

Geoffrey was silent, not knowing what to say.

"Have you got a jacket on?" he asked at last.

"What do you think? You've got hold of it."

41

"You're wet through, aren't you?"

"I shouldn't be dry, comin' through that teemin' rain. But 'e's not here, so I'll go."

"I mean," he said humbly, "are you wet through?"

She did not answer. He felt her shiver.

"Are you cold?" he asked, in surprise and concern.

She did not answer. He did not know what to say.

"Stop a minute," he said, and he fumbled in his pocket for his matches. He struck a light, holding it in the hollow of his large, hard palm. He was a big man, and he looked anxious. Shedding the light on her, he saw she was rather pale, and very weary looking. Her old sailor hat was sodden and drooping with rain. She wore a fawn-coloured jacket of smooth cloth. This jacket was black-wet where the rain had beaten, her skirt hung sodden, and dripped on to her boots. The match went out.

"Why, you're wet through!" he said.

She did not answer.

"Shall you stop in here while it gives over?" he asked. She did not answer.

"'Cause if you will, you'd better take your things off, an' have th' rug. There's a horse-rug in the box."

He waited, but she would not answer. So he lit his bicycle lamp, and rummaged in the box, pulling out a large brown blanket, striped with scarlet and yellow. She stood stock still. He shone the light on her. She was very pale, and trembling fitfully.

"Are you that cold?" he asked in concern. "Take your jacket off, and your hat, and put this right over you."

Mechanically, she undid the enormous fawn-coloured buttons, and unpinned her hat. With her black hair drawn back from her low, honest brow, she looked little more than a girl, like a girl driven hard with womanhood by stress of life. She was small, and natty, with neat little features. But she shivered convulsively.

"Is something a-matter with you?" he asked.

"I've walked to Bulwell and back," she quivered, "looking for him-an' I've not touched a thing since this morning." She did not weep-she was too dreary-hardened to cry. He looked at her in dismay, his mouth half open: "Gormin'", as Maurice would have said.

"'Aven't you had nothing to eat?" he said.

Then he turned aside to the box. There, the bread remaining was kept, and the great piece of cheese, and such things as sugar and salt, with all table utensils: there was some butter.

She sat down drearily on the bed of hay. He cut her a piece of bread and butter, and a piece of cheese. This she took, but ate listlessly.

"I want a drink," she said.

"We 'aven't got no beer," he answered. "My father doesn't have it."

"I want water," she said.

He took a can and plunged through the wet darkness, under the great black hedge, down to the trough. As he came back he saw her in the half-lit little cave sitting bunched together. The soaked grass wet his feet-he thought of her. When he gave her a cup of water, her hand touched his and he felt her fingers hot and glossy. She trembled so she spilled the water.

"Do you feel badly?" he asked.

"I can't keep myself still-but it's only with being tired and having nothing to eat."

He scratched his head contemplatively, waited while she ate her piece of bread and butter. Then he offered her another piece.

"I don't want it just now," she said.

"You'll have to eat summat," he said.

"I couldn't eat any more just now."

He put the piece down undecidedly on the box. Then there was another long pause. He stood up with bent head. The bicycle, like a restful animal, glittered behind him, turning towards the wall. The woman sat hunched on the hay, shivering.

"Can't you get warm?" he asked.

"I shall by an' by-don't you bother. I'm taking your seat-are you stopping here all night?"

"Yes."

"I'll be goin' in a bit," she said.

"Nay, I non want you to go. I'm thinkin' how you could get warm."

"Don't you bother about me," she remonstrated, almost irritably.

"I just want to see as the stacks is all right. You take your shoes an' stockin's an' all your wet things off: you can easy wrap yourself all over in that rug, there's not so much of you."

"It's raining-I s'll be all right-I s'll be going in a minute."

"I've got to see as the stacks is safe. Take your wet things off."

"Are you coming back?" she asked.

"I mightn't, not till morning."

"Well, I s'll be gone in ten minutes, then. I've no rights to be here, an' I s'll not let anybody be turned out for me."

"You won't be turning me out."

"Whether or no, I shan't stop."

"Well, shall you if I come back?" he asked. She did not answer.

He went. In a few moments, she blew the light out. The rain was falling steadily, and the night was a black gulf. All was intensely still. Geoffrey listened everywhere: no sound save the rain. He stood between the stacks, but only heard the trickle of water, and the light swish of rain. Everything was lost in blackness. He imagined death was like that, many things dissolved in silence and darkness, blotted out, but existing. In the dense blackness he felt himself almost extinguished. He was afraid he might not find things the same. Almost frantically, he stumbled, feeling his way, till his hand touched the wet metal. He had been looking for a gleam of light.

"Did you blow the lamp out?" he asked, fearful lest the silence should answer him.

"Yes," she answered humbly. He was glad to hear her voice. Groping into the pitch-dark shed, he knocked against the box, part of whose cover served as table. There was a clatter and a fall.

"That's the lamp, an' the knife, an' the cup," he said. He struck a match.

43

"Th' cup's not broke." He put it into the box.

"But th' oil's spilled out o' th' lamp. It always was a rotten old thing." He hastily blew out his match, which was burning his fingers. Then he struck another light.

"You don't want a lamp, you know you don't, and I s'll be going directly, so you come an' lie down an' get your night's rest. I'm not taking any of your place."

He looked at her by the light of another match. She was a queer little bundle, all brown, with gaudy border folding in and out, and her little face peering at him. As the match went out she saw him beginning to smile.

"I can sit right at this end," she said. "You lie down."

He came and sat on the hay, at some distance from her. After a spell of silence:

"Is he really your husband?" he asked.

"He is!" she answered grimly.

"Hm!" Then there was silence again.

After a while: "Are you warm now?"

"Why do you bother yourself?"

"I don't bother myself-do you follow him because you like him?" He put it very timidly. He wanted to know.

"I don't-I wish he was dead," this with bitter contempt. Then doggedly; "But he's my husband."

He gave a short laugh.

"By Gad!" he said.

Again, after a while: "Have you been married long?"

"Four years."

"Four years-why, how old are you?"

"Twenty-three."

"Are you turned twenty-three?"

"Last May."

"Then you're four month older than me." He mused over it. They were only two voices in the pitch-black night. It was eerie silence again.

"And do you just tramp about?" he asked.

"He reckons he's looking for a job. But he doesn't like work in any shape or form. He was a stableman when I married him, at Greenhalgh's, the horse-dealers, at Chesterfield, where I was housemaid. He left that job when the baby was only two month, and I've been badgered about from pillar to post ever sin'. They say a rolling stone gathers no moss . . ."

"An' where's the baby?"

"It died when it was ten month old."

Now the silence was clinched between them. It was quite a long time before Geoffrey ventured to say sympathetically: "You haven't much to look forward to."

"I've wished many a score time when I've started shiverin' an' shakin' at nights, as I was taken bad for death. But we're not that handy at dying."

He was silent. "But what ever shall you do?" he faltered.

"I s'll find him, if I drop by th' road."

44

"Why?" he asked, wondering, looking her way, though he saw nothing but solid darkness.

"Because I shall. He's not going to have it all his own road."

"But why don't you leave him?"

"Because he's not goin' to have it all his own road."

She sounded very determined, even vindictive. He sat in wonder, feeling uneasy, and vaguely miserable on her behalf. She sat extraordinarily still. She seemed like a voice only, a presence.

"Are you warm now?" he asked, half afraid.

"A bit warmer-but my feet!" She sounded pitiful.

"Let me warm them with my hands," he asked her. "I'm hot enough."

"No, thank you," she said, coldly.

Then, in the darkness, she felt she had wounded him. He was writhing under her rebuff, for his offer had been pure kindness.

"They're 'appen dirty," she said, half mocking.

"Well-mine is-an' I have a bath a'most every day," he answered.

"I don't know when they'll get warm," she moaned to herself.

"Well, then, put them in my hands."

She heard him faintly rattling the match-box, and then a phosphorescent glare began to fume in his direction. Presently he was holding two smoking, blue-green blotches of light towards her feet. She was afraid. But her feet ached so, and the impulse drove her on, so she placed her soles lightly on the two blotches of smoke. His large hands clasped over her instep, warm and hard.

"They're like ice!" he said, in deep concern.

He warmed her feet as best he could, putting them close against him. Now and again convulsive tremors ran over her. She felt his warm breath on the balls of her toes, that were bunched up in his hands. Leaning forward, she touched his hair delicately with her fingers. He thrilled. She fell to gently stroking his hair, with timid, pleading finger-tips.

"Do they feel any better?" he asked, in a low voice, suddenly lifting his face to her. This sent her hand sliding softly over his face, and her finger-tips caught on his mouth. She drew quickly away. He put his hand out to find hers, in his other palm holding both her feet. His wandering hand met her face. He touched it curiously. It was wet. He put his big fingers cautiously on her eyes, into two little pools of tears.

"What's a matter?" he asked, in a low, choked voice.

She leaned down to him, and gripped him tightly round the neck, pressing him to her bosom in a little frenzy of pain. Her bitter disillusionment with life, her unalleviated shame and degradation during the last four years, had driven her into loneliness, and hardened her till a large part of her nature was caked and sterile. Now she softened again, and her spring might be beautiful. She had been in a fair way to make an ugly old woman.

She clasped the head of Geoffrey to her breast, which heaved and fell, and heaved again. He was bewildered, full of wonder. He allowed the woman to do as she would with him. Her tears fell on his hair, as she wept

45

noiselessly; and he breathed deep as she did. At last she let go her clasp. He put his arms round her.

"Come and let me warm you," he said, folding her up on his knee, and lapping her with his heavy arms against himself. She was small and câline. He held her very warm and close. Presently she stole her arms round him.

"You are big," she whispered.

He gripped her hard, started, put his mouth down wanderingly, seeking her out. His lips met her temple. She slowly, deliberately turned her mouth to his, and with opened lips, met him in a kiss, his first love kiss.

V

It was breaking cold dawn when Geoffrey woke. The woman was still sleeping in his arms. Her face in sleep moved all his tenderness: the tight shutting of her mouth, as if in resolution to bear what was very hard to bear, contrasted so pitifully with the small mould of her features. Geoffrey pressed her to his bosom: having her, he felt he could bruise the lips of the scornful, and pass on erect, unabateable. With her to complete him, to form the core of him, he was firm and whole. Needing her so much, he loved her fervently.

Meanwhile the dawn came like death, one of those slow, livid mornings that seem to come in a cold sweat. Slowly, and painfully, the air began to whiten. Geoffrey saw it was not raining. As he was watching the ghastly transformation outside, he felt aware of something. He glanced down: she was open-eyed, watching him; she had golden-brown, calm eyes, that immediately smiled into his. He also smiled, bowed softly down and kissed her. They did not speak for some time. Then:

"What's thy name?" he asked curiously.

"Lydia," she said.

"Lydia!" he repeated, wonderingly. He felt rather shy.

"Mine's Geoffrey Wookey," he said.

She merely smiled at him.

They were silent for a considerable time. By morning light, things look small. The huge trees of the evening were dwindling to hoary, small, uncertain things, trespassing in the sick pallor of the atmosphere.

There was a dense mist, so that the light could scarcely breathe. Everything seemed to quiver with cold and sickliness.

"Have you often slept out?" he asked her.

"Not so very," she answered.

"You won't go after him?" he asked.

"I s'll have to," she replied, but she nestled in to Geoffrey. He felt a sudden panic.

"You musn't," he exclaimed, and she saw he was afraid for himself. She let it be, was silent.

46

"We couldn't get married?" he asked, thoughtfully.

"No."

He brooded deeply over this. At length:

"Would you go to Canada with me?"

"We'll see what you think in two months' time," she replied quietly, without bitterness.

"I s'll think the same," he protested, hurt.

She did not answer, only watched him steadily. She was there for him to do as he liked with; but she would not injure his fortunes; no, not to save his soul.

"Haven't you got no relations?" he asked.

"A married sister at Crick."

"On a farm?"

"No-married a farm labourer-but she's very comfortable. I'll go there, if you want me to, just till I can get another place in service."

He considered this.

"Could you get on a farm?" he asked wistfully.

"Greenhalgh's was a farm."

He saw the future brighten: she would be a help to him. She agreed to go to her sister, and to get a place of service-until Spring, he said, when they would sail for Canada. He waited for her assent.

"You will come with me, then?" he asked.

"When the time comes," she said.

Her want of faith made him bow his head: she had reason for it.

"Shall you walk to Crick, or go from Langley Mill to Ambergate? But it's only ten mile to walk. So we can go together up Hunt's Hill-you'd have to go past our lane-end, then I could easy nip down an' fetch you some money," he said, humbly.

"I've got half a sovereign by me-it's more than I s'll want."

"Let's see it," he said.

After a while, fumbling under the blanket, she brought out the piece of money. He felt she was independent of him. Brooding rather bitterly, he told himself she'd forsake him. His anger gave him courage to ask:

"Shall you go in service in your maiden name?"

"No."

He was bitterly wrathful with her-full of resentment.

"I bet I s'll niver see you again," he said, with a short, hard laugh. She put her arms round him, pressed him to her bosom, while the tears rose to her eyes. He was reassured, but not satisfied.

"Shall you write to me to-night?"

"Yes, I will."

"And can I write to you-who shall I write to?"

"Mrs Bredon."

"'Bredon'!" he repeated bitterly.

He was exceedingly uneasy.

The dawn had grown quite wan. He saw the hedges drooping wet down the grey mist. Then he told her about Maurice.

"Oh, you shouldn't!" she said. "You should ha' put the ladder up for them, you should."

"Well-I don't care."

"Go and do it now-and I'll go."

"No, don't you. Stop an' see our Maurice, go on, stop an' see him-then I s'll be able to tell him."

She consented in silence. He had her promise she would not go before he returned. She adjusted her dress, found her way to the trough, where she performed her toilet.

Geoffrey wandered round to the upper field. The stacks looked wet in the mist, the hedge was drenched. Mist rose like steam from the grass, and the near hills were veiled almost to a shadow. In the valley, some peaks of black poplar showed fairly definite, jutting up. He shivered with chill.

There was no sound from the stacks, and he could see nothing. After all, he wondered, were they up there. But he reared the ladder to the place whence it had been swept, then went down the hedge to gather dry sticks. He was breaking off thin dead twigs under a holly tree when he heard, on the perfectly still air: "Well I'm dashed!"

He listened intently. Maurice was awake.

"Sithee here!" the lad's voice exclaimed. Then, after a while, the foreign sound of the girl:

"What-oh, thair!"

"Aye, th' ladder's there, right enough."

"You said it had fall down."

"Well, I heard it drop-an' I couldna feel it nor see it."

"You said it had fall down-you lie, you liar."

"Nay, as true as I'm here-"

"You tell me lies-make me stay here-you tell me lies-" She was passionately indignant.

"As true as I'm standing here-" he began.

"Lies!-lies!-lies!" she cried. "I don't believe you, never. You mean, you mean, mean, mean!"

"A' raïght, then!" he was now incensed, in his turn.

"You are bad, mean, mean, mean."

"Are yer commin' down?" asked Maurice, coldly.

"No-I will not come with you-mean, to tell me lies."

"Are ter commin' down?"

"No, I don't want you."

"A' raïght, then!"

Geoffrey, peering through the holly tree, saw Maurice negotiating the ladder. The top rung was below the brim of the stack, and rested on the cloth, so it was dangerous to approach. The Fräulein watched him from the end of the stack, where the cloth thrown back showed the light, dry hay. He slipped slightly, she screamed. When he had got on to the ladder, he pulled the cloth away, throwing it back, making it easy for her to descend.

"Now are ter comin'?" he asked.

"No!" she shook her head violently, in a pet.

Geoffrey felt slightly contemptuous of her. But Maurice waited.

48

"Are ter comin'?" he called again.

"No," she flashed, like a wild cat.

"All right, then I'm going."

He descended. At the bottom, he stood holding the ladder.

"Come on, while I hold it steady," he said.

There was no reply. For some minutes he stood patiently with his foot on the bottom rung of the ladder. He was pale, rather washed-out in his appearance, and he drew himself together with cold.

"Are ter commin', or aren't ter?" he asked at length. Still there was no reply.

"Then stop up till tha'rt ready," he muttered, and he went away. Round the other side of the stacks he met Geoffrey.

"What, are thaïgh here?" he exclaimed.

"Bin here a' naïght," replied Geoffrey. "I come to help thee wi' th' cloth, but I found it on, an' th' ladder down, so I thowt tha'd gone."

"Did ter put th' ladder up?"

"I did a bit sin."

Maurice brooded over this, Geoffrey struggled with himself to get out his own news. At last he blurted:

"Tha knows that woman as wor here yis'day dinner-'er come back, an' stopped i' th' shed a' night, out o' th' rain."

"Oh-ah!" said Maurice, his eye kindling, and a smile crossing his pallor.

"An' I s'll gi'e her some breakfast."

"Oh-ah!" repeated Maurice.

"It's th' man as is good-for-nowt, not her," protested Geoffrey. Maurice did not feel in a position to cast stones.

"Tha pleases thysen," he said, "what ter does." He was very quiet, unlike himself. He seemed bothered and anxious, as Geoffrey had not seen him before.

"What's up wi' thee?" asked the elder brother, who in his own heart was glad, and relieved.

"Nowt," was the reply.

They went together to the hut. The woman was folding the blanket. She was fresh from washing, and looked very pretty. Her hair, instead of being screwed tightly back, was coiled in a knot low down, partly covering her ears. Before, she had deliberately made herself plain-looking: now she was neat and pretty, with a sweet, womanly gravity.

"Hello. I didn't think to find you here," said Maurice, very awkwardly, smiling. She watched him gravely without reply. "But it was better in shelter than outside, last night," he added.

"Yes," she replied.

"Shall you get a few more sticks?" Geoffrey asked him. It was a new thing for Geoffrey to be leader. Maurice obeyed. He wandered forth into the damp, raw morning. He did not go to the stack, as he shrank from meeting Paula.

At the mouth of the hut, Geoffrey was making the fire. The woman got out coffee from the box: Geoffrey set the tin to boil. They were arranging

49

breakfast when Paula appeared. She was hatless. Bits of hay stuck in her hair, and she was white-faced—altogether, she did not show to advantage.

"Ah—you!" she exclaimed, seeing Geoffrey.

"Hello!" he answered. "You're out early."

"Where's Maurice?"

"I dunno, he should be back directly."

Paula was silent.

"When have you come?" she asked.

"I come last night, but I could see nobody about. I got up half an hour sin', an' put th' ladder up ready to take the stack-cloth up."

Paula understood, and was silent. When Maurice returned with the faggots, she was crouched warming her hands. She looked up at him, but he kept his eyes averted from her. Geoffrey met the eyes of Lydia, and smiled. Maurice put his hands to the fire.

"You cold?" asked Paula tenderly.

"A bit," he answered, quite friendly, but reserved. And all the while the four sat round the fire, drinking their smoked coffee, eating each a small piece of toasted bacon, Paula watched eagerly for the eyes of Maurice, and he avoided her. He was gentle, but would not give his eyes to her looks. And Geoffrey smiled constantly to Lydia, who watched gravely.

The German girl succeeded in getting safely into the Vicarage, her escapade unknown to anyone save the housemaid. Before a week was out, she was openly engaged to Maurice, and when her month's notice expired, she went to live at the farm.

Geoffrey and Lydia kept faith one with the other.

MOTHER AND DAUGHTER

Virginia Bodoin had a good job: she was head of a department in a certain government office, held a responsible position, and earned, to imitate Balzac and be precise about it, seven hundred and fifty pounds a year. That is already something. Rachel Bodoin, her mother, had an income of about six hundred a year, on which she had lived in the capitals of Europe since the effacement of a never very important husband.

Now, after some years of virtual separation and "freedom", mother and daughter once more thought of settling down. They had become, in course of time, more like a married couple than mother and daughter. They knew one another very well indeed, and each was a little "nervous" of the other. They had lived together and parted several times. Virginia was now thirty, and she didn't look like marrying. For four years she had been as good as married to Henry Lubbock, a rather spoilt young man who was musical. Then Henry let her down: for two reasons. He couldn't stand her mother. Her mother couldn't stand him. And anybody whom Mrs Bodoin could not stand she managed to sit on, disastrously. So Henry had writhed horribly, feeling his mother-in-law sitting on him tight, and Virginia, after all, in a helpless sort of family loyalty, sitting alongside her mother. Virginia didn't really want to sit on Henry. But when her mother egged her on, she couldn't help it. For ultimately, her mother had power over her; a strange female power, nothing to do with parental authority. Virginia had long thrown parental authority to the winds. But her mother had another, much subtler form of domination, female and thrilling, so that when Rachel said: Let's squash him! Virginia had to rush wickedly and gleefully to the sport. And Henry knew quite well when he was being squashed. So that was one of his reasons for going back on Vinny.-He called her Vinny, to the superlative disgust of Mrs Bodoin, who always corrected him: My daughter Virginia-

The second reason was, again to be Balzacian, that Virginia hadn't a sou of her own. Henry had a sorry two hundred and fifty. Virginia, at the age of twenty-four, was already earning four hundred and fifty. But she was earning them. Whereas Henry managed to earn about twelve pounds per annum, by his precious music. He had realized that he would find it hard to earn more. So that marrying, except with a wife who could keep him, was rather out of the question. Vinny would inherit her mother's money. But then Mrs Bodoin had the health and muscular equipment of the Sphinx. She would live forever, seeking whom she might devour, and devouring him. Henry lived with Vinny for two years, in the married sense of the words: and Vinny felt they were married, minus a mere ceremony. But Vinny had her mother always in the background; often as far back as Paris or Biarritz, but still, within letter reach. And she never realized the funny little grin that came on her own elvish face when her mother, even in a letter, spread her skirts and calmly sat on Henry. She never realized that in spirit she promptly and mischievously sat on him too: she could no more have helped it than the tide can help turning to the moon. And she did not dream that he felt it, and was utterly mortified in his masculine vanity. Women, very often, hypnotize one another, and then, hypnotized, they proceed gently to wring the neck of the man they think they are loving with all their hearts. Then they call it utter perversity on his part, that he doesn't like having his neck wrung. They think he is repudiating a heart-felt love. For they are hypnotized. Women hypnotize one another, without knowing it.

In the end, Henry backed out. He saw himself being simply reduced to nothingness by two women, an old witch with muscles like the Sphinx, and a young, spell-bound witch, lavish, elvish and weak, who utterly spoilt him but who ate his marrow.

Rachel would write from Paris: My dear Virginia, as I had a windfall in the way of an investment, I am sharing it with you. You will find enclosed my cheque for twenty pounds. No doubt you will be needing it to buy Henry a suit of clothes, since the spring is apparently come, and the sunlight may be tempted to show him up for what he is worth. I don't want my daughter going around with what is presumably a street-corner musician, but please pay the tailor's bill yourself, or you may have to do it over again later.-Henry got a suit of clothes, but it was as good as a shirt of Nessus, eating him away with subtle poison.

So he backed out. He didn't jump out, or bolt, or carve his way out at the sword's point. He sort of faded out, distributing his departure over a year or more. He was fond of Vinny, and he could hardly do without her, and he was sorry for her. But at length he couldn't see her apart from her mother. She was a young, weak, spendthrift witch, accomplice of her tough-clawed witch of a mother.

Henry made other alliances, got a good hold on elsewhere, and gradually extricated himself. He saved his life, but he had lost, he felt, a good deal of his youth and marrow. He tended now to go fat, a little puffy, somewhat insignificant. And he had been handsome and striking-looking.

The two witches howled when he was lost to them. Poor Virginia was really half crazy, she didn't know what to do with herself. She had a violent recoil from her mother. Mrs Bodoin was filled with furious contempt for her daughter: that she should let such a hooked fish slip out of her hands! that she should allow such a person to turn her down!-"I don't quite see my daughter seduced and thrown over by a sponging individual such as Henry Lubbock," she wrote. "But if it has happened, I suppose it is somebody's fault-"

There was a mutual recoil, which lasted nearly five years. But the spell was not broken. Mrs Bodoin's mind never left her daughter, and Virginia was ceaselessly aware of her mother, somewhere in the universe. They wrote, and met at intervals, but they kept apart in recoil.

The spell, however, was between them, and gradually it worked. They felt more friendly. Mrs Bodoin came to London. She stayed in the same quiet hotel with her daughter: Virginia had had two rooms in an hotel for the past three years. And, at last, they thought of taking an apartment together.

Virginia was now over thirty. She was still thin and odd and elvish, with a very slight and piquant cast in one of her brown eyes, and she still had her odd, twisted smile, and her slow, rather deep-toned voice, that caressed a man like the stroking of subtle finger-tips. Her hair was still a natural tangle of curls, a bit dishevelled. She still dressed with a natural elegance which tended to go wrong and a tiny bit sluttish. She still might have a hole in her expensive and perfectly new stockings, and still she might have to take off her shoes in the drawing-room, if she came to tea, and sit there in her stockinged-feet. True, she had elegant feet: she was altogether elegantly shaped. But it wasn't that. It was neither coquetry nor vanity. It was simply that, after having gone to a good shoemaker and paid five guineas for a pair of perfectly simple and natural shoes, made to her feet, the said shoes would hurt her excruciatingly, when she had walked half a mile in them, and she would simply have to take them off, even if she sat on the kerb to do it. It was a fatality. There was a touch of the gamin in her very feet, a certain sluttishness that wouldn't let them stay properly in nice proper shoes. She practically always wore her mother's old shoes.-Of course I go through life in mother's old shoes. If she died and left me without a supply, I suppose I should have to go in a bathchair, she would say, with her odd twisted little grin. She was so elegant, and yet a slut. It was her charm, really.

Just the opposite of her mother. They could wear each other's shoes and each other's clothes, which seemed remarkable, for Mrs Bodoin seemed so much the bigger of the two. But Virginia's shoulders were broad, if she was thin, she had a strong frame, even when she looked a frail rag.

Mrs Bodoin was one of those women of sixty or so, with a terrible inward energy and a violent sort of vitality. But she managed to hide it. She sat with perfect repose, and folded hands. One thought: What a calm woman! Just as one may look at the snowy summit of a quiescent volcano, in the evening light, and think: What peace!

It was a strange muscular energy which possessed Mrs Bodoin, as it possesses, curiously enough, many women over fifty, and is usually distasteful in its manifestations. Perhaps it accounts for the lassitude of the young.

But Mrs Bodoin recognized the bad taste in her energetic coevals, so she cultivated repose. Her very way of pronouncing the word, in two syllables: re-pose, making the second syllable run on into the twilight, showed how much suppressed energy she had. Faced with the problem of iron-grey hair and black eyebrows, she was too clever to try dyeing herself back into youth. She studied her face, her whole figure, and decided that it was positive. There was no denying it. There was no wispiness, no hollowness, no limp frail blossom-on-a-bending-stalk about her. Her figure, though not stout, was full, strong, and cambré. Her face had an aristocratic arched nose, aristocratic, who-the-devil-are-you grey eyes, and cheeks rather long but also rather full. Nothing appealing or youthfully skittish here.

Like an independent woman, she used her wits, and decided most emphatically not to be either youthful or skittish or appealing. She would keep her dignity, for she was fond of it. She was positive. She liked to be positive. She was used to her positivity. So she would just be positive.

She turned to the positive period; to the eighteenth century, to Voltaire, to Ninon de l'Enclos and the Pompadour, to Madame la Duchesse and Monsieur le Marquis. She decided that she was not much in the line of la Pompadour or la Duchesse, but almost exactly in the line of Monsieur le Marquis. And she was right. With hair silvering to white, brushed back clean from her positive brow and temples, cut short, but sticking out a little behind, with her rather full, pink face and thin black eyebrows plucked to two fine, superficial crescents, her arching nose and her rather full insolent eyes she was perfectly eighteenth-century, the early half. That she was Monsieur le Marquis rather than Madame la Marquise made her really modern.

Her appearance was perfect. She wore delicate combinations of grey and pink, maybe with a darkening iron-grey touch, and her jewels were of soft old coloured paste. Her bearing was a sort of alert repose, very calm, but very assured. There was, to use a vulgarism, no getting past her.

She had a couple of thousand pounds she could lay hands on. Virginia, of course, was always in debt. But, after all, Virginia was not to be sniffed at. She made seven hundred and fifty a year.

Virginia was oddly clever, and not clever. She didn't really know anything, because anything and everything was interesting to her for the moment, and she picked it up at once. She picked up languages with extraordinary ease, she was fluent in a fortnight. This helped her enormously with her job. She could prattle away with heads of industry, let them come from where they liked. But she didn't know any language, not even her own. She picked things up in her sleep, so to speak, without knowing anything about them.

And this made her popular with men. With all her curious facility, they didn't feel small in front of her, because she was like an instrument. She had to be prompted. Some man had to set her in motion, and then she worked, really cleverly. She could collect the most valuable information. She was very useful. She worked with men, spent most of her time with men, her friends were practically all men. She didn't feel easy with women.

Yet she had no lover, nobody seemed eager to marry her, nobody seemed eager to come close to her at all. Mrs Bodoin said: I'm afraid Virginia is a one-man woman. I am a one-man woman. So was my mother, and so was my grandmother. Virginia's father was the only man in my life, the only one. And I'm afraid Virginia is the same, tenacious. Unfortunately, the man was what he was, and her life is just left there.

Henry had said, in the past, that Mrs Bodoin wasn't a one-man woman, she was a no-man woman, and that if she could have had her way, everything male would have been wiped off the face of the earth, and only the female element left.

However, Mrs Bodoin thought that it was now time to make a move. So she and Virginia took a quite handsome apartment in one of the old Bloomsbury Squares, fitted it up and furnished it with extreme care, and with some quite lovely things, got in a very good man, an Austrian, to cook, and they set up married life together, mother and daughter.

At first it was rather thrilling. The two reception-rooms, looking down on the dirty old trees of the square garden, were of splendid proportions, and each with three great windows coming down low, almost to the level of the knees. The chimney-piece was late eighteenth-century. Mrs Bodoin furnished the rooms with a gentle suggestion of Louis Seize merged with Empire, without keeping to any particular style. But she had, saved from her own home, a really remarkable Aubusson carpet. It looked almost new, as if it had been woven two years ago, and was startling, yet somehow rather splendid, as it spread its rose-red borders and wonderful florid array of silver-grey and gold-grey roses, lilies and gorgeous swans and trumpeting volutes away over the floor. Very aesthetic people found it rather loud, they preferred the worn, dim yellowish Aubusson in the big bedroom. But Mrs Bodoin loved her drawing-room carpet. It was positive, but it was not vulgar. It had a certain grand air in its floridity. She felt it gave her a proper footing. And it behaved very well with her painted cabinets and grey-and-gold brocade chairs and big Chinese vases, which she liked to fill with big flowers: single Chinese peonies, big roses, great tulips, orange lilies. The dim room of London, with all its atmospheric colour, would stand the big, free, fisticuffing flowers.

Virginia, for the first time in her life, had the pleasure of making a home. She was again entirely under her mother's spell, and swept away, thrilled to her marrow. She had had no idea that her mother had got such treasures as the carpets and painted cabinets and brocade chairs up her sleeve: many of them the débris of the Fitzpatrick home in Ireland, Mrs Bodoin being a Fitzpatrick. Almost like a child, like a bride, Virginia threw herself into the business of fixing up the rooms. "Of course, Virginia, I consider this is your apartment," said Mrs Bodoin. "I am nothing but your dame de compagnie, and shall carry out your wishes entirely, if you will only express them."

Of course Virginia expressed a few, but not many. She introduced some wild pictures bought from impecunious artists whom she patronized. Mrs Bodoin thought the pictures positive about the wrong things, but as far as possible, she let them stay: looking on them as the necessary element of modern ugliness. But by that element of modern ugliness, wilfully so, it was easy to see the things that Virginia had introduced into the apartment.

Perhaps nothing goes to the head like setting up house. You can get drunk on it. You feel you are creating something. Nowadays it is no longer the "home", the domestic nest. It is "my rooms", or "my house", the great garment which reveals and clothes "my personality". Mrs Bodoin, deliberately scheming for Virginia, kept moderately cool over it, but even she was thrilled to the marrow, and of an intensity and ferocity with the decorators and furnishers, astonishing. But Virginia was just all the time tipsy with it, as if she had touched some magic button on the grey wall of life, and with an Open Sesame! her lovely and coloured rooms had begun to assemble out of fairyland. It was far more vivid and wonderful to her than if she had inherited a duchy.

The mother and daughter, the mother in a sort of faded russet crimson and the daughter in silver, began to entertain. They had, of course, mostly

55

men. It filled Mrs Bodoin with a sort of savage impatience to entertain women. Besides, most of Virginia's acquaintances were men. So there were dinners and well-arranged evenings.

It went well, but something was missing. Mrs Bodoin wanted to be gracious, so she held herself rather back. She stayed a little distant, was calm, reposed, eighteenth-century, and determined to be a foil to the clever and slightly-elvish Virginia. It was a pose, and alas, it stopped something. She was very nice with the men, no matter what her contempt of them. But the men were uneasy with her: afraid.

What they all felt, all the men guests, was that for them, nothing really happened. Everything that happened was between mother and daughter. All the flow was between mother and daughter. A subtle, hypnotic spell encompassed the two women, and try as they might, the men were shut out. More than one young man, a little dazzled, began to fall in love with Virginia. But it was impossible. Not only was he shut out, he was, in some way, annihilated. The spontaneity was killed in his bosom. While the two women sat, brilliant and rather wonderful, in magnetic connection at opposite ends of the table, like two witches, a double Circe turning the men not into swine-the men would have liked that well enough-but into lumps.

It was tragic. Because Mrs Bodoin wanted Virginia to fall in love and marry. She really wanted it, and she attributed Virginia's lack of forthcoming to the delinquent Henry. She never realized the hypnotic spell, which of course encompassed her as well as Virginia, and made men just an impossibility to both women, mother and daughter alike.

At this time, Mrs Bodoin hid her humour. She had a really marvellous faculty of humorous imitation. She could imitate the Irish servants from her old home, or the American women who called on her, or the modern lady-like young men, the asphodels, as she called them: "Of course you know the asphodel is a kind of onion! Oh yes, just an over-bred onion": who wanted, with their murmuring voices and peeping under their brows, to make her feel very small and very bourgeois. She could imitate them all with a humour that was really touched with genius. But it was devastating. It demolished the objects of her humour so absolutely, smashed them to bits with a ruthless hammer, pounded them to nothing so terribly, that it frightened people, particularly men. It frightened men off.

So she hid it. She hid it. But there it was, up her sleeve, her merciless, hammer-like humour, which just smashed its object on the head and left him brained. She tried to disown it. She tried to pretend, even to Virginia, that she had the gift no more. But in vain; the hammer hidden up her sleeve hovered over the head of every guest, and every guest felt his scalp creep, and Virginia felt her inside creep with a little, mischievous, slightly idiotic grin, as still another fool male was mystically knocked on the head. It was a sort of uncanny sport.

No, the plan was not going to work: the plan of having Virginia fall in love and marry. Of course the men were such lumps, such oeufs farcies. There was one, at least, that Mrs Bodoin had real hopes of. He was a healthy and normal and very good-looking boy of good family, with no money, alas, but clerking to the House of Lords and very hopeful, and not very clever, but simply in love with Virginia's cleverness. He was just the one Mrs Bodoin would have married for herself. True, he was only twenty-six, to Virginia's thirty-one. But he had rowed in the Oxford eight, and adored horses, talked horses adorably, and was simply infatuated by Virginia's cleverness. To him Virginia had the finest mind on earth. She was as wonderful as Plato, but infinitely more attractive, because she was a woman, and winsome with it. Imagine a winsome Plato with untidy curls and the tiniest little brown-eyed squint and just a hint of woman's pathetic need for a protector, and you may imagine Adrian's feeling for Virginia. He adored her on his knees, but he felt he could protect her.

"Of course he's just a very nice boy!" said Mrs Bodoin. "He's a boy, and that's all you can say. And he always will be a boy. But that's the very nicest kind of man, the only kind you can live with: the eternal boy. Virginia, aren't you attracted to him?"

"Yes, Mother! I think he's an awfully nice boy, as you say," replied Virginia, in her rather slow, musical, whimsical voice. But the mocking little curl in the intonation put the lid on Adrian. Virginia was not marrying a nice boy! She could be malicious too, against her mother's taste. And Mrs Bodoin let escape her a faint gesture of impatience.

For she had been planning her own retreat, planning to give Virginia the apartment outright, and half of her own income, if she would marry Adrian. Yes, the mother was already scheming how best she could live with dignity on three hundred a year, once Virginia was happily married to that most attractive if slightly brainless boy.

A year later, when Virginia was thirty-two, Adrian, who had married a wealthy American girl and been transferred to a job in the legation at Washington in the meantime, faithfully came to see Virginia as soon as he was in London, faithfully kneeled at her feet, faithfully thought her the most wonderful spiritual being, and faithfully felt that she, Virginia, could have done wonders with him, which wonders would now never be done, for he had married in the meantime.

Virginia was looking haggard and worn. The scheme of a ménage à deux with her mother had not succeeded. And now, work was telling on the younger woman. It is true, she was amazingly facile. But facility wouldn't get her all the way. She had to earn her money, and earn it hard. She had to slog, and she had to concentrate. While she could work by quick intuition and without much responsibility, work thrilled her. But as soon as she had to get down to it, as they say, grip and slog and concentrate, in a really responsible position, it wore her out terribly. She had to do it all off her nerves. She hadn't the same sort of fighting power as a man. Where a man can summon his old Adam in him to fight through his work, a woman has to draw on her nerves, and on her nerves alone. For the old Eve in her will have nothing to do with such work. So that mental responsibility, mental concentration, mental slogging wear out a woman terribly, especially if she is head of a department, and not working for somebody.

So poor Virginia was worn out. She was thin as a rail. Her nerves were frayed to bits. And she could never forget her beastly work. She would come home at teatime speechless and done for. Her mother, tortured by the sight of her, longed to say: Has anything gone wrong, Virginia? Have you had anything particularly trying at the office today?-But she learned to hold her tongue, and say nothing. The question would be the last straw to Virginia's poor overwrought nerves, and there would be a little scene which, despite Mrs Bodoin's calm and forbearance, offended the elder woman to the quick. She had learned, by bitter experience, to leave her child alone, as one would leave a frail tube of vitriol alone. But of course, she could not keep her mind off Virginia. That was impossible. And poor Virginia, under the strain of work and the strain of her mother's awful ceaseless mind, was at the very end of her strength and resources.

Mrs Bodoin had always disliked the fact of Virginia's doing a job. But now she hated it. She hated the whole government office with violent and virulent hate. Not only was it undignified for Virginia to be tied up there, but it was turning her, Mrs Bodoin's daughter, into a thin, nagging, fearsome old maid. Could anything be more utterly English and humiliating to a well-born Irishwoman?

After a long day attending to the apartment, skilfully darning one of the brocade chairs, polishing the Venetian mirrors to her satisfaction, selecting flowers, doing certain shopping and housekeeping, attending perfectly to everything, then receiving callers in the afternoon, with never-ending energy, Mrs Bodoin would go up from the drawing-room after tea and write a few letters, take her bath, dress with great care-she enjoyed attending to her person-and come down to dinner as fresh as a daisy, but far more energetic than that quiet flower. She was ready now for a full evening.

She was conscious, with gnawing anxiety, of Virginia's presence in the house, but she did not see her daughter till dinner was announced. Virginia slipped in, and away to her room unseen, never going into the drawing-room to tea. If Mrs Bodoin heard her daughter's key in the latch, she quickly retired into one of the rooms till Virginia was safely through. It was too much for poor Virginia's nerves even to catch sight of anybody in the house, when she came in from the office. Bad enough to hear the murmur of visitors' voices behind the drawing-room door.

And Mrs Bodoin would wonder: How is she? How is she to-night? I wonder what sort of a day she's had?-And this thought would roam prowling through the house, to where Virginia was lying on her back in her room. But the mother would have to consume her anxiety till dinner-time. And then Virginia would appear, with black lines under her eyes, thin, tense, a young woman out of an office, the stigma upon her: badly dressed, a little acid in humour, with an impaired digestion, not interested in anything, blighted by her work. And Mrs Bodoin, humiliated at the very sight of her, would control herself perfectly, say nothing but the mere smooth nothings of casual speech, and sit in perfect form presiding at a carefully-cooked dinner thought out entirely to please Virginia. Then Virginia hardly noticed what she ate.

Mrs Bodoin was pining for an evening with life in it. But Virginia would lie on the couch and put on the loudspeaker. Or she would put a humorous record on the gramophone, and be amused, and hear it again, and be amused, and hear it again, six times, and six times be amused by a mildly funny record that Mrs Bodoin now knew off by heart. "Why, Virginia, I could repeat that record over to you, if you wished it, without your troubling to wind up that gramophone."-And Virginia, after a pause in which she seemed not to have heard what her mother said, would reply, "I'm sure you could, mother". And that simple speech would convey such volumes of contempt for all that Rachel Bodoin was or ever could be or ever had been, contempt for her energy, her vitality, her mind, her body, her very existence, that the elder woman would curl. It seemed as if the ghost of Robert Bodoin spoke out of the mouth of the daughter, in deadly venom.-Then Virginia would put on the record for the seventh time.

During the second ghastly year, Mrs Bodoin realized that the game was up. She was a beaten woman, a woman without object or meaning any more. The hammer of her awful female humour, which had knocked so many people on the head, all the people, in fact, that she had come into contact with, had at last flown backwards and hit herself on the head. For her daughter was her other self, her alter ego. The secret and the meaning and the power of Mrs Bodoin's whole life lay in the hammer, that hammer of her living humour which knocked everything on the head. That had been her lust and her passion, knocking everybody and everything humorously on the head. She had felt inspired in it: it was a sort of mission. And she had hoped to hand on the hammer to Virginia, her clever, unsolid but still actual daughter, Virginia. Virginia was the continuation of Rachel's own self. Virginia was Rachel's alter ego, her other self.

But, alas, it was a half-truth. Virginia had had a father. This fact, which had been utterly ignored by the mother, was gradually brought home to her by the curious recoil of the hammer. Virginia was her father's daughter. Could anything be more unseemly, horrid, more perverse in the natural scheme of things? For Robert Bodoin had been fully and deservedly knocked on the head by Rachel's hammer. Could anything, then, be more disgusting than that he should resurrect again in the person of Mrs Bodoin's own daughter, her own alter ego Virginia, and start hitting back with a little spiteful hammer that was David's pebble against Goliath's battle-axe!

But the little pebble was mortal. Mrs Bodoin felt it sink into her brow, her temple, and she was finished. The hammer fell nerveless from her hand.

The two women were now mostly alone. Virginia was too tired to have company in the evening. So there was the gramophone or loudspeaker, or else silence. Both women had come to loathe the apartment. Virginia felt it was the last grand act of bullying on her mother's part, she felt bullied by the assertive Aubusson carpet, by the beastly Venetian mirrors, by the big overcultured flowers. She even felt bullied by the excellent food, and longed again for a Soho restaurant and her two poky shabby rooms in the hotel. She loathed the apartment: she loathed everything. But she had not the energy to move. She had not the energy to do anything. She crawled to her work, and for the rest, she lay flat, gone.

It was Virginia's worn-out inertia that really finished Mrs Bodoin. That

59

was the pebble that broke the bone of her temple: "To have to attend my daughter's funeral, and accept the sympathy of all her fellow-clerks in her office, no, that is a final humiliation which I must spare myself. No! If Virginia must be a lady-clerk, she must be it henceforth on her own responsibility. I will retire from her existence."

Mrs Bodoin had tried hard to persuade Virginia to give up her work and come and live with her. She had offered her half her income. In vain. Virginia stuck to her office.

Very well! So be it!-The apartment was a fiasco, Mrs Bodoin was longing, longing to tear it to pieces again. One last and final blow of the hammer!-"Virginia, don't you think we'd better get rid of this apartment, and live around as we used to? Don't you think we'll do that?"-"But all the money you've put into it? And the lease for ten years!" cried Virginia, in a kind of inertia.-"Never mind! We had the pleasure of making it. And we've had as much pleasure out of living in it as we shall ever have. Now we'd better get rid of it-quickly-don't you think?"

Mrs Bodoin's arms were twitching to snatch the pictures off the walls, roll up the Aubusson carpet, take the china out of the ivory-inlaid cabinet there and then, at that very moment.

"Let us wait till Sunday before we decide," said Virginia.

"Till Sunday! Four days! As long as that? Haven't we already decided in our own minds?" said Mrs Bodoin.

"We'll wait till Sunday, anyhow," said Virginia.

The next evening, the Armenian came to dinner. Virginia called him Arnold, with the French pronunciation, Arnault. Mrs Bodoin, who barely tolerated him, and could never get his name, which seemed to have a lot of bouyoums in it, called him either the Armenian, or the Rahat Lakoum, after the name of the sweetmeat, or simply The Turkish Delight.

"Arnault is coming to dinner to-night, Mother."

"Really! The Turkish Delight is coming here to dinner? Shall I provide anything special?"-Her voice sounded as if she would suggest snails in aspic.

"I don't think so."

Virginia had seen a good deal of the Armenian at the office, when she had to negotiate with him on behalf of the Board of Trade. He was a man of about sixty, a merchant, had been a millionaire, was ruined during the war, but was now coming on again, and represented trade in Bulgaria. He wanted to negotiate with the British Government, and the British Government sensibly negotiated with him: at first through the medium of Virginia. Now things were going satisfactorily between Monsieur Arnault, as Virginia called him, and the Board of Trade, so that a sort of friendship had followed the official relations.

The Turkish Delight was sixty, grey-haired and fat. He had numerous grandchildren growing up in Bulgaria, but he was a widower. He had a grey moustache cut like a brush, and glazed brown eyes over which hung heavy lids with white lashes. His manner was humble, but in his bearing there was a certain dogged conceit. One notices the combination sometimes in Jews. He had been very wealthy and kow-towed to, he had been ruined and humiliated, terribly humiliated, and now, doggedly, he was rising up again, his sons backing him, away in Bulgaria. One felt he was not alone. He had his sons, his family, his tribe behind him, away in the Near East.

He spoke bad English, but fairly fluent guttural French. He did not speak much, but he sat. He sat, with his short, fat thighs, as if for eternity, there. There was a strange potency in his fat immobile sitting, as if his posterior were connected with the very centre of the earth. And his brain, spinning away at the one point in question, business, was very agile. Business absorbed him. But not in a nervous, personal way. Somehow the family, the tribe was always felt behind him. It was business for the family, the tribe.

With the English he was humble, for the English like such aliens to be humble, and he had had a long schooling from the Turks. And he was always an outsider. Nobody would ever take any notice of him in society. He would just be an outsider, sitting.

"I hope, Virginia, you won't ask that Turkish-carpet gentleman when we have other people. I can bear it," said Mrs Bodoin. "Some people might mind."

"Isn't it hard when you can't choose your own company in your own house!" mocked Virginia.

"No! I don't care. I can meet anything; and I'm sure, in the way of selling Turkish carpets, your acquaintance is very good. But I don't suppose you look on him as a personal friend-?"

"I do. I like him quite a lot."

"Well-! as you will. But consider your other friends."

Mrs Bodoin was really mortified this time. She looked on the Armenian as one looks on the fat Levantine in a fez who tries to sell one hideous tapestries at Port Said, or on the sea-front at Nice, as being outside the class of human beings, and in the class of insects. That he had been a millionaire, and might be a millionaire again, only added venom to her feeling of disgust at being forced into contact with such scum. She could not even squash him, or annihilate him. In scum, there is nothing to squash, for scum is only the unpleasant residue of that which was never anything but squashed.

However, she was not quite just. True, he was fat, and he sat, with short thighs, like a toad, as if seated for a toad's eternity. His colour was of a dirty sort of paste, his black eyes were glazed under heavy lids. And he never spoke until spoken to, waiting in his toad's silence, like a slave.

But his thick, fine white hair, which stood up on his head like a soft brush, was curiously virile. And his curious small hands, of the same soft dull paste, had a peculiar, fat, soft masculine breeding of their own. And his dull brown eye could glint with the subtlety of serpents, under the white brush of eyelash. He was tired, but he was not defeated. He had fought, and won, and lost, and was fighting again, always at a disadvantage. He belonged to a defeated race which accepts defeat, but which gets its own back by cunning. He was the father of sons, the head of a family, one of the heads of a defeated but indestructible tribe. He was not

61

alone, and so you could not lay your finger on him. His whole consciousness was patriarchal and tribal. And somehow, he was humble, but he was indestructible.

At dinner he sat half-effaced, humble, yet with the conceit of the humble. His manners were perfectly good, rather French. Virginia chattered to him in French, and he replied with that peculiar nonchalance of the boulevards, which was the only manner he could command when speaking French. Mrs Bodoin understood, but she was what one would call a heavy-footed linguist, so when she said anything, it was intensely in English. And the Turkish Delight replied in his clumsy English, hastily. It was not his fault that French was being spoken. It was Virginia's.

He was very humble, conciliatory, with Mrs Bodoin. But he cast at her sometimes that rapid glint of a reptilian glance as if to say: Yes! I see you! You are a handsome figure. As an objet de vertu you are almost perfect.-Thus his connoisseur's, antique-dealer's eye would appraise her. But then his thick white eyebrows would seem to add: But what, under holy Heaven, are you as a woman? You are neither wife nor mother nor mistress, you have no perfume of sex, you are more dreadful than a Turkish soldier or an English official. No man on earth could embrace you. You are a ghoul, you are a strange genie from the underworld!-And he would secretly invoke the holy names, to shield him.

Yet he was in love with Virginia. He saw, first and foremost, the child in her, as if she were a lost child in the gutter, a waif with a faint, fascinating cast in her brown eyes, waiting till someone would pick her up. A fatherless waif! And he was tribal father, father through all the ages.

Then, on the other hand, he knew her peculiar disinterested cleverness in affairs. That, too, fascinated him: that odd, almost second-sight cleverness about business, and entirely impersonal, entirely in the air. It seemed to him very strange. But it would be an immense help to him in his schemes. He did not really understand the English. He was at sea with them. But with her, he would have a clue to everything. For she was, finally, quite a somebody among these English, these English officials.

He was about sixty. His family was established, in the East, his grandsons were growing up. It was necessary for him to live in London, for some years. This girl would be useful. She had no money, save what she would inherit from her mother. But he would risk that: she would be an investment in his business. And then the apartment. He liked the apartment extremely. He recognized the cachet, and the lilies and swans of the Aubusson carpet really did something to him. Virginia said to him: Mother gave me the apartment.-So he looked on that as safe. And finally, Virginia was almost a virgin, probably quite a virgin, and, as far as the paternal oriental male like himself was concerned, entirely virgin. He had a very small idea of the silly puppy-sexuality of the English, so different from the prolonged male voluptuousness of his own pleasures. And last of all, he was physically lonely, getting old, and tired.

Virginia of course did not know why she liked being with Arnault. Her cleverness was amazingly stupid when it came to life, to living. She said he was "quaint". She said his nonchalant French of the boulevards was "amusing". She found his business cunning "intriguing", and the glint in his dark glazed eyes, under the white, thick lashes, "sheiky". She saw him quite often, had tea with him in his hotel, and motored with him one day down to the sea.

When he took her hand in his own soft still hands, there was something so caressing, so possessive in his touch, so strange and positive in his leaning towards her, that though she trembled with fear, she was helpless.- "But you are so thin, dear little thin thing, you need repose, repose, for the blossom to open, poor little blossom, to become a little fat!" he said in his French.

She quivered, and was helpless. It certainly was quaint! He was so strange and positive, he seemed to have all the power. The moment he realized that she would succumb into his power, he took full charge of the situation, he lost all his hesitation and his humility. He did not want just to make love to her: he wanted to marry her, for all his multifarious reasons. And he must make himself master of her.

He put her hand to his lips, and seemed to draw her life to his in kissing her thin hand. "The poor child is tired, she needs repose, she needs to be caressed and cared for," he said in his French. And he drew nearer to her.

She looked up in dread at his glinting, tired dark eyes under the white lashes. But he used all his will, looking back at her heavily and calculating that she must submit. And he brought his body quite near to her, and put his hand softly on her face, and made her lay her face against his breast, as he soothingly stroked her arm with his other hand, "Dear little thing! dear little thing! Arnault loves her so dearly! Arnault loves her! Perhaps she will marry her Arnault. Dear little girl, Arnault will put flowers in her life, and make her life perfumed with sweetness and content."

She leaned against his breast and let him caress her. She gave a fleeting, half poignant, half vindictive thought to her mother. Then she felt in the air the sense of destiny, destiny. Oh so nice, not to have to struggle. To give way to destiny.

"Will she marry her old Arnault? Eh? Will she marry him?" he asked in a soothing, caressing voice, at the same time compulsive.

She lifted her head and looked at him: the thick white brows, the glinting, tired dark eyes. How queer and comic! How comic to be in his power! And he was looking a little baffled.

"Shall I?" she said, with her mischievous twist of a grin.

"Mais oui!" he said, with all the sang froid of his old eyes. "Mais oui! Je te contenterai, tu le verras."

"Tu me contenteras!" she said, with a flickering smile of real amusement at his assurance. "Will you really content me?"

"But surely! I assure it you. And you will marry me?"

"You must tell mother," she said, and hid wickedly against his waistcoat again, while the male pride triumphed in him.

Mrs Bodoin had no idea that Virginia was intimate with the Turkish Delight: she did not inquire into her daughter's movements. During the famous dinner, she was calm and a little aloof, but entirely self-possessed. When, after coffee, Virginia left her alone with the Turkish Delight, she made no effort at conversation, only glanced at the rather short, stout man in correct dinner-jacket, and thought how his sort of fatness called for a fez and the full muslin breeches of a bazaar merchant in The Thief of Baghdad.

"Do you really prefer to smoke a hookah?" she asked him, with a slow drawl.

"What is a hookah, please?"

"One of those water-pipes. Don't you all smoke them, in the East?"

He only looked mystified and humble, and silence resumed. She little knew what was simmering inside his stillness.

"Madame," he said, "I want to ask you something."

"You do? Then why not ask it?" came her slightly melancholy drawl.

"Yes! It is this. I wish I may have the honour to marry your daughter. She is willing."

There was a moment's blank pause. Then Mrs Bodoin leaned towards him from her distance, with curious portentousness.

"What was that you said?" she asked. "Repeat it!"

"I wish I may have the honour to marry your daughter. She is willing to take me."

His dark, glazed eyes looked at her, then glanced away again. Still leaning forward, she gazed fixedly on him, as if spellbound, turned to stone. She was wearing pink topaz ornaments, but he judged they were paste, moderately good.

"Did I hear you say she is willing to take you?" came the slow, melancholy, remote voice.

"Madame, I think so," he said, with a bow.

"I think we'll wait till she comes," she said, leaning back.

There was silence. She stared at the ceiling. He looked closely round the room, at the furniture, at the china in the ivory-inlaid cabinet.

"I can settle five thousand pounds on Mademoiselle Virginia, Madame," came his voice. "Am I correct to assume that she will bring this apartment and its appointments into the marriage settlement?"

Absolute silence. He might as well have been on the moon. But he was a good sitter. He just sat until Virginia came in.

Mrs Bodoin was still staring at the ceiling. The iron had entered her soul finally and fully. Virginia glanced at her, but said:

"Have a whisky-and-soda, Arnault?"

He rose and came towards the decanters, and stood beside her: a rather squat, stout man with white head, silent with misgiving. There was the fizz of the syphon: then they came to their chairs.

"Arnault has spoken to you, Mother?" said Virginia.

Mrs Bodoin sat up straight, and gazed at Virginia with big, owlish eyes, haggard. Virginia was terrified, yet a little thrilled. Her mother was beaten.

"Is it true, Virginia, that you are willing to marry this-oriental gentleman?" asked Mrs Bodoin slowly.

"Yes, Mother, quite true," said Virginia, in her teasing soft voice.

Mrs Bodoin looked owlish and dazed.

"May I be excused from having any part in it, or from having anything to do with your future husband-I mean having any business to transact with him?" she asked dazedly, in her slow, distinct voice.

"Why, of course!" said Virginia, frightened, smiling oddly.

There was a pause. Then Mrs Bodoin, feeling old and haggard, pulled herself together again.

"Am I to understand that your future husband would like to possess this apartment?" came her voice.

Virginia smiled quickly and crookedly. Arnault just sat, planted on his posterior, and heard. She reposed on him.

"Well-perhaps!" said Virginia. "Perhaps he would like to know that I possessed it." She looked at him.

Arnault nodded gravely.

"And do you wish to possess it?" came Mrs Bodoin's slow voice. "If it your intention to inhabit it, with your husband?" She put eternities into her long, stressed words.

"Yes, I think it is," said Virginia. "You know you said the apartment was mine, Mother."

"Very well! It shall be so. I shall send my lawyer to this-oriental gentleman, if you will leave written instructions on my writing-table. May I ask when you think of getting-married?"

"When do you think, Arnault?" said Virginia.

"Shall it be, in two weeks?" he said, sitting erect, with his fists on his knees.

"In about a fortnight, Mother," said Virginia.

"I have heard! In two weeks! Very well! In two weeks everything shall be at your disposal. And now, please excuse me." She rose, made a slight general bow, and moved calmly and dimly from the room. It was killing her, that she could not shriek aloud and beat that Levantine out of the house. But she couldn't. She had imposed the restraint on herself.

Arnault stood and looked with glistening eyes round the room. It would be his. When his sons came to England, here he would receive them.

He looked at Virginia. She too was white and haggard, now. And she hung away from him, as if in resentment. She resented the defeat of her mother. She was still capable of dismissing him for ever, and going back to her mother.

"Your mother is a wonderful lady," he said, going to Virginia and taking her hand. "But she has no husband to shelter her, she is unfortunate. I am sorry she will be alone. I should be happy if she would like to stay here with us."

The sly old fox knew what he was about.

"I'm afraid there's no hope of that," said Virginia, with a return to her old irony.

She sat on the couch, and he caressed her softly and paternally, and the very incongruity of it, there in her mother's drawing-room, amused her. And because he saw that the things in the drawing-room were handsome and valuable, and now they were his, his blood flushed and he caressed the thin girl at his side with passion, because she represented these valuable surroundings, and brought them to his possession. And he said: "And with me you will be very comfortable, very content, oh, I shall make you content, not like Madame your mother. And you will get fatter, and bloom

65

like the rose. I shall make you bloom like the rose. And shall we say next week, hein? Shall it be next week, next Wednesday, that we marry? Wednesday is a good day. Shall it be then?"

"Very well!" said Virginia, caressed again into a luxurious sense of destiny, reposing on fate, having to make no effort, no more effort, all her life.

Mrs Bodoin moved into an hotel next day, and came into the apartment to pack up and extricate herself and her immediate personal belongings only when Virginia was necessarily absent. She and her daughter communicated by letter, as far as was necessary.

And in five days' time Mrs Bodoin was clear. All business that could be settled was settled, all her trunks were removed. She had five trunks, and that was all. Denuded and outcast, she would depart to Paris, to live out the rest of her days.

The last day, she waited in the drawing-room till Virginia should come home. She sat there in her hat and street things, like a stranger.

"I just waited to say good-bye," she said. "I leave in the morning for Paris. This is my address. I think everything is settled; if not, let me know and I'll attend to it. Well, good-bye!-and I hope you'll be very happy!"

She dragged out the last words sinisterly; which restored Virginia, who was beginning to lose her head.

"Why, I think I may be," said Virginia, with the twist of a smile.

"I shouldn't wonder," said Mrs Bodoin pointedly and grimly. "I think the Armenian grandpapa knows very well what he's about. You're just the harem type, after all." The words came slowly, dropping, each with a plop! of deep contempt.

"I suppose I am! Rather fun!" said Virginia. "But I wonder where I got it? Not from you, Mother-" she drawled mischievously.

"I should say not."

"Perhaps daughters go by contraries, like dreams," mused Virginia wickedly. "All the harem was left out of you, so perhaps it all had to be put back into me."

Mrs Bodoin flashed a look at her.

"You have all my pity!" she said.

"Thank you, dear. You have just a bit of mine."

NEW EVE AND OLD ADAM

I

"After all," she said, with a little laugh, "I can't see it was so wonderful of you to hurry home to me, if you are so cross when you do come."

"You would rather I stayed away?" he asked.

"I wouldn't mind."

"You would rather I had stayed a day or two in Paris-or a night or two."

She burst into a jeering "pouf!" of laughter.

"You!" she cried. "You and Parisian Nights' Entertainment! What a fool you would look."

"Still," he said, "I could try."

"You would!" she mocked. "You would go dribbling up to a woman. 'Please take me-my wife is so unkind to me!'"

He drank his tea in silence. They had been married a year. They had married quickly, for love. And during the last three months there had gone on almost continuously that battle between them which so many married people fight, without knowing why. Now it had begun again. He felt the physical sickness rising in him. Somewhere down in his belly the big, feverish pulse began to beat, where was the inflamed place caused by the conflict between them.

She was a beautiful woman of about thirty, fair, luxuriant, with proud shoulders and a face borne up by a fierce, native vitality. Her green eyes had a curiously puzzled contraction just now. She sat leaning on the table against the tea-tray, absorbed. It was as if she battled with herself in him. Her green dress reflected in the silver, against the red of the firelight. Leaning abstractedly forward, she pulled some primroses from the bowl, and threaded them at intervals in the plait which bound round her head in the peasant fashion. So, with her little starred fillet of flowers, there was something of the Gretchen about her. But her eyes retained the curious half-smile.

Suddenly her face lowered gloomily. She sank her beautiful arms, laying them on the table. Then she sat almost sullenly, as if she would not give in. He was looking away out of the window. With a quick movement she glanced down at her hands. She took off her wedding-ring, reached to the bowl for a long flower-stalk, and shook the ring glittering round and round upon it, regarding the spinning gold, and spinning it as if she would spurn it. Yet there was something about her of a fretful, naughty child as she did so.

The man sat by the fire, tired, but tense. His body seemed so utterly still because of the tension in which it was held. His limbs, thin and vigorous, lay braced like a listening thing, always vivid for action, yet held perfectly still. His face was set and expressionless. The wife was all the time, in spite of herself, conscious of him, as if the cheek that was turned towards him

67

had a sense which perceived him. They were both rendered elemental, like impersonal forces, by the battle and the suffering.

She rose and went to the window. Their flat was the fourth, the top storey of a large house. Above the high-ridged, handsome red roof opposite was an assembly of telegraph wires, a square, squat framework, towards which hosts of wires sped from four directions, arriving in darkly-stretched lines out of the white sky. High up, at a great height, a seagull sailed. There was a noise of traffic from the town beyond.

Then, from behind the ridge of the house-roof opposite a man climbed up into the tower of wires, belted himself amid the netted sky, and began to work, absorbedly. Another man, half-hidden by the roof-ridge, stretched up to him with a wire. The man in the sky reached down to receive it. The other, having delivered, sank out of sight. The solitary man worked absorbedly. Then he seemed drawn away from his task. He looked round almost furtively, from his lonely height, the space pressing on him. His eyes met those of the beautiful woman who stood in her afternoon-gown, with flowers in her hair, at the window.

"I like you," she said, in her normal voice.

Her husband, in the room with her, looked round slowly and asked: "Whom do you like?"

Receiving no answer, he resumed his tense stillness.

She remained watching at the window, above the small, quiet street of large houses. The man, suspended there in the sky, looked across at her and she at him. The city was far below. Her eyes and his met across the lofty space. Then, crouching together again into his forgetfulness, he hid himself in his work. He would not look again. Presently he climbed down, and the tower of wires was empty against the sky.

The woman glanced at the little park at the end of the clear, grey street. The diminished, dark-blue form of a soldier was seen passing between the green stretches of grass, his spurs giving the faintest glitter to his walk.

Then she turned hesitating from the window, as if drawn by her husband. He was sitting still motionless, and detached from her, hard; held absolutely away from her by his will. She wavered, then went and crouched on the hearth-rug at his feet, laying her head on his knee.

"Don't be horrid with me!" she pleaded, in a caressing, languid, impersonal voice. He shut his teeth hard, and his lips parted slightly with pain.

"You know you love me," she continued, in the same heavy, sing-song way. He breathed hard, but kept still.

"Don't you?" she said, slowly, and she put her arms round his waist, under his coat, drawing him to her. It was as if flames of fire were running under his skin.

"I have never denied it," he said woodenly.

"Yes," she pleaded, in the same heavy, toneless voice. "Yes. You are always trying to deny it." She was rubbing her cheek against his knee, softly. Then she gave a little laugh, and shook her head. "But it's no good." She looked up at him. There was a curious light in his eyes, of subtle victory. "It's no good, my love, is it?"

His heart ran hot. He knew it was no good trying to deny he loved her. But he saw her eyes, and his will remained set and hard. She looked away into the fire.

"You hate it that you have to love me," she said, in a pensive voice through which the triumph flickered faintly. "You hate it that you love me-and it is petty and mean of you. You hate it that you had to hurry back to me from Paris."

Her voice had become again quite impersonal, as if she were talking to herself.

"At any rate," he said, "it is your triumph."

She gave a sudden, bitter-contemptuous laugh.

"Ha!" she said. "What is triumph to me, you fool! You can have your triumph. I should be only too glad to give it you."

"And I to take it."

"Then take it," she cried, in hostility. "I offer it you often enough."

"But you never mean to part with it."

"It is a lie. It is you, you, who are too paltry to take a woman. How often do I fling myself at you-"

"Then don't-don't."

"Ha!-and if I don't-I get nothing out of you. Self! self! that is all you are."

His face remained set and expressionless. She looked up at him. Suddenly she drew him to her again, and hid her face against him.

"Don't kick me off, Pietro, when I come to you," she pleaded.

"You don't come to me," he answered stubbornly.

She lifted her head a few inches away from him and seemed to listen, or to think.

"What do I do, then?" she asked, for the first time quietly.

"You treat me as if I were a piece of cake, for you to eat when you wanted."

She rose from him with a mocking cry of scorn, that yet had something hollow in its sound.

"Treat you like a piece of cake, do I!" she cried. "I, who have done all I have for you!"

There was a knock, and the maid entered with a telegram. He tore it open.

"No answer," he said, and the maid softly closed the door.

"I suppose it is for you," he said, bitingly, rising and handing her the slip of paper. She read it, laughed, then read it again, aloud:

"'Meet me Marble Arch 7.30-theatre-Richard.' Who is Richard?" she asked, looking at her husband rather interested. He shook his head.

"Nobody of mine," he said. "Who is he?"

"I haven't the faintest notion," she said, flippantly.

"But," and his eyes went bullying, "you must know."

She suddenly became quiet, and jeering, took up his challenge.

"Why must I know?" she asked.

"Because it isn't for me, therefore it must be for you."

"And couldn't it be for anybody else?" she sneered.

69

"'Moest, 14 Merrilies Street,'" he read, decisively.

For a second she was puzzled into earnestness.

"Pah, you fool," she said, turning aside. "Think of your own friends," and she flung the telegram away.

"It is not for me," he said, stiffly and finally.

"Then it is for the man in the moon-I should think his name is Moest," she added, with a pouf of laughter against him.

"Do you mean to say you know nothing about it?" he asked.

"Do you mean to say," she mocked, mouthing the words, and sneering; "Yes, I do mean to say, poor little man."

He suddenly went hard with disgust.

"Then I simply don't believe you," he said coldly.

"Oh-don't you believe me!" she jeered, mocking the touch of sententiousness in his voice. "What a calamity. The poor man doesn't believe!"

"It couldn't possibly be any acquaintance of mine," he said slowly.

"Then hold your tongue!" she cried harshly. "I've heard enough of it."

He was silent, and soon she went out of the room. In a few minutes he heard her in the drawing-room, improvising furiously. It was a sound that maddened him: something yearning, yearning, striving, and something perverse, that counteracted the yearning. Her music was always working up towards a certain culmination, but never reaching it, falling away in a jangle. How he hated it. He lit a cigarette, and went across to the sideboard for a whisky and soda. Then she began to sing. She had a good voice, but she could not keep time. As a rule it made his heart warm with tenderness for her, hearing her ramble through the songs in her own fashion, making Brahms sound so different by altering his time. But to-day he hated her for it. Why the devil couldn't she submit to the natural laws of the stuff!

In about fifteen minutes she entered, laughing. She laughed as she closed the door, and as she came to him where he sat.

"Oh," she said, "you silly thing, you silly thing! Aren't you a stupid clown?"

She crouched between his knees and put her arms round him. She was smiling into his face, her green eyes looking into his, were bright and wide. But somewhere in them, as he looked back, was a little twist that could not come loose to him, a little cast, that was like an aversion from him, a strain of hate for him. The hot waves of blood flushed over his body, and his heart seemed to dissolve under her caresses. But at last, after many months, he knew her well enough. He knew that curious little strain in her eyes, which was waiting for him to submit to her, and then would spurn him again. He resisted her while ever it was there.

"Why don't you let yourself love me?" she asked, pleading, but a touch of mockery in her voice. His jaw set hard.

"Is it because you are afraid?"

He heard the slight sneer.

"Of what?" he asked.

"Afraid to trust yourself?"

70

There was silence. It made him furious that she could sit there caressing him and yet sneer at him.

"What have I done with myself?" he asked.

"Carefully saved yourself from giving all to me, for fear you might lose something."

"Why should I lose anything?" he asked.

And they were both silent. She rose at last and went away from him to get a cigarette. The silver box flashed red with firelight in her hands. She struck a match, bungled, threw the stick aside, lit another.

"What did you come running back for?" she asked, insolently, talking with half-shut lips because of the cigarette. "I told you I wanted peace. I've had none for a year. And for the last three months you've done nothing but try to destroy me."

"You have not gone frail on it," he answered sarcastically.

"Nevertheless," she said, "I am ill inside me. I am sick of you-sick. You make an eternal demand, and you give nothing back. You leave one empty." She puffed the cigarette in feminine fashion, then suddenly she struck her forehead with a wild gesture. "I have a ghastly, empty feeling in my head," she said. "I feel I simply must have rest-I must."

The rage went through his veins like flame.

"From your labours?" he asked, sarcastically, suppressing himself.

"From you-from you?" she cried, thrusting forward her head at him. "You, who use a woman's soul up, with your rotten life. I suppose it is partly your health, and you can't help it," she added, more mildly. "But I simply can't stick it-I simply can't, and that is all."

She shook her cigarette carelessly in the direction of the fire. The ash fell on the beautiful Asiatic rug. She glanced at it, but did not trouble. He sat, hard with rage.

"May I ask how I use you up, as you say?" he asked.

She was silent a moment, trying to get her feeling into words. Then she shook her hand at him passionately, and took the cigarette from her mouth.

"By-by following me about-by not leaving me alone. You give me no peace-I don't know what you do, but it is something ghastly."

Again the hard stroke of rage went down his mind.

"It is very vague," he said.

"I know," she cried. "I can't put it into words-but there it is. You-you don't love. I pour myself out to you, and then-there's nothing there-you simply aren't there."

He was silent for some time. His jaw set hard with fury and hate.

"We have come to the incomprehensible," he said. "And now, what about Richard?"

It had grown nearly dark in the room. She sat silent for a moment. Then she took the cigarette from her mouth and looked at it.

"I'm going to meet him," her voice, mocking, answered out of the twilight.

His head went molten, and he could scarcely breathe.

71

"Who is he?" he asked, though he did not believe the affair to be anything at all, even if there were a Richard.

"I'll introduce him to you when I know him a little better," she said. He waited.

"But who is he?"

"I tell you, I'll introduce him to you later."

There was a pause.

"Shall I come with you?"

"It would be like you," she answered, with a sneer.

The maid came in, softly, to draw the curtains and turn on the light. The husband and wife sat silent.

"I suppose," he said, when the door was closed again, "you are wanting a Richard for a rest?"

She took his sarcasm simply as a statement.

"I am," she said. "A simple, warm man who would love me without all these reservation and difficulties. That is just what I do want."

"Well, you have your own independence," he said.

"Ha," she laughed. "You needn't tell me that. It would take more than you to rob me of my independence."

"I meant your own income," he answered quietly, while his heart was plunging with bitterness and rage.

"Well," she said, "I will go and dress."

He remained without moving, in his chair. The pain of this was almost too much. For some moments the great, inflamed pulse struck through his body. It died gradually down, and he went dull. He had not wanted to separate from her at this point of their union; they would probably, if they parted in such a crisis, never come together again. But if she insisted, well then, it would have to be. He would go away for a month. He could easily make business in Italy. And when he came back, they could patch up some sort of domestic arrangement, as most other folk had to do.

He felt full and heavy inside, and without the energy for anything. The thought of having to pack and take a train to Milan appalled him; it would mean such an effort of will. But it would have to be done, and so he must do it. It was no use his waiting at home. He might stay in town a night, at his brother-in-law's, and go away the next day. It were better to give her a little time to come to herself. She was really impulsive. And he did not really want to go away from her.

He was still sitting thinking, when she came downstairs. She was in costume and furs and toque. There was a radiant, half-wistful, half-perverse look about her. She was a beautiful woman, her bright, fair face set among the black furs.

"Will you give me some money?" she said. "There isn't any."

He took two sovereigns, which she put in her little black purse. She would go without a word of reconciliation. It made his heart set hard again.

"You would like me to go away for a moment?" he said, calmly.

"Yes," she answered, stubbornly.

"All right, then, I will. I must stop in town for to-morrow, but I will sleep at Edmund's."

72

"You could do that, couldn't you?" she said, accepting his suggestion, a little bit hesitating.

"If you want me to."

"I'm so tired!" she lamented.

But there was exasperation and hate in the last word, too.

"Very well," he answered.

She finished buttoning her glove.

"You'll go, then?" she said suddenly, brightly, turning to depart. "Good-bye."

He hated her for the flippant insult of her leave-taking.

"I shall be at Edmund's to-morrow," he said.

"You will write to me from Italy, won't you?"

He would not answer the unnecessary question.

"Have you taken the dead primroses out of your hair?" he asked.

"I haven't," she said.

And she unpinned her hat.

"Richard would think me cracked," she said, picking out the crumpled, creamy fragments. She strewed the withered flowers carelessly on the table, set her hat straight.

"Do you want me to go?" he asked, again, rather yearning.

She knitted her brows. It irked her to resist the appeal. Yet she had in her breast a hard, repellent feeling for him. She had loved him, too. She had loved him dearly. And-he had not seemed to realise her. So that now she did want to be free of him for a while. Yet the love, the passion she had had for him clung about her. But she did want, first and primarily, to be free of him again.

"Yes," she said, half pleading.

"Very well," he answered.

She came across to him, and put her arms round his neck. Her hatpin caught his head, but he moved, and she did not notice.

"You don't mind very much, do you, my love?" she said caressingly.

"I mind all the world, and all I am," he said.

She rose from him, fretted, miserable, and yet determined.

"I must have some rest," she repeated.

He knew that cry. She had had it, on occasions, for two months now. He had cursed her, and refused either to go away or to let her go. Now he knew it was no use.

"All right," he said. "Go and get it from Richard."

"Yes." She hesitated. "Good-bye," she called, and was gone.

He heard her cab whirr away. He had no idea whither she was gone-but probably to Madge, her friend.

He went upstairs to pack. Their bedroom made him suffer. She used to say, at first, that she would give up anything rather than her sleeping with him. And still they were always together. A kind of blind helplessness drove them to one another, even when, after he had taken her, they only felt more apart than ever. It had seemed to her that he had been mechanical and barren with her. She felt a horrible feeling of aversion from him, inside her, even while physically she still desired him. His body

73

had always a kind of fascination for her. But had hers for him? He seemed, often, just to have served her, or to have obeyed some impersonal instinct for which she was the only outlet, in his loving her. So at last she rose against him, to cast him off. He seemed to follow her so, to draw her life into his. It made her feel she would go mad. For he seemed to do it just blindly, without having any notion of her herself. It was as if she were sucked out of herself by some non-human force. As for him, he seemed only like an instrument for his work, his business, not like a person at all. Sometimes she thought he was a big fountain-pen which was always sucking at her blood for ink.

He could not understand anything of this. He loved her-he could not bear to be away from her. He tried to realise her and to give her what she wanted. But he could not understand. He could not understand her accusations against him. Physically, he knew, she loved him, or had loved him, and was satisfied by him. He also knew that she would have loved another man nearly as well. And for the rest, he was only himself. He could not understand what she said about his using her and giving her nothing in return. Perhaps he did not think of her, as a separate person from himself, sufficiently. But then he did not see, he could not see that she had any real personal life, separate from himself. He tried to think of her in every possible way, and to give her what she wanted. But it was no good; she was never at peace. And lately there had been growing a breach between them. They had never come together without his realising it, afterwards. Now he must submit, and go away.

And her quilted dressing-gown-it was a little bit torn, like most of her things-and her pearl-backed mirror, with one of the pieces of pearl missing-all her untidy, flimsy, lovable things hurt him as he went about the bedroom, and made his heart go hard with hate, in the midst of his love.

II

Instead of going to his brother-in-law's, he went to an hotel for the night. It was not till he stood in the lift, with the attendant at his side, that he began to realise that he was only a mile or so away from his own home, and yet farther away than any miles could make him. It was about nine o'clock. He hated his bedroom. It was comfortable, and not ostentatious; its only fault was the neutrality necessary to an hotel apartment. He looked round. There was one semi-erotic Florentine picture of a lady with cat's eyes, over the bed. It was not bad. The only other ornament on the walls was the notice of hours and prices of meals and rooms. The couch sat correctly before the correct little table, on which the writing-sachet and ink-stand stood mechanically. Down below, the quiet street was half illuminated, the people passed sparsely, like stunted shadows. And of all times of the night, it was a quarter-past nine. He thought he would go to bed. Then he looked at the white-and-glazed doors which shut him off from the bath. He would bath, to pass the time away. In the bath-closet everything was so comfortable and white and warm-too warm; the level, unvarying heat of the atmosphere, from which there was no escape anywhere, seemed so hideously hotel-like; this central-heating forced a unity into the great building, making it more than ever like an enormous box with incubating cells. He loathed it. But at any rate the bath-closet was human, white and business-like and luxurious.

He was trying, with the voluptuous warm water, and the exciting thrill of the shower-bath, to bring back the life into his dazed body. Since she had begun to hate him, he had gradually lost that physical pride and pleasure in his own physique which the first months of married life had given him. His body had gone meaningless to him again, almost as if it were not there. It had wakened up, there had been the physical glow and satisfaction about his movements of a creature which rejoices in itself; a glow which comes on a man who loves and is loved passionately and successfully. Now this was going again. All the life was accumulating in his mental consciousness, and his body felt like a piece of waste. He was not aware of this. It was instinct which made him want to bathe. But that, too, was a failure. He went under the shower-spray with his mind occupied by business, or some care of affairs, taking the tingling water almost without knowing it, stepping out mechanically, as a man going through a barren routine. He was dry again, and looking out of the window, without having experienced anything during the last hour.

Then he remembered that she did not know his address. He scribbled a note and rang to have it posted.

As soon as he had turned out the light, and there was nothing left for his mental consciousness to flourish amongst, it dropped, and it was dark inside him as without. It was his blood, and the elemental male in it, that now rose from him; unknown instincts suffocated him, and he could not bear it, that he was shut in this great, warm building. He wanted to be outside, with space springing from him. But, again, the reasonable being in him knew it was ridiculous, and he remained staring at the dark, having the horrible sensation of a roof low down over him; whilst that dark, unknown being, which lived below all his consciousness in the eternal gloom of his blood, heaved and raged blindly against him.

It was not his thoughts that represented him. They spun like straws or the iridescence of oil on a dark stream. He thought of her, sketchily, spending an evening of light amusement with the symbolical Richard. That did not mean much to him. He did not really speculate about Richard. He had the dark, powerful sense of her, how she wanted to get away from him and from the deep, underneath intimacy which had gradually come between them, back to the easy, everyday life where one knows nothing of the underneath, so that it takes its way apart from the consciousness. She did not want to have the deeper part of herself in direct contact with or under the influence of any other intrinsic being. She wanted, in the deepest sense, to be free of him. She could not bear the close, basic intimacy into which she had been drawn. She wanted her life for herself. It was true, her strongest desire had been previously to know the contact through the whole of her being, down to the very bottom. Now it troubled her. She wanted to disengage his roots. Above, in the open, she would live. But she must live perfectly free of herself, and not, at her source, be connected with anybody. She was using this symbolical Richard as a spade to dig him away from her. And he felt like a thing whose roots are all straining on their hold, and whose elemental life, that blind source, surges backwards and forwards darkly, in a chaos, like something which is threatened with spilling out of its own vessel.

This tremendous swaying of the most elemental part of him continued through the hours, accomplishing his being, whilst superficially he thought of the journey, of the Italian he would speak, how he had left his coat in the train, and the rascally official interpreter had tried to give him twenty lire for a sovereign-how the man in the hat-shop in the Strand had given him the wrong change-of the new shape in hats, and the new felt-and so on. Underneath it all, like the sea under a pleasure pier, his elemental, physical soul was heaving in great waves through his blood and his tissue, the sob, the silent lift, the slightly-washing fall away again. So his blood, out of whose darkness everything rose, being moved to its depth by her revulsion, heaved and swung towards its own rest, surging blindly to its own re-settling.

Without knowing it, he suffered that night almost more than he had ever suffered during his life. But it was all below his consciousness. It was his life itself at storm, not his mind and his will engaged at all.

In the morning he got up, thin and quiet, without much movement anywhere, only with some of the clearing afterstorm. His body felt like a clean, empty shell. His mind was limpidly clear. He went through the business of the toilet with a certain accuracy, and at breakfast, in the restaurant, there was about him that air of neutral correctness which makes men seem so unreal.

At lunch, there was a telegram for him. It was like her to telegraph.

"Come to tea, my dear love."

As he read it, there was a great heave of resistance in him. But then he faltered. With his consciousness, he remembered how impulsive and eager she was when she dashed off her telegram, and he relaxed. It went without saying that he would go.

III

When he stood in the lift going up to his own flat, he was almost blind with the hurt of it all. They had loved each other so much in his first home. The parlour-maid opened to him, and he smiled at her affectionately. In the golden-brown and cream-coloured hall-Paula would have nothing heavy or sombre about her-a bush of rose-coloured azaleas shone, and a little tub of lilies twinkled naïvely.

She did not come out to meet him.

76

"Tea is in the drawing-room," the maid said, and he went in while she was hanging up his coat. It was a big room, with a sense of space, and a spread of whity carpet almost the colour of unpolished marble-and grey and pink border; of pink roses on big white cushions, pretty Dresden china, and deep chintz-covered chairs and sofas which looked as if they were used freely. It was a room where one could roll in soft, fresh-comfort, a room which had not much breakable in it, and which seemed, in the dusky spring evening, fuller of light than the streets outside.

Paula rose, looking queenly and rather radiant, as she held out her hand. A young man whom Peter scarcely noticed rose on the other side of the hearth.

"I expected you an hour ago," she said, looking into her husband's eyes. But though she looked at him, she did not see him. And he sank his head.

"This is another Moest," she said, presenting the stranger. "He knows Richard, too."

The young man, a German of about thirty, with a clean-shaven æsthetic face, long black hair brushed back a little wearily or bewildered from his brow, and inclined to fall in an odd loose strand again, so that he nervously put it back with his fine hand, looked at Moest and bowed. He had a finely-cut face, but his dark-blue eyes were strained, as if he did not quite know where he was. He sat down again, and his pleasant figure took a self-conscious attitude, of a man whose business it was to say things that should be listened to. He was not conceited or affected-naturally sensitive and rather naïve; but he could only move in an atmosphere of literature and literary ideas; yet he seemed to know there was something else, vaguely, and he felt rather at a loss. He waited for the conversation to move his way, as, inert, an insect waits for the sun to set it flying.

"Another Moest," Paula was pronouncing emphatically. "Actually another Moest, of whom we have never heard, and under the same roof with us."

The stranger laughed, his lips moving nervously over his teeth.

"You are in this house?" Peter asked, surprised.

The young man shifted in his chair, dropped his head, looked up again.

"Yes," he said, meeting Moest's eyes as if he were somewhat dazzled. "I am staying with the Lauriers, on the second floor."

He spoke English slowly, with a quaint, musical quality in his voice, and a certain rhythmic enunciation.

"I see; and the telegram was for you?" said the host.

"Yes," replied the stranger, with a nervous little laugh.

"My husband," broke in Paula, evidently repeating to the German what she had said before, for Peter's benefit this time, "was quite convinced I had an affaire"-she pronounced it in the French fashion-"with this terrible Richard."

The German gave his little laugh, and moved, painfully self-conscious, in his chair.

"Yes," he said, glancing at Moest.

"Did you spend a night of virtuous indignation?" Paula laughed to her husband, "imagining my perfidy?"

77

"I did not," said her husband. "Were you at Madge's?"

"No," she said. Then, turning to her guest: "Who is Richard, Mr. Moest?"

"Richard," began the German, word by word, "is my cousin." He glanced quickly at Paula, to see if he were understood. She rustled her skirts, and arranged herself comfortably, lying, or almost squatting, on the sofa by the fire. "He lives in Hampstead."

"And what is he like?" she asked, with eager interest.

The German gave his little laugh. Then he moved his fingers across his brow, in his dazed fashion. Then he looked, with his beautiful blue eyes, at his beautiful hostess.

"I-" He laughed again nervously. "He is a man whose parts-are not very much-very well known to me. You see," he broke forth, and it was evident he was now conversing to an imaginary audience-"I cannot easily express myself in English. I-I never have talked it. I shall speak, because I know nothing of modern England, a kind of Renaissance English."

"How lovely!" cried Paula. "But if you would rather, speak German. We shall understand sufficiently."

"I would rather hear some Renaissance English," said Moest.

Paula was quite happy with the new stranger. She listened to descriptions of Richard, shifting animatedly on her sofa. She wore a new dress, of a rich red-tile colour, glossy and long and soft, and she had threaded daisies, like buttons, in the braided plait of her hair. Her husband hated her for these familiarities. But she was beautiful too, and warm-hearted. Only, through all her warmth and kindliness, lay, he said, at the bottom, an almost feline selfishness, a coldness.

She was playing to the stranger-nay, she was not playing, she was really occupied by him. The young man was the favourite disciple of the most famous present-day German poet and Meister. He himself was occupied in translating Shakespeare. Having been always a poetic disciple, he had never come into touch with life save through literature, and for him, since he was a rather fine-hearted young man, with a human need to live, this was a tragedy. Paula was not long in discovering what ailed him, and she was eager to come to his rescue.

It pleased her, nevertheless, to have her husband sitting by, watching her. She forgot to give tea to anyone. Moest and the German both helped themselves, and the former attended also to his wife's cup. He sat rather in the background, listening, and waiting. She had made a fool of him with her talk to this stranger of "Richard"; lightly and flippantly she had made a fool of him. He minded, but was used to it. Now she had absorbed herself in this dazed, starved, literature-bewildered young German, who was, moreover, really lovable, evidently a gentleman. And she was seeing in him her mission-"just as", said Moest bitterly to himself, "she saw her mission in me, a year ago. She is no woman. She's got a big heart for everybody, but it must be like a common-room; she's got no private, sacred heart, except perhaps for herself, where there's no room for a man in it."

At length the stranger rose to go, promising to come again.

"Isn't he adorable?" cried Paula, as her husband returned to the drawing-room. "I think he is simply adorable."

"Yes!" said Moest.

"He called this morning to ask about the telegram. But, poor devil, isn't it a shame what they've done to him?"

"What who have done to him?" her husband asked coldly, jealous.

"Those literary creatures. They take a young fellow like that, and stick him up among the literary gods, like a mantelpiece ornament, and there he has to sit, being a minor ornament, while all his youth is gone. It is criminal."

"He should get off the mantelpiece, then," said Moest.

But inside him his heart was black with rage against her. What had she, after all, to do with this young man, when he himself was being smashed up by her? He loathed her pity and her kindliness, which was like a charitable institution. There was no core to the woman. She was full of generosity and bigness and kindness, but there was no heart in her, no security, no place for one single man. He began to understand now sirens and sphinxes and the other Greek fabulous female things. They had not been created by fancy, but out of bitter necessity of the man's human heart to express itself.

"Ha!" she laughed, half contemptuous. "Did you get off your miserable, starved isolation by yourself?-you didn't. You had to be fetched down, and I had to do it."

"Out of your usual charity," he said.

"But you can sneer at another man's difficulties," she said.

"Your name ought to be Panacea, not Paula," he replied.

He felt furious and dead against her. He could even look at her without the tenderness coming. And he was glad. He hated her. She seemed unaware. Very well; let her be so.

"Oh, but he makes me so miserable, to see him!" she cried. "Self-conscious, can't get into contact with anybody, living a false literary life like a man who takes poetry as a drug.-One ought to help him."

She was really earnest and distressed.

"Out of the frying-pan into the fire," he said.

"I'd rather be in the fire any day, than in a frying-pan," she said, abstractedly, with a little shudder. She never troubled to see the meaning of her husband's sarcasms.

They remained silent. The maid came in for the tray, and to ask him if he would be in to dinner. He waited for his wife to answer. She sat with her chin in her hands, brooding over the young German, and did not hear. The rage flashed up in his heart. He would have liked to smash her out of this false absorption.

"No," he said to the maid. "I think not. Are you at home for dinner, Paula?"

"Yes," she said.

And he knew by her tone, easy and abstracted, that she intended him to stay, too. But she did not trouble to say anything.

At last, after some time, she asked:

"What did you do?"

"Nothing-went to bed early," he replied.

"Did you sleep well?"

"Yes, thank you."

And he recognised the ludicrous civilities of married people, and he wanted to go. She was silent for a time. Then she asked, and her voice had gone still and grave:

"Why don't you ask me what I did?"

"Because I don't care-you just went to somebody's for dinner."

"Why don't you care what I do? Isn't it your place to care?"

"About the things you do to spite me?-no!"

"Ha!" she mocked. "I did nothing to spite you. I was in deadly earnest."

"Even with your Richard?"

"Yes," she cried. "There might have been a Richard. What did you care!"

"In that case you'd have been a liar and worse, so why should I care about you then?"

"You don't care about me," she said, sullenly.

"You say what you please," he answered.

She was silent for some time.

"And did you do absolutely nothing last night?" she asked.

"I had a bath and went to bed."

Then she pondered.

"No," she said, "you don't care for me."

He did not trouble to answer. Softly, a little china clock rang six.

"I shall go to Italy in the morning," he said.

"Yes."

"And," he said, slowly, forcing the words out, "I shall stay at the Aquila Nera at Milan-you know my address."

"Yes," she answered.

"I shall be away about a month. Meanwhile you can rest."

"Yes," she said, in her throat, with a little contempt of him and his stiffness. He, in spite of himself, was breathing heavily. He knew that this parting was the real separation of their souls, marked the point beyond which they could go no farther, but accepted the marriage as a comparative failure. And he had built all his life on his marriage. She accused him of not loving her. He gripped the arms of his chair. Was there something in it? Did he only want the attributes which went along with her, the peace of heart which a man has in living to one woman, even if the love between them be not complete; the singleness and unity in his life that made it easy; the fixed establishment of himself as a married man with a home; the feeling that he belonged somewhere, that one woman existed-not was paid but existed-really to take care of him; was it these things he wanted, and not her? But he wanted her for these purposes-her, and nobody else. But was that not enough for her? Perhaps he wronged her-it was possible. What she said against him was in earnest. And what she said in earnest he had to believe, in the long run, since it was the utterance of her being. He felt miserable and tired.

When he looked at her, across the gathering twilight of the room, she

80

was staring into the fire and biting her finger-nail, restlessly, restlessly, without knowing. And all his limbs went suddenly weak, as he realised that she suffered too, that something was gnawing at her. Something in the look of her, the crouching, dogged, wondering look made him faint with tenderness for her.

"Don't bite your finger-nails," he said quietly, and, obediently, she took her hand from her mouth. His heart was beating quickly. He could feel the atmosphere of the room changing. It had stood aloof, the room, like something placed round him, like a great box. Now everything got softer, as if it partook of the atmosphere, of which he partook himself, and they were all one.

His mind reverted to her accusations, and his heart beat like a caged thing against what he could not understand. She said he did not love her. But he knew that in his way, he did. In his way-but was his way wrong? His way was himself, he thought, struggling. Was there something wrong, something missing in his nature, that he could not love? He struggled, as if he were in a mesh, and could not get out. He did not want to believe that he was deficient in his nature. Wherein was he deficient? It was nothing physical. She said he would not come out of himself, that he was no good to her, because he could not get outside himself. What did she mean? Not outside himself! It seemed like some acrobatic feat, some slippery, contortionist trick. No, he could not understand. His heart flashed hot with resentment. She did nothing but find fault with him. What did she care about him, really, when she could taunt him with not being able to take a light woman when he was in Paris? Though his heart, forced to do her justice, knew that for this she loved him, really.

But it was too complicated and difficult, and already, as they sat thinking, it had gone wrong between them and things felt twisted, horribly twisted, so that he could not breathe. He must go. He could dine at the hotel and go to the theatre.

"Well," he said casually, "I must go. I think I shall go and see The 'Black Sheep'."

She did not answer. Then she turned and looked at him with a queer, half-bewildered, half-perverse smile that seemed conscious of pain. Her eyes, shining rather dilated and triumphant, and yet with something heavily yearning behind them, looked at him. He could not understand, and, between her appeal and her defiant triumph, he felt as if his chest was crushed so that he could not breathe.

"My love," she said, in a little singing, abstract fashion, her lips somehow sipping towards him, her eyes shining dilated; and yet he felt as if he were not in it, himself.

His heart was a flame that prevented his breathing. He gripped the chair like a man who is going to be put under torture.

"What?" he said, staring back at her.

"Oh, my love!" she said softly, with a little, intense laugh on her face, that made him pant. And she slipped from her sofa and came across to him quickly, and put her hand hesitating on his hair. The blood struck like flame across his consciousness, and the hurt was keen like joy, like the releasing of something that hurts as the pressure is relaxed and the movement comes, before the peace. Afraid, his fingers touched her hand, and she sank swiftly between his knees, and put her face on his breast. He held her head hard against his chest, and again and again the flame went down his blood, as he felt her round, small, nut of a head between his hands pressing into his chest where the hurt had been bruised in so deep. His wrists quivered as he pressed her head to him, as he felt the deadness going out of him; the real life released, flowing into his body again. How hard he had shut it off, against her, when she hated him. He was breathing heavily with relief, blindly pressing her head against him. He believed in her again.

She looked up, laughing, childish, inviting him with her lips. He bent to kiss her, and as his eyes closed, he saw hers were shut. The feeling of restoration was almost unbearable.

"Do you love me?" she whispered, in a little ecstasy.

He did not answer, except with the quick tightening of his arms, clutching her a little closer against him. And he loved the silkiness of her hair, and its natural scent. And it hurt him that the daisies she had threaded in should begin to wither. He resented their hurting her by their dying.

He had not understood. But the trouble had gone off. He was quiet, and he watched her from out of his sensitive stillness, a little bit dimly, unable to recover. She was loving to him, protective, and bright, laughing like a glad child too.

"We must tell Maud I shall be in to dinner," he said.

That was like him-always aware of the practical side of the case, and the appearances. She laughed a little bit ironically. Why should she have to take her arm from round him, just to tell Maud he would be in to dinner?

"I'll go," she said.

He drew the curtains and turned on the light in the big lamp that stood in a corner. The room was dim, and palely warm. He loved it dearly.

His wife, when she came back, as soon as she had closed the door, lifted her arms to him in a little ecstasy, coming to him. They clasped each other closer, body to body. And the intensity of his feeling was so fierce, he felt himself going dim, fusing into something soft and plastic between her hands. And this connection with her was bigger than life or death. And at the bottom of his heart was a sob.

She was gay and winsome at the dinner. Like lovers, they were just deliciously waiting for the night to come up. But there remained in him always the slightly broken feeling which the night before had left.

"And you won't go to Italy," she said, as if it were an understood thing.

She gave him the best things to eat, and was solicitous for his welfare-which was not usual with her. It gave him deep, shy pleasure. He remembered a verse she was often quoting as one she loved. He did not know it for himself:

"On my breasts I warm thy foot-soles;
Wine I pour, and dress thy meats;

82

Humbly, when my lord disposes,
Lie with him on perfumed sheets."

She said it to him sometimes, looking up at him from the pillow. But it never seemed real to him. She might, in her sudden passion, put his feet between her breasts. But he never felt like a lord, never more pained and insignificant than at those times. As a little girl, she must have subjected herself before her dolls. And he was something like her lordliest plaything. He liked that too. If only . . .

Then, seeing some frightened little way of looking at him which she had, the pure pain came back. He loved her, and it would never be peace between them; she would never belong to him, as a wife. She would take him and reject him, like a mistress. And perhaps for that reason he would love her all the more; it might be so.

But then, he forgot. Whatever was or was not, now she loved him. And whatever came after, this evening he was the lord. What matter if he were deposed to-morrow, and she hated him!

Her eyes, wide and candid, were staring at him a little bit wondering, a little bit forlorn. She knew he had not quite come back. He held her close to him.

"My love," she murmured consolingly. "My love."

And she put her fingers through his hair, arranging it in little, loose curves, playing with it and forgetting everything else. He loved that dearly, to feel the light lift and touch-touch of her finger-tips making his hair, as she said, like an Apollo's. She lifted his face to see how he looked, and, with a little laugh of love, kissed him. And he loved to be made much of by her. But he had the dim, hurting sense that she would not love him to-morrow, that it was only her great need to love that exalted him to-night. He knew he was no king; he did not feel a king, even when she was crowning and kissing him.

"Do you love me?" she asked, playfully whispering.

He held her fast and kissed her, while the blood hurt in his heart-chambers.

"You know," he answered, with a struggle.

Later, when he lay holding her with a passion intense like pain, the words blurted from him:

"Flesh of my flesh. Paula!-Will you-?"

"Yes, my love," she answered consolingly.

He bit his mouth with pain. For him it was almost an agony of appeal.

"But, Paula-I mean it-flesh of my flesh-a wife?"

She tightened her arms round him without answering. And he knew, and she knew, that she put him off like that.

IV

Two months later, she was writing to him in Italy: "Your idea of your woman is that she is an expansion, no, a rib of yourself, without any existence of her own. That I am a being by myself is more than you can grasp. I wish I could absolutely submerge myself in a man-and so I do. I always loved you . . .

"You will say 'I was patient.' Do you call that patient, hanging on for your needs, as you have done? The innermost life you have always had of me, and you held yourself aloof because you were afraid.

"The unpardonable thing was you told me you loved me.-Your feelings have hated me these three months, which did not prevent you from taking my love and every breath from me.-Underneath you undermined me, in some subtle, corrupt way that I did not see because I believed you, when you told me you loved me . . .

"The insult of the way you took me these last three months I shall never forgive you. I honestly did give myself, and always in vain and rebuffed. The strain of it all has driven me quite mad.

"You say I am a tragédienne, but I don't do any of your perverse undermining tricks. You are always luring one into the open like a clever enemy, but you keep safely under cover all the time.

"This practically means, for me, that life is over, my belief in life-I hope it will recover, but it never could do so with you . . ."

To which he answered: "If I kept under cover it is funny, for there isn't any cover now.-And you can hope, pretty easily, for your own recovery apart from me. For my side, without you, I am done . . . But you lie to yourself. You wouldn't love me, and you won't be able to love anybody else-except yourself."

RAWDON'S ROOF

Rawdon was the sort of man who said, privately, to his men friends, over a glass of wine after dinner: "No woman shall sleep again under my roof!"

He said it with pride, rather vaunting, pursing his lips. "Even my housekeeper goes home to sleep."

But the housekeeper was a gentle old thing of about sixty, so it seemed a little fantastic. Moreover, the man had a wife, of whom he was secretly rather proud, as a piece of fine property, and with whom he kept up a very witty correspondence, epistolary, and whom he treated with humorous gallantry when they occasionally met for half an hour. Also he had a love affair going on. At least, if it wasn't a love affair, what was it? However!

"No, I've come to the determination that no woman shall ever sleep under my roof again-not even a female cat!"

One looked at the roof, and wondered what it had done amiss. Besides, it wasn't his roof. He only rented the house. What does a man mean, anyhow, when he says "my roof"? My roof! The only roof I am conscious of having, myself, is the top of my head. However, he hardly can have meant that no woman should sleep under the elegant dome of his skull. Though there's no telling. You see the top of a sleek head through a window, and you say: "By Jove, what a pretty girl's head!" And after all, when the individual comes out, it's in trousers.

The point, however, is that Rawdon said so emphatically-no, not emphatically, succinctly: "No woman shall ever again sleep under my roof." It was a case of futurity. No doubt he had had his ceilings whitewashed, and their memories put out. Or rather, repainted, for it was a handsome wooden ceiling. Anyhow, if ceilings have eyes, as walls have ears, then Rawdon had given his ceilings a new outlook, with a new coat of paint, and all memory of any woman's having slept under them-for after all, in decent circumstances we sleep under ceilings, not under roofs-was wiped out for ever.

"And will you neither sleep under any woman's roof?"

That pulled him up rather short. He was not prepared to sauce his gander as he had sauced his goose. Even I could see the thought flitting through his mind, that some of his pleasantest holidays depended on the charm of his hostess. Even some of the nicest hotels were run by women.

"Ah! Well! That's not quite the same thing, you know. When one leaves one's own house one gives up the keys of circumstance, so to speak. But, as far as possible, I make it a rule not to sleep under a roof that is openly, and obviously, and obtrusively a woman's roof!"

"Quite!" said I with a shudder. "So do I!"

Now I understood his mysterious love affair less than ever. He was never known to speak of this love affair: he did not even write about it to his wife. The lady-for she was a lady-lived only five minutes' walk from Rawdon. She had a husband, but he was in diplomatic service or

85

something like that, which kept him occupied in the sufficiently-far distance. Yes, far enough. And, as a husband, he was a complete diplomat. A balance of power. If he was entitled to occupy the wide field of the world, she, the other and contrasting power, might concentrate and consolidate her position at home.

She was a charming woman, too, and even a beautiful woman. She had two charming children, long-legged, stalky, clove-pink-half-opened sort of children. But really charming. And she was a woman with a certain mystery. She never talked. She never said anything about herself. Perhaps she suffered; perhaps she was frightfully happy, and made that her cause for silence. Perhaps she was wise enough even to be beautifully silent about her happiness. Certainly she never mentioned her sufferings, or even her trials: and certainly she must have a fair handful of the latter, for Alec Drummond sometimes fled home in the teeth of a gale of debts. He simply got through his own money and through hers, and, third and fatal stride, through other people's as well. Then something had to be done about it. And Janet, dear soul, had to put her hat on and take journeys. But she never said anything of it. At least, she did just hint that Alec didn't quite make enough money to meet expenses. But after all, we don't go about with our eyes shut, and Alec Drummond, whatever else he did, didn't hide his prowess under a bushel.

Rawdon and he were quite friendly, but really! None of them ever talked. Drummond didn't talk, he just went off and behaved in his own way. And though Rawdon would chat away till the small hours, he never "talked". Not to his nearest male friend did he ever mention Janet save as a very pleasant woman and his neighbour: he admitted he adored her children. They often came to see him.

And one felt about Rawdon, he was making a mystery of something. And that was rather irritating. He went every day to see Janet, and of course we saw him going: going or coming. How can one help but see? But he always went in the morning, at about eleven, and did not stay for lunch: or he went in the afternoon, and came home to dinner. Apparently he was never there in the evening. Poor Janet, she lived like a widow.

Very well, if Rawdon wanted to make it so blatantly obvious that it was only platonic, purely platonic, why wasn't he natural? Why didn't he say simply: "I'm very fond of Janet Drummond, she is my very dear friend?" Why did he sort of curl up at the very mention of her name, and curdle into silence: or else say rather forcedly: "Yes, she is a charming woman. I see a good deal of her, but chiefly for the children's sake. I'm devoted to the children!" Then he would look at one in such a curious way, as if he were hiding something. And after all, what was there to hide? If he was the woman's friend, why not? It could be a charming friendship. And if he were her lover, why, heaven bless me, he ought to have been proud of it, and showed just a glint, just an honest man's glint.

But no, never a glint of pride or pleasure in the relation either way. Instead of that, this rather theatrical reserve. Janet, it is true, was just as reserved. If she could, she avoided mentioning his name. Yet one knew, sure as houses, she felt something. One suspected her of being more in love with Rawdon than ever she had been with Alec. And one felt that there was a hush put upon it all. She had had a hush put upon her. By whom? By both the men? Or by Rawdon only? Or by Drummond? Was it for her husband's sake? Impossible! For her children's? But why! Her children were devoted to Rawdon.

It had now become the custom for them to go to him three times a week, for music. I don't mean he taught them the piano. Rawdon was a very refined musical amateur. He had them sing, in their delicate girlish voices, delicate little songs, and really he succeeded wonderfully with them; he made them so true, which children rarely are, musically, and so pure and effortless, like little flamelets of sound. It really was rather beautiful, and sweet of him. And he taught them music, the delicacy of the feel of it. They had a regular teacher for the practice.

Even the little girls, in their young little ways, were in love with Rawdon! So if their mother were in love too, in her ripened womanhood, why not?

Poor Janet! She was so still, and so elusive: the hush upon her! She was rather like a half-opened rose that somebody had tied a string round, so that it couldn't open any more. But why? Why? In her there was a real touch of mystery. One could never ask her, because one knew her heart was too keenly involved: or her pride.

Whereas there was, really, no mystery about Rawdon, refined and handsome and subtle as he was. He had no mystery: at least, to a man. What he wrapped himself up in was a certain amount of mystification.

Who wouldn't be irritated to hear a fellow saying, when for months and months he has been paying a daily visit to a lonely and very attractive woman-nay, lately even a twice-daily visit, even if always before sundown-to hear him say, pursing his lips after a sip of his own very moderate port: "I've taken a vow that no woman shall sleep under my roof again!"

I almost snapped out: "Oh, what the hell! And what about your Janet?" But I remembered in time, it was not my affair, and if he wanted to have his mystifications, let him have them.

If he meant he wouldn't have his wife sleep under his roof again, that one could understand. They were really very witty with one another, he and she, but fatally and damnably married.

Yet neither wanted a divorce. And neither put the slightest claim to any control over the other's behaviour. He said: "Women live on the moon, men on the earth." And she said: "I don't mind in the least if he loves Janet Drummond, poor thing. It would be a change for him, from loving himself. And a change for her, if somebody loved her-"

Poor Janet! But he wouldn't have her sleep under his roof, no, not for any money. And apparently he never slept under hers-if she could be said to have one. So what the deuce?

Of course, if they were friends, just friends, all right! But then in that case, why start talking about not having a woman sleep under your roof? Pure mystification!

The cat never came out of the bag. But one evening I distinctly heard it mewing inside its sack, and I even believe I saw a claw through the canvas.

It was in November-everything much as usual-myself pricking my ears to hear if the rain had stopped, and I could go home, because I was just a little bored about "cornemuse" music. I had been having dinner with Rawdon, and listening to him ever since on his favourite topic: not, of course, women, and why they shouldn't sleep under his roof, but fourteenth-century melody and windbag accompaniment.

It was not late-not yet ten o'clock-but I was restless, and wanted to go home. There was no longer any sound of rain. And Rawdon was perhaps going to make a pause in his monologue.

Suddenly there was a tap at the door, and Rawdon's man, Hawken, edged in. Rawdon, who had been a major in some fantastic capacity during the war, had brought Hawken back with him. This fresh-faced man of about thirty-five appeared in the doorway with an intensely blank and bewildered look on his face. He was really an extraordinarily good actor.

"A lady, sir!" he said, with a look of utter blankness.

"A what?" snapped Rawdon.

"A lady!"-then with a most discreet drop in his voice: "Mrs. Drummond, sir!" He looked modestly down at his feet.

Rawdon went deathly white, and his lips quivered.

"Mrs. Drummond! Where?"

Hawken lifted his eyes to his master in a fleeting glance.

"I showed her into the dining-room, there being no fire in the drawing-room."

Rawdon got to his feet and took two or three agitated strides. He could not make up his mind. At last he said, his lips working with agitation:

"Bring her in here."

Then he turned with a theatrical gesture to me.

"What this is all about, I don't know," he said.

"Let me clear out," said I, making for the door.

He caught me by the arm.

"No, for God's sake! For God's sake, stop and see me through!"

He gripped my arm till it really hurt, and his eyes were quite wild. I did not know my Olympic Rawdon.

Hastily I backed away to the side of the fire-we were in Rawdon's room, where the books and piano were-and Mrs. Drummond appeared in the doorway. She was much paler than usual, being a rather warm-coloured woman, and she glanced at me with big reproachful eyes, as much as to say: You intruder! You interloper! For my part, I could do nothing but stare. She wore a black wrap, which I knew quite well, over her black dinner-dress.

"Rawdon!" she said, turning to him and blotting out my existence from her consciousness. Hawken softly closed the door, and I could feel him standing on the threshold outside, listening keen as a hawk.

"Sit down, Janet," said Rawdon, with a grimace of a sour smile, which he could not get rid of once he had started it, so that his face looked very odd indeed, like a mask which he was unable either to fit on or take off. He had several conflicting expressions all at once, and they had all stuck.

She let her wrap slip back on her shoulders, and knitted her white fingers against her skirt, pressing down her arms, and gazing at him with a terrible gaze. I began to creep to the door.

Rawdon started after me.

"No, don't go! Don't go! I specially want you not to go," he said in extreme agitation.

I looked at her. She was looking at him with a heavy, sombre kind of stare. Me she absolutely ignored. Not for a second could she forgive me for existing on the earth. I slunk back to my post behind the leather armchair, as if hiding.

"Do sit down, Janet," he said to her again. "And have a smoke. What will you drink?"

"Nothanks!" she said, as if it were one word slurred out. "Nothanks."

And she proceeded again to fix him with that heavy, portentous stare.

He offered her a cigarette, his hand trembling as he held out the silver box.

"Nothanks!" she slurred out again, not even looking at the box, but keeping him fixed with that dark and heavy stare.

He turned away, making a great delay lighting a cigarette, with his back to her, to get out of the stream of that stare. He carefully went for an ash-tray, and put it carefully within reach-all the time trying not to be swept away on that stare. And she stood with her fingers locked, her straight, plump, handsome arms pressed downwards against her skirt, and she gazed at him.

He leaned his elbow on the mantelpiece abstractedly for a moment-then he started suddenly, and rang the bell. She turned her eyes from him for a moment, to watch his middle finger pressing the bell-button. Then there was a tension of waiting, an interruption in the previous tension. We waited. Nobody came. Rawdon rang again.

"That's very curious!" he murmured to himself. Hawken was usually so prompt. Hawken, not being a woman, slept under the roof, so there was no excuse for his not answering the bell. The tension in the room had now changed quality, owing to this new suspense. Poor Janet's sombre stare became gradually loosened, so to speak. Attention was divided. Where was Hawken? Rawdon rang the bell a third time, a long peal. And now Janet was no longer the centre of suspense. Where was Hawken? The question loomed large over every other.

"I'll just look in the kitchen," said I, making for the door.

"No, no. I'll go," said Rawdon.

But I was in the passage-and Rawdon was on my heels. The kitchen was very tidy and cheerful, but empty; only a bottle of beer and two glasses stood on the table. To Rawdon the kitchen was as strange a world as to me-he never entered the servants' quarters. But to me it was curious that the bottle of beer was empty, and both the glasses had been used. I knew Rawdon wouldn't notice.

"That's very curious!" said Rawdon: meaning the absence of his man.

At that moment we heard a step on the servants' stairs, and Rawdon

89

opened the door to reveal Hawken descending with an armful of sheets and things.

"What are you doing?"

"Why!-" and a pause. "I was airing the clean laundry, like-not to waste the fire last thing."

Hawken descended into the kitchen with a very flushed face and very bright eyes and rather ruffled hair, and proceeded to spread the linen on chairs before the fire.

"I hope I've not done wrong, sir," he said in his most winning manner. "Was you ringing?"

"Three times! Leave that linen and bring a bottle of the fizz."

"I'm sorry, sir. You can't hear the bell from the front, sir."

It was perfectly true. The house was small, but it had been built for a very nervous author, and the servants' quarters were shut off, padded from the rest of the house.

Rawdon said no more about the sheets and things, but he looked more peaked than ever.

We went back to the music-room. Janet had gone to the hearth, and stood with her hand on the mantel. She looked round at us, baffled.

"We're having a bottle of fizz," said Rawdon. "Do let me take your wrap."

"And where was Hawken?" she asked satirically.

"Oh, busy somewhere upstairs."

"He's a busy young man, that!" she said sardonically. And she sat uncomfortably on the edge of the chair where I had been sitting.

When Hawken came with the tray, she said:

"I'm not going to drink."

Rawdon appealed to me, so I took a glass. She looked inquiringly at the flushed and bright-eyed Hawken, as if she understood something.

The manservant left the room. We drank our wine, and the awkwardness returned.

"Rawdon!" she said suddenly, as if she were firing a revolver at him. "Alec came home to-night in a bigger mess than ever, and wanted to make love to me to get it off his mind. I can't stand it any more. I'm in love with you, and I simply can't stand Alec getting too near to me. He's dangerous when he's crossed-and when he's worked up. So I just came here. I didn't see what else I could do."

She left off as suddenly as a machine-gun leaves off firing. We were just dazed.

"You are quite right," Rawdon began, in a vague and neutral tone. . . .

"I am, am I not?" she said eagerly.

"I'll tell you what I'll do," he said. "I'll go round to the hotel to-night, and you can stay here."

"Under the kindly protection of Hawken, you mean!" she said, with quiet sarcasm.

"Why!-I could send Mrs. Betts, I suppose," he said.

Mrs. Betts was his housekeeper.

"You couldn't stay and protect me yourself?" she said quietly.

"I! I! Why, I've made a vow-haven't I, Joe?"-he turned to me-"not to have any woman sleep under my roof again."-He got the mixed sour smile on his face.

She looked up at the ceiling for a moment, then lapsed into silence. Then she said:

"Sort of monastery, so to speak!"

And she rose and reached for her wrap, adding:

"I'd better go, then."

"Joe will see you home," he said.

She faced round on me.

"Do you mind not seeing me home, Mr. Bradley?" she said, gazing at me.

"Not if you don't want me," said I.

"Hawken will drive you," said Rawdon.

"Oh, no, he won't!" she said. "I'll walk. Good-night."

"I'll get my hat," stammered Rawdon, in an agony. "Wait! Wait! The gate will be locked."

"It was open when I came," she said.

He rang for Hawken to unlock the iron doors at the end of the short drive, whilst he himself huddled into a greatcoat and scarf, fumbling for a flashlight.

"You won't go till I come back, will you?" he pleaded to me. "I'd be awfully glad if you'd stay the night. The sheets will be aired."

I had to promise-and he set off with an umbrella, in the rain, at the same time asking Hawken to take a flashlight and go in front. So that was how they went, in single file along the path over the fields to Mrs. Drummond's house, Hawken in front, with flashlight and umbrella, curving round to light up in front of Mrs. Drummond, who, with umbrella only, walked isolated between two lights, Rawdon shining his flashlight on her from the rear from under his umbrella. I turned indoors.

So that was over! At least, for the moment!

I thought I would go upstairs and see how damp the bed in the guest-chamber was before I actually stayed the night with Rawdon. He never had guests-preferred to go away himself.

The guest-chamber was a good room across a passage and round a corner from Rawdon's room-its door just opposite the padded service-door. This latter service-door stood open, and a light shone through. I went into the spare bedroom, switching on the light.

To my surprise, the bed looked as if it had just been left-the sheets tumbled, the pillows pressed. I put in my hands under the bedclothes, and it was warm. Very curious!

As I stood looking round in mild wonder, I heard a voice call softly: "Joe!"

"Yes!" said I instinctively, and, though startled, strode at once out of the room and through the servants' door, towards the voice. Light shone from the open doorway of one of the servants' rooms.

There was a muffled little shriek, and I was standing looking into what was probably Hawken's bedroom, and seeing a soft and pretty white leg and a pretty feminine posterior very thinly dimmed in a rather short night-dress, just in the act of climbing into a narrow little bed, and, then arrested, the owner of the pretty posterior burying her face in the bed-clothes, to be invisible, like the ostrich in the sand.

I discreetly withdrew, went downstairs and poured myself a glass of wine. And very shortly Rawdon returned looking like Hamlet in the last act.

He said nothing, neither did I. We sat and merely smoked. Only as he was seeing me upstairs to bed, in the now immaculate bedroom, he said pathetically:

"Why aren't women content to be what a man wants them to be?"

"Why aren't they!" said I wearily.

"I thought I had made everything clear," he said.

"You start at the wrong end," said I.

And as I said it, the picture came into my mind of the pretty feminine butt-end in Hawken's bedroom. Yes, Hawken made better starts, wherever he ended.

When he brought me my cup of tea in the morning, he was very soft and cat-like. I asked him what sort of day it was, and he asked me if I'd had a good night, and was I comfortable.

"Very comfortable!" said I. "But I turned you out, I'm afraid."

"Me, sir?" He turned on me a face of utter bewilderment.

But I looked him in the eye.

"Is your name Joe?" I asked him.

"You're right, sir."

"So is mine," said I. "However, I didn't see her face, so it's all right. I suppose you were a bit tight, in that little bed!"

"Well, sir!" and he flashed me a smile of amazing impudence, and lowered his tone to utter confidence. "This is the best bed in the house, this is." And he touched it softly.

"You've not tried them all, surely?"

A look of indignant horror on his face!

"No, sir, indeed I haven't."

That day, Rawdon left for London, on his way to Tunis, and Hawken was to follow him. The roof of his house looked just the same.

The Drummonds moved too-went away somewhere, and left a lot of unsatisfied tradespeople behind.

STRIKE-PAY

Strike-money is paid in the Primitive Methodist Chapel. The crier was round quite early on Wednesday morning to say that paying would begin at ten o'clock.

The Primitive Methodist Chapel is a big barn of a place, built, designed, and paid for by the colliers themselves. But it threatened to fall down from its first form, so that a professional architect had to be hired at last to pull the place together.

It stands in the Square. Forty years ago, when Bryan and Wentworth opened their pits, they put up the "squares" of miners' dwellings. They are two great quadrangles of houses, enclosing a barren stretch of ground, littered with broken pots and rubbish, which forms a square, a great, sloping, lumpy playground for the children, a drying-ground for many women's washing.

Wednesday is still wash-day with some women. As the men clustered round the Chapel, they heard the thud-thud-thud of many pouches, women pounding away at the wash-tub with a wooden pestle. In the Square the white clothes were waving in the wind from a maze of clothes-lines, and here and there women were pegging out, calling to the miners, or to the children who dodged under the flapping sheets.

Ben Townsend, the Union agent, has a bad way of paying. He takes the men in order of his round, and calls them by name. A big, oratorical man with a grey beard, he sat at the table in the Primitive school-room, calling name after name. The room was crowded with colliers, and a great group pushed up outside. There was much confusion. Ben dodged from the Scargill Street list to the Queen Street. For this Queen Street men were not prepared. They were not to the fore.

"Joseph Grooby-Joseph Grooby! Now, Joe, where are you?"

"Hold on a bit, Sorry!" cried Joe from outside. "I'm shovin' up."

There was a great noise from the men.

"I'm takin' Queen Street. All you Queen Street men should be ready. Here you are, Joe," said the Union agent loudly.

"Five children!" said Joe, counting the money suspiciously.

"That's right, I think," came the mouthing voice. "Fifteen shillings, is it not?"

"A bob a kid," said the collier.

"Thomas Sedgwick-How are you, Tom? Missis better?"

"Ay, 'er's shapin' nicely. Tha'rt hard at work to-day, Ben." This was sarcasm on the idleness of a man who had given up the pit to become a Union agent.

"Yes. I rose at four to fetch the money."

"Dunna hurt thysen," was the retort, and the men laughed.

"No-John Merfin!"

But the colliers, tired with waiting, excited by the strike spirit, began to

93

rag. Merfin was young and dandiacal. He was choir-master at the Wesleyan Chapel.

"Does your collar cut, John?" asked a sarcastic voice out of the crowd.

"Hymn Number Nine.

> 'Diddle-diddle dumpling, my son John
> Went to bed with his best suit on,'"

came the solemn announcement.

Mr. Merfin, his white cuffs down to his knuckles, picked up his half-sovereign, and walked away loftily.

"Sam Coutts!" cried the paymaster.

"Now, lad, reckon it up," shouted the voice of the crowd, delighted.

Mr. Coutts was a straight-backed ne'er-do-well. He looked at his twelve shillings sheepishly.

"Another two-bob-he had twins a-Monday night-get thy money, Sam, tha's earned it-tha's addled it, Sam; dunna go be-out it. Let him ha' the two bob for 'is twins, mister," came the clamour from the men around.

Sam Coutts stood grinning awkwardly.

"You should ha' given us notice, Sam," said the paymaster suavely. "We can make it all right for you next week-"

"Nay, nay, nay," shouted a voice. "Pay on delivery-the goods is there right enough."

"Get thy money, Sam, tha's addled it," became the universal cry, and the Union agent had to hand over another florin, to prevent a disturbance. Sam Coutts grinned with satisfaction.

"Good shot, Sam," the men exclaimed.

"Ephraim Wharmby," shouted the pay-man.

A lad came forward.

"Gi' him sixpence for what's on t'road," said a sly voice.

"Nay, nay," replied Ben Townsend; "pay on delivery."

There was a roar of laughter. The miners were in high spirits.

In the town they stood about in gangs, talking and laughing. Many sat on their heels in the market-place. In and out of the public-houses they went, and on every bar the half-sovereigns clicked.

"Comin' ter Nottingham wi' us, Ephraim?" said Sam Coutts to the slender, pale young fellow of about twenty-two.

"I'm non walkin' that far of a gleamy day like this."

"He has na got the strength," said somebody, and a laugh went up.

"How's that?" asked another pertinent voice.

"He's a married man, mind yer," said Chris Smitheringale, "an' it ta'es a bit o' keepin' up."

The youth was teased in this manner for some time.

"Come on ter Nottingham wi's; tha'll be safe for a bit," said Coutts.

A gang set off, although it was only eleven o'clock. It was a nine-mile walk. The road was crowded with colliers travelling on foot to see the match between Notts and Aston Villa. In Ephraim's gang were Sam Coutts, with his fine shoulders and his extra florin, Chris Smitheringale, fat and smiling, and John Wharmby, a remarkable man, tall, erect as a soldier, black-haired and proud; he could play any musical instrument, he declared.

"I can play owt from a comb up'ards. If there's music to be got outer a thing, I back I'll get it. No matter what shape or form of instrument you set before me, it doesn't signify if I nivir clapped eyes on it before, I's warrant I'll have a tune out of it in five minutes."

He beguiled the first two miles so. It was true, he had caused a sensation by introducing the mandoline into the townlet, filling the hearts of his fellow-colliers with pride as he sat on the platform in evening dress, a fine soldierly man, bowing his black head, and scratching the mewing mandoline with hands that had only to grasp the "instrument" to crush it entirely.

Chris stood a can round at the "White Bull" at Gilt Brook. John Wharmby took his turn at Kimberley top.

"We wunna drink again," they decided, "till we're at Cinder Hill. We'll non stop i' Nuttall."

They swung along the high-road under the budding trees. In Nuttall churchyard the crocuses blazed with yellow at the brim of the balanced, black yews. White and purple crocuses dipt up over the graves, as if the churchyard were bursting out in tiny tongues of flame.

"Sithee," said Ephraim, who was an ostler down pit, "sithee, here comes the Colonel. Sithee at his 'osses how they pick their toes up, the beauties!"

The Colonel drove past the men, who took no notice of him.

"Hast heard, Sorry," said Sam, "as they're com'n out i' Germany, by the thousand, an' begun riotin'?"

"An' comin' out i' France simbitar," cried Chris.

The men all gave a chuckle.

"Sorry," shouted John Wharmby, much elated, "we oughtna ter go back under a twenty per cent rise."

"We should get it," said Chris.

"An' easy! They can do nowt bi-out us, we'n on'y ter stop out long enough."

"I'm willin'," said Sam, and there was a laugh. The colliers looked at one another. A thrill went through them as if an electric current passed.

"We'n on'y ter stick out, an' we s'll see who's gaffer."

"Us!" cried Sam. "Why, what can they do again' us, if we come out all over th' world?"

"Nowt!" said John Wharmby. "Th' mesters is bobbin' about like corks on a cassivoy a'ready." There was a large natural reservoir, like a lake, near Bestwood, and this supplied the simile.

Again there passed through the men that wave of elation, quickening their pulses. They chuckled in their throats. Beyond all consciousness was this sense of battle and triumph in the hearts of the working-men at this juncture.

It was suddenly suggested at Nuttall that they should go over the fields to Bulwell, and into Nottingham that way. They went single file across the fallow, past the wood, and over the railway, where now no trains were

95

running. Two fields away was a troop of pit ponies. Of all colours, but chiefly of red or brown, they clustered thick in the field, scarcely moving, and the two lines of trodden earth patches showed where fodder was placed down the field.

"Theer's the pit 'osses," said Sam. "Let's run 'em."

"It's like a circus turned out. See them skewbawd 'uns-seven skewbawd," said Ephraim.

The ponies were inert, unused to freedom. Occasionally one walked round. But there they stood, two thick lines of ruddy brown and piebald and white, across the trampled field. It was a beautiful day, mild, pale blue, a "growing day", as the men said, when there was the silence of swelling sap everywhere.

"Let's ha'e a ride," said Ephraim.

The younger men went up to the horses.

"Come on-co-oop, Taffy-co-oop, Ginger."

The horses tossed away. But having got over the excitement of being above-ground, the animals were feeling dazed and rather dreary. They missed the warmth and the life of the pit. They looked as if life were a blank to them.

Ephraim and Sam caught a couple of steeds, on whose backs they went careering round, driving the rest of the sluggish herd from end to end of the field. The horses were good specimens, on the whole, and in fine condition. But they were out of their element.

Performing too clever a feat, Ephraim went rolling from his mount. He was soon up again, chasing his horse. Again he was thrown. Then the men proceeded on their way.

They were drawing near to miserable Bulwell, when Ephraim, remembering his turn was coming to stand drinks, felt in his pocket for his beloved half-sovereign, his strike-pay. It was not there. Through all his pockets he went, his heart sinking like lead.

"Sam," he said, "I believe I'n lost that ha'ef a sovereign."

"Tha's got it somewheer about thee," said Chris.

They made him take off his coat and waistcoat. Chris examined the coat, Sam the waistcoat, whilst Ephraim searched his trousers.

"Well," said Chris, "I'n foraged this coat, an' it's non theer."

"An' I'll back my life as th' on'y bit a metal on this wa'scoat is the buttons," said Sam.

"An' it's non in my breeches," said Ephraim. He took off his boots and his stockings. The half-sovereign was not there. He had not another coin in his possession.

"Well," said Chris, "we mun go back an' look for it."

Back they went, four serious-hearted colliers, and searched the field, but in vain.

"Well," said Chris, "we s'll ha'e ter share wi' thee, that's a'."

"I'm willin'," said John Wharmby.

"An' me," said Sam.

"Two bob each," said Chris.

Ephraim, who was in the depths of despair, shamefully accepted their six shillings.

In Bulwell they called in a small public-house, which had one long room with a brick floor, scrubbed benches and scrubbed tables. The central space was open. The place was full of colliers, who were drinking. There was a great deal of drinking during the strike, but not a vast amount drunk. Two men were playing skittles, and the rest were betting. The seconds sat on either side the skittle-board, holding caps of money, sixpences and coppers, the wagers of the "backers".

Sam, Chris, and John Wharmby immediately put money on the man who had their favour. In the end Sam declared himself willing to play against the victor. He was the Bestwood champion. Chris and John Wharmby backed him heavily, and even Ephraim the Unhappy ventured sixpence.

In the end, Sam had won half a crown, with which he promptly stood drinks and bread and cheese for his comrades. At half-past one they set off again.

It was a good match between Notts and Villa-no goals at half-time, two-none for Notts at the finish. The colliers were hugely delighted, especially as Flint, the forward for Notts, who was an Underwood man well known to the four comrades, did some handsome work, putting the two goals through.

Ephraim determined to go home as soon as the match was over. He knew John Wharmby would be playing the piano at the "Punch Bowl", and Sam, who had a good tenor voice, singing, while Chris cut in with witticisms, until evening. So he bade them farewell, as he must get home. They, finding him somewhat of a damper on their spirits, let him go.

He was the sadder for having witnessed an accident near the football-ground. A navvy, working at some drainage, carting an iron tip-tub of mud and emptying it, had got with his horse on to the deep deposit of ooze which was crusted over. The crust had broken, the man had gone under the horse, and it was some time before the people had realised he had vanished. When they found his feet sticking out, and hauled him forth, he was dead, stifled dead in the mud. The horse was at length hauled out, after having its neck nearly pulled from the socket.

Ephraim went home vaguely impressed with a sense of death, and loss, and strife. Death was loss greater than his own, the strike was a battle greater than that he would presently have to fight.

He arrived home at seven o'clock, just when it had fallen dark. He lived in Queen Street with his young wife, to whom he had been married two months, and with his mother-in-law, a widow of sixty-four. Maud was the last child remaining unmarried, the last of eleven.

Ephraim went up the entry. The light was burning in the kitchen. His mother-in-law was a big, erect woman, with wrinkled, loose face, and cold blue eyes. His wife was also large, with very vigorous fair hair, frizzy like unravelled rope. She had a quiet way of stepping, a certain cat-like stealth, in spite of her large build. She was five months pregnant.

"Might we ask wheer you've been to?" inquired Mrs. Marriott, very erect, very dangerous. She was only polite when she was very angry.

"I' bin ter th' match."

"Oh, indeed!" said the mother-in-law. "And why couldn't we be told as you thought of jaunting off?"

"I didna know mysen," he answered, sticking to his broad Derbyshire.

"I suppose it popped into your mind, an' so you darted off," said the mother-in-law dangerously.

"I didna. It wor Chris Smitheringale who exed me."

"An' did you take much invitin'?"

"I didna want ter goo."

"But wasn't there enough man beside your jacket to say no?"

He did not answer. Down at the bottom he hated her. But he was, to use his own words, all messed up with having lost his strike-pay and with knowing the man was dead. So he was more helpless before his mother-in-law, whom he feared. His wife neither looked at him nor spoke, but kept her head bowed. He knew she was with her mother.

"Our Maud's been waitin' for some money, to get a few things," said the mother-in-law.

In silence, he put five-and-sixpence on the table.

"Take that up, Maud," said the mother.

Maud did so.

"You'll want it for us board, shan't you?" she asked, furtively, of her mother.

"Might I ask if there's nothing you want to buy yourself, first?"

"No, there's nothink I want," answered the daughter.

Mrs. Marriott took the silver and counted it.

"And do you," said the mother-in-law, towering upon the shrinking son, but speaking slowly and statelily, "do you think I'm going to keep you and your wife for five and sixpence a week?"

"It's a' I've got," he answered sulkily.

"You've had a good jaunt, my sirs, if it's cost four and sixpence. You've started your game early, haven't you?"

He did not answer.

"It's a nice thing! Here's our Maud an' me been sitting since eleven o'clock this morning! Dinner waiting and cleared away, tea waiting and washed up; then in he comes crawling with five and sixpence. Five and sixpence for a man an' wife's board for a week, if you please!"

Still he did not say anything.

"You must think something of yourself, Ephraim Wharmby!" said his mother-in-law. "You must think something of yourself. You suppose, do you, I'm going to keep you an' your wife, while you make a holiday, off on the nines to Nottingham, drink an' women."

"I've neither had drink nor women, as you know right well," he said.

"I'm glad we know summat about you. For you're that close, anybody'd think we was foreigners to you. You're a pretty little jockey, aren't you? Oh, it's a gala time for you, the strike is. That's all men strike for, indeed. They enjoy themselves, they do that. Ripping and racing and drinking, from morn till night, my sirs!"

"Is there on'y tea for me?" he asked, in a temper.

"Hark at him! Hark-ye! Should I ask you whose house you think you're

98

in? Kindly order me about, do. Oh, it makes him big, the strike does. See him land home after being out on the spree for hours, and give his orders, my sirs! Oh, strike sets the men up, it does. Nothing have they to do but guzzle and gallivant to Nottingham. Their wives'll keep them, oh yes. So long as they get something to eat at home, what more do they want! What more should they want, prithee? Nothing! Let the women and children starve and scrape, but fill the man's belly, and let him have his fling. My sirs, indeed, I think so! Let tradesmen go-what do they matter! Let rent go. Let children get what they can catch. Only the man will see he's all right. But not here, though!"

"Are you goin' ter gi'e me ony bloody tea?"

His mother-in-law started up.

"If tha dares ter swear at me, I'll lay thee flat."

"Are yer-goin' ter-gi'e me-any blasted, rotten, còssed, blòody tèa?" he bawled, in a fury, accenting every other word deliberately.

"Maud!" said the mother-in-law, cold and stately, "If you gi'e him any tea after that, you're a trollops." Whereupon she sailed out to her other daughters.

Maud quietly got the tea ready.

"Shall y'ave your dinner warmed up?" she asked.

"Ay."

She attended to him. Not that she was really meek. But-he was her man, not her mother's.

THE BLUE MOCCASINS

The fashion in women changes nowadays even faster than women's fashions. At twenty, Lina M'Leod was almost painfully modern. At sixty almost obsolete!

She started off in life to be really independent. In that remote day, forty years ago, when a woman said she was going to be independent, it meant she was having no nonsense with men. She was kicking over the masculine traces, and living her own life, manless.

To-day, when a girl says she is going to be independent, it means she is going to devote her attentions almost exclusively to men; though not necessarily to "a man".

Miss M'Leod had an income from her mother. Therefore, at the age of twenty, she turned her back on that image of tyranny, her father, and went to Paris to study art. Art having been studied, she turned her attention to the globe of earth. Being terribly independent, she soon made Africa look small; she dallied energetically with vast hinterlands of China; and she knew the Rocky Mountains and the deserts of Arizona as if she had been married to them. All this, to escape mere man.

It was in New Mexico she purchased the blue moccasins, blue bead moccasins, from an Indian who was her guide and her subordinate. In her independence she made use of men, of course, but merely as servants, subordinates.

When the war broke out she came home. She was then forty-five, and already going grey. Her brother, two years older than herself, but a bachelor, went off to the war; she stayed at home in the small family mansion in the country, and did what she could. She was small and erect and brief in her speech, her face was like pale ivory, her skin like a very delicate parchment, and her eyes were very blue. There was no nonsense about her, though she did paint pictures. She never even touched her delicately parchment face with pigment. She was good enough as she was, honest-to-God, and the country town had a tremendous respect for her.

In her various activities she came pretty often into contact with Percy Barlow, the clerk at the bank, He was only twenty-two when she first set eyes on him in 1914, and she immediately liked him. He was a stranger in the town, his father being a poor country vicar in Yorkshire. But he was of the confiding sort. He soon confided in Miss M'Leod, for whom he had a towering respect, how he disliked his step-mother, how he feared his father, was but as wax in the hands of that downright woman, and how, in consequence, he was homeless. Wrath shone in his pleasant features, but somehow it was an amusing wrath; at least to Miss M'Leod.

He was distinctly a good-looking boy, with stiff dark hair and odd, twinkling grey eyes under thick dark brows, and a rather full mouth and a queer, deep voice that had a caressing touch of hoarseness. It was his voice that somehow got behind Miss M'Leod's reserve. Not that he had the

100

faintest intention of so doing. He looked up to her immensely: "She's miles above me."

When she watched him playing tennis, letting himself go a bit too much, hitting too hard, running too fast, being too nice to his partner, her heart yearned over him. The orphan in him! Why should he go and be shot? She kept him at home as long as possible, working with her at all kinds of war-work. He was so absolutely willing to do everything she wanted: devoted to her.

But at last the time came when he must go. He was now twenty-four and she was forty-seven. He came to say good-bye, in his awkward fashion. She suddenly turned away, leaned her forehead against the wall, and burst into bitter tears. He was frightened out of his wits. Before he knew what was happening he had his arm in front of his face and was sobbing too.

She came to comfort him. "Don't cry, dear, don't! It will all be all right,"

At last he wiped his face on his sleeve and looked at her sheepishly. "It was you crying as did me in," he said. Her blue eyes were brilliant with tears. She suddenly kissed him.

"You are such a dear!" she said wistfully. Then she added, flushing suddenly vivid pink under her transparent parchment skin: "It wouldn't be right for you to marry an old thing like me, would it?"

He looked at her dumbfounded.

"No, I'm too old," she added hastily.

"Don't talk about old! You're not old!" he said hotly.

"At least I'm too old for that," she said sadly.

"Not as far as I'm concerned," he said. "You're younger than me, in most ways, I'm hanged if you're not!"

"Are you hanged if I'm not?" she teased wistfully.

"I am," he said. "And if I thought you wanted me, I'd be jolly proud if you married me. I would, I assure you."

"Would you?" she said, still teasing him.

Nevertheless, the next time he was home on leave she married him, very quietly, but very definitely. He was a young lieutenant. They stayed in her family home, Twybit Hall, for the honeymoon. It was her house now, her brother being dead. And they had a strangely happy month. She had made a strange discovery: a man.

He went off to Gallipoli, and became a captain. He came home in 1919, still green with malaria, but otherwise sound. She was in her fiftieth year. And she was almost white-haired; long, thick, white hair, done perfectly, and perfectly creamy, colourless face, with very blue eyes.

He had been true to her, not being very forward with women. But he was a bit startled by her white hair. However, he shut his eyes to it, and loved her. And she, though frightened and somewhat bewildered, was happy. But she was bewildered. It always seemed awkward to her, that he should come wandering into her room in his pyjamas when she was half dressed, and brushing her hair. And he would sit there silent, watching her brush the long swinging river of silver, of her white hair, the bare, ivory-white, slender arm working with a strange mechanical motion, sharp and forcible, brushing down the long silvery stream of hair. He would sit as if

101

mesmerised, just gazing. And she would at last glance round sharply, and he would rise, saying some little casual thing to her and smiling to her oddly with his eyes. Then he would go out, his thin cotton pyjamas hitching up over his hips, for he was a rather big-built fellow. And she would feel dazed, as if she did not quite know her own self any more. And the queer, ducking motion of his silently going out of her door impressed her ominously, his curious cat head, his big hips and limbs.

They were alone in the house, save for the servants. He had no work. They lived modestly, for a good deal of her money had been lost during the war. But she still painted pictures. Marriage had only stimulated her to this. She painted canvases of flowers, beautiful flowers that thrilled her soul. And he would sit, pipe in fist, silent, and watch her. He had nothing to do. He just sat and watched her small, neat figure and her concentrated movements as she painted. Then he knocked out his pipe and filled it again.

She said that at last she was perfectly happy. And he said that he was perfectly happy. They were always together. He hardly went out, save riding in the lanes. And practically nobody came to the house.

But still, they were very silent with one another. The old chatter had died out. And he did not read much. He just sat still, and smoked, and was silent. It got on her nerves sometimes, and she would think as she had thought in the past, that the highest bliss a human being can experience is perhaps the bliss of being quite alone, quite, quite alone.

His bank firm offered to make him manager of the local branch, and, at her advice, he accepted. Now he went out of the house every morning and came home every evening, which was much more agreeable. The rector begged him to sing again in the church choir: and again she advised him to accept. These were the old grooves in which his bachelor life had run. He felt more like himself.

He was popular: a nice, harmless fellow, everyone said of him. Some of the men secretly pitied him. They made rather much of him, took him home to luncheon, and let him loose with their daughters. He was popular among the daughters too: naturally, for if a girl expressed a wish, he would instinctively say: "What! Would you like it? I'll get it for you." And if he were not in a position to satisfy the desire, he would say: "I only wish I could do it for you. I'd do it like a shot." All of which he meant.

At the same time, though he got on so well with the maidens of the town, there was no coming forward about him. He was, in some way, not wakened up. Good-looking, and big, and serviceable, he was inwardly remote, without self-confidence, almost without a self at all.

The rector's daughter took upon herself to wake him up. She was exactly as old as he was, a smallish, rather sharp-faced young woman who had lost her husband in the war, and it had been a grief to her. But she took the stoic attitude of the young: You've got to live, so you may as well do it! She was a kindly soul, in spite of her sharpness. And she had a very perky little red-brown Pomeranian dog that she had bought in Florence in the street, but which had turned out a handsome little fellow. Miss M'Leod looked down a bit on Alice Howells and her pom, so Mrs. Howells felt no special love for Miss M'Leod-"Mrs. Barlow, that is!" she would add sharply. "For it's quite impossible to think of her as anything but Miss M'Leod!"

Percy was really more at ease at the rectory, where the pom yapped and Mrs. Howells changed her dress three or four times a day, and looked it, than in the semi-cloisteral atmosphere of Twybit Hall, where Miss M'Leod wore tweeds and a natural knitted jumper, her skirts rather long, her hair done up pure silver, and painted her wonderful flower pictures in the deepening silence of the daytime. At evening she would go up to change, after he came home. And though it thrilled her to have a man coming into her room as he dressed, snapping his collar-stud, to tell her something trivial as she stood bare-armed in her silk slip, rapidly coiling up the rope of silver hair behind her head, still, it worried her. When he was there, he couldn't keep away from her. And he would watch her, watch her, watch her as if she was the ultimate revelation. Sometimes it made her irritable. She was so absolutely used to her own privacy. What was he looking at? She never watched him. Rather she looked the other way. His watching tried her nerves. She was turned fifty. And his great silent body loomed almost dreadful.

He was quite happy playing tennis or croquet with Alice Howells and the rest. Alice was choir-mistress, a bossy little person outwardly, inwardly rather forlorn and affectionate, and not very sure that life hadn't let her down for good. She was now over thirty-and had no one but the pom and her father and the parish-nothing in her really intimate life. But she was very cheerful, busy, even gay, with her choir and school work, her dancing, and flirting, and dressmaking.

She was intrigued by Percy Barlow. "How can a man be so nice to everybody?" she asked him, a little exasperated. "Well, why not?" he replied, with the odd smile of his eyes. "It's not why he shouldn't, but how he manages to do it! How can you have so much good-nature? I have to be catty to some people, but you're nice to everybody."

"Oh, am I!" he said ominously.

He was like a man in a dream, or in a cloud. He was quite a good bank-manager, in fact very intelligent. Even in appearance, his great charm was his beautifully-shaped head. He had plenty of brains, really. But in his will, in his body, he was asleep. And sometimes this lethargy, or coma, made him look haggard. And sometimes it made his body seem inert and despicable, meaningless.

Alice Howells longed to ask him about his wife. "Do you love her? Can you really care for her?" But she daren't. She daren't ask him one word about his wife. Another thing she couldn't do, she couldn't persuade him to dance. Never, not once. But in everything else he was pliable as wax.

Mrs. Barlow-Miss M'Leod-stayed out at Twybit all the time. She did not even come in to church on Sunday. She had shaken off church, among other things. And she watched Percy depart, and felt just a little humiliated. He was going to sing in the choir! Yes, marriage was also a humiliation to her. She had distinctly married beneath her.

The years had gone by: she was now fifty-seven, Percy was thirty-four. He was still, in many ways, a boy. But in his curious silence, he was

103

ageless. She managed him with perfect ease. If she expressed a wish, he acquiesced at once. So now it was agreed he should not come to her room any more. And he never did. But sometimes she went to him in his room, and was winsome in a pathetic, heart-breaking way.

She twisted him round her little finger, as the saying goes. And yet secretly she was afraid of him. In the early years he had displayed a clumsy but violent sort of passion, from which she had shrunk away. She felt it had nothing to do with her. It was just his indiscriminating desire for Woman, and for his own satisfaction. Whereas she was not just unidentified Woman, to give him his general satisfaction. So she had recoiled, and withdrawn herself. She had put him off. She had regained the absolute privacy of her room.

He was perfectly sweet about it. Yet she was uneasy with him now. She was afraid of him; or rather, not of him, but of a mysterious something in him. She was not a bit afraid of him, oh no! And when she went to him now, to be nice to him, in her pathetic winsomeness of an unused woman of fifty-seven, she found him sweet-natured as ever, but really indifferent. He saw her pathos and her winsomeness. In some way, the mystery of her, her thick white hair, her vivid blue eyes, her ladylike refinement still fascinated him. But his bodily desire for her had gone, utterly gone. And secretly, she was rather glad. But as he looked at her, looked at her, as he lay there so silent, she was afraid, as if some finger were pointed at her. Yet she knew, the moment she spoke to him, he would twist his eyes to that good-natured and "kindly" smile of his.

It was in the late, dark months of this year that she missed the blue moccasins. She had hung them on a nail in his room. Not that he ever wore them: they were too small. Nor did she: they were too big. Moccasins are male footwear, among the Indians, not female. But they were of a lovely turquoise-blue colour, made all of little turquoise beads, with little forked flames of dead-white and dark-green. When, at the beginning of their marriage, he had exclaimed over them, she had said: "Yes! Aren't they a lovely colour! So blue!" And he had replied: "Not as blue as your eyes, even then."

So, naturally, she had hung them up on the wall in his room, and there they had stayed. Till, one November day, when there were no flowers, and she was pining to paint a still-life with something blue in it-oh, so blue, like delphiniums!-she had gone to his room for the moccasins. And they were not there. And though she hunted, she could not find them. Nor did the maids know anything of them.

So she asked him: "Percy, do you know where those blue moccasins are, which hung in your room?" There was a moment's dead silence. Then he looked at her with his good-naturedly twinkling eyes, and said: "No, I know nothing of them." There was another dead pause. She did not believe him. But being a perfect lady, she only said, as she turned away: "Well then, how curious it is!" And there was another dead pause. Out of which he asked her what she wanted them for, and she told him. Whereon the matter lapsed.

It was November, and Percy was out in the evening fairly often now. He

104

was rehearsing for a "play" which was to be given in the church schoolroom at Christmas. He had asked her about it. "Do you think it's a bit infra dig., if I play one of the characters?" She had looked at him mildly, disguising her real feeling. "If you don't feel personally humiliated," she said, "then there's nothing else to consider." And he had answered: "Oh, it doesn't upset me at all." So she mildly said: "Then do it, by all means." Adding at the back of her mind: If it amuses you, child!-but she thought, a change had indeed come over the world, when the master of Twybit Hall, or even, for that matter, the manager of the dignified Stubb's Bank, should perform in public on a schoolroom stage in amateur theatricals. And she kept calmly aloof, preferring not to know any details. She had a world of her own.

When he had said to Alice Howells: "You don't think other folk'll mind-clients of the bank and so forth-think it beneath my dignity?" she had cried, looking up into his twinkling eyes: "Oh, you don't have to keep your dignity on ice, Percy-any more than I do mine."

The play was to be performed for the first time on Christmas Eve: and after the play, there was the midnight service in church. Percy therefore told his wife not to expect him home till the small hours, at least. So he drove himself off in the car.

As night fell, and rain, Miss M'Leod felt a little forlorn. She was left out of everything. Life was slipping past her. It was Christmas Eve, and she was more alone than she had ever been. Percy only seemed to intensify her aloneness, leaving her in this fashion.

She decided not to be left out. She would go to the play too. It was past six o'clock, and she had worked herself into a highly nervous state. Outside was darkness and rain: inside was silence, forlornness. She went to the telephone and rang up the garage in Shrewbury. It was with great difficulty she got them to promise to send a car for her: Mr. Slater would have to fetch her himself in the two-seater runabout: everything else was out.

She dressed nervously, in a dark-green dress with a few modest jewels. Looking at herself in the mirror, she still thought herself slim, young-looking and distinguished. She did not see how old-fashioned she was, with her uncompromising erectness, her glistening knob of silver hair sticking out behind, and her long dress.

It was a three-mile drive in the rain, to the small country town. She sat next to old Slater, who was used to driving horses and was nervous and clumsy with a car, without saying a word. He thankfully deposited her at the gate of St. Barnabas' School.

It was almost half-past-seven. The schoolroom was packed and buzzing with excitement. "I'm afraid we haven't a seat left, Mrs. Barlow!" said Jackson, one of the church sidesmen, who was standing guard in the school porch, where people were still fighting to get in. He faced her in consternation. She faced him in consternation. "Well, I shall have to stay somewhere, till Mr. Barlow can drive me home," she said. "Couldn't you put me a chair somewhere?"

Worried and flustered, he went worrying and flustering the other people in charge. The schoolroom was simply packed solid. But Mr.

Simmons, the leading grocer, gave up his chair in the front row to Mrs. Barlow, whilst he sat in a chair right under the stage, where he couldn't see a thing. But he could see Mrs. Barlow seated between his wife and daughter, speaking a word or two to them occasionally, and that was enough.

The lights went down: The Shoes of Shagput was about to begin. The amateur curtains were drawn back, disclosing the little amateur stage with a white amateur back-cloth daubed to represent a Moorish courtyard. In stalked Percy, dressed as a Moor, his face darkened. He looked quite handsome, his pale grey eyes queer and startling in his dark face. But he was afraid of the audience-he spoke away from them, stalking around clumsily. After a certain amount of would-be funny dialogue, in tripped the heroine, Alice Howells, of course. She was an Eastern houri, in white gauze Turkish trousers, silver veil, and-the blue moccasins. The whole stage was white, save for her blue moccasins, Percy's dark-green sash, and a negro boy's red fez.

When Mrs. Barlow saw the blue moccasins, a little bomb of rage exploded in her. This, of all places! The blue moccasins that she had bought in the western deserts! The blue moccasins that were not so blue as her own eyes! Her blue moccasins! On the feet of that creature, Mrs. Howells.

Alice Howells was not afraid of the audience. She looked full at them, lifting her silver veil. And of course she saw Mrs. Barlow, sitting there like the Ancient of Days in judgment, in the front row. And a bomb of rage exploded in her breast too.

In the play, Alice was the wife of the grey-bearded old Caliph, but she captured the love of the young Ali, otherwise Percy, and the whole business was the attempt of these two to evade Caliph and negro-eunuchs and ancient crones, and get into each other's arms. The blue shoes were very important: for while the sweet Lelia wore them, the gallant Ali was to know there was danger. But when she took them off, he might approach her.

It was all quite childish, and everybody loved it, and Miss M'Leod might have been quite complacent about it all, had not Alice Howells got her monkey up, so to speak. Alice with a lot of make-up, looked boldly handsome. And suddenly bold she was, bold as the devil. All these years the poor young widow had been "good", slaving in the parish, and only even flirting just to cheer things up, never going very far and knowing she could never get anything out of it, but determined never to mope.

Now the sight of Miss M'Leod sitting there so erect, so coolly "higher plane", and calmly superior, suddenly let loose a devil in Alice Howells. All her limbs went suave and molten, as her young sex, long pent up, flooded even to her finger-tips. Her voice was strange, even to herself, with its long, plaintive notes. She felt all her movements soft and fluid, she felt herself like living liquid. And it was lovely. Underneath it all was the sting of malice against Miss M'Leod, sitting there so erect, with her great knob of white hair.

Alice's business, as the lovely Leila, was to be seductive to the rather heavy Percy. And seductive she was. In two minutes, she had him spellbound. He saw nothing of the audience. A faint, fascinated grin came on to his face, as he acted up to the young woman in the Turkish trousers. His rather full, hoarse voice changed and became clear, with a new, naked clang in it. When the two sang together, in the simple banal duets of the play, it was with a most fascinating intimacy. And when, at the end of Act One, the lovely Leila kicked off the blue moccasins, saying: "Away, shoes of bondage, shoes of sorrow!" and danced a little dance all alone, barefoot, in her Turkish trousers, in front of her fascinated hero, his smile was so spellbound that everybody else was spellbound too.

Miss M'Leod's indignation knew no bounds. When the blue moccasins were kicked across the stage by the brazen Alice, with the words: "Away, shoes of bondage, shoes of sorrow!" the elder woman grew pink with fury, and it was all she could do not to rise and snatch the moccasins from the stage, and bear them away. She sat in speechless indignation during the brief curtain between Act One and Act Two. Her moccasins! Her blue moccasins! Of the sacred blue colour, the turquoise of heaven.

But there they were, in Act Two, on the feet of the bold Alice. It was becoming too much. And the love-scenes between Percy and the young woman were becoming nakedly shameful. Alice grew worse and worse. She was worked up now, caught in her own spell, and unconscious of everything save of him, and the sting of that other woman, who presumed to own him. Own him? Ha-ha! For he was fascinated. The queer smile on his face, the concentrated gleam of his eyes, the queer way he leaned forward from his loins towards her, the new, reckless, throaty twang in his voice-the audience had before their eyes a man spellbound and lost in passion.

Miss M'Leod sat in shame and torment, as if her chair was red-hot. She too was fast losing her normal consciousness, in the spell of rage. She was outraged. The second Act was working up to its climax. The climax came. The lovely Leila kicked off the blue shoes: "Away, shoes of bondage, away!" and flew barefoot to the enraptured Ali, flinging herself into his arms. And if ever a man was gone in sheer desire, it was Percy, as he pressed the woman's lithe form against his body, and seemed unconsciously to envelop her, unaware of everything else. While she, blissful in his spell, but still aware of the audience and of the superior Miss M'Leod, let herself be wrapped closer and closer.

Miss M'Leod rose to her feet and looked towards the door. But the way out was packed, with people standing holding their breath as the two on the stage remained wrapped in each other's arms, and the three fiddles and the flute softly woke up. Miss M'Leod could not bear it. She was on her feet, and beside herself. She could not get out. She could not sit down again.

"Percy!" she said, in a low clear voice. "Will you hand me my moccasins?"

He lifted his face like a man startled in a dream, lifted his face from the shoulder of his Leila. His gold-grey eyes were like softly-startled flames. He looked in sheer horrified wonder at the little white-haired woman standing below.

"Eh?" he said, purely dazed

"Will you please hand me my moccasins!"-and she pointed to where they lay on the stage.

Alice had stepped away from him, and was gazing at the risen viper of the little elderly woman on the tip of the audience. Then she watched him move across the stage, bending forward from the loins in his queer mesmerised way, pick up the blue moccasins, and stoop down to hand them over the edge of the stage to his wife, who reached up for them.

"Thank you!" said Miss M'Leod, seating herself, with the blue moccasins in her lap.

Alice recovered her composure, gave a sign to the little orchestra, and began to sing at once, strong and assured, to sing her part in the duet that closed the Act. She knew she could command public opinion in her favour.

He too recovered at once, the little smile came back on his face, he calmly forgot his wife again as he sang his share in the duet. It was finished. The curtains were pulled to. There was immense cheering. The curtains opened, and Alice and Percy bowed to the audience, smiling both of them their peculiar secret smile, while Miss M'Leod sat with the blue moccasins in her lap.

The curtains were closed, it was the long interval. After a few moments of hesitation, Mrs. Barlow rose with dignity, gathered her wrap over her arm, and with the blue moccasins in her hand, moved towards the door. Way was respectfully made for her.

"I should like to speak to Mr. Barlow," she said to Jackson, who had anxiously ushered her in, and now would anxiously usher her out.

"Yes, Mrs. Barlow."

He led her round to the smaller class-room at the back, that acted as dressing-room. The amateur actors were drinking lemonade, and chattering freely. Mrs. Howells came forward, and Jackson whispered the news to her. She turned to Percy.

"Percy, Mrs. Barlow wants to speak to you. Shall I come with you?"

"Speak to me? Aye, come on with me."

The two followed the anxious Jackson into the other half-lighted class-room, where Mrs. Barlow stood in her wrap, holding the moccasins. She was very pale, and she watched the two butter-muslin Turkish figures enter, as if they could not possibly be real. She ignored Mrs. Howells entirely.

"Percy," she said, "I want you to drive me home."

"Drive you home!" he echoed.

"Yes, please!"

"Why-when?" he said, with vague bluntness.

"Now-if you don't mind-"

"What-in this get-up?" He looked at himself.

"I could wait while you changed."

There was a pause. He turned and looked at Alice Howells, and Alice Howells looked at him. The two women saw each other out of the corners of their eyes: but it was beneath notice. He turned to his wife, his black face ludicrously blank, his eyebrows cocked.

108

"Well, you see," he said, "it's rather awkward. I can hardly hold up the third Act while I've taken you home and got back here again, can I?"

"So you intend to play in the third Act?" she asked with cold ferocity.

"Why, I must, mustn't I?" he said blankly.

"Do you wish to?" she said, in all her intensity.

"I do, naturally. I want to finish the thing up properly," he replied, in the utter innocence of his head; about his heart he knew nothing.

She turned sharply away.

"Very well!" she said. And she called to Jackson, who was standing dejectedly near the door: "Mr Jackson, will you please find some car or conveyance to take me home?"

"Aye! I say, Mr. Jackson," called Percy in his strong, democratic voice, going forward to the man. "Ask Tom Lomas if he'll do me a good turn and get my car out of the rectory garage, to drive Mrs. Barlow home. Aye, ask Tom Lomas! And if not him, ask Mr. Pilkington-Leonard. The key's there. You don't mind, do you? I'm ever so much obliged-"

The three were left awkwardly alone again.

"I expect you've had enough with two acts," said Percy soothingly to his wife. "These things aren't up to your mark. I know it. They're only child's play. But, you see, they please the people. We've got a packed house, haven't we?"

His wife had nothing to answer. He looked so ludicrous, with his dark-brown face and butter-muslin bloomers. And his mind was so ludicrously innocent. His body, however, was not so ridiculously innocent as his mind, as she knew when he turned to the other woman.

"You and I, we're more on the nonsense level, aren't we?" he said, with the new, throaty clang of naked intimacy in his voice. His wife shivered.

"Absolutely on the nonsense level," said Alice, with easy assurance.

She looked into his eyes, then she looked at the blue moccasins in the hand of the other woman. He gave a little start, as if realising something for himself.

At that moment Tom Lomas looked in, saying heartily: "Right you are, Percy! I'll have my car here in half a tick. I'm more handy with it than yours."

"Thanks, old man! You're a Christian."

"Try to be-especially when you turn Turk! Well-" He disappeared.

"I say, Lina," said Percy in his most amiable democratic way, "would you mind leaving the moccasins for the next act? We s'll be in a bit of a hole without them."

Miss M'Leod faced him and stared at him with the full blast of her forget-me-not blue eyes, from her white face.

"Will you pardon me if I don't?" she said.

"What!" he exclaimed. "Why? Why not? It's nothing but play, to amuse the people. I can't see how it can hurt the moccasins. I understand you don't quite like seeing me make a fool of myself. But, anyhow, I'm a bit of a born fool. What?"-and his blackened face laughed with a Turkish laugh. "Oh, yes, you have to realise I rather enjoy playing the fool," he resumed. "And, after all, it doesn't really hurt you, now does it? Shan't you leave us those moccasins for the last act?"

She looked at him, then at the moccasins in her hand. No, it was useless to yield to so ludicrous a person. The vulgarity of his wheedling, the commonness of the whole performance! It was useless to yield even the moccasins. It would be treachery to herself.

"I'm sorry," she said. "But I'd so much rather they weren't used for this kind of thing. I never intended them to be." She stood with her face averted from the ridiculous couple.

He changed as if she had slapped his face. He sat down on top of the low pupils' desk and gazed with glazed interest round the class-room. Alice sat beside him, in her white gauze and her bedizened face. They were like two rebuked sparrows on one twig, he with his great, easy, intimate limbs, she so light and alert. And as he sat he sank into an unconscious physical sympathy with her. Miss M'Leod walked towards the door.

"You'll have to think of something as'll do instead," he muttered to Alice in a low voice, meaning the blue moccasins. And leaning down, he drew off one of the grey shoes she had on, caressing her foot with the slip of his hand over its slim, bare shape. She hastily put the bare foot behind her other, shod foot.

Tom Lomas poked in his head, his overcoat collar turned up to his ears.

"Car's here," he said.

"Right-o! Tom! I'll chalk it up to thee, lad!" said Percy with heavy breeziness. Then, making a great effort with himself, he rose heavily and went across to the door, to his wife, saying to her, in the same stiff voice of false heartiness:

"You'll be as right as rain with Tom. You won't mind if I don't come out? No! I'd better not show myself to the audience. Well-I'm glad you came, if only for a while. Good-bye then! I'll be home after the service-but I shan't disturb you. Good-bye! Don't get wet now-" And his voice, falsely cheerful, stiff with anger, ended in a clang of indignation.

Alice Howells sat on the infants' bench in silence. She was ignored. And she was unhappy, uneasy, because of the scene.

Percy closed the door after his wife. Then he turned with a looming slowness to Alice, and said in a hoarse whisper: "Think o' that, now!"

She looked up at him anxiously. His face, in its dark pigment, was transfigured with indignant anger. His yellow-grey eyes blazed, and a great rush of anger seemed to be surging up volcanic in him. For a second his eyes rested on her upturned, troubled, dark-blue eyes, then glanced away, as if he didn't want to look at her in his anger. Even so, she felt a touch of tenderness in his glance.

"And that's all she's ever cared about-her own things and her own way," he said, in the same hoarse whisper, hoarse with suddenly-released rage. Alice Howells hung her head in silence.

"Not another damned thing, but what's her own, her own-and her own holy way-damned holy-holy-holy, all to herself." His voice shook with hoarse, whispering rage, burst out at last.

Alice Howells looked up at him in distress.

"Oh, don't say it!" she said. "I'm sure she's fond of you."

"Fond of me! Fond of me!" he blazed, with a grin of transcendent irony.

110

"It makes her sick to look at me. I am a hairy brute, I own it. Why, she's never once touched me to be fond of me-never once-though she pretends sometimes. But a man knows-" and he made a grimace of contempt. "He knows when a woman's just stroking him, good doggie!-and when she's really a bit woman-fond of him. That woman's never been real fond of anybody or anything, all her life-she couldn't, for all her show of kindness. She's limited to herself, that woman is; and I've looked up to her as if she was God. More fool me! If God's not good-natured and good-hearted, then what is He-?"

Alice sat with her head dropped, realising once more that men aren't really fooled. She was upset, shaken by his rage, and frightened, as if she too were guilty. He had sat down blankly beside her. She glanced up at him.

"Never mind!" she said soothingly. "You'll like her again to-morrow."

He looked down at her with a grin, a grey sort of grin. "Are you going to stroke me 'good doggie!' as well?" he said.

"Why?" she asked, blank.

But he did not answer. Then after a while he resumed: "Wouldn't even leave the moccasins! And she's hung them up in my room, left them there for years-any man'd consider they were his. And I did want this show to-night to be a success! What are you going to do about it?"

"I've sent over for a pair of pale-blue satin bed-slippers of mine-they'll do just as well," she replied.

"Aye! For all that, it's done me in."

"You'll get over it."

"Happen so! She's curdled my inside, for all that. I don't know how I'm going to be civil to her."

"Perhaps you'd better stay at the rectory to-night," she said softly.

He looked into her eyes. And in that look, he transferred his allegiance.

"You don't want to be drawn in, do you?" he asked, with troubled tenderness.

But she only gazed with wide, darkened eyes into his eyes, so she was like an open, dark doorway to him. His heart beat thick, and the faint, breathless smile of passion came into his eyes again.

"You'll have to go on, Mrs. Howells. We can't keep them waiting any longer."

It was Jim Stokes, who was directing the show. They heard the clapping and stamping of the impatient audience.

"Goodness!" cried Alice Howells, darting to the door.

THE MORTAL COIL

I

She stood motionless in the middle of the room, something tense in her reckless bearing. Her gown of reddish stuff fell silkily about her feet; she looked tall and splendid in the candlelight. Her dark-blond hair was gathered loosely in a fold on top of her head, her young, blossom-fresh face was lifted. From her throat to her feet she was clothed in the elegantly-made dress of silky red stuff, the colour of red earth. She looked complete and lovely, only love could make her such a strange, complete blossom. Her cloak and hat were thrown across a table just in front of her.

Quite alone, abstracted, she stood there arrested in a conflict of emotions. Her hand, down against her skirt, worked irritably, the ball of the thumb rubbing, rubbing across the tips of the fingers. There was a slight tension between her lifted brows.

About her the room glowed softly, reflecting the candlelight from its whitewashed walls, and from the great, bowed, whitewashed ceiling. It was a large attic, with two windows, and the ceiling curving down on either side, so that both the far walls were low. Against one, on one side, was a single bed, opened for the night, the white over-bolster piled back. Not far from this was the iron stove. Near the window closest to the bed was a table with writing materials, and a handsome cactus-plant with clear scarlet blossoms threw its bizarre shadow on the wall. There was another table near the second window, and opposite was the door on which hung a military cloak. Along the far wall, were guns and fishing-tackle, and some clothes too, hung on pegs-all men's clothes, all military. It was evidently the room of a man, probably a young lieutenant.

The girl, in her pure red dress that fell about her feet, so that she looked a woman, not a girl, at last broke from her abstraction and went aimlessly to the writing-table. Her mouth was closed down stubbornly, perhaps in anger, perhaps in pain. She picked up a large seal made of agate, looked at the ingraven coat of arms, then stood rubbing her finger across the cut-out stone, time after time. At last she put the seal down, and looked at the other things-a beautiful old beer-mug used as a tobacco-jar, a silver box like an urn, old and of exquisite shape, a bowl of sealing wax. She fingered the pieces of wax. This, the dark-green, had sealed her last letter. Ah, well! She carelessly turned over the blotting book, which again had his arms stamped on the cover. Then she went away to the window. There, in the window-recess, she stood and looked out. She opened the casement and took a deep breath of the cold night air. Ah, it was good! Far below was the street, a vague golden milky way beneath her, its tiny black figures moving and crossing and re-crossing with marionette, insect-like intentness. A small horse-car rumbled along the lines, so belittled, it was an absurdity. So much for the world! . . . he did not come.

She looked overhead. The stars were white and flashing, they looked nearer than the street, more kin to her, more real. She stood pressing her breast on her arms, her face lifted to the stars, in the long, anguished suspense of waiting. Noises came up small from the street, as from some insect-world. But the great stars overhead struck white and invincible, infallible. Her heart felt cold like the stars.

At last she started. There was a noisy knocking at the door, and a female voice calling:

"Anybody there?"

"Come in," replied the girl.

She turned round, shrinking from this intrusion, unable to bear it, after the flashing stars.

There entered a thin, handsome dark girl dressed in an extravagantly-made gown of dark purple silk and dark blue velvet. She was followed by a small swarthy, inconspicuous lieutenant in pale-blue uniform.

"Ah you! . . . alone?" cried Teresa, the newcomer, advancing into the room. "Where's the Fritz, then?"

The girl in red raised her shoulders in a shrug, and turned her face aside, but did not speak.

"Not here! You don't know where he is? Ach, the dummy, the lout!" Teresa swung round on her companion.

"Where is he?" she demanded.

He also lifted his shoulders in a shrug.

"He said he was coming in half an hour," the young lieutenant replied.

"Ha!-half an hour! Looks like it! How long is that ago-two hours?"

Again the young man only shrugged. He had beautiful black eye-lashes, and steady eyes. He stood rather deprecatingly, whilst his girl, golden like a young panther, hung over him.

"One knows where he is," said Teresa, going and sitting on the opened bed. A dangerous contraction came between the brows of Marta, the girl in red, at this act.

"Wine, Women and Cards!" said Teresa, in her loud voice. "But they prefer the women on the cards.

'My love he has four Queenies,
Four Queenies has my lo-o-ove,'"

she sang. Then she broke off, and turned to Podewils. "Was he winning when you left him, Karl?"

Again the young baron raised his shoulders.

"Tant pis que mal,' he replied, cryptically.

"Ah, you!" cried Teresa, "with your tant pis que mal! Are you tant pis que mal?" She laughed her deep, strange laugh. "Well," she added, "he'll be coming in with a fortune for you, Marta-"

There was a vague, unhappy silence.

"I know his fortunes," said Marta.

"Yes," said Teresa, in sudden sober irony, "he's a horse-shoe round your neck, is that young jockey.-But what are you going to do, Matzen dearest? You're not going to wait for him any longer?-Don't dream of it! The idea,

113

waiting for that young gentleman as if you were married to him!-Put your hat on, dearest, and come along with us . . . Where are we going, Karl, you pillar of salt?-Eh?-Geier's?-To Geier's, Marta, my dear. Come, quick, up-you've been martyred enough, Marta, my martyr-haw!-haw!!-put your hat on. Up-away!"

Teresa sprang up like an explosion, anxious to be off.

"No, I'll wait for him," said Marta, sullenly.

"Don't be such a fool!" cried Teresa, in her deep voice. "Wait for him! I'd give him wait for him. Catch this little bird waiting." She lifted her hand and blew a little puff across the fingers. "Choo-fly!" she sang, as if a bird had just flown.

The young lieutenant stood silent with smiling dark eyes. Teresa was quick, and golden as a panther.

"No, but really, Marta, you're not going to wait any more-really! It's stupid for you to play Gretchen-your eyes are much too green. Put your hat on, there's a darling."

"No," said Marta, her flower-like face strangely stubborn. "I'll wait for him. He'll have to come some time."

There was a moment's uneasy pause.

"Well," said Teresa, holding her long shoulders for her cloak, "so long as you don't wait as long as Lenora-fuhr-ums-Morgenrot-! Adieu, my dear, God be with you."

The young lieutenant bowed a solicitous bow, and the two went out, leaving the girl in red once more alone.

She went to the writing table, and on a sheet of paper began writing her name in stiff Gothic characters, time after time:

Marta Hohenest
Marta Hohenest
Marta Hohenest.

The vague sounds from the street below continued. The wind was cold. She rose and shut the window. Then she sat down again.

At last the door opened, and a young officer entered. He was buttoned up in a dark-blue great-coat, with large silver buttons going down on either side of the breast. He entered quickly, glancing over the room, at Marta, as she sat with her back to him. She was marking with a pencil on paper. He closed the door. Then with fine beautiful movements he divested himself of his coat and went to hang it up. How well Marta knew the sound of his movements, the quick light step! But she continued mechanically making crosses on the paper, her head bent forward between the candles, so that her hair made fine threads and mist of light, very beautiful. He saw this, and it touched him. But he could not afford to be touched any further.

"You have been waiting?" he said formally. The insulting futile question! She made no sign, as if she had not heard. He was absorbed in the tragedy of himself, and hardly heeded her.

He was a slim, good-looking youth, clear-cut and delicate in mould. His features now were pale, there was something evasive in his dilated, vibrating eyes. He was barely conscious of the girl, intoxicated with his own desperation, that held him mindless and distant.

114

To her, the atmosphere of the room was almost unbreathable, since he had come in. She felt terribly bound, walled up. She rose with a sudden movement that tore his nerves. She looked to him tall and bright and dangerous, as she faced round on him.

"Have you come back with a fortune?" she cried, in mockery, her eyes full of dangerous light.

He was unfastening his belt, to change his tunic. She watched him up and down, all the time. He could not answer, his lips seemed dumb. Besides, silence was his strength.

"Have you come back with a fortune?" she repeated, in her strong, clear voice of mockery.

"No," he said, suddenly turning. "Let it please you that-that I've come back at all."

He spoke desperately, and tailed off into silence. He was a man doomed. She looked at him: he was insignificant in his doom. She turned in ridicule. And yet she was afraid; she loved him.

He had stood long enough exposed, in his helplessness. With difficulty he took a few steps, went and sat down at the writing-table. He looked to her like a dog with its tail between its legs.

He saw the paper, where her name was repeatedly written. She must find great satisfaction in her own name, he thought vaguely. Then he picked up the seal and kept twisting it round in his fingers, doing some little trick. And continually the seal fell on to the table with a sudden rattle that made Marta stiffen cruelly. He was quite oblivious of her.

She stood watching as he sat bent forward in his stupefaction. The fine cloth of his uniform showed the moulding of his back. And something tortured her as she saw him, till she could hardly bear it: the desire of his finely-shaped body, the stupefaction and the abjectness of him now, his immersion in the tragedy of himself, his being unaware of her. All her will seemed to grip him, to bruise some manly nonchalance and attention out of him.

"I suppose you're in a fury with me, for being late?" he said, with impotent irony in his voice. Her fury over trifles, when he was lost in calamity! How great was his real misery, how trivial her small offendedness!

Something in his tone burned her, and made her soul go cold.

"I'm not exactly pleased," she said coldly, turning away to a window.

Still he sat bent over the table, twisting something with his fingers. She glanced round on him. How nervy he was! He had beautiful hands, and the big topaz signet-ring on his finger made yellow lights. Ah, if only his hands were really dare-devil and reckless! They always seemed so guilty, so cowardly.

"I'm done for now," he said suddenly, as if to himself, tilting back his chair a little. In all his physical movement he was so fine and poised, so sensitive! Oh, and it attracted her so much!

"Why?" she said, carelessly.

An anger burned in him. She was so flippant. If he were going to be shot, she would not be moved more than about half a pound of sweets.

115

"Why!" he repeated laconically. "The same unimportant reason as ever."

"Debts?" she cried, in contempt.

"Exactly."

Her soul burned in anger.

"What have you done now?-lost more money?"

"Three thousand marks."

She was silent in deep wrath.

"More fool you!" she said. Then, in her anger, she was silent for some minutes. "And so you're done for, for three thousand marks?" she exclaimed, jeering at him. "You go pretty cheap."

"Three thousand-and the rest," he said, keeping up a manly sang froid."

"And the rest!" she repeated in contempt. "And for three thousand-and the rest, your life is over!"

"My career," he corrected her.

"Oh," she mocked, "only your career! I thought it was a matter of life and death. Only your career? Oh, only that!"

His eyes grew furious under her mockery.

"My career is my life," he said.

"Oh, is it!-You're not a man then, you are only a career?"

"I am a gentleman."

"Oh, are you! How amusing! How very amusing, to be a gentleman, and not a man!-I suppose that's what it means, to be a gentleman, to have no guts outside your career?"

"Outside my honour-none."

"And might I ask what is your honour?" She spoke in extreme irony.

"Yes, you may ask," he replied coolly. "But if you don't know without being told, I'm afraid I could never explain it."

"Oh, you couldn't! No, I believe you-you are incapable of explaining it, it wouldn't bear explaining." There was a long, tense pause. "So you've made too many debts, and you're afraid they'll kick you out of the army, therefore your honour is gone, is it?-And what then-what after that?"

She spoke in extreme irony. He winced again at her phrase "kick you out of the army". But he tilted his chair back with assumed nonchalance.

"I've made too many debts, and I know they'll kick me out of the army," he repeated, thrusting the thorn right home to the quick. "After that-I can shoot myself. Or I might even be a waiter in a restaurant-or possibly a clerk, with twenty-five shillings a week."

"Really!-All those alternatives!-Well, why not, why not be a waiter in the Germania? It might be awfully jolly."

"Why not?" he repeated ironically. "Because it wouldn't become me."

She looked at him, at his aristocratic fineness of physique, his extreme physical sensitiveness. And all her German worship for his old, proud family rose up in her. No, he could not be a waiter in the Germania: she could not bear it. He was too refined and beautiful a thing.

"Ha!" she cried suddenly. "It wouldn't come to that, either. If they kick you out of the army, you'll find somebody to get round-you're like a cat, you'll land on your feet."

But this was just what he was not. He was not like a cat. His self-mistrust was too deep. Ultimately he had no belief in himself, as a separate isolated being. He knew he was sufficiently clever, an aristocrat, good-looking, the sensitive superior of most men. The trouble was, that apart from the social fabric he belonged to, he felt himself nothing, a cipher. He bitterly envied the common working-men for a certain manly aplomb, a grounded, almost stupid self-confidence he saw in them. Himself-he could lead such men through the gates of hell-for what did he care about danger or hurt to himself, whilst he was leading? But-cut him off from all this, and what was he? A palpitating rag of meaningless human life.

But she, coming from the people, could not fully understand. And it was best to leave her in the dark. The free indomitable self-sufficient being which a man must be in his relation to a woman who loves him-this he could pretend. But he knew he was not it. He knew that the world of man from which he took his value was his mistress beyond any woman. He wished, secretly, cravingly, almost cravenly, in his heart, it was not so. But so it was.

Therefore, he heard her phrase "you're like a cat," with some bitter envy.

"Whom shall I get round?-some woman, who will marry me?" he said.

This was a way out. And it was almost the inevitable thing, for him. But he felt it the last ruin of his manhood, even he.

The speech hurt her mortally, worse than death. She would rather he died, because then her own love would not turn to ash.

"Get married, then, if you want to," she said, in a small broken voice.

"Naturally," he said.

There was a long silence, a foretaste of barren hopelessness.

"Why is it so terrible to you," she asked at length, "to come out of the army and trust to your own resources? Other men are strong enough."

"Other men are not me," he said.

Why would she torture him? She seemed to enjoy torturing him. The thought of his expulsion from the army was an agony to him, really worse than death. He saw himself in the despicable civilian clothes, engaged in some menial occupation. And he could not bear it. It was too heavy a cross.

Who was she to talk? She was herself, an actress, daughter of a tradesman. He was himself. How should one of them speak for the other? It was impossible. He loved her. He loved her far better than men usually loved their mistresses. He really cared.-And he was strangely proud of his love for her, as if it were a distinction to him . . . But there was a limit to her understanding. There was a point beyond which she had nothing to do with him, and she had better leave him alone. Here in this crisis, which was his crisis, his downfall, she should not presume to talk, because she did not understand.-But she loved to torture him, that was the truth.

"Why should it hurt you to work?" she reiterated.

He lifted his face, white and tortured, his grey eyes flaring with fear and hate.

"Work!" he cried. "What do you think I am worth?-Twenty-five shillings a week, if I am lucky."

117

His evident anguish penetrated her. She sat dumbfounded, looking at him with wide eyes. He was white with misery and fear; his hand, that lay loose on the table, was abandoned in nervous ignominy. Her mind filled with wonder, and with deep, cold dread. Did he really care so much? But did it really matter so much to him? When he said he was worth twenty-five shillings a week, he was like a man whose soul is pierced. He sat there, annihilated. She looked for him, and he was nothing then. She looked for the man, the free being that loved her. And he was not, he was gone, this blank figure remained. Something with a blanched face sat there in the chair, staring at nothing.

His amazement deepened with intolerable dread. It was as if the world had fallen away into chaos. Nothing remained. She seemed to grasp the air for foothold.

He sat staring in front of him, a dull numbness settled on his brain. He was watching the flame of the candle. And, in his detachment, he realized the flame was a swiftly travelling flood, flowing swiftly from the source of the wick through a white surge and on into the darkness above. It was like a fountain suddenly foaming out, then running on dark and smooth. Could one dam the flood? He took a piece of paper, and cut off the flame for a second.

The girl in red started at the pulse of the light. She seemed to come to, from some trance. She saw his face, clear now, attentive, abstract, absolved. He was quite absolved from his temporal self.

"It isn't true," she said, "is it? It's not so tragic, really?-It's only your pride is hurt, your silly little pride?" She was rather pleading.

He looked at her with clear steady eyes.

"My pride!" he said. "And isn't my pride me? What am I without my pride?"

"You are yourself," she said. "If they take your uniform off you, and turn you naked into the street, you are still yourself."

His eyes grew hot. Then he cried:

"What does it mean, myself! It means I put on ready-made civilian clothes and do some dirty drudging elsewhere: that is what myself amounts to."

She knitted her brows.

"But what you are to me-that naked self which you are to me-that is something, isn't it?-everything," she said.

"What is it, if it means nothing?" he said: "What is it, more than a pound of chocolate dragées?-It stands for nothing-unless as you say, a petty clerkship, at twenty-five shillings a week."

These were all wounds to her, very deep. She looked in wonder for a few moments.

"And what does it stand for now?" she said. "A magnificent second-lieutenant!"

He made a gesture of dismissal with his hand.

She looked at him from under lowered brows.

"And our love!" she said. "It means nothing to you, nothing at all?"

"To me as a menial clerk, what does it mean? What does love mean!

118

Does it mean that a man shall be no more than a dirty rag in the world?-What worth do you think I have in love, if in life I am a wretched inky subordinate clerk?"

"What does it matter?"

"It matters everything."

There was silence for a time, then the anger flashed up in her.

"It doesn't matter to you what I feel, whether I care or not," she cried, her voice rising. "They'll take his little uniform with buttons off him, and he'll have to be a common little civilian, so all he can do is to shoot himself!-It doesn't matter that I'm there-"

He sat stubborn and silent. He thought her vulgar. And her raving did not alter the situation in the least.

"Don't you see what value you put on me, you clever little man?" she cried in fury. "I've loved you, loved you with all my soul, for two years-and you've lied, and said you loved me. And now, what do I get? He'll shoot himself, because his tuppenny vanity is wounded.-Ah, fool-!"

He lifted his head and looked at her. His face was fixed and superior.

"All of which," he said, "leaves the facts of the case quite untouched!"

She hated his cool little speeches.

"Then shoot yourself," she cried, "and you'll be worth less than twenty-five shillings a week!"

There was a fatal silence.

"Then there'll be no question of worth," he said.

"Ha!" she ejaculated in scorn.

She had finished. She had no more to say. At length, after they had both sat motionless and silent, separate, for some time, she rose and went across to her hat and cloak. He shrank in apprehension. Now, he could not bear her to go. He shrank as if he were being whipped. She put her hat on, roughly, then swung her warm plaid cloak over her shoulders. Her hat was of black glossy silk, with a sheeny heap of cocks-feathers, her plaid cloak was dark green and blue, it swung open above her clear harsh-red dress. How beautiful she was, like a fiery Madonna!

"Good-bye," she said, in her voice of mockery. "I'm going now."

He sat motionless, as if loaded with fetters. She hesitated, then moved towards the door.

Suddenly, with a spring like a cat, he was confronting her, his back to the door. His eyes were full and dilated, like a cat's, his face seemed to gleam at her. She quivered, as some subtle fluid ran through her nerves.

"Let me go," she said dumbly. "I've had enough." His eyes, with a wide, dark electric pupil, like a cat's, only watched her objectively. And again a wave of female submissiveness went over her.

"I want to go," she pleaded. "You know it's no good.-You know this is no good."

She stood humbly before him. A flexible little grin quivered round his mouth.

"You know you don't want me," she persisted. "You know you don't really want me.-You only do this to show your power over me-which is a mean trick."

119

But he did not answer, only his eyes narrowed in a sensual, cruel smile. She shrank, afraid, and yet she was fascinated.

"You won't go yet," he said.

She tried in vain to rouse her real opposition.

"I shall call out," she threatened. "I shall shame you before people."

His eyes narrowed again in the smile of vindictive, mocking indifference.

"Call then," he said.

And at the sound of his still, cat-like voice, an intoxication ran over her veins.

"I will," she said, looking defiantly into his eyes. But the smile in the dark, full, dilated pupils made her waver into submission again.

"Won't you let me go?" she pleaded sullenly.

Now the smile went openly over his face.

"Take your hat off," he said.

And with quick, light fingers he reached up and drew out the pins of her hat, unfastened the clasp of her cloak, and laid her things aside.

She sat down in a chair. Then she rose again, and went to the window. In the street below, the tiny figures were moving just the same. She opened the window, and leaned out, and wept.

He looked round at her in irritation as she stood in her long, clear-red dress in the window-recess, leaning out. She was exasperating.

"You will be cold," he said.

She paid no heed. He guessed, by some tension in her attitude, that she was crying. It irritated him exceedingly, like a madness. After a few minutes of suspense, he went across to her, and took her by the arm. His hand was subtle, soft in its touch, and yet rather cruel than gentle.

"Come away," he said. "Don't stand there in the air-come away."

He drew her slowly away to the bed, she sat down, and he beside her.

"What are you crying for?" he said in his strange, penetrating voice, that had a vibration of exultancy in it. But her tears only ran faster.

He kissed her face, that was soft, and fresh, and yet warm, wet with tears. He kissed her again, and again, in pleasure of the soft, wet saltness of her. She turned aside and wiped her face with her handkerchief, and blew her nose. He was disappointed-yet the way she blew her nose pleased him.

Suddenly she slid away to the floor, and hid her face in the side of the bed, weeping and crying loudly:

"You don't love me-Oh, you don't love me-I thought you did, and you let me go on thinking it-but you don't, no, you don't, and I can't bear it.-Oh, I can't bear it."

He sat and listened to the strange, animal sound of her crying. His eyes flickered with exultancy, his body seemed full and surcharged with power. But his brows were knitted in tension. He laid his hand softly on her head, softly touched her face, which was buried against the bed.

She suddenly rubbed her face against the sheets, and looked up once more.

"You've deceived me," she said, as she sat beside him.

120

"Have I? Then I've deceived myself." His body felt so charged with male vigour, he was almost laughing in his strength.

"Yes," she said enigmatically, fatally. She seemed absorbed in her thoughts. Then her face quivered again.

"And I loved you so much," she faltered, the tears rising. There was a clangour of delight in his heart.

"I love you," he said softly, softly touching her, softly kissing her, in a sort of subtle, restrained ecstasy.

She shook her head stubbornly. She tried to draw away. Then she did break away, and turned to look at him, in fear and doubt. The little, fascinating, fiendish lights were hovering in his eyes like laughter.

"Don't hurt me so much," she faltered, in a last protest.

A faint smile came on his face. He took her face between his hands and covered it with soft, blinding kisses, like a soft, narcotic rain. He felt himself such an unbreakable fountain-head of powerful blood. He was trembling finely in all his limbs, with mastery.

When she lifted her face and opened her eyes, her face was wet, and her greenish-golden eyes were shining, it was like sudden sunshine in wet foliage. She smiled at him like a child of knowledge, through the tears, and softly, infinitely softly he dried her tears with his mouth and his soft young moustache.

"You'd never shoot yourself, because you're mine, aren't you!" she said, knowing the fine quivering of his body, in mastery.

"Yes," he said.

"Quite mine?" she said, her voice rising in ecstasy.

"Yes."

"Nobody else but mine-nothing at all-?"

"Nothing at all," he re-echoed.

"But me?" came her last words of ecstasy.

"Yes."

And she seemed to be released free into the infinite of ecstasy.

II

They slept in fulfilment through the long night. But then strange dreams began to fill them both, strange dreams that were neither waking nor sleeping;-only, in curious weariness, through her dreams, she heard at last a continual low rapping. She awoke with difficulty. The rapping began again-she started violently. It was at the door-it would be the orderly rapping for Friedeburg. Everything seemed wild and unearthly. She put her hand on the shoulder of the sleeping man, and pulled him roughly, waited a moment, then pushed him, almost violently, to awake him. He woke with a sense of resentment at her violent handling. Then he heard the knocking of the orderly. He gathered his senses.

"Yes, Heinrich!" he said.

121

Strange, the sound of a voice! It seemed a far-off tearing sound. Then came the muffled voice of the servant.

"Half past four, Sir."

"Right!" said Friedeburg, and automatically he got up and made a light. She was suddenly as wide awake as if it were daylight. But it was a strange, false day, like a delirium. She saw him put down the match, she saw him moving about, rapidly dressing. And the movement in the room was a trouble to her. He himself was vague and unreal, a thing seen but not comprehended. She watched all the acts of his toilet, saw all the motions, but never saw him. There was only a disturbance about her, which fretted her, she was not aware of any presence. Her mind, in its strange, hectic clarity, wanted to consider things in absolute detachment. For instance, she wanted to consider the cactus plant. It was a curious object with pure scarlet blossoms. Now, how did these scarlet blossoms come to pass, upon that earthly-looking unliving creature? Scarlet blossoms! How wonderful they were! What were they, then, how could one lay hold on their being? Her mind turned to him. Him, too, how could one lay hold on him, to have him? Where was he, what was he? She seemed to grasp at the air.

He was dipping his face in the cold water-the slight shock was good for him. He felt as if someone had stolen away his being in the night, he was moving about a light, quick shell, with all his meaning absent. His body was quick and active, but all his deep understanding, his soul was gone. He tried to rub it back into his face. He was quite dim, as if his spirit had left his body.

"Come and kiss me," sounded the voice from the bed. He went over to her automatically. She put her arms around him and looked into his face with her clear brilliant, grey-green eyes, as if she too were looking for his soul.

"How are you?" came her meaningless words.

"All right."

"Kiss me."

He bent down and kissed her.

And still her clear, rather frightening eyes seemed to be searching for him inside himself. He was like a bird transfixed by her pellucid, grey-green, wonderful eyes. She put her hands into his soft, thick, fine hair, and gripped her hands full of his hair. He wondered with fear at her sudden painful clutching.

"I shall be late," he said.

"Yes," she answered. And she let him go.

As he fastened his tunic he glanced out of the window. It was still night: a night that must have lasted since eternity. There was a moon in the sky. In the streets below the yellow street-lamps burned small at intervals. This was the night of eternity.

There came a knock at the door, and the orderly's voice.

"Coffee, Sir."

"Leave it there."

They heard the faint jingle of the tray as it was set down outside.

Friedeburg sat down to put on his boots. Then, with a man's solid tread, he went and took in the tray. He felt properly heavy and secure now in his accoutrement. But he was always aware of her two wonderful, clear, unfolded eyes, looking on his heart, out of her uncanny silence.

There was a strong smell of coffee in the room.

"Have some coffee?" His eyes could not meet hers.

"No, thank you."

"Just a drop?"

"No, thank you."

Her voice sounded quite gay. She watched him dipping his bread in the coffee and eating quickly, absently. He did not know what he was doing, and yet the dipped bread and hot coffee gave him pleasure. He gulped down the remainder of his drink, and rose to his feet.

"I must go," he said.

There was a curious, poignant smile in her eyes. Her eyes drew him to her. How beautiful she was, and dazzling, and frightening, with this look of brilliant tenderness seeming to glitter from her face. She drew his head down to her bosom, and held it fast prisoner there, murmuring with tender, triumphant delight: "Dear! Dear!"

At last she let him lift his head, and he looked into her eyes, that seemed to concentrate in a dancing, golden point of vision in which he felt himself perish.

"Dear!" she murmured. "You love me, don't you?"

"Yes," he said mechanically.

The golden point of vision seemed to leap to him from her eyes, demanding something. He sat slackly, as if spellbound. Her hand pushed him a little.

"Mustn't you go?" she said.

He rose. She watched him fastening the belt round his body, that seemed soft under the fine clothes. He pulled on his great-coat, and put on his peaked cap. He was again a young officer.

But he had forgotten his watch. It lay on the table near the bed. She watched him slinging it on his chain. He looked down at her. How beautiful she was, with her luminous face and her fine, stray hair! But he felt far away.

"Anything I can do for you?" he asked.

"No, thank you-I'll sleep," she replied, smiling. And the strange golden spark danced on her eyes again, again he felt as if his heart were gone, destroyed out of him. There was a fine pathos too in her vivid, dangerous face.

He kissed her for the last time, saying:

"I'll blow the candles out, then?"

"Yes, my love-and I'll sleep."

"Yes-sleep as long as you like."

The golden spark of her eyes seemed to dance on him like a destruction, she was beautiful, and pathetic. He touched her tenderly with his finger-tips, then suddenly blew out the candles, and walked across in the faint moonlight to the door.

He was gone. She heard his boots click on the stone stairs-she heard the far below tread of his feet on the pavement. Then he was gone. She lay quite still, in a swoon of deathly peace. She never wanted to move any more. It was finished. She lay quite still, utterly, utterly abandoned.

But again she was disturbed. There was a little tap at the door, then Teresa's voice saying, with a shuddering sound because of the cold:

"Ugh!-I'm coming to you, Marta my dear. I can't stand being left alone."

"I'll make a light," said Marta, sitting up and reaching for the candle. "Lock the door, will you, Resie, and then nobody can bother us."

She saw Teresa, loosely wrapped in her cloak, two thick ropes of hair hanging untidily. Teresa looked voluptuously sleepy and easy, like a cat running home to the warmth.

"Ugh!" she said, "it's cold!"

And she ran to the stove. Marta heard the chink of the little shovel, a stirring of coals, then a clink of the iron door. Then Teresa came running to the bed, with a shuddering little run, she puffed out the light and slid in beside her friend.

"So cold!" she said, with a delicious shudder at the warmth. Marta made place for her, and they settled down.

"Aren't you glad you're not them?" said Resie, with a little shudder at the thought. "Ugh!-poor devils!"

"I am," said Marta.

"Ah, sleep-sleep, how lovely!" said Teresa, with deep content. "Ah, it's so good!"

"Yes," said Marta.

"Good morning, good night, my dear," said Teresa, already sleepily.

"Good night," responded Marta.

Her mind flickered a little. Then she sank unconsciously to sleep. The room was silent.

Outside, the setting moon made peaked shadows of the high-roofed houses; from twin towers that stood like two dark, companion giants in the sky, the hour trembled out over the sleeping town. But the footsteps of hastening officers and cowering soldiers rang on the frozen pavements. Then a lantern appeared in the distance, accompanied by the rattle of a bullock wagon. By the light of the lantern on the wagon-pole could be seen the delicately moving feet and the pale, swinging dewlaps of the oxen. They drew slowly on, with a rattle of heavy wheels, the banded heads of the slow beasts swung rhythmically.

Ah, this was life! How sweet, sweet each tiny incident was! How sweet to Friedeburg, to give his orders ringingly on the frosty air, to see his men like bears shambling and shuffling into their places, with little dancing movements of uncouth playfulness and resentment, because of the pure cold.

Sweet, sweet it was to be marching beside his men, sweet to hear the great thresh-thresh of their heavy boots in the unblemished silence, sweet to feel the immense mass of living bodies co-ordinated into oneness near him, to catch the hot waft of their closeness, their breathing. Friedeburg was like a man condemned to die, catching at every impression as at an inestimable treasure.

Sweet it was to pass through the gates of the town, the scanty, loose

124

suburb, into the open darkness and space of the country. This was almost best of all. It was like emerging in the open plains of eternal freedom.

They saw a dark figure hobbling along under the dark side of a shed. As they passed, through the open door of the shed, in the golden light were seen the low rafters, the pale, silken sides of the cows, evanescent. And a woman with a red kerchief bound round her head lifted her face from the flank of the beast she was milking, to look at the soldiers threshing like multitudes of heavy ghosts down the darkness. Some of the men called to her, cheerfully, impudently. Ah, the miraculous beauty and sweetness of the merest trifles like these!

They tramped on down a frozen, rutty road, under lines of bare trees. Beautiful trees! Beautiful frozen ruts in the road! Ah, even, in one of the ruts there was a silver of ice and of moon-glimpse. He heard ice tinkle as a passing soldier purposely put his toe in it. What a sweet noise!

But there was a vague uneasiness. He heard the men arguing as to whether dawn were coming. There was the silver moon, still riding on the high seas of the sky. A lovely thing she was, a jewel! But was there any blemish of day? He shrank a little from the rawness of the day to come. This night of morning was so rare and free.

Yes, he was sure. He saw a colourless paleness on the horizon. The earth began to look hard, like a great, concrete shadow. He shrank into himself. Glancing at the ranks of his men, he could see them like a company of rhythmic ghosts. The pallor was actually reflected on their livid faces. This was the coming day. It frightened him.

The dawn came. He saw the rosiness of it hang trembling with light, above the east. Then a strange glamour of scarlet passed over the land. At his feet, glints of ice flashed scarlet, even the hands of the men were red as they swung, sinister, heavy, reddened.

The sun surged up, her rim appeared, swimming with fire, hesitating, surging up. Suddenly there were shadows from trees and ruts, and grass was hoar and ice was gold against the ebony shadow. The faces of the men were alight, kindled with life. Ah, it was magical, it was all too marvellous! If only it were always like this!

When they stopped at the inn for breakfast, at nine o'clock, the smell of the inn went raw and ugly to his heart: beer and yesterday's tobacco!

He went to the door to look at the men biting huge bites from their hunks of grey bread, or cutting off pieces with their clasp-knives. This made him still happy. Women were going to the fountain for water, the soldiers were chaffing them coarsely. He liked all this.

But the magic was going, inevitably, the crystal delight was thawing to desolation in his heart, his heart was cold, cold mud. Ah, it was awful. His face contracted, he almost wept with cold, stark despair.

Still he had the work, the day's hard activity with the men. Whilst this lasted, he could live. But when this was over, and he had to face the horror of his own cold-thawing mud of despair: ah, it was not to be thought of. Still, he was happy at work with the men: the wild desolate place, the hard activity of mock warfare. Would to God it were real: war, with the prize of death!

By afternoon the sky had gone one dead, livid level of grey. It seemed low down, and oppressive. He was tired, the men were tired, and this let the heavy cold soak in to them like despair. Life could not keep it out.

And now, when his heart was so heavy it could sink no more, he must glance at his own situation again. He must remember what a fool he was, his new debts like half thawed mud in his heart. He knew, with the cold misery of hopelessness, that he would be turned out of the army. What then?-what then but death? After all, death was the solution for him. Let it be so.

They marched on and on, stumbling with fatigue under a great leaden sky, over a frozen dead country. The men were silent with weariness, the heavy motion of their marching was like an oppression. Friedeburg was tired too, and deadened, as his face was deadened by the cold air. He did not think any more; the misery of his soul was like a frost inside him.

He heard someone say it was going to snow. But the words had no meaning for him. He marched as a clock ticks, with the same monotony, everything numb and cold-soddened.

They were drawing near to the town. In the gloom of the afternoon he felt it ahead, as unbearable oppression on him. Ah the hideous suburb! What was his life, how did it come to pass that life was lived in a formless, hideous grey structure of hell! What did it all mean? Pale, sulphur-yellow lights spotted the livid air, and people, like soddened shadows, passed in front of the shops that were lit up ghastly in the early twilight. Out of the colourless space, crumbs of snow came and bounced animatedly off the breast of his coat.

At length he turned away home, to his room, to change and get warm and renewed, for he felt as cold-soddened as the grey, cold, heavy bread which felt hostile in the mouths of the soldiers. His life was to him like this dead, cold bread in his mouth.

As he neared his own house, the snow was peppering thinly down. He became aware of some unusual stir about the house-door. He looked-a strange, closed-in wagon, people, police. The sword of Damocles that had hung over his heart, fell. O God, a new shame, some new shame, some new torture! His body moved on. So it would move on through misery upon misery, as is our fate. There was no emergence, only this progress through misery unto misery, till the end. Strange, that human life was so tenacious! Strange, that men had made of life a long, slow process of torture to the soul. Strange, that it was no other than this! Strange, that but for man, this misery would not exist. For it was not God's misery, but the misery of the world of man.

He saw two officials push something white and heavy into the cart, shut the doors behind with a bang, turn the silver handle, and run round to the front of the wagon. It moved off. But still most of the people lingered. Friedeburg drifted near in that inevitable motion which carries us through all our shame and torture. He knew the people talked about him. He went up the steps and into the square hall.

There stood a police-officer, with a note-book in his hand, talking to Herr Kapell, the housemaster. As Friedeburg entered through the swing door, the housemaster, whose brow was wrinkled in anxiety and perturbation, made a gesture with his hand, as if to point out a criminal.

"Ah!-the Herr Baron von Friedeburg!" he said, in self-exculpation.

The police officer turned, saluted politely, and said, with the polite, intolerable suffisance of officialdom:

"Good evening! Trouble here!"

"Yes?" said Friedeburg.

He was so frightened, his sensitive constitution was so lacerated, that something broke in him, he was a subservient, murmuring ruin.

"Two young ladies found dead in your room," said the police-official, making an official statement. But under his cold impartiality of officialdom, what obscene unction! Ah, what obscene exposures now!

"Dead!" ejaculated Friedeburg, with the wide eyes of a child. He became quite child-like, the official had him completely in his power. He could torture him as much as he liked.

"Yes." He referred to his note-book. "Asphyxiated by fumes from the stove."

Friedeburg could only stand wide-eyed and meaningless.

"Please-will you go upstairs?"

The police-official marshalled Friedburg in front of himself. The youth slowly mounted the stairs, feeling as if transfixed through the base of the spine, as if he would lose the use of his legs. The official followed close on his heels.

They reached the bedroom. The policeman unlocked the door. The housekeeper followed with a lamp. Then the official examination began.

"A young lady slept here last night?"

"Yes."

"Name, please?"

"Marta Hohenest."

"H-o-h-e-n-e-s-t," spelled the official. "-And address?"

Friedeburg continued to answer. This was the end of him. The quick of him was pierced and killed. The living dead answered the living dead in obscene antiphony. Question and answer continued, the note-book worked as the hand of the old dead wrote in it the replies of the young who was dead.

The room was unchanged from the night before. There was her heap of clothing, the lustrous, pure-red dress lying soft where she had carelessly dropped it. Even, on the edge of the chair-back, her crimson silk garters hung looped.

But do not look, do not see. It is the business of the dead to bury their dead. Let the young dead bury their own dead, as the old dead have buried theirs. How can the dead remember, they being dead? Only the living can remember, and are at peace with their living who have passed away.

THE OLD ADAM

The maid who opened the door was just developing into a handsome womanhood. Therefore she seemed to have the insolent pride of one newly come to an inheritance. She would be a splendid woman to look at, having just enough of Jewish blood to enrich her comeliness into beauty. At nineteen her fine grey eyes looked challenge, and her warm complexion, her black hair looped up slack, enforced the sensuous folding of her mouth.

She wore no cap nor apron, but a well-looking sleeved overall such as even very ladies don.

The man she opened to was tall and thin, but graceful in his energy. He wore white flannels, carried a tennis-racket. With a light bow to the maid he stepped beside her on the threshold. He was one of those who attract by their movement, whose movement is watched unconsciously, as we watch the flight of a sea-bird waving its wing leisurely. Instead of entering the house, the young man stood beside the maid-servant and looked back into the blackish evening. When in repose, he had the diffident, ironic bearing so remarkable in the educated youth of to-day, the very reverse of that traditional aggressiveness of youth.

"It is going to thunder, Kate," he said.

"Yes, I think it is," she replied, on an even footing.

The young man stood a moment looking at the trees across the road, and on the oppressive twilight.

"Look," he said, "there's not a trace of colour in the atmosphere, though it's sunset; all a dark, lustrous grey; and those oaks kindle green like a low fire-see!"

"Yes," said Kate, rather awkwardly.

"A troublesome sort of evening; must be, because it's your last with us."

"Yes," said the girl, flushing and hardening.

There was another pause; then:

"Sorry you're going?" he asked, with a faint tang of irony.

"In some ways," she replied, rather haughtily.

He laughed, as if he understood what was not said, then, with an "Ah well!" he passed along the hall.

The maid stood for a few moments clenching her young fists, clenching her very breast in revolt. Then she closed the door.

Edward Severn went into the dining-room. It was eight o'clock, very dark for a June evening; on the dusk-blue walls only the gilt frames of the pictures glinted pale. The clock occupied the room with its delicate ticking.

The door opened into a tiny conservatory that was lined with a grapevine. Severn could hear, from the garden beyond, the high prattling of a child. He went to the glass door.

Running down the grass by the flower-border was a little girl of three, dressed in white. She was very bonny, very quick and intent in her movements; she reminded him of a fieldmouse which plays alone in the corn, for sheer joy. Severn lounged in the doorway, watching her. Suddenly

128

she perceived him. She started, flashed into greeting, gave a little gay jump, and stood quite still again, as if pleading.

"Mr. Severn," she cried, in wonderfully coaxing tones: "Come and see this."

"What?" he asked.

"Com' and see it," she pleaded.

He laughed, knowing she only wanted to coax him into the garden; and he went.

"Look," she said, spreading out her plump little arm.

"What?" he asked.

The baby was not going to admit that she had tricked him thither for her amusement.

"All gone up to buds," she said, pointing to the closed marigolds. Then "See!" she shrieked, flinging herself at his legs, grasping the flannel of his trousers, and tugging at him wildly. She was a wild little Mænad. She flew shrieking like a revelling bird down the garden, glancing back to see if he were coming. He had not the heart to desist, but went swiftly after her. In the obscure garden, the two white figures darted through the flowering plants, the baby, with her full silk skirts, scudding like a ruffled bird, the man, lithe and fleet, snatching her up and smothering his face in hers. And all the time her piercing voice reechoed from his low calls of warning and of triumph as he hunted her. Often she was really frightened of him; then she clung fast round his neck, and he laughed and mocked her in a low, stirring voice, whilst she protested.

The garden was large for a London suburb. It was shut in by a high dark embankment, that rose above a row of black poplar trees. And over the spires of the trees, high up, slid by the golden-lighted trains, with the soft movement of caterpillars and a hoarse, subtle noise.

Mrs. Thomas stood in the dark doorway watching the night, the trains, the flash and run of the two white figures.

"And now we must go in," she heard Severn say.

"No," cried the baby, wild and defiant as a bacchanal. She clung to him like a wild-cat.

"Yes," he said. "Where's your mother?"

"Give me a swing," demanded the child.

He caught her up. She strangled him hard with her young arms.

"I said, where's your mother?" he persisted, half smothered.

"She's op'tairs," shouted the child. "Give me a swing."

"I don't think she is," said Severn.

"She is. Give me a swing, a swi-i-ing!"

He bent forward, so that she hung from his neck like a great pendant. Then he swung her, laughing low to himself while she shrieked with fear. As she slipped he caught her to his breast.

"Mary!" called Mrs. Thomas, in that low, songful tone of a woman when her heart is roused and happy.

"Mary!" she called, long and sweet.

"Oh, no!" cried the child quickly.

But Severn bore her off. Laughing, he bowed his head and offered to the mother the baby who clung round his neck.

"Come along here," said Mrs. Thomas roguishly, clasping the baby's waist with her hands.

"Oh, no," cried the child, tucking her head into the young man's neck.

"But it's bed-time," said the mother. She laughed as she drew at the child to pull her loose from Severn. The baby clung tighter, and laughed, feeling no determination in her mother's grip. Severn bent his head to loosen the child's hold, bowed, and swung the heavy baby on his neck. The child clung to him, bubbling with laughter; the mother drew at her baby, laughing low, while the man swung gracefully, giving little jerks of laughter.

"Let Mr. Severn undress me," said the child, hugging close to the young man, who had come to lodge with her parents when she was scarce a month old.

"You're in high favour to-night," said the mother to Severn. He laughed, and all three stood a moment watching the trains pass and repass in the sky beyond the garden-end. Then they went indoors, and Severn undressed the child.

She was a beautiful girl, a bacchanal with her wild, dull-gold hair tossing about like a loose chaplet, her hazel eyes shining daringly, her small, spaced teeth glistening in little passions of laughter within her red, small mouth. The young man loved her. She was such a little bright wave of wilfulness, so abandoned to her impulses, so white and smooth as she lay at rest, so startling as she flashed her naked limbs about. But she was growing too old for a young man to undress.

She sat on his knee in her high-waisted night-gown, eating her piece of bread-and-butter with savage little bites of resentment: she did not want to go to bed. But Severn made her repeat a Pater Noster. She lisped over the Latin, and Mrs. Thomas, listening, flushed with pleasure; although she was a Protestant, and although she deplored the unbelief of Severn, who had been a Catholic.

The mother took the baby to carry her to bed. Mrs. Thomas was thirty-four years old, full-bosomed and ripe. She had dark hair that twined lightly round her low, white brow. She had a clear complexion, and beautiful brows, and dark-blue eyes. The lower part of her face was heavy.

"Kiss me," said Severn to the child.

He raised his face as he sat in the rocking-chair. The mother stood beside, looking down at him, and holding the laughing rogue of a baby against her breast. The man's face was uptilted, his heavy brows set back from the laughing tenderness of his eyes, which looked dark, because the pupil was dilated. He pursed up his handsome mouth, his thick close-cut moustache roused.

He was a man who gave tenderness, but who did not ask for it. All his own troubles he kept, laughingly, to himself. But his eyes were very sad when quiet, and he was too quick to understand sorrow, not to know it.

Mrs. Thomas watched his fine mouth lifted for kissing. She leaned forward, lowering the baby, and suddenly, by a quick change in his eyes,

130

she knew he was aware of her heavy woman's breasts approaching down to him. The wild rogue of a baby bent her face to his, and then, instead of kissing him, suddenly licked his cheek with her wet, soft tongue. He started back in aversion, and his eyes and his teeth flashed with a dangerous laugh.

"No, no," he laughed, in low strangled tones. "No dog-lick, my dear, oh no!"

The baby chuckled with glee, gave one wicked jerk of laughter, that came out like a bubble escaping.

He put up his mouth again, and again his face was horizontal below the face of the young mother. She looked down on him as if by a kind of fascination.

"Kiss me, then," he said with thick throat.

The mother lowered the baby. She felt scarcely sure of her balance. Again the child, when near to his face, darted out her tongue to lick him. He swiftly averted his face, laughing in his throat.

Mrs. Thomas turned her face aside; she would see no more.

"Come then," she said to the child. "If you won't kiss Mr. Severn nicely"

The child laughed over the mother's shoulder like a squirrel crouched there. She was carried to bed.

It was still not quite dark; the clouds had opened slightly. The young man flung himself into an arm-chair, with a volume of French verse. He read one lyric, then he lay still.

"What, all in the dark!" exclaimed Mrs. Thomas, coming in. "And reading by this light." She rebuked him with timid affectionateness. Then, glancing at his white-flannelled limbs sprawled out in the gloom, she went to the door. There she turned her back to him, looking out.

"Don't these flags smell strongly in the evening?" she said at length.

He replied with a few lines of the French he had been reading.

She did not understand. There was a peculiar silence.

"A peculiar, brutal, carnal scent, iris," he drawled at length. "Isn't it?"

She laughed shortly, saying: "Eh, I don't know about that."

"It is," he asserted calmly.

He rose from his chair, went to stand beside her at the door.

There was a great sheaf of yellow iris near the window. Farther off, in the last twilight, a gang of enormous poppies balanced and flapped their gold-scarlet, which even the darkness could not quite put out.

"We ought to be feeling very sad," she said after a while.

"Why?" he asked.

"Well-isn't it Kate's last night?" she said, slightly mocking.

"She's a tartar, Kate," he said.

"Oh, she's too rude, she is really! The way she criticises the things you do, and her insolence-"

"The things I do?" he asked.

"Oh no; you can't do anything wrong. It's the things I do." Mrs. Thomas sounded very much incensed.

"Poor Kate, she'll have to lower her key," said Severn.

"Indeed she will, and a good thing too."

131

There was silence again.

"It's lightning," he said at last.

"Where?" she asked, with a suddenness that surprised him. She turned, met his eyes for a second. He sank his head, abashed.

"Over there in the north-east," he said, keeping his face from her. She watched his hand rather than the sky.

"Oh," she said uninterestedly.

"The storm will wheel round, you'll see," he said.

"I hope it wheels the other way, then."

"Well, it won't. You don't like lightning, do you? You'd even have to take refuge with Kate if I weren't here."

She laughed quietly at his irony.

"No," she said, quite bitterly. "Mr. Thomas is never in when he's wanted."

"Well, as he won't be urgently required, we'll acquit him, eh?"

At that moment a white flash fell across the blackness. They looked at each other, laughing. The thunder came broken and hesitatingly.

"I think we'll shut the door," said Mrs. Thomas, in normal, sufficiently distant tones. A strong woman, she locked and bolted the stiff fastenings easily. Severn pressed on the light. Mrs. Thomas noticed the untidiness of the room. She rang, and presently Kate appeared.

"Will you clear baby's things away?" she said, in the contemptuous tone of a hostile woman. Without answering, and in her superb, unhastening way, Kate began to gather up the small garments. Both women were aware of the observant, white figure of the man standing on the hearth. Severn balanced with a fine, easy poise, and smiled to himself, exulting a little to see the two women in this state of hostility. Kate moved about with bowed defiant head. Severn watched her curiously; he could not understand her. And she was leaving to-morrow. When she had gone out of the room, he remained still standing, thinking. Something in his lithe, vigorous balance, so alert, and white, and independent, caused Mrs. Thomas to glance at him from her sewing.

"I will let the blinds down," he said, becoming aware that he was attracting attention.

"Thank you," she replied conventionally.

He let the lattice blinds down, then flung himself into his chair.

Mrs. Thomas sat at the table, near him, sewing. She was a good-looking woman, well made. She sat under the one light that was turned on. The lamp-shade was of red silk lined with yellow. She sat in the warm-gold light. There was established between the two a peculiar silence, like suspense, almost painful to each of them, yet which neither would break. Severn listened to the snap of her needle, looked from the movement of her hand to the window, where the lightning beat and fluttered through the lattice. The thunder was as yet far off.

"Look," he said, "at the lightning."

Mrs. Thomas started at the sound of his voice, and some of the colour went from her face. She turned to the window.

There, between the cracks of the Venetian blinds, came the white flare

132

of lightning, then the dark. Several storms were in the sky. Scarcely had one sudden glare fluttered and palpitated out, than another covered the window with white. It dropped, and another flew up, beat like a moth for a moment, then vanished. Thunder met and overlapped; two battles were fought together in the sky.

Mrs. Thomas went very pale. She tried not to look at the window, yet, when she felt the lightning blench the lamplight, she watched, and each time a flash leaped on the window, she shuddered. Severn, all unconsciously, was smiling with roused eyes.

"You don't like it?" he said, at last, gently.

"Not much," she answered, and he laughed.

"Yet all the storms are a fair way off," he said. "Not one near enough to touch us."

"No, but," she replied, at last laying her hands in her lap, and turning to him, "it makes me feel worked up. You don't know how it makes me feel, as if I couldn't contain myself."

She made a helpless gesture with her hand. He was watching her closely. She seemed to him pathetically helpless and bewildered; she was eight years older than he. He smiled in a strange, alert fashion, like a man who feels in jeopardy. She bent over her work, stitching nervously. There was a silence in which neither of them could breathe freely.

Presently a bigger flash than usual whitened through the yellow lamplight. Both glanced at the window, then at each other. For a moment it was a look of greeting; then his eyes dilated to a smile, wide with recklessness. He felt her waver, lose her composure, become incoherent. Seeing the faint helplessness of coming tears, he felt his heart thud to a crisis. She had her face at her sewing.

Severn sank in his chair, half suffocated by the beating of his heart. Yet, time after time, as the flashes came, they looked at each other, till in the end they both were panting, and afraid, not of the lightning but of themselves and of each other.

He was so much moved that he became conscious of his perturbation. "What the deuce is up?" he asked himself, wondering. At twenty-seven, he was quite chaste. Being highly civilised, he prized women for their intuition, and because of the delicacy with which he could transfer to them his thoughts and feelings, without cumbrous argument. From this to a state of passion he could only proceed by fine gradations, and such a procedure he had never begun. Now he was startled, astonished, perturbed, yet still scarcely conscious of his whereabouts. There was a pain in his chest that made him pant, and an involuntary tension in his arms, as if he must press someone to his breast. But the idea that this someone was Mrs. Thomas would have shocked him too much had he formed it. His passion had run on subconsciously, till now it had come to such a pitch it must drag his conscious soul into allegiance. This, however, would probably never happen; he would not yield allegiance, and blind emotion, in this direction, could not carry him alone.

Towards eleven o'clock Mr. Thomas came in.

133

"I wonder you come home at all," Severn heard Mrs. Thomas say as her husband stepped indoors.

"I left the office at half-past ten," the voice of Thomas replied, disagreeably.

"Oh, don't try to tell me that old tale," the woman answered contemptuously.

"I didn't try anything at all, Gertie," he replied with sarcasm. "Your question was answered."

Severn imagined him bowing with affected, magisterial dignity, and he smiled. Mr. Thomas was something in the law.

Mrs. Thomas left her husband in the hall, came and sat down again at table, where she and Severn had just finished supper, both of them reading the while.

Thomas came in, flushed very red. He was of middle stature, a thickly-built man of forty, good-looking. But he had grown round-shouldered with thrusting forward his chin in order to look the aggressive, strong-jawed man. He had a good jaw; but his mouth was small and nervously pinched. His brown eyes were of the emotional, affectionate sort, lacking pride or any austerity.

He did not speak to Severn nor Severn to him. Although as a rule the two men were very friendly, there came these times when, for no reason whatever, they were sullenly hostile. Thomas sat down heavily, and reached his bottle of beer. His hands were thick, and in their movement rudimentary. Severn watched the thick fingers grasp the drinking-glass as if it were a treacherous enemy.

"Have you had supper, Gertie?" he asked, in tones that sounded like an insult. He could not bear that these two should sit reading as if he did not exist.

"Yes," she replied, looking up at him in impatient surprise. "It's late enough." Then she buried herself again in her book.

Severn ducked low and grinned. Thomas swallowed a mouthful of beer.

"I wish you could answer my questions, Gertie, without superfluous detail," he said nastily, thrusting out his chin at her as if cross-examining.

"Oh," she said indifferently, not looking up. "Wasn't my answer right, then?"

"Quite-I thank you," he answered, bowing with great sarcasm. It was utterly lost on his wife.

"Hm-hm!" she murmured in abstraction, continuing to read.

Silence resumed. Severn was grinning to himself, chuckling.

"I had a compliment paid me to-night, Gertie," said Thomas, quite amicably, after a while. He still ignored Severn.

"Hm-hm!" murmured his wife. This was a well-known beginning. Thomas valiantly struggled on with his courtship of his wife, swallowing his spleen.

"Councillor Jarndyce, in full committee-Are you listening, Gertie?"

"Yes," she replied, looking up for a moment.

"You know Councillor Jarndyce's style," Thomas continued, in the tone of a man determined to be patient and affable: "-the courteous Old English Gentleman-"

"Hm-hm!" replied Mrs. Thomas.

"He was speaking in reply to . . ." Thomas gave innumerable wearisome details, which no one heeded.

"Then he bowed to me, then to the Chairman-'I am compelled to say, Mr. Chairman, that we have one cause for congratulation; we are inestimably fortunate in one member of our staff; there is one point of which we can always be sure-the point of law; and it is an important point, Mr. Chairman.'

"He bowed to the Chairman, he bowed to me. And you should have heard the applause all round that Council Chamber-that great, horseshoe table, you don't know how impressive it is. And every face turned to me, and all round the board: 'Hear-Hear!' You don't know what respect I command in business, Mrs. Thomas."

"Then let it suffice you," said Mrs. Thomas, calmly indifferent.

Mr. Thomas bit his bread-and-butter.

"The fat-head's had two drops of Scotch, so he's drawing on his imagination," thought Severn chuckling deeply.

"I thought you said there was no meeting to-night," Mrs. Thomas suddenly and innocently remarked after a while.

"There was a meeting, in camera," replied her husband, drawing himself up with official dignity. His excessive and wounded dignity convulsed Severn; the lie disgusted Mrs. Thomas in spite of herself.

Presently Thomas, always courting his wife and insultingly overlooking Severn, raised a point of politics, passed a lordly opinion very offensive to the young man. Severn had risen, stretched himself, and laid down his book. He was leaning on the mantelpiece in an indifferent manner, as if he scarcely noticed the two talkers. But hearing Thomas pronounce like a boor upon the Woman's Bill, he roused himself, and coolly contradicted his landlord. Mrs. Thomas shot a look of joy at the white-clad young man who lounged so scornfully on the hearth. Thomas cracked his knuckles one after another, and lowered his brown eyes, which were full of hate. After a sufficient pause, for his timidity was stronger than his impulse, he replied with a phrase that sounded final. Severn flipped the sense out of it with a few words. In the argument Severn, more cultured and far more nimble-witted than his antagonist, who hauled up his answers with a lawyer's show of invincibility, but who had not any fineness of perception, merely spiked his opponent's pieces and smiled at him. Also the young man enjoyed himself by looking down scornfully, straight into the brown eyes of his senior all the time, so that Thomas writhed.

Mrs. Thomas, meantime, took her husband's side against women, without reserve. Severn was angry; he was scornfully angry with her. Mrs. Thomas glanced at him from time to time, a little ecstasy lighting her fine blue eyes. The irony of her part was delicious to her. If she had sided with Severn, that young man would have pitied the forlorn man, and been gentle with him.

The battle of words had got quieter and more intense. Mrs. Thomas made no move to check it. At last Severn was aware he and Thomas were both getting overheated. Thomas had doubled and dodged painfully, like a half-frenzied rabbit that will not realise it is trapped. Finally his efforts had moved even his opponent to pity. Mrs. Thomas was not pitiful. She scorned her husband's dexterity of argument, when his intellectual dishonesty was so evident to her. Severn uttered his last phrases, and would say no more. Then Thomas cracked his knuckles one after the other, turned aside, consumed with morbid humiliation, and there was silence.

"I will go to bed," said Severn. He would have spoken some conciliatory words to his landlord; he lingered with that purpose; but he could not bring his throat to utter his purpose.

"Oh, before you go, do you mind, Mr. Severn, helping Mr. Thomas down with Kate's box? You may be gone before he's up in the morning, and the cab comes at ten. Do you mind?"

"Why should I?" replied Severn.

"Are you ready, Joe?" she asked her husband.

Thomas rose with the air of a man who represses himself and is determined to be patient.

"Where is it?" he asked.

"On the top landing. I'll tell Kate, and then we shan't frighten her. She has gone to bed."

Mrs. Thomas was quite mistress of the situation; both men were humble before her. She led the way, with a candle, to the third floor. There on the little landing, outside the closed door, stood a large tin trunk. The three were silent because of the baby.

"Poor Kate," Severn thought. "It's a shame to kick her out into the world, and all for nothing." He felt an impulse of hate towards womankind.

"Shall I go first, Mr. Severn?" asked Thomas.

It was surprising how friendly the two men were, as soon as they had something to do together, or when Mrs. Thomas was absent. Then they were comrades, Thomas, the elder, the thick-set, playing the protector's part, though always deferential to the younger, whimsical man.

"I had better go first," said Thomas kindly. "And if you put this round the handle, it won't cut your fingers."

He offered the young man a little flexible book from his pocket. Severn had such small, fine hands that Thomas pitied them.

Severn raised one end of the trunk. Leaning back, and flashing a smile to Mrs. Thomas, who stood with the candle, he whispered: "Kate's got a lot more impediments than I have."

"I know it's heavy," laughed Mrs. Thomas.

Thomas, waiting at the brink of the stairs, saw the young man tilting his bare throat towards the smiling woman, and whispering words which pleased her.

"At your pleasure, sir," he said in his most grating and official tones.

"Sorry," Severn flung out scornfully.

The elder man retreated very cautiously, stiffly lowering himself down one stair, looking anxiously behind.

"Are you holding the light for me, Gertie?" he snapped sarcastically, when he had managed one stair. She lifted the candle with a swoop. He was in a bustle and a funk, Severn, always indifferent, smiled slightly, and lowered the box with negligent ease of movement. As a matter of fact, three-quarters of the heavy weight: pressed on Thomas. Mrs. Thomas watched the two figures from above.

"If I slip now," thought Severn, as he noticed the anxious, red face of his landlord, "I should squash him like a shrimp," and he laughed to himself.

"Don't come yet," he called softly to Mrs. Thomas, whom he heard following. "If you slip, your husband's bottom-most under the smash. 'Beware the fearful avalanche!'"

He laughed, and Mrs. Thomas gave a little chuckle. Thomas, very red and flustered, glanced irritably back at them, but said nothing.

Near the bottom of the staircase there was a twist in the stairs. Severn was feeling particularly reckless. When he came to the turn, he chuckled to himself, feeling his house-slippers unsafe on the narrowed, triangular stairs. He loved a risk above all things, and a subconscious instinct made the risk doubly sweet when his rival was under the box. Though Severn would not knowingly have hurt a hair of his landlord's head.

When Thomas was beginning to sweat with relief, being only one step from the landing, Severn did slip, quite accidentally. The great box crashed as if in pain, Severn glissaded down the stairs. Thomas was flung backwards across the landing, and his head went thud against the banister post. Severn, seeing no great harm done, was struggling to his feet, laughing and saying: "I'm awfully sorry-" when Thomas got up. The elder man was infuriated like a bull. He saw the laughing face of Severn and he went mad. His brown eyes flared.

"You --, you did it on purpose!" he shouted, and straightway he fetched the young man two heavy blows, upon the jaw and ear. Thomas, a footballer and a boxer in his youth, had been brought up among the roughs of Swansea; Severn in a religious college in France. The young man had never been struck in the face before. He instantly went white and mad with rage. Thomas stood on guard, fists up. But on the small, lumbered landing there was no room for fight. Moreover, Severn had no instinct of fisticuffs. With open, stiff fingers, the young man sprang on his adversary. In spite of the blow he received, but did not feel, he flung himself again forward, and then, catching Thomas's collar, brought him down with a crash. Instantly his exquisite hands were dug in the other's thick throat, the linen collar having been torn open. Thomas fought madly, with blind, brute strength. But the other lay wrapped on him like a white steel, his rare intelligence concentrated, not scattered; concentrated on strangling Thomas swiftly. He pressed forward, forcing his landlord's head over the edge of the next flight of stairs. Thomas, stout and full-blooded, lost every trace of self-possession; he struggled like an animal at slaughter. The blood came out of his nose over his face; he made horrid choking sounds as he struggled.

Suddenly Severn felt his face turned between two hands. With a shock of real agony, he met the eyes of Kate. She bent forward, she captured his eyes.

"What do you think you're doing?" she cried in frenzy of indignation.

She leaned over him in her night-dress, her two black plaits hanging perpendicular. He hid his face, and took his hands away. As he kneeled to rise, he glanced up the stairs. Mrs. Thomas stood against the banisters, motionless in a trance of horror and remorse. He saw the remorse plainly. Severn turned away his face, and was wild with shame. He saw his landlord kneeling, his hands at his throat, choking, rattling, and gasping. The young man's heart filled with remorse and grief. He put his arms round the heavy man, and raised him, saying tenderly:

"Let me help you up."

He had got Thomas up against the wall, when the choked man began to slide down again in collapse, gasping all the time pitifully.

"No, stand up; you're best standing up," commanded Severn sharply, rearing his landlord up again. Thomas managed to obey, stupidly. His nose still bled, he still held his throat and gasped with a crowing sound. But his breathing was getting deeper.

"Water, Kate-and sponge-cold," said Severn.

Kate was back in an instant. The young man bathed his landlord's face and temples and throat. The bleeding ceased directly, the stout man's breathing became a series of irregular, jerky gasps, like a child that has been sobbing hard. At last he took a long breath, and his breast settled into regular stroke, with little fluttering interruptions. Still holding his hand to his throat, he looked up with dazed, piteous brown eyes, mutely wretched and appealing. He moved his tongue as if to try it, put back his head a little, and moved the muscles of his throat. Then he replaced his hands on the place that ached.

Severn was grief-stricken. He would willingly, at that moment, have given his right hand for the man he had hurt.

Mrs. Thomas, meanwhile, stood on the stairs, watching: for a long time she dared not move, knowing she would sink down. She watched. One of the crises of her life was passing. Full of remorse, she passed over into the bitter land of repentance. She must no longer allow herself to hope for anything for herself. The rest of her life must be spent in self-abnegation: she must seek for no sympathy, must ask for no grace in love, no grace and harmony in living. Henceforward, as far as her own desires went, she was dead. She took a fierce joy in the anguish of it.

"Do you feel better?" Severn asked of the sick man. Thomas looked at the questioner with tragic brown eyes, in which was no anger, only mute self-pity. He did not answer, but looked like a wounded animal, very pitiable. Mrs. Thomas quickly repressed an impulse of impatient scorn, replacing it with a numb, abstract sense of duty, lofty and cold.

"Come," said Severn, full of pity, and gentle as a woman. "Let me help you to bed."

Thomas, leaning heavily on the young man, whose white garments were dabbed with blood and water, stumbled forlornly into his room. There Severn unlaced his boots and got off the remnant of his collar. At this point Mrs. Thomas came in. She had taken her part; she was weeping also.

"Thank you, Mr. Severn," she said coldly. Severn, dismissed, slunk out of the room. She went up to her husband, took his pathetic head upon her

138

bosom, and pressed it there. As Severn went downstairs, he heard the few sobs of the husband, among the quick sniffing of the wife's tears. And he saw Kate, who had stood on the stairs to see all went well, climb up to her room with cold, calm face.

He locked up the house, put everything in order. Then he heated some water to bathe his face, which was swelling painfully. Having finished his fomentations, he sat thinking bitterly, with a good deal of shame.

As he sat, Mrs. Thomas came down for something. Her bearing was cold and hostile. She glanced round to see all was safe. Then:

"You will put out the light when you go to bed, Mr. Severn," she said, more formally than a landlady at the seaside would speak. He was insulted: any ordinary being would turn off the light on retiring. Moreover, almost every night it was he who locked up the house, and came last to bed.

"I will, Mrs. Thomas," he answered. He bowed, his eyes flickering with irony, because he knew his face was swollen.

She returned again after having reached the landing.

"Perhaps you wouldn't mind helping me down with the box," she said, quietly and coldly. He did not reply, as he would have done an hour before, that he certainly should not help her, because it was a man's job, and she must not do it. Now, he rose, bowed, and went upstairs with her. Taking the greater part of the weight, he came quickly downstairs with the load.

"Thank you; it's very good of you. Good-night," said Mrs. Thomas, and she retired.

In the morning Severn rose late. His face was considerably swollen. He went in his dressing-gown across to Thomas's room. The other man lay in bed, looking much the same as ever, but mournful in aspect, though pleased within himself at being coddled.

"How are you this morning?" Severn asked.

Thomas smiled, looked almost with tenderness up at his friend.

"Oh, I'm all right, thanks," he replied.

He looked at the other's swollen and bruised cheek, then again, affectionately, into Severn's eyes.

"I'm sorry"-with a glance of indication-"for that," he said simply. Severn smiled with his eyes, in his own winsome manner.

"I didn't know we were such essential brutes," he said. "I thought I was so civilised ..."

Again he smiled, with a wry, stiff mouth. Thomas gave a deprecating little grunt of a laugh.

"Oh, I don't know," he said. "It shows a man's got some fight in him."

He looked up in the other's face appealingly. Severn smiled, with a touch of bitterness. The two men grasped hands.

To the end of their acquaintance, Severn and Thomas were close friends, with a gentleness in their bearing, one towards the other. On the other hand, Mrs. Thomas was only polite and formal with Severn, treating him as if he were a stranger.

Kate, her fate disposed of by her "betters", passed out of their three lives.

139

THE OVERTONE

His wife was talking to two other women. He lay on the lounge pretending to read. The lamps shed a golden light, and, through the open door, the night was lustrous, and a white moon went like a woman, unashamed and naked across the sky. His wife, her dark hair tinged with grey looped low on her white neck, fingered as she talked the pearl that hung in a heavy, naked drop against the bosom of her dress. She was still a beautiful woman, and one who dressed like the night, for harmony. Her gown was of silk lace, all in flakes, as if the fallen, pressed petals of black and faded-red poppies were netted together with gossamer about her. She was fifty-one, and he was fifty-two. It seemed impossible. He felt his love cling round her like her dress, like a garment of dead leaves. She was talking to a quiet woman about the suffrage. The other girl, tall, rather aloof, sat listening in her chair, with the posture of one who neither accepts nor rejects, but who allows things to go on around her, and will know what she thinks only when she must act. She seemed to be looking away into the night. A scent of honeysuckle came through the open door. Then a large grey moth blundered into the light.

It was very still, almost too silent, inside the room. Mrs. Renshaw's quiet, musical voice continued:

"But think of a case like Mrs. Mann's now. She is a clever woman. If she had slept in my cradle, and I in hers, she would have looked a greater lady than I do at this minute. But she married Mann, and she has seven children by him, and goes out charring. Her children she can never leave. So she must stay with a dirty, drunken brute like Mann. If she had an income of two pounds a week, she could say to him: 'Sir, good-bye to you,' and she would be well rid. But no, she is tied to him for ever."

They were discussing the State-endowment of mothers. She and Mrs. Hankin were bitterly keen upon it. Elsa Laskell sat and accepted their talk as she did the scent of the honeysuckle or the blundering adventure of the moth round the silk: it came burdened, not with the meaning of the words, but with the feeling of the woman's heart as she spoke. Perhaps she heard a nightingale in the park outside-perhaps she did. And then this talk inside drifted also to the girl's heart, like a sort of inarticulate music. Then she was vaguely aware of the man sprawled in his homespun suit upon the lounge. He had not changed for dinner: he was called unconventional.

She knew he was old enough to be her father, and yet he looked young enough to be her lover. They all seemed young, the beautiful hostess, too, but with a meaningless youth that cannot ripen, like an unfertilised flower which lasts a long time. He was a man she classed as a Dane-with fair, almost sandy hair, blue eyes, long loose limbs, and a boyish activity. But he was fifty-two-and he lay looking out on the night, with one of his hands swollen from hanging so long inert, silent. The women bored him.

Elsa Laskell sat in a sort of dreamy state, and the feelings of her hostess, and the feeling of her host drifted like iridescence upon the quick of her soul, among the white touch of that moon out there, and the exotic heaviness of the honeysuckle, and the strange flapping of the moth. So still, it was, behind the murmur of talk: a silence of being. Of the third woman, Mrs Hankin, the girl had no sensibility. But the night and the moon, the moth, Will Renshaw and Edith Renshaw and herself were all in full being, a harmony.

To him it was six months after his marriage, and the sky was the same, and the honeysuckle in the air. He was living again his crisis, as we all must, fretting and fretting against our failure, till we have worn away the thread of our life. It was six months after his marriage, and they were down at the little bungalow on the bank of the Soar. They were comparatively poor, though her father was rich, and his was well-to-do. And they were alone in the little two-roomed bungalow that stood on its wild bank over the river, among the honeysuckle bushes. He had cooked the evening meal, they had eaten the omelette and drank the coffee, and all was settling into stillness.

He sat outside, by the remnants of the fire, looking at the country lying level and lustrous grey opposite him. Trees hung like vapour in a perfect calm under the moonlight. And that was the moon so perfectly naked and unfaltering, going her errand simply through the night. And that was the river faintly rustling. And there, down the darkness, he saw a flashing of activity white betwixt black twigs. It was the water mingling and thrilling with the moon. So! It made him quiver, and reminded him of the starlit rush of a hare. There was vividness then in all this lucid night, things flashing and quivering with being, almost as the soul quivers in the darkness of the eye. He could feel it. The night's great circle was the pupil of an eye, full of the mystery, and the unknown fire of life, that does not burn away, but flickers unquenchable.

So he rose, and went to look for his wife. She sat with her dark head bent into the light of a reading lamp, in the little hut. She wore a white dress, and he could see her shoulders' softness and curve through the lawn. Yet she did not look up when he moved. He stood in the doorway, knowing that she felt his presence. Yet she gave no sign.

"Will you come out?" he asked.

She looked up at him as if to find out what he wanted, and she was rather cold to him. But when he had repeated his request, she had risen slowly to acquiesce, and a tiny shiver had passed down her shoulders. So he unhung from its peg her beautiful Paisley shawl, with its tempered colours that looked as if they had faltered through the years and now were here in their essence, and put it round her. They sat again outside the little hut, under the moonlight. He held both her hands. They were heavy with rings. But one ring was his wedding ring. He had married her, and there was nothing more to own. He owned her, and the night was the pupil of her eye, in which was everything. He kissed her fingers, but she sat and made no sign. It was as he wished. He kissed her fingers again.

Then a corncrake began to call in the meadow across the river, a strange, dispassionate sound, that made him feel not quite satisfied, not quite sure. It was not all achieved. The moon, in her white and naked candour, was beyond him. He felt a little numbness, as one who has gloves on. He could not feel that clear, clean moon. There was something betwixt him and her, as if he had gloves on. Yet he ached for the clear touch, skin to skin-even of the moonlight. He wanted a further purity, a newer cleanness and nakedness. The corncrake cried too. And he watched the moon, and he watched her light on his hands. It was like a butterfly on his glove, that he could see, but not feel. And he wanted to unglove himself. Quite clear, quite, quite bare to the moon, the touch of everything, he wanted to be. And after all, his wife was everything-moon, vapour of trees, trickling water and drift of perfume-it was all his wife. The moon glistened on her finger-tips as he cherished them, and a flash came out of a diamond, among the darkness. So, even here in the quiet harmony, life was at a flash with itself.

"Come with me to the top of the red hill," he said to his wife quietly.

"But why?" she asked.

"Do come."

And dumbly she acquiesced, and her shawl hung gleaming above the white flash of her skirt. He wanted to hold her hand, but she was walking apart from him, in her long shawl. So he went to her side, humbly. And he was humble, but he felt it was great. He had looked into the whole of the night, as into the pupil of an eye. And now, he would come perfectly clear out of all his embarrassments of shame and darkness, clean as the moon who walked naked across the night, so that the whole night was as an effluence from her, the whole of it was hers, held in her effluence of moonlight, which was her perfect nakedness, uniting her to everything. Covering was barrier, like cloud across the moon.

The red hill was steep, but there was a tiny path from the bungalow, which he had worn himself. And in the effort of climbing, he felt he was struggling nearer and nearer to himself. Always he looked half round, where, just behind him, she followed, in the lustrous obscurity of her shawl. Her steps came with a little effort up the steep hill, and he loved her feet, he wanted to kiss them as they strove upwards in the gloom. He put aside the twigs and branches. There was a strong scent of honeysuckle like a thick strand of gossamer over his mouth.

He knew a place on the ledge of the hill, on the lip of the cliff, where the trees stood back and left a little dancing-green, high up above the water, there in the midst of miles of moonlit, lonely country. He parted the boughs, sure as a fox that runs to its lair. And they stood together on this little dancing-green presented towards the moon, with the red cliff cumbered with bushes going down to the river below, and the haze of moon-dust on the meadows, and the trees behind them, and only the moon could look straight into the place he had chosen.

She stood always a little way behind him. He saw her face all compounded of shadows and moonlight, and he dared not kiss her yet.

"Will you," he said, "will you take off your things and love me here?"

"I can't," she said.

He looked away to the moon. It was difficult to ask her again, yet it meant so much to him. There was not a sound in the night. He put his hand to his throat and began to unfasten his collar.

"Take off all your things and love me," he pleaded.

For a moment she was silent.

"I can't," she said.

Mechanically, he had taken off his flannel collar and pushed it into his pocket. Then he stood on the edge of the land, looking down into all that gleam, as into the living pupil of an eye. He was bareheaded to the moon. Not a breath of air ruffled his bare throat. Still, in the dropping folds of her shawl, she stood, a thing of dusk and moonlight, a little back. He ached with the earnestness of his desire. All he wanted was to give himself, clean and clear, into this night, this time. Of which she was all, she was everything. He could go to her now, under the white candour of the moon, without shame or shadow, but in his completeness loving her completeness, without a stain, without a shadow between them such as even a flower could cast. For this he yearned as never in his life he could yearn more deeply.

"Do take me," he said, gently parting the shawl on her breast. But she held it close, and her voice went hard.

"No-I can't," she said.

"Why?"

"I can't-let us go back."

He looked again over the countryside of dimness, saying in a low tone, his back towards her:

"But I love you-and I want you so much-like that, here and now. I'll never ask you anything again," he said quickly, passionately, as he turned to her. "Do this for me," he said. "I'll never trouble you for anything again. I promise."

"I can't," she said stubbornly, with some hopelessness in her voice.

"Yes," he said. "Yes. You trust me, don't you?"

"I don't want it. Not here-not now," she said.

"Do," he said. "Yes."

"You can have me in the bungalow. Why do you want me here?" she asked.

"But I do. Have me, Edith. Have me now."

"No," she said, turning away. "I want to go down."

"And you won't?"

"No-I can't."

There was something like fear in her voice. They went down the hill together. And he did not know how he hated her, as if she had kept him out of the promised land that was justly his. He thought he was too generous to bear her a grudge. So he had always held himself deferential to her. And later that evening he had loved her. But she had hated it, it had been really his hate ravaging her. Why had he lied, calling it love? Ever since, it had seemed the same, more or less. So that he had ceased to come to her, gradually. For one night she had said: "I think a man's body is ugly-all in parts with mechanical joints." And now he had scarcely had her for some years. For she thought him an ugliness. And there were no children.

Now that everything was essentially over for both of them, they lived on the surface, and had good times. He drove to all kinds of unexpected places in his motor-car, bathed where he liked, said what he liked, and did what he liked. But nobody minded very much his often aggressive unconventionality. It was only fencing with the foils. There was no danger in his thrusts. He was a castrated bear. So he prided himself on being a bear, on being known as an uncouth bear.

It was not often he lay and let himself drift. But always when he did, he held it against her that on the night when they climbed the red bank, she refused to have him. There were perhaps many things he might have held against her, but this was the only one that remained: his real charge against her on the Judgment Day. Why had she done it? It had been, he might almost say, a holy desire on his part. It had been almost like taking off his shoes before God. Yet she refused him, she who was his religion to him. Perhaps she had been afraid, she who was so good-afraid of the big righteousness of it-as if she could not trust herself so near the Burning Bush, dared not go near for transfiguration, afraid of herself.

It was a thought he could not bear. Rising softly, because she was still talking, he went out into the night.

Elsa Laskell stirred uneasily in her chair. Mrs. Renshaw went on talking like a somnambule, not because she really had anything to say about the State-endowment of mothers, but because she had a weight on her heart that she wanted to talk away. The girl heard, and lifted her hand, and stirred her fingers uneasily in the dark-purple porphyry bowl, where pink rose-leaves and crimson, thrown this morning from the stem, lay gently shrivelling. There came a slight acrid scent of new rose-petals. And still the girl lifted her long white fingers among the red and pink in the dark bowl, as if they stirred in blood.

And she felt the nights behind like a purple bowl into which the woman's heart-beats were shed, like rose-leaves fallen and left to wither and go brown. For Mrs. Renshaw had waited for him. During happy days of stillness and blueness she had moved, while the sunshine glancing through her blood made flowers in her heart, like blossoms underground thrilling with expectancy, lovely fragrant things that would have delight to appear. And all day long she had gone secretly and quietly saying, saying: "To-night-to-night they will blossom for him. To-night I shall be a bed of blossom for him, all narcissi and fresh fragrant things shaking for joy, when he comes with his deeper sunshine, when he turns the darkness like mould, and brings them forth with his sunshine for spade. Yea, there are two suns; him in the sky and that other, warmer one whose beams are our radiant bodies. He is a sun to me, shining full on my heart when he comes, and everything stirs." But he had come like a bitter morning. He had never bared the sun of himself to her-a sullen day he had been on her heart, covered with cloud impenetrable. She had waited so heavy anxious, with such a wealth of possibility. And he in his blindness had never known. He could never let the real rays of his love through the cloud of fear and mistrust. For once she had denied him. And all her flowers had been shed inwards so that her heart was like a heap of leaves, brown, withered, almost scentless petals that had never given joy to anyone. And yet again she had come to him pregnant with beauty and love, but he had been

144

afraid. When she lifted her eyes to him, he had looked aside. The kisses she needed like warm raindrops he dared not give, till she was parched and gone hard, and did not want them. Then he gave kisses enough. But he never trusted himself. When she was open and eager to him, he was afraid. When she was shut, it was like playing at pride, to pull her petals apart, a game that gave him pleasure.

So they had been mutually afraid of each other, but he most often. Whenever she had needed him at some mystery of love, he had overturned her censers and her sacraments, and made profane love in her sacred place. Which was why, at last, she had hated his body; but perhaps she had hated it at first, or feared it so much that it was hate.

And he had said to her: "If we don't have children, you might have them by another man-" which was surely one of the cruellest things a woman ever heard from her husband. For so little was she his, that he would give her a caller and not mind. This was all the wife she was to him. He was a free and easy man, and brought home to dinner any man who pleased him, from a beggar upwards. And his wife was to be as public as his board.

Nay, to the very bowl of her heart, any man might put his lips and he would not mind. And so, she sadly set down the bowl from between her two hands of offering, and went always empty, and aloof.

Yet they were married, they were good friends. It was said they were the most friendly married couple in the county. And this was it. And all the while, like a scent, the bitter psalm of the woman filled the room.

"Like a garden in winter, I was full of bulbs and roots, I was full of little flowers, all conceived inside me.

"And they were all shed away unborn, little abortions of flowers.

"Every day I went like a bee gathering honey from the sky and among the stars I rummaged for yellow honey, filling it in my comb.

"Then I broke the comb, and put it to your lips. But you turned your mouth aside and said: 'You have made my face unclean, and smeared my mouth.'

"And week after week my body was a vineyard, my veins were vines. And as the grapes, the purple drops grew full and sweet, I crushed them in a bowl, I treasured the wine.

"Then when the bowl was full I came with joy to you. But you in fear started away, and the bowl was thrown from my hands, and broke in pieces at my feet.

"Many times, and many times, I said: 'The hour is striking,' but he answered: 'Not yet.'

"Many times and many times he has heard the cock crow, and gone out and wept, he knew not why.

"I was a garden and he ran in me as in the grass.

"I was a stream, and he threw his waste in me.

"I held the rainbow balanced on my outspread hands, and he said: 'You open your hands and give me nothing.'

"What am I now but a bowl of withered leaves, but a kaleidoscope of broken beauties, but an empty bee-hive, yea, a rich garment rusted that no one has worn, a dumb singer, with the voice of a nightingale yet making discord.

"And it was over with me, and my hour is gone. And soon like a barren sea-shell on the strand, I shall be crushed underfoot to dust.

"But meanwhile I sing to those that listen with their ear against me, of the sea that gave me form and being, the everlasting sea, and in my song is nothing but bitterness, for of the fluid life of the sea I have no more, but I am to be dust, that powdery stuff the sea knows not. I am to be dead, who was born of life, silent who was made a mouth, formless who was all of beauty. Yea, I was a seed that held the heavens lapped up in bud, with a whirl of stars and a steady moon.

"And the seed is crushed that never sprouted, there is a heaven lost, and stars and a moon that never came forth.

"I was a bud that never was discovered, and in my shut chalice, skies and lake water and brooks lie crumbling, and stars and the sun are smeared out, and birds are a little powdery dust, and their singing is dry air, and I am a dark chalice."

And the girl, hearing the hostess talk, still talk, and yet her voice like the sound of a sea-shell whispering hoarsely of despair, rose and went out into the garden, timidly, beginning to cry. For what should she do for herself?

Renshaw, leaning on the wicket that led to the paddock, called:

"Come on, don't be alarmed-Pan is dead."

And then she bit back her tears. For when he said, "Pan is dead," he meant Pan was dead in his own long, loose Dane's body. Yet she was a nymph still, and if Pan were dead, she ought to die. So with tears she went up to him.

"It's all right out here," he said. "By Jove, when you see a night like this, how can you say that life's tragedy-or death either, for that matter?"

"What is it then?" she asked.

"Nay, that's one too many-a joke, eh?"

"I think," she said, "one has no business to be irreverent."

"Who?" he asked.

"You," she said, "and me, and all of us."

Then he leaned on the wicket, thinking till he laughed.

"Life's a real good thing," he said.

"But why protest it?" she answered.

And again he was silent.

"If the moon came nearer and nearer," she said, "and were a naked woman, what would you do?"

"Fetch a wrap, probably," he said.

"Yes-you would do that," she answered.

"And if he were a man, ditto?" he teased.

"If a star came nearer and were a naked man, I should look at him."

"That is surely very improper," he mocked, with still a tinge of yearning.

"If he were a star come near-" she answered.

Again he was silent.

"You are a queer fish of a girl," he said.

146

They stood at the gate, facing the silver-grey paddock. Presently their hostess came out, a long shawl hanging from her shoulders.

"So you are here," she said. "Were you bored?"

"I was," he replied amiably. "But there, you know I always am."

"And I forgot," replied the girl.

"What were you talking about?" asked Mrs. Renshaw, simply curious. She was not afraid of her husband's running loose.

"We were just saying 'Pan is dead'," said the girl.

"Isn't that rather trite?" asked the hostess.

"Some of us miss him fearfully," said the girl.

"For what reason?" asked Mrs. Renshaw.

"Those of us who are nymphs-just lost nymphs among farm-lands and suburbs. I wish Pan were alive."

"Did he die of old age?" mocked the hostess.

"Don't they say, when Christ was born, a voice was heard in the air saying: 'Pan is dead.' I wish Christ needn't have killed Pan."

"I wonder how He managed it," said Renshaw.

"By disapproving of him, I suppose," replied his wife. And her retort cut herself, and gave her a sort of fakir pleasure.

"The men are all women now," she said, "since the fauns died in a frost one night."

"A frost of disapproval," said the girl.

"A frost of fear," said Renshaw.

There was a silence.

"Why was Christ afraid of Pan?" said the girl suddenly.

"Why was Pan so much afraid of Christ that he died?" asked Mrs. Renshaw bitterly.

"And all his fauns in a frost one night," mocked Renshaw. Then a light dawned on him. "Christ was woman and Pan was man," he said. It gave him a real joy to say this bitterly, keenly-a thrust into himself, and into his wife. "But the fauns and satyrs are there-you have only to remove the surplices that all men wear nowadays."

"Nay," said Mrs. Renshaw, "it is not true-the surplices have grown into their limbs, like Hercules's garment."

"That his wife put on him," said Renshaw.

"Because she was afraid of him-not because she loved him," said the girl.

"She imagined that all her lonely wasted hours wove him a robe of love," said Mrs. Renshaw. "It was to her horror she was mistaken. You can't weave love out of waste."

"When I meet a man," said the girl, "I shall look down the pupil of his eye, for a faun. And after a while it will come, skipping-"

"Perhaps a satyr," said Mrs. Renshaw bitterly.

"No," said the girl, "because satyrs are old, and I have seen some fearfully young men."

"Will is young even now-quite a boy," said his wife.

"Oh no!" cried the girl. "He says that neither life nor death is a tragedy. Only somebody very old could say that."

There was a tension in the night. The man felt something give way inside him.

"Yes, Edith," he said, with a quiet, bitter joy of cruelty, "I am old."

The wife was frightened.

"You are always preposterous," she said quickly, crying inside herself. She knew she herself had been never young.

"I shall look in the eyes of my man for the faun," the girl continued in a sing-song, "and I shall find him. Then I shall pretend to run away from him. And both our surplices, and all the crucifix, will be outside the wood. Inside nymph and faun, Pan and his satyrs-ah, yes: for Christ and the Cross is only for day-time, and bargaining. Christ came to make us deal honourably.

"But love is no deal, nor merchant's bargaining, and Christ neither spoke of it nor forbade it. He was afraid of it. If once His faun, the faun of the young Jesus had run free, seen one white nymph's brief breast, He would not have been content to die on a Cross-and then the men would have gone on cheating the women in life's business, all the time. Christ made one bargain in mankind's business-and He made it for the women's sake-I suppose for His mother's, since He was fatherless. And Christ made a bargain for me, and I shall avail myself of it. I won't be cheated by my man. When between my still hands I weave silk out of the air, like a cocoon, He shall not take it to pelt me with. He shall draw it forth and weave it up. For I want to finger the sunshine I have drawn through my body, stroke it, and have joy of the fabric.

"And when I run wild on the hills, with Dionysus, and shall come home like a bee that has rolled in floury crocuses, he must see the wonder on me, and make bread of it.

"And when I say to him, 'It is harvest in my soul', he shall look in my eyes and lower his nets where the shoal moves in a throng in the dark, and lift out the living blue silver for me to see, and know, and taste.

"All this, my faun in commerce, my faun at traffic with me.

"And if he cheat me, he must take his chance.

"But I will not cheat him, in his hour, when he runs like a faun after me. I shall flee, but only to be overtaken. I shall flee, but never out of the wood to the crucifix. For that is to deny I am a nymph; since how can a nymph cling at the crucifix? Nay, the cross is the sign I have on my money, for honesty.

"In the morning, when we come out of the wood, I shall say to him: 'Touch the cross, and prove you will deal fairly,' and if he will not, I will set the dogs of anger and judgment on him, and they shall chase him. But if, perchance, some night he contrive to crawl back into the wood, beyond the crucifix, he will be faun and I nymph, and I shall have no knowledge what happened outside, in the realm of the crucifix. But in the morning, I shall say: 'Touch the cross, and prove you will deal fairly.' And being renewed, he will touch the cross.

"Many a dead faun I have seen, like dead rabbits poisoned lying about the paths, and many a dead nymph, like swans that could not fly and the dogs destroyed.

"But I am a nymph and a woman, and Pan is for me, and Christ is for me.

"For Christ I cover myself in my robe, and weep, and vow my vow of honesty.

"For Pan I throw my coverings down and run headlong through the leaves, because of the joy of running.

"And Pan will give me my children and joy, and Christ will give me my pride.

"And Pan will give me my man, and Christ my husband.

"To Pan I am nymph, to Christ I am woman.

"And Pan is in the darkness, and Christ in the pale light.

"And night shall never be day, and day shall never be night.

"But side by side they shall go, day and night, night and day, for ever apart, for ever together.

"Pan and Christ, Christ and Pan.

"Both moving over me, so when in the sunshine I go in my robes among my neighbours, I am a Christian. But when I run robeless through the dark-scented woods alone, I am Pan's nymph.

"Now I must go, for I want to run away. Not run away from myself, but to myself.

"For neither am I a lamp that stands in the way in the sunshine.

"Now am I a sundial foolish at night.

"I am myself, running through light and shadow for ever, a nymph and a Christian; I, not two things, but an apple with a gold side and a red, a freckled deer, a stream that tinkles and a pool where light is drowned; I, no fragment, no half-thing like the day, but a blackbird with a white breast and underwings, a peewit, a wild thing, beyond understanding."

"I wonder if we shall hear the nightingale to-night," said Mrs. Renshaw.

"He's a gurgling fowl-I'd rather hear a linnet," said Renshaw. "Come a drive with me to-morrow, Miss Laskell."

And the three went walking back to the house. And Elsa Laskell was glad to get away from them.

THE PRINCESS

To her father, she was The Princess. To her Boston aunts and uncles she was just Dollie Urquhart, poor little thing.

Colin Urquhart was just a bit mad. He was of an old Scottish family, and he claimed royal blood. The blood of Scottish kings flowed in his veins. On this point, his American relatives said, he was just a bit "off". They could not bear any more to be told which royal blood of Scotland blued his veins. The whole thing was rather ridiculous, and a sore point. The only fact they remembered was that it was not Stuart.

He was a handsome man, with a wide-open blue eye that seemed sometimes to be looking at nothing, soft black hair brushed rather low on his low, broad brow, and a very attractive body. Add to this a most beautiful speaking voice, usually rather hushed and diffident, but sometimes resonant and powerful like bronze, and you have the sum of his charms. He looked like some old Celtic hero. He looked as if he should have worn a greyish kilt and a sporran, and shown his knees. His voice came direct out of the hushed Ossianic past.

For the rest, he was one of those gentlemen of sufficient but not excessive means who fifty years ago wandered vaguely about, never arriving anywhere, never doing anything, and never definitely being anything, yet well received in the good society of more than one country.

He did not marry till he was nearly forty, and then it was a wealthy Miss Prescott, from New England. Hannah Prescott at twenty-two was fascinated by the man with the soft black hair not yet touched by grey, and the wide, rather vague blue eyes. Many women had been fascinated before her. But Colin Urquhart, by his very vagueness, had avoided any decisive connection.

Mrs. Urquhart lived three years in the mist and glamour of her husband's presence. And then it broke her. It was like living with a fascinating spectre. About most things he was completely, even ghostly oblivious. He was always charming, courteous, perfectly gracious in that hushed, musical voice of his. But absent. When all came to all, he just wasn't there. "Not all there," as the vulgar say.

He was the father of the little girl she bore at the end of the first year. But this did not substantiate him the more. His very beauty and his haunting musical quality became dreadful to her after the first few months. The strange echo: he was like a living echo! His very flesh, when you touched it, did not seem quite the flesh of a real man.

Perhaps it was that he was a little bit mad. She thought it definitely the night her baby was born.

"Ah, so my little princess has come at last!" he said, in his throaty, singing Celtic voice, like a glad chant, swaying absorbed.

It was a tiny, frail baby, with wide, amazed blue eyes. They christened it Mary Henrietta. She called the little thing My Dollie. He called it always My Princess.

150

It was useless to fly at him. He just opened his wide blue eyes wider, and took a child-like, silent dignity there was no getting past.

Hannah Prescott had never been robust. She had no great desire to live. So when the baby was two years old she suddenly died.

The Prescotts felt a deep but unadmitted resentment against Colin Urquhart. They said he was selfish. Therefore they discontinued Hannah's income, a month after her burial in Florence, after they had urged the father to give the child over to them, and he had courteously, musically, but quite finally refused. He treated the Prescotts as if they were not of his world, not realities to him: just casual phenomena, or gramophones, talking-machines that had to be answered. He answered them. But of their actual existence he was never once aware.

They debated having him certified unsuitable to be guardian of his own child. But that would have created a scandal. So they did the simplest thing, after all-washed their hands of him. But they wrote scrupulously to the child, and sent her modest presents of money at Christmas, and on the anniversary of the death of her mother.

To The Princess her Boston relatives were for many years just a nominal reality. She lived with her father, and he travelled continually, though in a modest way, living on his moderate income. And never going to America. The child changed nurses all the time. In Italy it was a contadina; in India she had an ayah; in Germany she had a yellow-haired peasant girl.

Father and child were inseparable. He was not a recluse. Wherever he went he was to be seen paying formal calls going out to luncheon or to tea, rarely to dinner. And always with the child. People called her Princess Urquhart, as if that were her christened name.

She was a quick, dainty little thing with dark gold hair that went a soft brown, and wide, slightly prominent blue eyes that were at once so candid and so knowing. She was always grown up; she never really grew up. Always strangely wise, and always childish.

It was her father's fault.

"My little Princess must never take too much notice of people and the things they say and do," he repeated to her. "People don't know what they are doing and saying. They chatter-chatter, and they hurt one another, and they hurt themselves very often, till they cry. But don't take any notice, my little Princess. Because it is all nothing. Inside everybody there is another creature, a demon which doesn't care at all. You peel away all the things they say and do and feel, as cook peels away the outside of the onions. And in the middle of everybody there is a green demon which you can't peel away. And this green demon never changes, and it doesn't care at all about all the things that happen to the outside leaves of the person, all the chatter-chatter, and all the husbands and wives and children, and troubles and fusses. You peel everything away from people, and there is a green, upright demon in every man and woman; and this demon is a man's real self, and a woman's real self. It doesn't really care about anybody, it belongs to the demons and the primitive fairies, who never care. But, even so, there are big demons and mean demons, and splendid demonish fairies, and vulgar ones. But there are no royal fairy women left. Only you, my little Princess. You are the last of the royal race of the old people; the last, my Princess. There are no others. You and I are the last. When I am dead there will be only you. And that is why, darling, you will never care for any of the people in the world very much. Because their demons are all dwindled and vulgar. They are not royal. Only you are royal, after me. Always remember that. And always remember, it is a great secret. If you tell people, they will try to kill you, because they will envy you for being a Princess. It is our great secret, darling. I am a prince, and you a princess, of the old, old blood. And we keep our secret between us, all alone. And so, darling, you must treat all people very politely, because noblesse oblige. But you must never forget that you alone are the last of Princesses, and that all other are less than you are, less noble, more vulgar. Treat them politely and gently and kindly, darling. But you are the Princess, and they are commoners. Never try to think of them as if they were like you. They are not. You will find, always, that they are lacking, lacking in the royal touch, which only you have-"

The Princess learned her lesson early-the first lesson, of absolute reticence, the impossibility of intimacy with any other than her father; the second lesson, of naïve, slightly benevolent politeness. As a small child, something crystallised in her character, making her clear and finished, and as impervious as crystal.

"Dear child!" her hostesses said of her. "She is so quaint and old-fashioned; such a lady, poor little mite!"

She was erect, and very dainty. Always small, nearly tiny in physique, she seemed like a changeling beside her big, handsome, slightly mad father. She dressed very simply, usually in blue or delicate greys, with little collars of old Milan point, or very finely-worked linen. She had exquisite little hands, that made the piano sound like a spinet when she played. She was rather given to wearing cloaks and capes, instead of coats, out of doors, and little eighteenth-century sort of hats. Her complexion was pure apple-blossom.

She looked as if she had stepped out of a picture. But no one, to her dying day, ever knew exactly the strange picture her father had framed her in and from which she never stepped.

Her grandfather and grandmother and her Aunt Maud demanded twice to see her, once in Rome and once in Paris. Each time they were charmed, piqued, and annoyed. She was so exquisite and such a little virgin. At the same time so knowing and so oddly assured. That odd, assured touch of condescension, and the inward coldness, infuriated her American relations.

Only she really fascinated her grandfather. He was spellbound; in a way, in love with the little faultless thing. His wife would catch him brooding, musing over his grandchild, long months after the meeting, and craving to see her again. He cherished to the end the fond hope that she might come to live with him and her grandmother.

"Thank you so much, grandfather. You are so very kind. But Papa and I are such an old couple, you see, such a crochety old couple, living in a world of our own."

Her father let her see the world-from the outside. And he let her read. When she was in her teens she read Zola and Maupassant, and with the eyes of Zola and Maupassant she looked on Paris. A little later she read Tolstoi and Dostoevsky. The latter confused her. The others, she seemed to understand with a very shrewd, canny understanding, just as she understood the Decameron stories as she read them in their old Italian, or the Nibelung poems. Strange and uncanny, she seemed to understand things in a cold light perfectly, with all the flush of fire absent. She was something like a changeling, not quite human.

This earned her, also, strange antipathies. Cabmen and railway porters, especially in Paris and Rome, would suddenly treat her with brutal rudeness, when she was alone. They seemed to look on her with sudden violent antipathy. They sensed in her curious impertinence, an easy, sterile impertinence towards the things they felt most. She was so assured, and her flower of maidenhood was so scentless. She could look at a lusty, sensual Roman cabman as if he were a sort of grotesque, to make her smile. She knew all about him, in Zola. And the peculiar condescension with which she would give him her order, as if she, frail, beautiful thing, were the only reality, and he, coarse monster, was a sort of Caliban floundering in the mud on the margin of the pool of the perfect lotus, would suddenly enrage the fellow, the real Mediterranean who prided himself on his beauté male, and to whom the phallic mystery was still the only mystery. And he would turn a terrible face on her, bully her in a brutal, coarse fashion-hideous. For to him she had only the blasphemous impertinence of her own sterility.

Encounters like these made her tremble, and made her know she must have support from the outside. The power of her spirit did not extend to these low people, and they had all the physical power. She realised an implacability of hatred in their turning on her. But she did not lose her head. She quietly paid out money and turned away.

Those were dangerous moments, though, and she learned to be prepared for them. The Princess she was, and the fairy from the North, and could never understand the volcanic phallic rage with which coarse people could turn on her in a paroxysm of hatred. They never turned on her father like that. And quite early she decided it was the New England mother in her whom they hated. Never for one minute could she see with the old Roman eyes, see herself as sterility, the barren flower taking on airs and an intolerable impertinence. This was what the Roman cabman saw in her. And he longed to crush the barren blossom. Its sexless beauty and its authority put him in a passion of brutal revolt.

When she was nineteen her grandfather died, leaving her a considerable fortune in the safe hands of responsible trustees. They would deliver her her income, but only on condition that she resided for six months in the year in the United States.

"Why should they make me conditions?" she said to her father. "I refuse to be imprisoned six months in the year in the United States. We will tell them to keep their money."

"Let us be wise, my little Princess, let us be wise. No, we are almost poor, and we are never safe from rudeness. I cannot allow anybody to be rude to me. I hate it, I hate it!" His eyes flamed as he said it. "I could kill any man or woman who is rude to me. But we are in exile in the world. We are powerless. If we were really poor, we should be quite powerless, and then I should die. No, my Princess. Let us take their money, then they will not dare to be rude to us. Let us take it, as we put on clothes, to cover ourselves from their aggressions."

There began a new phase, when the father and daughter spent their summers on the Great Lakes or in California, or in the South-West. The father was something of a poet, the daughter something of a painter. He wrote poems about the lakes or the redwood trees, and she made dainty drawings. He was physically a strong man, and he loved the out-of-doors. He would go off with her for days, paddling in a canoe and sleeping by a camp-fire. Frail little Princess, she was always undaunted, always undaunted. She would ride with him on horseback over the mountain trails till she was so tired she was nothing but a bodiless consciousness sitting astride her pony. But she never gave in. And at night he folded her in her blanket on a bed of balsam pine twigs, and she lay and looked at the stars unmurmuring. She was fulfilling her rôle.

People said to her as the years passed, and she was a woman of twenty-five, then a woman of thirty, and always the same virgin dainty Princess, 'knowing' in a dispassionate way, like an old woman, and utterly intact:

"Don't you ever think what you will do when your father is no longer with you?"

She looked at her interlocutor with that cold, elfin detachment of hers:

"No, I never think of it," she said.

She had a tiny, but exquisite little house in London, and another small, perfect house in Connecticut, each with a faithful housekeeper. Two homes, if she chose. And she knew many interesting literary and artistic people. What more?

So the years passed imperceptibly. And she had that quality of the sexless fairies, she did not change. At thirty-three she looked twenty-three.

Her father, however, was ageing, and becoming more and more queer. It was now her task to be his guardian in his private madness. He spent the last three years of life in the house in Connecticut. He was very much estranged, sometimes had fits of violence which almost killed the little Princess. Physical violence was horrible to her; it seemed to shatter her heart. But she found a woman a few years younger than herself, well-educated and sensitive, to be a sort of nurse-companion to the mad old man. So the fact of madness was never openly admitted. Miss Cummins, the companion, had a passionate loyalty to the Princess, and a curious affection, tinged with love, for the handsome, white-haired, courteous old man, who was never at all aware of his fits of violence once they had passed.

154

The Princess was thirty-eight years old when her father died. And quite unchanged. She was still tiny, and like a dignified, scentless flower. Her soft brownish hair, almost the colour of beaver fur, was bobbed, and fluffed softly round her apple-blossom face, that was modelled with an arched nose like a proud old Florentine portrait. In her voice, manner and bearing she was exceedingly still, like a flower that has blossomed in a shadowy place. And from her blue eyes looked out the Princess's eternal laconic challenge, that grew almost sardonic as the years passed. She was the Princess, and sardonically she looked out on a princeless world.

She was relieved when her father died, and at the same time, it was as if everything had evaporated around her. She had lived in a sort of hot-house, in the aura of her father's madness. Suddenly the hot-house had been removed from around her, and she was in the raw, vast, vulgar open air.

Quoi faire? What was she to do? She seemed faced with absolute nothingness. Only she had Miss Cummins, who shared with her the secret, and almost the passion for her father. In fact, the Princess felt that her passion for her mad father had in some curious way transferred itself largely to Charlotte Cummins during the last years. And now Miss Cummins was the vessel that held the passion for the dead man. She herself, the Princess, was an empty vessel.

An empty vessel in the enormous warehouse of the world.

Quoi faire? What was she to do? She felt that, since she could not evaporate into nothingness, like alcohol from an unstoppered bottle, she must do something. Never before in her life had she felt the incumbency. Never, never had she felt she must do anything. That was left to the vulgar.

Now her father was dead, she found herself on the fringe of the vulgar crowd, sharing their necessity to do something. It was a little humiliating. She felt herself becoming vulgarised. At the same time she found herself looking at men with a shrewder eye: an eye to marriage. Not that she felt any sudden interest in men, or attraction towards them. No. She was still neither interested nor attracted towards men vitally. But marriage, that peculiar abstraction, had imposed a sort of spell on her. She thought that marriage, in the blank abstract, was the thing she ought to do. That marriage implied a man she also knew. She knew all the facts. But the man seemed a property of her own mind rather than a thing in himself, another thing.

Her father died in the summer, the month after her thirty-eighth birthday. When all was over, the obvious thing to do, of course, was to travel. With Miss Cummins. The two women knew each other intimately, but they were always Miss Urquhart and Miss Cummins to one another, and a certain distance was instinctively maintained. Miss Cummins, from Philadelphia, of scholastic stock, and intelligent but untravelled, four years younger than the Princess, felt herself immensely the junior of her 'lady'. She had a sort of passionate veneration for the Princess, who seemed to her ageless, timeless. She could not see the rows of tiny, dainty, exquisite shoes in the Princess's cupboard without feeling a stab at the heart, a stab of tenderness and reverence, almost of awe.

Miss Cummins also was virginal, but with a look of puzzled surprise in her brown eyes. Her skin was pale and clear, her features well modelled, but there was a certain blankness in her expression, where the Princess had an odd touch of Renaissance grandeur. Miss Cummins's voice was also hushed almost to a whisper; it was the inevitable effect of Colin Urquhart's room. But the hushedness had a hoarse quality.

The Princess did not want to go to Europe. Her face seemed turned west. Now her father was gone, she felt she would go west, westwards, as if for ever. Following, no doubt, the March of Empire, which is brought up rather short on the Pacific coast, among swarms of wallowing bathers.

No, not the Pacific coast. She would stop short of that. The South-West was less vulgar. She would go to New Mexico.

She and Miss Cummins arrived at the Rancho del Cerro Gordo towards the end of August, when the crowd was beginning to drift back east. The ranch lay by a stream on the desert some four miles from the foot of the mountains, a mile away from the Indian pueblo of San Cristobal. It was a ranch for the rich; the Princess paid thirty dollars a day for herself and Miss Cummins. But then she had a little cottage to herself, among the apple trees of the orchard, with an excellent cook. She and Miss Cummins, however, took dinner at evening in the large guest-house. For the Princess still entertained the idea of marriage.

The guests at the Rancho del Cerro Gordo were of all sorts, except the poor sort. They were practically all rich, and many were romantic. Some were charming, others were vulgar, some were movie people, quite quaint and not unattractive in their vulgarity, and many were Jews. The Princess did not care for Jews, though they were usually the most interesting to talk to. So she talked a good deal with the Jews, and painted with the artists, and rode with the young men from college, and had altogether quite a good time. And yet she felt something of a fish out of water, or a bird in the wrong forest. And marriage remained still completely in the abstract. No connecting it with any of these young men, even the nice ones.

The Princess looked just twenty-five. The freshness of her mouth, the hushed, delicate-complexioned virginity of her face gave her not a day more. Only a certain laconic look in her eyes was disconcerting. When she was forced to write her age, she put twenty-eight, making the figure two rather badly, so that it just avoided being a three.

Men hinted marriage at her. Especially boys from college suggested it from a distance. But they all failed before the look of sardonic ridicule in the Princess's eyes. It always seemed to her rather preposterous, quite ridiculous, and a tiny bit impertinent on their part.

The only man that intrigued her at all was one of the guides, a man called Romero—Domingo Romero. It was he who had sold the ranch itself to the Wilkiesons, ten years before, for two thousand dollars. He had gone away, then reappeared at the old place. For he was the son of the old Romero, the last of the Spanish family that had owned miles of land around San Cristobal. But the coming of the white man and the failure of the vast flocks of sheep, and the fatal inertia which overcomes all men, at last, on the desert near the mountains, had finished the Romero family. The last descendants were just Mexican peasants.

Domingo, the heir, had spent his two thousand dollars, and was working for white people. He was now about thirty years old, a tall, silent fellow, with a heavy closed mouth and black eyes that looked across at one almost sullenly. From behind he was handsome, with a strong, natural body, and the back of his neck very dark and well-shapen, strong with life. But his dark face was long and heavy, almost sinister, with that peculiar heavy meaninglessness in it, characteristic of the Mexicans of his own locality. They are strong, they seem healthy. They laugh and joke with one another. But their physique and their natures seem static, as if there were nowhere, nowhere at all for their energies to go, and their faces, degenerating to misshapen heaviness, seem to have no raison d'être, no radical meaning. Waiting either to die or to be aroused into passion and hope. In some of the black eyes a queer, haunting mystic quality, sombre and a bit gruesome, the skull-and-cross-bones look of the Penitentes. They had found their raison d'être in self-torture and death-worship. Unable to wrest a positive significance for themselves from the vast, beautiful, but vindictive landscape they were born into, they turned on their own selves, and worshipped death through self-torture. The mystic gloom of this showed in their eyes.

But as a rule the dark eyes of the Mexicans were heavy and half alive, sometimes hostile, sometimes kindly, often with the fatal Indian glaze on them, or the fatal Indian glint.

Domingo Romero was almost a typical Mexican to look at, with the typical heavy, dark, long face, clean-shaven, with an almost brutally heavy mouth. His eyes were black and Indian-looking. Only, at the centre of their hopelessness was a spark of pride, or self-confidence, or dauntlessness. Just a spark in the midst of the blackness of static despair.

But this spark was the difference between him and the mass of men. It gave a certain alert sensitiveness to his bearing and a certain beauty to his appearance. He wore a low-crowned black hat, instead of the ponderous headgear of the usual Mexican, and his clothes were thinnish and graceful. Silent, aloof, almost imperceptible in the landscape, he was an admirable guide, with a startling quick intelligence that anticipated difficulties about to rise. He could cook, too, crouching over the camp-fire and moving his lean deft brown hands. The only fault he had was that he was not forthcoming, he wasn't chatty and cosy.

"Oh, don't send Romero with us," the Jews would say. "One can't get any response from him."

Tourists come and go, but they rarely see anything, inwardly. None of them ever saw the spark at the middle of Romero's eye; they were not alive enough to see it.

The Princess caught it one day, when she had him for a guide. She was fishing for trout in the canyon, Miss Cummins was reading a book, the horses were tied under the trees, Romero was fixing a proper fly on her line. He fixed the fly and handed her the line, looking up at her. And at that

157

moment she caught the spark in his eye. And instantly she knew that he was a gentleman, that his 'demon', as her father would have said, was a fine demon. And instantly her manner towards him changed.

He had perched her on a rock over a quiet pool, beyond the cotton-wood trees. It was early September, and the canyon already cool, but the leaves of the cottonwoods were still green. The Princess stood on her rock, a small but perfectly-formed figure, wearing a soft, close grey sweater and neatly-cut grey riding-breeches, with tall black boots, her fluffy brown hair straggling from under a little grey felt hat. A woman? Not quite. A changeling of some sort, perched in outline there on the rock, in the bristling wild canyon. She knew perfectly well how to handle a line. Her father had made a fisherman of her.

Romero, in a black shirt and with loose black trousers pushed into wide black riding-boots, was fishing a little farther down. He had put his hat on a rock behind him; his dark head was bent a little forward, watching the water. He had caught three trout. From time to time he glanced up-stream at the Princess, perched there so daintily. He saw she had caught nothing.

Soon he quietly drew in his line and came up to her. His keen eye watched her line, watched her position. Then, quietly, he suggested certain changes to her, putting his sensitive brown hand before her. And he withdrew a little, and stood in silence, leaning against a tree, watching her. He was helping her across the distance. She knew it, and thrilled. And in a moment she had a bite. In two minutes she landed a good trout. She looked round at him quickly, her eyes sparkling, the colour heightened in her cheeks. And as she met his eyes a smile of greeting went over his dark face, very sudden, with an odd sweetness.

She knew he was helping her. And she felt in his presence a subtle, insidious male kindliness she had never known before waiting upon her. Her cheek flushed, and her blue eyes darkened.

After this, she always looked for him, and for that curious dark beam of a man's kindliness which he could give her, as it were, from his chest, from his heart. It was something she had never known before.

A vague, unspoken intimacy grew up between them. She liked his voice, his appearance, his presence. His natural language was Spanish; he spoke English like a foreign language, rather slow, with a slight hesitation, but with a sad, plangent sonority lingering over from his Spanish. There was a certain subtle correctness in his appearance; he was always perfectly shaved; his hair was thick and rather long on top, but always carefully groomed behind. And his fine black cashmere shirt, his wide leather belt, his well-cut, wide black trousers going into the embroidered cowboy boots had a certain inextinguishable elegance. He wore no silver rings or buckles. Only his boots were embroidered and decorated at the top with an inlay of white suède. He seemed elegant, slender, yet he was very strong.

And at the same time, curiously, he gave her the feeling that death was not far from him. Perhaps he too was half in love with death. However that may be, the sense she had that death was not far from him made him 'possible' to her.

158

Small as she was, she was quite a good horsewoman. They gave her at the ranch a sorrel mare, very lovely in colour, and well-made, with a powerful broad neck and the hollow back that betokens a swift runner. Tansy, she was called. Her only fault was the usual mare's failing, she was inclined to be hysterical.

So that every day the Princess set off with Miss Cummins and Romero, on horseback, riding into the mountains. Once they went camping for several days, with two more friends in the party.

"I think I like it better," the Princess said to Romero, "when we three go alone."

And he gave her one of his quick, transfiguring smiles.

It was curious no white man had ever showed her this capacity for subtle gentleness, this power to help her in silence across a distance, if she were fishing without success, or tired of her horse, or if Tansy suddenly got scared. It was as if Romero could send her from his heart a dark beam of succour and sustaining. She had never known this before, and it was very thrilling.

Then the smile that suddenly creased his dark face, showing the strong white teeth. It creased his face almost into a savage grotesque. And at the same time there was in it something so warm, such a dark flame of kindliness for her, she was elated into her true Princess self.

Then that vivid, latent spark in his eye, which she had seen, and which she knew he was aware she had seen. It made an inter-recognition between them, silent and delicate. Here he was delicate as a woman in this subtle inter-recognition.

And yet his presence only put to flight in her the idée fixe of 'marriage'. For some reason, in her strange little brain, the idea of marrying him could not enter. Not for any definite reason. He was in himself a gentleman, and she had plenty of money for two. There was no actual obstacle. Nor was she conventional.

No, now she came down to it, it was as if their two 'dæmons' could marry, were perhaps married. Only their two selves, Miss Urquhart and Señor Domingo Romero, were for some reason incompatible. There was a peculiar subtle intimacy of inter-recognition between them. But she did not see in the least how it would lead to marriage. Almost she could more easily marry one of the nice boys from Harvard or Yale.

The time passed, and she let it pass. The end of September came, with aspens going yellow on the mountain heights, and oak-scrub going red. But as yet the cottonwoods in the valley and canyons had not changed.

"When will you go away?" Romero asked her, looking at her fixedly, with a blank black eye.

"By the end of October," she said. "I have promised to be in Santa Barbara at the beginning of November."

He was hiding the spark in his eye from her. But she saw the peculiar sullen thickening of his heavy mouth.

She had complained to him many times that one never saw any wild animals, except chipmunks and squirrels, and perhaps a skunk and a porcupine. Never a deer, or a bear, or a mountain lion.

159

"Are there no bigger animals in these mountains?" she asked, dissatisfied.

"Yes," he said. "There are deer-I see their tracks. And I saw the tracks of a bear."

"But why can one never see the animals themselves?" She looked dissatisfied and wistful like a child.

"Why, it's pretty hard for you to see them. They won't let you come close. You have to keep still, in a place where they come. Or else you have to follow their tracks a long way."

"I can't bear to go away till I've seen them: a bear, or a deer-"

The smile came suddenly on his face, indulgent.

"Well, what do you want? Do you want to go up into the mountains to some place, to wait till they come?"

"Yes," she said, looking up at him with a sudden naïve impulse of recklessness.

And immediately his face became sombre again, responsible.

"Well," he said, with slight irony, a touch of mockery of her. "You will have to find a house. It's very cold at night now. You would have to stay all night in a house."

"And there are no houses up there?" she said.

"Yes," he replied. "There is a little shack that belongs to me, that a miner built a long time ago, looking for gold. You can go there and stay one night, and maybe you see something. Maybe! I don't know. Maybe nothing come."

"How much chance is there?"

"Well, I don't know. Last time when I was there I see three deer come down to drink at the water, and I shot two raccoons. But maybe this time we don't see anything."

"Is there water there?" she asked.

"Yes, there is a little round pond, you know, below the spruce trees. And the water from the snow runs into it."

"Is it far away?" she asked.

"Yes, pretty far. You see that ridge there"-and turning to the mountains he lifted his arm in the gesture which is somehow so moving, out in the West, pointing to the distance-"that ridge where there are no trees, only rock"-his black eyes were focussed on the distance, his face impassive, but as if in pain-"you go round that ridge, and along, then you come down through the spruce trees to where that cabin is. My father bought that placer claim from a miner who was broke, but nobody ever found any gold or anything, and nobody ever goes there. Too lonesome!"

The Princess watched the massive, heavy-sitting, beautiful bulk of the Rocky Mountains. It was early in October, and the aspens were already losing their gold leaves; high up, the spruce and pine seemed to be growing darker; the great flat patches of oak scrub on the heights were red like gore.

"Can I go over there?" she asked, turning to him and meeting the spark in his eye.

His face was heavy with responsibility.

160

"Yes," he said, "you can go. But there'll be snow over the ridge, and it's awful cold, and awful lonesome."

"I should like to go," she said, persistent.

"All right," he said. "You can go if you want to."

She doubted, though, if the Wilkiesons would let her go; at least alone with Romero and Miss Cummins.

Yet an obstinacy characteristic of her nature, an obstinacy tinged perhaps with madness, had taken hold of her. She wanted to look over the mountains into their secret heart. She wanted to descend to the cabin below the spruce trees, near the tarn of bright green water. She wanted to see the wild animals move about in their wild unconsciousness.

"Let us say to the Wilkiesons that we want to make the trip round the Frijoles canyon," she said.

The trip round the Frijoles canyon was a usual thing. It would not be strenuous, nor cold, nor lonely: they could sleep in the log house that was called an hotel.

Romero looked at her quickly.

"If you want to say that," he replied, "you can tell Mrs. Wilkieson. Only I know she'll be mad with me if I take you up in the mountains to that place. And I've got to go there first with a pack-horse, to take lots of blankets and some bread. Maybe Miss Cummins can't stand it. Maybe not. It's a hard trip."

He was speaking, and thinking, in the heavy, disconnected Mexican fashion.

"Never mind!" The Princess was suddenly very decisive and stiff with authority. "I want to do it. I will arrange with Mrs. Wilkieson. And we'll go on Saturday."

He shook his head slowly.

"I've got to go up on Sunday with a pack-horse and blankets," he said. "Can't do it before."

"Very well!" she said, rather piqued. "Then we'll start on Monday."

She hated being thwarted even the tiniest bit.

He knew that if he started with the pack on Sunday at dawn he would not be back until late at night. But he consented that they should start on Monday morning at seven. The obedient Miss Cummins was told to prepare for the Frijoles trip. On Sunday Romero had his day off. He had not put in an appearance when the Princess retired on Sunday night, but on Monday morning, as she was dressing, she saw him bringing in the three horses from the corral. She was in high spirits.

The night had been cold. There was ice at the edges of the irrigation ditch, and the chipmunks crawled into the sun and lay with wide, dumb, anxious eyes, almost too numb to run.

"We may be away two or three days," said the Princess.

"Very well. We won't begin to be anxious about you before Thursday, then," said Mrs. Wilkieson, who was young and capable: from Chicago. "Anyway," she added, "Romero will see you through. He's so trustworthy."

The sun was already on the desert as they set off towards the mountains, making the greasewood and the sage pale as pale-grey sands,

161

luminous the great level around them. To the right glinted the shadows of the adobe pueblo, flat and almost invisible on the plain, earth of its earth. Behind lay the ranch and the tufts of tall, plumy cottonwoods, whose summits were yellowing under the perfect blue sky.

Autumn breaking into colour in the great spaces of the South-West.

But the three trotted gently along the trail, towards the sun that sparkled yellow just above the dark bulk of the ponderous mountains. Side-slopes were already gleaming yellow, flaming with a second light, under coldish blue of the pale sky. The front slopes were in shadow, with submerged lustre of red oak scrub and dull-gold aspens, blue-black pines and grey-blue rock. While the canyon was full of a deep blueness.

They rode single file, Romero first, on a black horse. Himself in black, made a flickering black spot in the delicate pallor of the great landscape, where even pine trees at a distance take a film of blue paler than their green. Romero rode on in silence past the tufts of furry greasewood. The Princess came next, on her sorrel mare. And Miss Cummins, who was not quite happy on horseback, came last, in the pale dust that the others kicked up. Sometimes her horse sneezed, and she started.

But on they went at a gentle trot. Romero never looked round. He could hear the sound of the hoofs following, and that was all he wanted.

For the rest, he held ahead. And the Princess, with that black, unheeding figure always travelling away from her, felt strangely helpless, withal elated.

They neared the pale, round foot-hills, dotted with the round dark piñon and cedar shrubs. The horses clinked and trotted among the stones. Occasionally a big round greasewood held out fleecy tufts of flowers, pure gold. They wound into blue shadow, then up a steep stony slope, with the world lying pallid away behind and below. Then they dropped into the shadow of the San Cristobal canyon.

The stream was running full and swift. Occasionally the horses snatched at a tuft of grass. The trail narrowed and became rocky; the rocks closed in; it was dark and cool as the horses climbed and climbed upwards, and the tree trunks crowded in the shadowy, silent tightness of the canyon. They were among cottonwood trees that ran straight up and smooth and round to an extraordinary height. Above, the tips were gold, and it was sun. But away below, where the horses struggled up the rocks and wound among the trunks, there was still blue shadow by the sound of waters and an occasional grey festoon of old man's beard, and here and there a pale, dripping crane's-bill flower among the tangle and the débris of the virgin place. And again the chill entered the Princess's heart as she realised what a tangle of decay and despair lay in the virgin forests.

They scrambled downwards, splashed across stream, up rocks and along the trail of the other side. Romero's black horse stopped, looked down quizzically at the fallen trees, then stepped over lightly. The Princess's sorrel followed, carefully. But Miss Cummins's buckskin made a fuss, and had to be got round.

In the same silence, save for the clinking of the horses and the splashing as the trail crossed stream, they worked their way upwards in the

162

tight, tangled shadow of the canyon. Sometimes, crossing stream, the Princess would glance upwards, and then always her heart caught in her breast. For high up, away in heaven, the mountain heights shone yellow, dappled with dark spruce firs, clear almost as speckled daffodils against the pale turquoise blue lying high and serene above the dark-blue shadow where the Princess was. And she would snatch at the blood-red leaves of the oak as her horse crossed a more open slope, not knowing what she felt.

They were getting fairly high, occasionally lifted above the canyon itself, in the low groove below the speckled, gold-sparkling heights which towered beyond. Then again they dipped and crossed stream, the horses stepping gingerly across a tangle of fallen, frail aspen stems, then suddenly floundering in a mass of rocks. The black emerged ahead, his black tail waving. The Princess let her mare find her own footing; then she too emerged from the clatter. She rode on after the black. Then came a great frantic rattle of the buckskin behind. The Princess was aware of Romero's dark face looking round, with a strange, demon-like watchfulness, before she herself looked round, to see the buckskin scrambling rather lamely beyond the rocks, with one of his pale buff knees already red with blood.

"He almost went down!" called Miss Cummins.

But Romero was already out of the saddle and hastening down the path. He made quiet little noises to the buckskin, and began examining the cut knee.

"Is he hurt?" cried Miss Cummins anxiously, and she climbed hastily down.

"Oh, my goodness!" she cried, as she saw the blood running down the slender buff leg of the horse in a thin trickle. "Isn't that awful?" She spoke in a stricken voice, and her face was white.

Romero was still carefully feeling the knee of the buckskin. Then he made him walk a few paces. And at last he stood up straight and shook his head.

"Not very bad!" he said. "Nothing broken."

Again he bent and worked at the knees. Then he looked up at the Princess.

"He can go on," he said. "It's not bad."

The Princess looked down at the dark face in silence.

"What, go on right up here?" cried Miss Cummins. "How many hours?"

"About five!" said Romero simply.

"Five hours!" cried Miss Cummins. "A horse with a lame knee! And a steep mountain! Why-y!"

"Yes, it's pretty steep up there," said Romero, pushing back his hat and staring fixedly at the bleeding knee. The buckskin stood in a stricken sort of dejection. "But I think he'll make it all right," the man added.

"Oh!" cried Miss Cummins, her eyes bright with sudden passion of unshed tears. "I wouldn't think of it. I wouldn't ride him up there, not for any money."

"Why wouldn't you?" asked Romero.

"It hurts him."

Romero bent down again to the horse's knee.

163

"Maybe it hurts him a little," he said. "But he can make it all right, and his leg won't get stiff."

"What! Ride him five hours up the steep mountains?" cried Miss Cummins. "I couldn't. I just couldn't do it. I'll lead him a little way and see if he can go. But I couldn't ride him again. I couldn't. Let me walk."

"But Miss Cummins, dear, if Romero says he'll be all right?" said the Princess.

"I know it hurts him. Oh, I just couldn't bear it."

There was no doing anything with Miss Cummins. The thought of a hurt animal always put her into a sort of hysterics.

They walked forward a little, leading the buckskin. He limped rather badly. Miss Cummins sat on a rock.

"Why, it's agony to see him!" she cried. "It's cruel!"

"He won't limp after a bit, if you take no notice of him," said Romero. "Now he plays up, and limps very much, because he wants to make you see."

"I don't think there can be much playing up," said Miss Cummins bitterly. "We can see how it must hurt him."

"It don't hurt much," said Romero.

But now Miss Cummins was silent with antipathy.

It was a deadlock. The party remained motionless on the trail, the Princess in the saddle, Miss Cummins seated on a rock, Romero standing black and remote near the drooping buckskin.

"Well!" said the man suddenly at last. "I guess we go back, then."

And he looked up swiftly at his horse, which was cropping at the mountain herbage and treading on the trailing reins.

"No!" cried the Princess. "Oh no!" Her voice rang with a great wail of disappointment and anger. Then she checked herself.

Miss Cummins rose with energy.

"Let me lead the buckskin home," she said, with cold dignity, "and you two go on."

This was received in silence. The Princess was looking down at her with a sardonic, almost cruel gaze.

"We've only come about two hours," said Miss Cummins. "I don't mind a bit leading him home. But I couldn't ride him. I couldn't have him ridden with that knee."

This again was received in dead silence. Romero remained impassive, almost inert.

"Very well, then," said the Princess. "You lead him home. You'll be quite all right. Nothing can happen to you, possibly. And say to them that we have gone on and shall be home tomorrow-or the day after."

She spoke coldly and distinctly. For she could not bear to be thwarted.

"Better all go back, and come again another day," said Romero-noncommittal.

"There will never be another day," cried the Princess. "I want to go on."

She looked at him square in the eyes, and met the spark in his eye.

He raised his shoulders slightly.

"If you want it," he said. "I'll go on with you. But Miss Cummins can ride my horse to the end of the canyon, and I lead the buckskin. Then I come back to you."

It was arranged so. Miss Cummins had her saddle put on Romero's black horse, Romero took the buckskin's bridle, and they started back. The Princess rode very slowly on, upwards, alone. She was at first so angry with Miss Cummins that she was blind to everything else. She just let her mare follow her own inclinations.

The peculiar spell of anger carried the Princess on, almost unconscious, for an hour or so. And by this time she was beginning to climb pretty high. Her horse walked steadily all the time. They emerged on a bare slope, and the trail wound through frail aspen stems. Here a wind swept, and some of the aspens were already bare. Others were fluttering their discs of pure, solid yellow leaves, so nearly like petals, while the slope ahead was one soft, glowing fleece of daffodil yellow; fleecy like a golden foxskin, and yellow as daffodils alive in the wind and the high mountain sun.

She paused and looked back. The near great slopes were mottled with gold and the dark hue of spruce, like some unsinged eagle, and the light lay gleaming upon them. Away through the gap of the canyon she could see the pale blue of the egg-like desert, with the crumpled dark crack of the Rio Grande Canyon. And far, far off, the blue mountains like a fence of angels on the horizon.

And she thought of her adventure. She was going on alone with Romero. But then she was very sure of herself, and Romero was not the kind of man to do anything to her against her will. This was her first thought. And she just had a fixed desire to go over the brim of the mountains, to look into the inner chaos of the Rockies. And she wanted to go with Romero, because he had some peculiar kinship with her; there was some peculiar link between the two of them. Miss Cummins anyhow would have been only a discordant note.

She rode on, and emerged at length in the lap of the summit. Beyond her was a great concave of stone and stark, dead-grey trees, where the mountain ended against the sky. But nearer was the dense black, bristling spruce, and at her feet was the lap of the summit, a flat little valley of sere grass and quiet-standing yellow aspens, the stream trickling like a thread across.

It was a little valley or shell from which the stream was gently poured into the lower rocks and trees of the canyon. Around her was a fairy-like gentleness, the delicate sere grass, the groves of delicate-stemmed aspens dropping their flakes of bright yellow. And the delicate, quick little stream threading through the wild, sere grass.

Here one might expect deer and fawns and wild things, as in a little paradise. Here she was to wait for Romero, and they were to have lunch.

She unfastened her saddle and pulled it to the ground with a crash, letting her horse wander with a long rope. How beautiful Tansy looked, sorrel, among the yellow leaves that lay like a patina on the sere ground. The Princess herself wore a fleecy sweater of a pale, sere buff, like the grass, and riding-breeches of a pure orange-tawny colour. She felt quite in the picture.

From her saddle-pouches she took the packages of lunch, spread a little cloth, and sat to wait for Romero. Then she made a little fire. Then she ate a devilled egg. Then she ran after Tansy, who was straying across-stream. Then she sat in the sun, in the stillness near the aspens, and waited.

The sky was blue. Her little alp was soft and delicate as fairy-land. But beyond and up jutted the great slopes, dark with the pointed feathers of spruce, bristling with grey dead trees among grey rock, or dappled with dark and gold. The beautiful, but fierce, heavy cruel mountains, with their moments of tenderness.

She saw Tansy start, and begin to run. Two ghost-like figures on horseback emerged from the black of the spruce across the stream. It was two Indians on horseback, swathed like seated mummies in their pale-grey cotton blankets. Their guns jutted beyond the saddles. They rode straight towards her, to her thread of smoke.

As they came near, they unswathed themselves and greeted her, looking at her curiously from their dark eyes. Their black hair was somewhat untidy, the long rolled plaits on their shoulders were soiled. They looked tired.

They got down from their horses near her little fire-a camp was a camp-swathed their blankets round their hips, pulled the saddles from their ponies and turned them loose, then sat down. One was a young Indian whom she had met before, the other was an older man.

"You all alone?" said the younger man.

"Romero will be here in a minute," she said, glancing back along the trail.

"Ah, Romero! You with him? Where are you going?"

"Round the ridge," she said. "Where are you going?"

"We going down to Pueblo."

"Been out hunting? How long have you been out?"

"Yes. Been out five days." The young Indian gave a little meaningless laugh.

"Got anything?"

"No. We see tracks of two deer-but not got nothing."

The Princess noticed a suspicious-looking bulk under one of the saddles-surely a folded-up deer. But she said nothing.

"You must have been cold," she said.

"Yes, very cold in the night. And hungry. Got nothing to eat since yesterday. Eat it all up." And again he laughed his little meaningless laugh. Under their dark skins, the two men looked peaked and hungry. The Princess rummaged for food among the saddle-bags. There was a lump of bacon-the regular stand-back-and some bread. She gave them this, and they began toasting slices of it on long sticks at the fire. Such was the little camp Romero saw as he rode down the slope: the Princess in her orange breeches, her head tied in a blue-and-brown silk kerchief, sitting opposite the two dark-headed Indians across the camp-fire, while one of the Indians was leaning forward toasting bacon, his two plaits of braid-hair dangling as if wearily.

Romero rode up, his face expressionless. The Indians greeted him in Spanish. He unsaddled his horse, took food from the bags, and sat down at the camp to eat. The Princess went to the stream for water, and to wash her hands.

"Got coffee?" asked the Indians.

"No coffee this outfit," said Romero.

They lingered an hour or more in the warm midday sun. Then Romero saddled the horses. The Indians still squatted by the fire. Romero and the Princess rode away, calling Adios! to the Indians over the stream and into the dense spruce whence two strange figures had emerged.

When they were alone, Romero turned and looked at her curiously, in a way she could not understand, with such a hard glint in his eyes. And for the first time she wondered if she was rash.

"I hope you don't mind going alone with me," she said.

"If you want it," he replied.

They emerged at the foot of the great bare slope of rocky summit, where dead spruce trees stood sparse and bristling like bristles on a grey dead hog. Romero said the Mexicans, twenty years back, had fired the mountains, to drive out the whites. This grey concave slope of summit was corpse-like.

The trail was almost invisible. Romero watched for the trees which the Forest Service had blazed. And they climbed the stark corpse slope, among dead spruce, fallen and ash-grey, into the wind. The wind came rushing from the west, up the funnel of the canyon, from the desert. And there was the desert, like a vast mirage tilting slowly upwards towards the west, immense and pallid, away beyond the funnel of the canyon. The Princess could hardly look.

For an hour their horses rushed the slope, hastening with a great working of the haunches upwards, and halting to breathe, scrambling again, and rowing their way up length by length, on the livid, slanting wall. While the wind blew like some vast machine.

After an hour they were working their way on the incline, no longer forcing straight up. All was grey and dead around them; the horses picked their way over the silver-grey corpses of the spruce. But they were near the top, near the ridge.

Even the horses made a rush for the last bit. They had worked round to a scrap of spruce forest near the very top. They hurried in, out of the huge, monstrous, mechanical wind, that whistled inhumanly and was palely cold. So, stepping through the dark screen of trees, they emerged over the crest.

In front now was nothing but mountains, ponderous, massive, down-sitting mountains, in a huge and intricate knot, empty of life or soul. Under the bristling black feathers of spruce near-by lay patches of white snow. The lifeless valleys were concaves of rock and spruce, the rounded summits and the hog-backed summits of grey rock crowded one behind the other like some monstrous herd in arrest.

It frightened the Princess, it was so inhuman. She had not thought it

167

could be so inhuman, so, as it were, anti-life. And yet now one of her desires was fulfilled. She had seen it, the massive, gruesome, repellent core of the Rockies. She saw it there beneath her eyes, in its gigantic, heavy gruesomeness.

And she wanted to go back. At this moment she wanted to turn back. She had looked down into the intestinal knot of these mountains. She was frightened. She wanted to go back.

But Romero was riding on, on the lee side of the spruce forest, above the concaves of the inner mountains. He turned round to her and pointed at the slope with a dark hand.

"Here a miner has been trying for gold," he said. It was a grey scratched-out heap near a hole-like a great badger hole. And it looked quite fresh.

"Quite lately?" said the Princess.

"No, long ago-twenty, thirty years." He had reined in his horse and was looking at the mountains. "Look!" he said. "There goes the Forest Service trail-along those ridges, on the top, way over there till it comes to Lucytown, where is the Goverment road. We go down there-no trail-see behind that mountain-you see the top, no trees, and some grass?"

His arm was lifted, his brown hand pointing, his dark eyes piercing into the distance, as he sat on his black horse twisting round to her. Strange and ominous, only the demon of himself, he seemed to her. She was dazed and a little sick, at that height, and she could not see any more. Only she saw an eagle turning in the air beyond, and the light from the west showed the pattern on him underneath.

"Shall I ever be able to go so far?" asked the Princess faintly, petulantly.

"Oh yes! All easy now. No more hard places."

They worked along the ridge, up and down, keeping on the lee side, the inner side, in the dark shadow. It was cold. Then the trail laddered up again, and they emerged on a narrow ridge-track, with the mountain slipping away enormously on either side. The Princess was afraid. For one moment she looked out, and saw the desert, the desert ridges, more desert, more blue ridges, shining pale and very vast, far below, vastly palely tilting to the western horizon. It was ethereal and terrifying in its gleaming, pale, half-burnished immensity, tilted at the west. She could not bear it. To the left was the ponderous, involved mass of mountains all kneeling heavily.

She closed her eyes and let her consciousness evaporate away. The mare followed the trail. So on and on, in the wind again.

They turned their backs to the wind, facing inwards to the mountains. She thought they had left the trail; it was quite invisible.

"No," he said, lifting his hand and pointing. "Don't you see the blazed trees?"

And making an effort of consciousness, she was able to perceive on a pale-grey dead spruce stem the old marks where an axe had chipped a piece away. But with the height, the cold, the wind, her brain was numb.

They turned again and began to descend; he told her they had left the trail. The horses slithered in the loose stones, picking their way downward. It was afternoon, the sun stood obtrusive and gleaming in the lower heavens-about four o'clock. The horses went steadily, slowly, but obstinately onwards. The air was getting colder. They were in among the lumpish peaks and steep concave valleys. She was barely conscious at all of Romero.

He dismounted and came to help her from her saddle. She tottered, but would not betray her feebleness.

"We must slide down here," he said. "I can lead the horses."

They were on a ridge, and facing a steep bare slope of pallid, tawny mountain grass on which the western sun shone full. It was steep and concave. The Princess felt she might start slipping, and go down like a toboggan into the great hollow.

But she pulled herself together. Her eye blazed up again with excitement and determination. A wind rushed past her; she could hear the shriek of spruce trees far below. Bright spots came on her cheeks as her hair blew across. She looked a wild, fairy-like little thing.

"No," she said. "I will take my horse."

"Then mind she doesn't slip down on top of you," said Romero. And away he went, nimbly dropping down the pale, steep incline, making from rock to rock, down the grass, and following any little slanting groove. His horse hopped and slithered after him, and sometimes stopped dead, with forefeet pressed back, refusing to go farther. He, below his horse, looked up and pulled the reins gently, and encouraged the creature. Then the horse once more dropped his forefeet with a jerk, and the descent continued.

The Princess set off in blind, reckless pursuit, tottering and yet nimble. And Romero, looking constantly back to see how she was faring, saw her fluttering down like some queer little bird, her orange breeches twinkling like the legs of some duck, and her head, tied in the blue and buff kerchief, bound round and round like the head of some blue-topped bird. The sorrel mare rocked and slipped behind her. But down came the Princess in a reckless intensity, a tiny, vivid spot on the great hollow flank of the tawny mountain. So tiny! Tiny as a frail bird's egg. It made Romero's mind go blank with wonder.

But they had to get down, out of that cold and dragging wind. The spruce trees stood below, where a tiny stream emerged in stones. Away plunged Romero, zigzagging down. And away behind, up the slope, fluttered the tiny, bright-coloured Princess, holding the end of the long reins, and leading the lumbering, four-footed, sliding mare.

At last they were down. Romero sat in the sun, below the wind, beside some squaw-berry bushes. The Princess came near, the colour flaming in her cheeks, her eyes dark blue, much darker than the kerchief on her head, and glowing unnaturally.

"We make it," said Romero.

"Yes," said the Princess, dropping the reins and subsiding on to the grass, unable to speak, unable to think.

But, thank heaven, they were out of the wind and in the sun.

In a few minutes her consciousness and her control began to come back. She drank a little water. Romero was attending to the saddles. Then they set off again, leading the horses still a little farther down the tiny stream-bed. Then they could mount.

They rode down a bank and into a valley grove dense with aspens. Winding through the thin, crowding, pale-smooth stems, the sun shone flickering beyond them, and the disc-like aspen leaves, waving queer mechanical signals, seemed to be splashing the gold light before her eyes. She rode on in a splashing dazzle of gold.

Then they entered shadow and the dark, resinous spruce trees. The fierce boughs always wanted to sweep her off her horse. She had to twist and squirm past.

But there was a semblance of an old trail. And all at once they emerged in the sun on the edge of the spruce grove, and there was a little cabin, and the bottom of a small, naked valley with grey rock and heaps of stones, and a round pool of intense green water, dark green. The sun was just about to leave it.

Indeed, as she stood, the shadow came over the cabin and over herself; they were in the lower gloom, a twilight. Above, the heights still blazed.

It was a little hole of a cabin, near the spruce trees, with an earthen floor and an unhinged door. There was a wooden bed-bunk, three old sawn-off log-lengths to sit on as stools, and a sort of fireplace; no room for anything else. The little hole would hardly contain two people. The roof had gone-but Romero had laid on thick spruce boughs.

The strange squalor of the primitive forest pervaded the place, the squalor of animals and their droppings, the squalor of the wild. The Princess knew the peculiar repulsiveness of it. She was tired and faint.

Romero hastily got a handful of twigs, set a little fire going in the stove grate, and went out to attend to the horses. The Princess vaguely, mechanically, put sticks on the fire, in a sort of stupor, watching the blaze, stupefied and fascinated. She could not make much fire-it would set the whole cabin alight. And smoke oozed out of the dilapidated mud-and-stone chimney.

When Romero came in with the saddle-pouches and saddles, hanging the saddles on the wall, there sat the little Princess on her stump of wood in front of the dilapidated fire-grate, warming her tiny hands at the blaze, while her oranges breeches glowed almost like another fire. She was in a sort of stupor.

"You have some whisky now, or some tea? Or wait for some soup?" he asked.

She rose and looked at him with bright, dazed eyes, half comprehending; the colour glowing hectic in her cheeks.

"Some tea," she said, "with a little whisky in it. Where's the kettle?"

"Wait," he said. "I'll bring the things."

She took her cloak from the back of her saddle, and followed him into the open. It was a deep cup of shadow. But above the sky was still shining, and the heights of the mountains were blazing with aspen like fire blazing.

Their horses were cropping the grass among the stones. Romero clambered up a heap of grey stones and began lifting away logs and rocks, till he had opened the mouth of one of the miner's little old workings. This

170

was his cache. He brought out bundles of blankets, pans for cooking, a little petrol camp-stove, an axe, the regular camp outfit. He seemed so quick and energetic and full of force. This quick force dismayed the Princess a little.

She took a saucepan and went down the stones to the water. It was very still and mysterious, and of a deep green colour, yet pure, transparent as glass. How cold the place was! How mysterious and fearful.

She crouched in her dark cloak by the water, rinsing the saucepan, feeling the cold heavy above her, the shadow like a vast weight upon her, bowing her down. The sun was leaving the mountain-tops, departing, leaving her under profound shadow. Soon it would crush her down completely.

Sparks? Or eyes looking at her across the water? She gazed, hypnotised. And with her sharp eyes she made out in the dusk the pale form of a bob-cat crouching by the water's edge, pale as the stones among which it crouched, opposite. And it was watching her with cold, electric eyes of strange intentness, a sort of cold, icy wonder and fearlessness. She saw its museau pushed forward, its tufted ears pricking intensely up. It was watching her with cold, animal curiosity, something demonish and conscienceless.

She made a swift movement, spilling her water. And in a flash the creature was gone, leaping like a cat that is escaping; but strange and soft in its motion, with its little bob-tail. Rather fascinating. Yet that cold, intent, demonish watching! She shivered with cold and fear. She knew well enough the dread and repulsiveness of the wild.

Romero carried in the bundles of bedding and the camp outfit. The windowless cabin was already dark inside. He lit a lantern, and then went out again with the axe. She heard him chopping wood as she fed sticks to the fire under her water. When he came in with an armful of oak-scrub faggots, she had just thrown the tea into the water.

"Sit down," she said, "and drink tea."

He poured a little bootleg whisky into the enamel cups, and in the silence the two sat on the log-ends, sipping the hot liquid and coughing occasionally from the smoke.

"We burn these oak sticks," he said. "They don't make hardly any smoke."

Curious and remote he was, saying nothing except what had to be said. And she, for her part, was as remote from him. They seemed far, far apart, worlds apart, now they were so near.

He unwrapped one bundle of bedding, and spread the blankets and the sheepskin in the wooden bunk.

"You lie down and rest," he said, "and I make the supper."

She decided to do so. Wrapping her cloak round her, she lay down in the bunk, turning her face to the wall. She could hear him preparing supper over the little petrol stove. Soon she could smell the soup he was heating; and soon she heard the hissing of fried chicken in a pan.

"You eat your supper now?" he said.

171

With a jerky, despairing movement, she sat up in the bunk, tossing back her hair. She felt cornered.

"Give it me here," she said.

He handed her first the cupful of soup. She sat among the blankets, eating it slowly. She was hungry. Then he gave her an enamel plate with pieces of fried chicken and currant jelly, butter and bread. It was very good. As they ate the chicken he made the coffee. She said never a word. A certain resentment filled her. She was cornered.

When supper was over he washed the dishes, dried them, and put everything away carefully, else there would have been no room to move in the hole of a cabin. The oak-wood gave out a good bright heat.

He stood for a few moments at a loss. Then he asked her:

"You want to go to bed soon?"

"Soon," she said. "Where are you going to sleep?"

"I make my bed here-" he pointed to the floor along the wall. "Too cold out of doors."

"Yes," she said. "I suppose it is."

She sat immobile, her cheeks hot, full of conflicting thoughts. And she watched him while he folded the blankets on the floor, a sheepskin underneath. Then she went out into night.

The stars were big. Mars sat on the edge of a mountain, for all the world like the blazing eye of a crouching mountain lion. But she herself was deep, deep below in a pit of shadow. In the intense silence she seemed to hear the spruce forest crackling with electricity and cold. Strange, foreign stars floated on that unmoving water. The night was going to freeze. Over the hills came the far sobbing-singing howling of the coyotes. She wondered how the horses would be.

Shuddering a little, she turned to the cabin. Warm light showed through its chinks. She pushed at the rickety, half-opened door.

"What about the horses?" she said.

"My black, he won't go away. And your mare will stay with him. You want to go to bed now?"

"I think I do."

"All right. I feed the horses some oats."

And he went out into the night.

He did not come back for some time. She was lying wrapped up tight in the bunk.

He blew out the lantern, and sat down on his bedding to take off his clothes. She lay with her back turned. And soon, in the silence, she was asleep.

She dreamed it was snowing, and the snow was falling on her through the roof, softly, softly, helplessly, and she was going to be buried alive. She was growing colder and colder, the snow was weighing down on her. The snow was going to absorb her.

She awoke with a sudden convulsion, like pain. She was really very cold; perhaps the heavy blankets had numbed her. Her heart seemed unable to beat, she felt she could not move.

With another convulsion she sat up. It was intensely dark. There was

172

not even a spark of fire, the light wood had burned right away. She sat in thick oblivious darkness. Only through a chink she could see a star.

What did she want? Oh, what did she want? She sat in bed and rocked herself woefully. She could hear the steady breathing of the sleeping man. She was shivering with cold; her heart seemed as if it could not beat. She wanted warmth, protection, she wanted to be taken away from herself. And at the same time, perhaps more deeply than anything, she wanted to keep herself intact, intact, untouched, that no one should have any power over her, or rights to her. It was a wild necessity in her that no one, particularly no man, should have any rights or power over her, that no one and nothing should possess her.

Yet that other thing! And she was so cold, so shivering, and her heart could not beat. Oh, would not someone help her heart to beat?

She tried to speak, and could not. Then she cleared her throat.

"Romero," she said strangely, "it is so cold."

Where did her voice come from, and whose voice was it, in the dark?

She heard him at once sit up, and his voice, startled, with a resonance that seemed to vibrate against her, saying:

"You want me to make you warm?"

"Yes."

As soon as he had lifted her in his arms, she wanted to scream to him not to touch her. She stiffened herself. Yet she was dumb.

And he was warm, but with a terrible animal warmth that seemed to annihilate her. He panted like an animal with desire. And she was given over to this thing.

She had never, never wanted to be given over to this. But she had willed that it should happen to her. And according to her will, she lay and let it happen. But she never wanted it. She never wanted to be thus assailed and handled, and mauled. She wanted to keep herself to herself.

However, she had willed it to happen, and it had happened. She panted with relief when it was over.

Yet even now she had to lie within the hard, powerful clasp of this other creature, this man. She dreaded to struggle to go away. She dreaded almost too much the icy cold of that other bunk.

"Do you want to go away from me?" asked his strange voice. Oh, if it could only have been a thousand miles away from her! Yet she had willed to have it thus close.

"No," she said.

And she could feel a curious joy and pride surging up again in him: at her expense. Because he had got her. She felt like a victim there. And he was exulting in his power over her, his possession, his pleasure.

When dawn came, he was fast asleep. She sat up suddenly.

"I want a fire," she said.

He opened his brown eyes wide, and smiled with a curious tender luxuriousness.

"I want you to make a fire," she said.

He glanced at the chinks of light. His brown face hardened to the day.

"All right," he said. "I'll make it."

She did her face while he dressed. She could not bear to look at him. He was so suffused with pride and luxury. She hid her face almost in despair. But feeling the cold blast of air as he opened the door, she wriggled down into the warm place where he had been. How soon the warmth ebbed, when he had gone!

He made a fire and went out, returning after a while with water.

"You stay in bed till the sun comes," he said. "It very cold."

"Hand me my cloak."

She wrapped the cloak fast round her, and sat up among the blankets. The warmth was already spreading from the fire.

"I suppose we will start back as soon as we've had breakfast?"

He was crouching at his camp-stove making scrambled eggs. He looked up suddenly, transfixed, and his brown eyes, so soft and luxuriously widened, looked straight at her.

"You want to?" he said.

"We'd better get back as soon as possible," she said, turning aside from his eyes.

"You want to get away from me?" he asked, repeating the question of the night in a sort of dread.

"I want to get away from here," she said decisively. And it was true. She wanted supremely to get away, back to the world of people.

He rose slowly to his feet, holding the aluminium frying-pan.

"Don't you like last night?" he asked.

"Not really," she said. "Why? Do you?"

He put down the frying-pan and stood staring at the wall. She could see she had given him a cruel blow. But she did not relent. She was getting her own back. She wanted to regain possession of all herself, and in some mysterious way she felt that he possessed some part of her still.

He looked round at her slowly, his face greyish and heavy.

"You Americans," he said, "you always want to do a man down."

"I am not American," she said. "I am British. And I don't want to do any man down. I only want to go back now."

"And what will you say about me, down there?"

"That you were very kind to me, and very good."

He crouched down again, and went on turning the eggs. He gave her her plate, and her coffee, and sat down to his own food.

But again he seemed not to be able to swallow. He looked up at her.

"You don't like last night?" he asked.

"Not really," she said, though with some difficulty. "I don't care for that kind of thing."

A blank sort of wonder spread over his face at these words, followed immediately by a black look of anger, and then a stony, sinister despair.

"You don't?" he said, looking her in the eyes.

"Not really," she replied, looking back with steady hostility into his eyes.

Then a dark flame seemed to come from his face.

"I make you," he said, as if to himself.

He rose and reached her clothes, that hung on a peg: the fine linen

174

underwear, the orange breeches, the fleecy jumper, the blue-and-bluff kerchief; then he took up her riding-boots and her bead moccasins. Crushing everything in his arms, he opened the door. Sitting up, she saw him stride down to the dark-green pool in the frozen shadow of that deep cup of a valley. He tossed the clothing and the boots out on the pool. Ice had formed. And on the pure, dark green mirror, in the slaty shadow, the Princess saw her things lying, the white linen, the orange breeches, the black boots, the blue moccasins, a tangled heap of colour. Romero picked up rocks and heaved them out at the ice, till the surface broke and the fluttering clothing disappeared in the rattling water, while the valley echoed and shouted again with the sound.

She sat in despair among the blankets, hugging tight her pale-blue cloak. Romero strode straight back to the cabin.

"Now you stay here with me," he said.

She was furious. Her blue eyes met his. They were like two demons watching one another. In his face, beyond a sort of unrelieved gloom, was a demonish desire for death.

He saw her looking round the cabin, scheming. He saw her eyes on his rifle. He took the gun and went out with it. Returning, he pulled out her saddle, carried it to the tarn, and threw it in. Then he fetched his own saddle, and did the same.

"Now will you go away?" he said, looking at her with a smile.

She debated within herself whether to coax him and wheedle him. But she knew he was already beyond it. She sat among her blankets in a frozen sort of despair, hard as hard ice with anger.

He did the chores, and disappeared with the gun. She got up in her blue pyjamas, huddled in her cloak, and stood in the doorway. The dark-green pool was motionless again, the stony slopes were pallid and frozen. Shadow still lay, like an after-death, deep in this valley. Always in the distance she saw the horses feeding. If she could catch one! The brilliant yellow sun was half-way down the mountain. It was nine o'clock.

All day she was alone, and she was frightened. What she was frightened of she didn't know. Perhaps the crackling in the dark spruce wood. Perhaps just the savage, heartless wildness of the mountains. But all day she sat in the sun in the doorway of the cabin, watching, watching for hope. And all the time her bowels were cramped with fear.

She saw a dark spot that probably was a bear, roving across the pale grassy slope in the far distance, in the sun.

When, in the afternoon, she saw Romero approaching, with silent suddenness, carrying his gun and a dead deer, the cramp in her bowels relaxed, then became colder. She dreaded him with a cold dread.

"There is deer-meat," he said, throwing the dead doe at her feet.

"You don't want to go away from here," he said. "This is a nice place."

She shrank into the cabin.

"Come into the sun," he said, following her. She looked up at him with hostile, frightened eyes.

"Come into the sun," he repeated, taking her gently by the arm, in a powerful grasp.

175

She knew it was useless to rebel. Quietly he led her out, and seated himself in the doorway, holding her still by the arm.

"In the sun it is warm," he said. "Look, this is a nice place. You are such a pretty white woman, why do you want to act mean to me? Isn't this a nice place? Come! Come here! It is sure warm here."

He drew her to him, and in spite of her stony resistance, he took her cloak from her, holding her in her thin blue pyjamas.

"You sure are a pretty little white woman, small and pretty," he said. "You sure won't act mean to me-you don't want to, I know you don't."

She, stony and powerless, had to submit to him. The sun shone on her white, delicate skin.

"I sure don't mind hell fire," he said. "After this."

A queer, luxurious good humour seemed to possess him again. But though outwardly she was powerless, inwardly she resisted him, absolutely and stonily.

When later he was leaving her again, she said to him suddenly:

"You think you can conquer me this way. But you can't. You can never conquer me."

He stood arrested, looking back at her, with many emotions conflicting in his face-wonder, surprise, a touch of horror, and an unconscious pain that crumpled his face till it was like a mask. Then he went out without saying a word, hung the dead deer on a bough, and started to flay it. While he was at this butcher's work, the sun sank and cold night came on again.

"You see," he said to her as he crouched, cooking the supper, "I ain't going to let you go. I reckon you called to me in the night, and I've some right. If you want to fix it up right now with me, and say you want to be with me, we'll fix it up now and go down to the ranch to-morrow and get married or whatever you want. But you've got to say you want to be with me. Else I shall stay right here, till something happens."

She waited a while before she answered:

"I don't want to be with anybody against my will. I don't dislike you; at least, I didn't, till you tried to put your will over mine. I won't have anybody's will put over me. You can't succeed. Nobody could. You can never get me under your will. And you won't have long to try, because soon they will send someone to look for me."

He pondered this last, and she regretted having said it. Then, sombre, he bent to the cooking again.

He could not conquer her, however much he violated her. Because her spirit was hard and flawless as a diamond. But he could shatter her. This she knew. Much more, and she would be shattered.

In a sombre, violent excess he tried to expend his desire for her. And she was racked with an agony, and felt each time she would die. Because, in some peculiar way, he had got hold of her, some unrealised part of her which she never wished to realise. Racked with a burning, tearing anguish, she felt that the thread of her being would break, and she would die. The burning heat that racked her inwardly.

If only, only she could be alone again, cool and intact! If only she could recover herself again, cool and intact! Would she ever, ever, ever be able to bear herself again?

Even now she did not hate him. It was beyond that. Like some racking, hot doom. Personally he hardly existed.

The next day he would not let her have any fire, because of attracting attention with the smoke. It was a grey day, and she was cold. He stayed round, and heated soup on the petrol stove. She lay motionless in the blankets.

And in the afternoon she pulled the clothes over her head and broke into tears. She had never really cried in her life. He dragged the blankets away and looked to see what was shaking her. She sobbed in helpless hysterics. He covered her over again and went outside, looking at the mountains, where clouds were dragging and leaving a little snow. It was a violent, windy, horrible day, the evil of winter rushing down.

She cried for hours. And after this a great silence came between them. They were two people who had died. He did not touch her any more. In the night she lay and shivered like a dying dog. She felt that her very shivering would rupture something in her body, and she would die.

At last she had to speak.

"Could you make a fire? I am so cold," she said, with chattering teeth.

"Want to come over here?" came his voice.

"I would rather you made me a fire," she said, her teeth knocking together and chopping the words in two.

He got up and kindled a fire. At last the warmth spread, and she could sleep.

The next day was still chilly, with some wind. But the sun shone. He went about in silence, with a dead-looking face. It was now so dreary and so like death she wished he would do anything rather than continue in this negation. If now he asked her to go down with him to the world and marry him, she would do it. What did it matter? Nothing mattered any more.

But he would not ask her. His desire was dead and heavy like ice within him. He kept watch around the house.

On the fourth day as she sat huddled in the doorway in the sun, hugged in a blanket, she saw two horsemen come over the crest of the grassy slope-small figures. She gave a cry. He looked up quickly and saw the figures. The men had dismounted. They were looking for the trail.

"They are looking for me," she said.

"Muy bien," he answered in Spanish.

He went and fetched his gun, and sat with it across his knees.

"Oh!" she said. "Don't shoot!"

He looked across at her.

"Why?" he said. "You like staying with me?"

"No," she said. "But don't shoot."

"I ain't going to Pen," he said.

"You won't have to go to Pen," she said. "Don't shoot!"

"I'm going to shoot," he muttered.

And straightaway he kneeled and took very careful aim. The Princess sat on in an agony of helplessness and hopelessness.

The shot rang out. In an instant she saw one of the horses on the pale grassy slope rear and go rolling down. The man had dropped in the grass, and was invisible. The second man clambered on his horse, and on that precipitous place went at a gallop in a long swerve towards the nearest spruce tree cover. Bang! Bang! went Romero's shots. But each time he missed, and the running horse leaped like a kangaroo towards cover.

It was hidden. Romero now got behind a rock; tense silence, in the brilliant sunshine. The Princess sat on the bunk inside the cabin, crouching, paralysed. For hours, it seemed, Romero knelt behind this rock, in his black shirt, bare-headed, watching. He had a beautiful, alert figure. The Princess wondered why she did not feel sorry for him. But her spirit was hard and cold, her heart could not melt. Though now she would have called him to her, with love.

But no, she did not love him. She would never love any man. Never! It was fixed and sealed in her, almost vindictively.

Suddenly she was so startled she almost fell from the bunk. A shot rang out quite close from behind the cabin. Romero leaped straight into the air, his arms fell outstretched, turning as he leaped. And even while he was in the air, a second shot rang out, and he fell with a crash, squirming, his hands clutching the earth towards the cabin door.

The Princess sat absolutely motionless, transfixed, staring at the prostrate figure. In a few moments the figure of a man in the Forest Service appeared close to the house; a young man in a broad-brimmed Stetson hat, dark flannel shirt, and riding-boots, carrying a gun. He strode over to the prostrate figure.

"Got you, Romero!" he said aloud. And he turned the dead man over. There was already a little pool of blood where Romero's breast had been.

"H'm!" said the Forest Service man. "Guess I got you nearer than I thought."

And he squatted there, staring at the dead man.

The distant calling of his comrade aroused him. He stood up.

"Hullo, Bill!" he shouted. "Yep! Got him! Yep! Done him in, apparently."

The second man rode out of the forest on a grey horse. He had a ruddy, kind face, and round brown eyes, dilated with dismay.

"He's not passed out?" he asked anxiously.

"Looks like it," said the first young man coolly.

The second dismounted and bent over the body. Then he stood up again, and nodded.

"Yea-a!" he said. "He's done in all right. It's him all right, boy! It's Domingo Romero."

"Yep! I know it!" replied the other.

Then in perplexity he turned and looked into the cabin, where the Princess squatted, staring with big owl eyes from her red blanket.

"Hello!" he said, coming towards the hut. And he took his hat off. Oh, the sense of ridicule she felt! Though he did not mean any.

But she could not speak, no matter what she felt.

"What'd this man start firing for?" he asked.

She fumbled for words, with numb lips.

"He had gone out of his mind!" she said, with solemn, stammering conviction.

"Good Lord! You mean to say he'd gone out of his mind? Whew! That's pretty awful! That explains it then. H'm!"

He accepted the explanation without more ado.

With some difficulty they succeeded in getting the Princess down to the ranch. But she, too, was not a little mad.

"I'm not quite sure where I am," she said to Mrs. Wilkieson, as she lay in bed. "Do you mind explaining?"

Mrs. Wilkieson explained tactfully.

"Oh yes!" said the Princess. "I remember. And I had an accident in the mountains, didn't I? Didn't we meet a man who'd gone mad, and who shot my horse from under me?"

"Yes, you met a man who had gone out of his mind."

The real affair was hushed up. The Princess departed east in a fortnight's time, in Miss Cummins's care. Apparently she had recovered herself entirely. She was the Princess, and a virgin intact.

But her bobbed hair was grey at the temples, and her eyes were a little mad. She was slightly crazy.

"Since my accident in the mountains, when a man went mad and shot my horse from under me, and my guide had to shoot him dead, I have never felt quite myself."

So she put it.

Later, she married an elderly man, and seemed pleased.

THE WITCH A LA MODE

When Bernard Coutts alighted at East Croydon he knew he was tempting Providence.

"I may just as well," he said to himself, "stay the night here, where I am used to the place, as go to London. I can't get to Connie's forlorn spot to-night, and I'm tired to death, so why shouldn't I do what is easiest?"

He gave his luggage to a porter.

Again, as he faced the approaching tram-car: "I don't see why I shouldn't go down to Purley. I shall just be in time for tea."

Each of these concessions to his desires he made against his conscience. But beneath his sense of shame his spirit exulted.

It was an evening of March. In the dark hollow below Crown Hill the buildings accumulated, bearing the black bulk of the church tower up into the rolling and smoking sunset.

"I know it so well," he thought. "And love it," he confessed secretly in his heart.

The car ran on familiarly. The young man listened for the swish, watched for the striking of the blue splash overhead, at the bracket. The sudden fervour of the spark, splashed out of the mere wire, pleased him.

"Where does it come from?" he asked himself, and a spark struck bright again. He smiled a little, roused.

The day was dying out. One by one the arc lamps fluttered or leaped alight, the strand of copper overhead glistened against the dark sky that now was deepening to the colour of monkshood. The tram-car dipped as it ran, seeming to exult. As it came clear of the houses, the young man, looking west, saw the evening star advance, a bright thing approaching from a long way off, as if it had been bathing in the surf of the daylight, and now was walking shorewards to the night. He greeted the naked star with a bow of the head, his heart surging as the car leaped.

"It seems to be greeting me across the sky-the star," he said, amused by his own vanity.

Above the colouring of the afterglow the blade of the new moon hung sharp and keen. Something recoiled in him.

"It is like a knife to be used at a sacrifice," he said to himself. Then, secretly: "I wonder for whom?"

He refused to answer this question, but he had the sense of Constance, his betrothed, waiting for him in the Vicarage in the north. He closed his eyes.

Soon the car was running full-tilt from the shadow to the fume of yellow light at the terminus, where shop on shop and lamp beyond lamp heaped golden fire on the floor of the blue night. The car, like an eager dog, ran in home, sniffing with pleasure the fume of lights.

Coutts flung away uphill. He had forgotten he was tired. From the distance he could distinguish the house, by the broad white cloth of alyssum flowers that hung down the garden walls. He ran up the steep path to the door, smelling the hyacinths in the dark, watching for the pale fluttering of daffodils and the steadier show of white crocuses on the grassy banks.

Mrs. Braithwaite herself opened the door to him.

"There!" she exclaimed. "I expected you. I had your card saying you would cross from Dieppe to-day. You wouldn't make up your mind to come here, not till the last minute, would you? No-that's what I expected. You know where to put your things; I don't think we've altered anything in the last year."

Mrs. Braithwaite chattered on, laughing all the time. She was a young widow, whose husband had been dead two years. Of medium height, sanguine in complexion and temper, there was a rich oily glisten in her skin and in her black hair, suggesting the flesh of a nut. She was dressed for the evening in a long gown of soft, mole-coloured satin.

"Of course, I'm delighted you've come," she said at last, lapsing into conventional politeness, and then, seeing his eyes, she began to laugh at her attempt at formality.

She let Coutts into a small, very warm room that had a dark, foreign sheen, owing to the black of the curtains and hangings covered thick with glistening Indian embroidery, and to the sleekness of some Indian ware. A rosy old gentleman, with exquisite white hair and side-whiskers, got up shakily and stretched out his hand. His cordial expression of welcome was rendered strange by a puzzled, wondering look of old age, and by a certain stiffness of his countenance, which now would only render a few expressions. He wrung the newcomer's hand heartily, his manner contrasting pathetically with his bowed and trembling form.

"Oh, why-why, yes, it's Mr. Coutts! H'm-ay. Well, and how are you-h'm? Sit down, sit down." The old man rose again, bowing, waving the young man into a chair. "Ay! well, and how are you? . . . What? Have some tea-come on, come along; here's the tray. Laura, ring for fresh tea for Mr. Courts. But I will do it." He suddenly remembered his old gallantry, forgot his age and uncertainty. Fumbling, he rose to go to the bell-pull.

"It's done, Pater-the tea will be in a minute," said his daughter in high, distinct tones. Mr. Cleveland sank with relief into his chair.

"You know, I'm beginning to be troubled with rheumatism," he explained in confidential tones. Mrs. Braithwaite glanced at the young man and smiled. The old gentleman babbled and chattered. He had no knowledge of his guest beyond the fact of his presence; Coutts might have been any other young man, for all his host was aware.

"You didn't tell us you were going away. Why didn't you?" asked Laura, in her distinct tones, between laughing and reproach. Coutts looked at her ironically, so that she fidgeted with some crumbs on the cloth.

"I don't know," he said. "Why do we do things?"

"I'm sure I don't know. Why do we? Because we want to, I suppose," and she ended again with a little run of laughter. Things were so amusing, and she was so healthy.

"Why do we do things, Pater?" she suddenly asked in a loud voice, glancing with a little chuckle of laughter at Coutts.

181

"Ay-why do we do things? What things?" said the old man, beginning to laugh with his daughter.

"Why, any of the things that we do."

"Eh? Oh!" The old man was illuminated, and delighted. "Well, now, that's a difficult question. I remember, when I was a little younger, we used to discuss Free Will-got very hot about it . . ." He laughed, and Laura laughed, then said, in a high voice:

"Oh! Free Will! We shall really think you're passé, if you revive that, Pater."

Mr. Cleveland looked puzzled for a moment. Then, as if answering a conundrum, he repeated:

"Why do we do things? Now, why do we do things?"

"I suppose," he said, in all good faith, "it's because we can't help it-eh? What?"

Laura laughed. Coutts showed his teeth in a smile.

"That's what I think, Pater," she said loudly.

"And are you still engaged to your Constance?" she asked of Coutts, with a touch of mockery this time. Coutts nodded.

"And how is she?" asked the widow.

"I believe she is very well-unless my delay has upset her," said Coutts, his tongue between his teeth. It hurt him to give pain to his fiancée, and yet he did it wilfully.

"Do you know, she always reminds me of a Bunbury-I call her your Miss Bunbury," Laura laughed.

Coutts did not answer.

"We missed you so much when you first went away," Laura began, reestablishing the proprieties.

"Thank you," he said. She began to laugh wickedly.

"On Friday evenings," she said, adding quickly: "Oh, and this is Friday evening, and Winifred is coming just as she used to-how long ago?-ten months?"

"Ten months," Coutts corroborated.

"Did you quarrel with Winifred?" she asked suddenly.

"Winifred never quarrels," he answered.

"I don't believe she does. Then why did you go away? You are such a puzzle to me, you know-and I shall never rest till I have had it out of you. Do you mind?"

"I like it," he said, quietly, flashing a laugh at her.

She laughed, then settled herself in a dignified, serious way.

"No, I can't make you out at all-nor can I Winifred. You are a pair! But it's you who are the real wonder. When are you going to be married?"

"I don't know-When I am sufficiently well off."

"I asked Winifred to come to-night," Laura confessed. The eyes of the man and woman met.

"Why is she so ironic to me?-does she really like me?" Coutts asked of himself. But Laura looked too bonny and jolly to be fretted by love.

"And Winifred won't tell me a word," she said.

"There is nothing to tell," he replied.

182

Laura looked at him closely for a few moments. Then she rose and left the room.

Presently there arrived a German lady with whom Coutts was slightly acquainted. At about half-past seven came Winifred Varley. Courts heard the courtly old gentleman welcoming her in the hall, heard her low voice in answer. When she entered, and saw him, he knew it was a shock to her, though she hid it as well as she could. He suffered too. After hesitating for a second in the doorway, she came forward, shook hands without speaking, only looking at him with rather frightened blue eyes. She was of medium height, sturdy in build. Her face was white and impassive, without the least trace of a smile. She was a blonde of twenty-eight, dressed in a white gown just short enough not to touch the ground. Her throat was solid and strong, her arms heavy and white and beautiful, her blue eyes heavy with unacknowledged passion. When she had turned away from Coutts, she flushed vividly. He could see the pink in her arms and throat, and he flushed in answer.

"That blush would hurt her," he said to himself, wincing.

"I did not expect to see you," she said, with a reedy timbre of voice, as if her throat were half-closed. It made his nerves tingle.

"No-nor I you. At least . . ." He ended indefinitely.

"You have come down from Yorkshire?" she asked. Apparently she was cold and self-possessed. Yorkshire meant the Rectory where his fiancée lived; he felt the sting of sarcasm.

"No," he answered. "I am on my way there."

There was a moment's pause. Unable to resolve the situation, she turned abruptly to her hostess.

"Shall we play, then?"

They adjourned to the drawing-room. It was a large room upholstered in dull yellow. The chimney-piece took Coutts' attention. He knew it perfectly well, but this evening it had a new, lustrous fascination. Over the mellow marble of the mantel rose an immense mirror, very translucent and deep, like deep grey water. Before this mirror, shining white as moons on a soft grey sky, was a pair of statues in alabaster, two feet high. Both were nude figures. They glistened under the side lamps, rose clean and distinct from their pedestals. The Venus leaned slightly forward, as if anticipating someone's coming. Her attitude of suspense made the young man stiffen. He could see the clean suavity of her shoulders and waist reflected white on the deep mirror. She shone, catching, as she leaned forward, the glow of the lamp on her lustrous marble loins.

Laura played Brahms; the delicate, winsome German lady played Chopin; Winifred played on her violin a Grieg sonata, to Laura's accompaniment. After having sung twice, Coutts listened to the music. Unable to criticise, he listened till he was intoxicated. Winifred, as she played, swayed slightly. He watched the strong forward thrust of her neck, the powerful and angry striking of her arm. He could see the outline of her figure; she wore no corsets; and he found her of resolute independent build. Again he glanced at the Venus bending in suspense. Winifred was blonde with a solid whiteness, an isolated woman.

All the evening, little was said, save by Laura. Miss Syfurt exclaimed continually: "Oh, that is fine! You play gra-and, Miss Varley, don't you know. If I could play the violin-ah! the violin!"

It was not later than ten o'clock when Winifred and Miss Syfurt rose to go, the former to Croydon, the latter to Ewell.

"We can go by car together to West Croydon," said the German lady, gleefully, as if she were a child. She was a frail, excitable little woman of forty, naïve and innocent. She gazed with bright brown eyes of admiration on Coutts.

"Yes, I am glad," he answered.

He took up Winifred's violin, and the three proceeded downhill to the tram-terminus. There a car was on the point of departure. They hurried forward. Miss Syfurt mounted the step. Coutts waited for Winifred. The conductor called:

"Come along, please, if you're going."

"No," said Winifred. "I prefer to walk this stage."

"We can walk from West Croydon," said Coutts.

The conductor rang the bell.

"Aren't you coming?" cried the frail, excitable little lady, from the footboard. "Aren't you coming?-Oh!"

"I walk from West Croydon every day; I prefer to walk here, in the quiet," said Winifred.

"Aw! aren't you coming with me?" cried the little lady, quite frightened. She stepped back, in supplication, towards the footboard. The conductor impatiently buzzed the bell. The car started forward, Miss Syfurt staggered, was caught by the conductor.

"Aw!" she cried, holding her hand out to the two who stood on the road, and breaking almost into tears of disappointment. As the tram darted forward she clutched at her hat. In a moment she was out of sight.

Coutts stood wounded to the quick by this pain given to the frail, child-like lady.

"We may as well," said Winifred, "walk over the hill to 'The Swan'." Her note had that intense reedy quality which always set the man on edge; it was the note of her anger, or, more often, of her tortured sense of discord. The two turned away, to climb the hill again. He carried the violin; for a long time neither spoke.

"Ah, how I hate her, how I hate her!" he repeated in his heart. He winced repeatedly at the thought of Miss Syfurt's little cry of supplication. He was in a position where he was not himself, and he hated her for putting him there, forgetting that it was he who had come, like a moth to the candle. For half a mile he walked on, his head carried stiffly, his face set, his heart twisted with painful emotion. And all the time, as she plodded, head down, beside him, his blood beat with hate of her, drawn to her, repelled by her.

At last, on the high-up, naked down, they came upon those meaningless pavements that run through the grass, waiting for the houses to line them. The two were thrust up into the night above the little flowering of the lamps in the valley. In front was the daze of light from London, rising midway to the zenith, just fainter than the stars. Across the valley, on the blackness of the opposite hill, little groups of lights like gnats seemed to be floating in the darkness. Orion was heeled over the West. Below, in a cleft in the night, the long, low garland of arc lamps strung down the Brighton Road, where now and then the golden tram-cars flew along the track, passing each other with a faint, angry sound.

"It is a year last Monday since we came over here," said Winifred, as they stopped to look about them.

"I remember-but I didn't know it was then," he said. There was a touch of hardness in his voice. "I don't remember our dates."

After a wait, she said in a very low, passionate tones:

"It is a beautiful night."

"The moon has set, and the evening star," he answered; "both were out as I came down."

She glanced swiftly at him to see if this speech was a bit of symbolism. He was looking across the valley with a set face. Very slightly, by an inch or two, she nestled towards him.

"Yes," she said, half-stubborn, half-pleading. "But the night is a very fine one, for all that."

"Yes," he replied, unwillingly.

Thus, after months of separation, they dove-tailed into the same love and hate.

"You are staying down here?" she asked at length, in a forced voice. She never intruded a hair's-breadth on the most trifling privacy; in which she was Laura's antithesis; so that this question was almost an impertinence for her. He felt her shrink.

"Till the morning-then Yorkshire," he said cruelly.

He hated it that she could not bear outspokenness.

At that moment a train across the valley threaded the opposite darkness with its gold thread. The valley re-echoed with vague threat. The two watched the express, like a gold-and-black snake, curve and dive seawards into the night. He turned, saw her full, fine face tilted up to him. It showed pale, distinct, and firm, very near to him. He shut his eyes and shivered.

"I hate trains," he said, impulsively.

"Why?" she asked, with a curious, tender little smile that caressed, as it were, his emotion towards her.

"I don't know; they pitch one about here and there . . ."

"I thought," she said, with faint irony, "that you preferred change."

"I do like life. But now I should like to be nailed to something, if it were only a cross."

She laughed sharply, and said, with keen sarcasm:

"Is it so difficult, then, to let yourself be nailed to a cross? I thought the difficulty lay in getting free."

He ignored her sarcasm on his engagement.

"There is nothing now that matters," he said, adding quickly, to forestall her: "Of course I'm wild when dinner's late, and so on; but . . . apart from those things . . . nothing seems to matter."

185

She was silent.

"One goes on-remains in office, so to speak; and life's all right-only, it doesn't seem to matter."

"This does sound like complaining of trouble because you've got none," she laughed.

"Trouble . . ." he repeated. "No, I don't suppose I've got any. Vexation, which most folk call trouble; but something I really grieve about in my soul-no, nothing. I wish I had."

She laughed again sharply; but he perceived in her laughter a little keen despair.

"I find a lucky pebble. I think, now I'll throw it over my left shoulder, and wish. So I spit over my little finger, and throw the white pebble behind me, and then, when I want to wish, I'm done. I say to myself: 'Wish,' and myself says back: 'I don't want anything.' I say again: 'Wish, you fool,' but I'm as dumb of wishes as a newt. And then, because it rather frightens me, I say in a hurry: 'A million of money.' Do you know what to wish for when you see the new moon?"

She laughed quickly.

"I think so," she said. "But my wish varies."

"I wish mine did," he said, whimsically lugubrious.

She took his hand in a little impulse of love.

They walked hand in hand on the ridge of the down, bunches of lights shining below, the big radiance of London advancing like a wonder in front.

"You know . . ." he began, then stopped.

"I don't . . ." she ironically urged.

"Do you want to?" he laughed.

"Yes; one is never at peace with oneself till one understands."

"Understands what?" he asked brutally. He knew she meant that she wanted to understand the situation he and she were in.

"How to resolve the discord," she said, balking the issue. He would have liked her to say: "What you want of me."

"Your foggy weather of symbolism, as usual," he said.

"The fog is not of symbols," she replied, in her metallic voice of displeasure. "It may be symbols are candles in a fog."

"I prefer my fog without candles. I'm the fog, eh? Then I'll blow out your candle, and you'll see me better. Your candles of speech, symbols and so forth, only lead you more wrong. I'm going to wander blind, and go by instinct, like a moth that flies and settles on the wooden box his mate is shut up in."

"Isn't it an ignis fatuus you are flying after, at that rate?" she said.

"Maybe, for if I breathe outwards, in the positive movement towards you, you move off. If I draw in a vacant sigh of soulfulness, you flow nearly to my lips."

"This is a very interesting symbol," she said, with sharp sarcasm.

He hated her, truly. She hated him. Yet they held hands fast as they walked.

"We are just the same as we were a year ago," he laughed. But he hated her, for all his laughter.

When, at the "Swan and Sugar-Loaf", they mounted the car, she climbed to the top, in spite of the sharp night. They nestled side by side, shoulders caressing, and all the time that they ran under the round lamps neither spoke.

At the gate of a small house in a dark tree-lined street, both waited a moment. From her garden leaned an almond tree whose buds, early this year, glistened in the light of the street lamp, with theatrical effect. He broke off a twig.

"I always remember this tree," he said; "how I used to feel sorry for it when it was full out, and so lively, at midnight in the lamplight. I thought it must be tired."

"Will you come in?" she asked tenderly.

"I did get a room in town," he answered, following her.

She opened the door with her latch-key, showing him, as usual, into the drawing-room. Everything was just the same; cold in colouring, warm in appointment; ivory-coloured walls, blond, polished floor, with thick ivory-coloured rugs; three deep arm-chairs in pale amber, with large cushions; a big black piano, a violin-stand beside it; and the room very warm with a clear red fire, the brass shining hot. Coutts, according to his habit, lit the piano-candles and lowered the blinds.

"I say," he said; "this is a variation from your line!"

He pointed to a bowl of magnificent scarlet anemones that stood on the piano.

"Why?" she asked, pausing in arranging her hair at the small mirror.

"On the piano!" he admonished.

"Only while the table was in use," she smiled, glancing at the litter of papers that covered her table.

"And then-red flowers!" he said.

"Oh, I thought they were such a fine piece of colour," she replied.

"I would have wagered you would buy freesias," he said.

"Why?" she smiled. He pleased her thus.

"Well-for their cream and gold and restrained, bruised purple, and their scent. I can't believe you bought scentless flowers!"

"What!" She went forward, bent over the flowers.

"I had not noticed," she said, smiling curiously, "that they were scentless."

She touched the velvet black centres.

"Would you have bought them had you noticed?" he asked.

She thought for a moment, curiously.

"I don't know . . . probably I should not."

"You would never buy scentless flowers," he averred. "Any more than you'd love a man because he was handsome."

"I did not know," she smiled. She was pleased.

The housekeeper entered with a lamp, which she set on a stand.

"You will illuminate me?" he said to Winifred. It was her habit to talk to him by candle-light.

187

"I have thought about you-now I will look at you," she said quietly, smiling.

"I see-To confirm your conclusions?" he asked.

Her eyes lifted quickly in acknowledgment of his guess.

"That is so," she replied.

"Then," he said, "I'll wash my hands."

He ran upstairs. The sense of freedom, of intimacy, was very fascinating. As he washed, the little everyday action of twining his hands in the lather set him suddenly considering his other love. At her house he was always polite and formal; gentlemanly, in short. With Connie he felt the old, manly superiority; he was the knight, strong and tender, she was the beautiful maiden with a touch of God on her brow. He kissed her, he softened and selected his speech for her, he forbore from being the greater part of himself. She was his betrothed, his wife, his queen, whom he loved to idealise, and for whom he carefully modified himself. She should rule him later on-that part of him which was hers. But he loved her, too, with a pitying, tender love. He thought of her tears upon her pillow in the northern Rectory, and he bit his lip, held his breath under the strain of the situation. Vaguely he knew she would bore him. And Winifred fascinated him. He and she really played with fire. In her house, he was roused and keen. But she was not, and never could be, frank. So he was not frank, even to himself. Saying nothing, betraying nothing, immediately they were together they began the same game. Each shuddered, each defenceless and exposed, hated the other by turns. Yet they came together again. Coutts felt a vague fear of Winifred. She was intense and unnatural-and he became unnatural and intense, beside her.

When he came downstairs she was fingering the piano from the score of "Walküre".

"First wash in England," he announced, looking at his hands. She laughed swiftly. Impatient herself of the slightest soil, his indifference to temporary grubbiness amused her.

He was a tall, bony man, with small hands and feet. His features were rough and rather ugly, but his smile was taking. She was always fascinated by the changes in him. His eyes, particularly, seemed quite different at times; sometimes hard, insolent, blue; sometimes dark, full of warmth and tenderness; sometimes flaring like an animal's.

He sank wearily into a chair.

"My chair," he said, as if to himself.

She bowed her head. Of compact physique, uncorseted, her figure bowed richly to the piano. He watched the shallow concave between her shoulders, marvelling at its rich solidity. She let one arm fall loose, he looked at the shadows in the dimples of her elbow. Slowly smiling a look of brooding affection, of acknowledgment upon him for a forgetful moment, she said:

"And what have you done lately?"

"Simply nothing," he replied quietly. "For all that these months have been so full of variety, I think they will sink out of my life; they will evaporate and leave no result; I shall forget them."

Her blue eyes were dark and heavy upon him, watching. She did not answer. He smiled faintly at her.

"And you?" he said, at length.

"With me it is different," she said quietly.

"You sit with your crystal," he laughed.

"While you tilt . . ." She hung on her ending.

He laughed, sighed, and they were quiet awhile.

"I've got such a skinful of heavy visions, they come sweating through my dreams," he said.

"Whom have you read?" She smiled.

"Meredith. Very healthy," he laughed.

She laughed quickly at being caught.

"Now, have you found out all you want?" he asked.

"Oh, no," she cried with full throat.

"Well, finish, at any rate. I'm not diseased. How are you?"

"But . . . but . . ." she stumbled on doggedly. "What do you intend to do?"

He hardened the line of his mouth and eyes, only to retort with immediate lightness:

"Just go on."

This was their battlefield: she could not understand how he could marry: it seemed almost monstrous to her; she fought against his marriage. She looked up at him, witch-like, from under bent brows. Her eyes were dark blue and heavy. He shivered, shrank with pain. She was so cruel to that other, common, everyday part of him.

"I wonder you dare go on like it," she said.

"Why dare?" he replied. "What's the odds?"

"I don't know," she answered, in deep, bitter displeasure.

"And I don't care," he said.

"But . . ." she continued, slowly, gravely pressing the point: "You know what you intend to do."

"Marry-settle-be a good husband, good father, partner in the business; get fat, be an amiable gentleman-Q.E.F."

"Very good," she said, deep and final.

"Thank you."

"I did not congratulate you," she said.

"Ah!" His voice tailed off into sadness and self-mistrust. Meanwhile she watched him heavily. He did not mind being scrutinised: it flattered him.

"Yes, it is, or may be, very good," she began; "but why all this?-why?"

"And why not? And why?-Because I want to."

He could not leave it thus flippantly.

"You know, Winifred, we should only drive each other into insanity, you and I: become abnormal."

"Well," she said, "and even so, why the other?"

"My marriage?-I don't know. Instinct."

"One has so many instincts," she laughed bitterly.

That was a new idea to him.

She raised her arms, stretched them above her head, in a weary gesture.

They were fine, strong arms. They reminded Coutts of Euripides' "Bacchae": white, round arms, long arms. The lifting of her arms lifted her breasts. She dropped suddenly as if inert, lolling her arms against the cushions.

"I really don't see why you should be," she said drearily, though always with a touch of a sneer, "why we should always-be fighting."

"Oh, yes, you do," he replied. It was a deadlock which he could not sustain.

"Besides," he laughed, "it's your fault."

"Am I so bad?" she sneered.

"Worse," he said.

"But"-she moved irritably-"is this to the point?"

"What point?" he answered; then, smiling: "You know you only like a wild-goose chase."

"I do," she answered plaintively. "I miss you very much. You snatch things from the Kobolds for me."

"Exactly," he said in a biting tone. "Exactly! That's what you want me for. I am to be your crystal, your 'genius'. My length of blood and bone you don't care a rap for. Ah, yes, you like me for a crystal-glass, to see things in: to hold up to the light. I'm a blessed Lady-of-Shalott looking-glass for you."

"You talk to me," she said, dashing his fervour, "of my fog of symbols!"

"Ah, well, if so, 'tis your own asking."

"I did not know it." She looked at him coldly. She was angry.

"No," he said.

Again, they hated each other.

"The old ancients," he laughed, "gave the gods the suet and intestines: at least, I believe so. They ate the rest. You shouldn't be a goddess."

"I wonder, among your rectory acquaintances, you haven't learned better manners," she answered in cold contempt. He closed his eyes, lying back in his chair, his legs sprawled towards her.

"I suppose we're civilised savages," he said sadly. All was silent. At last, opening his eyes again, he said: "I shall have to be going directly, Winifred; it is past eleven . . ." Then the appeal in his voice changed to laughter. "Though I know I shall be winding through all the Addios in 'Traviata' before you can set me travelling." He smiled gently at her, then closed his eyes once more, conscious of deep, but vague, suffering. She lay in her chair, her face averted, rosily, towards the fire. Without glancing at her he was aware of the white approach of her throat towards her breast. He seemed to perceive her with another, unknown sense that acted all over his body. She lay perfectly still and warm in the fire-glow. He was dimly aware that he suffered.

"Yes," she said at length; "if we were linked together we should only destroy each other."

He started, hearing her admit, for the first time, this point of which he was so sure.

"You should never marry anyone," he said.

"And you," she asked in irony, "must offer your head to harness and be bridled and driven?"

190

"There's the makings of quite a good, respectable trotter in me," he laughed. "Don't you see it's what I want to be?"

"I'm not sure," she laughed in return.

"I think so."

They were silent for a time. The white lamp burned steadily as moonlight, the red fire like sunset; there was no stir or flicker.

"And what of you?" he asked.

She crooned a faint, tired laugh.

"If you are jetsam, as you say you are," she answered, "I am flotsam. I shall lie stranded."

"Nay," he pleaded. "When were you wrecked?"

She laughed quickly, with a sound like a tinkle of tears.

"Oh, dear Winifred!" he cried despairingly.

She lifted her arms towards him, hiding her face between them, looking up through the white closure with dark, uncanny eyes, like an invocation. His breast lifted towards her uptilted arms. He shuddered, shut his eyes, held himself rigid. He heard her drop her arms heavily.

"I must go," he said in a dull voice.

The rapidly-chasing quivers that ran in tremors down the front of his body and limbs made him stretch himself, stretch hard.

"Yes," she assented gravely; "you must go."

He turned to her. Again looking up darkly, from under her lowered brows, she lifted her hands like small white orchids towards him. Without knowing, he gripped her wrists with a grasp that circled his blood-red nails with white rims.

"Good-bye," he said, looking down at her. She made a small, moaning noise in her throat, lifting her face so that it came open and near to him like a suddenly-risen flower, borne on a strong white stalk. She seemed to extend, to fill the world, to become atmosphere and all. He did not know what he was doing. He was bending forward, his mouth on hers, her arms round his neck, and his own hands, still fastened on to her wrists, almost bursting the blood under his nails with the intensity of their grip. They remained for a few moments thus, rigid. Then, weary of the strain, she relaxed. She turned her face, offered him her throat, white, hard, and rich, below the ear. Stooping still lower, so that he quivered in every fibre at the strain, he laid his mouth to the kiss. In the intense silence, he heard the deep, dull pulsing of her blood, and a minute click of a spark within the lamp.

Then he drew her from the chair up to him. She came, arms always round his neck, till at last she lay along his breast as he stood, feet planted wide, clasping her tight, his mouth on her neck. She turned suddenly to meet his full, red mouth in a kiss. He felt his moustache prick back into his lips. It was the first kiss she had genuinely given. Dazed, he was conscious of the throb of one great pulse, as if his whole body were a heart that contracted in throbs. He felt, with an intolerable ache, as if he, the heart, were setting the pulse in her, in the very night, so that everything beat from the throb of his overstrained, bursting body.

The hurt became so great it brought him out of the reeling stage to

191

distinct consciousness. She clipped her lips, drew them away, leaving him her throat. Already she had had enough. He opened his eyes as he bent with his mouth on her neck, and was startled; there stood the objects of the room, stark; there, close below his eyes, were the half-sunk lashes of the woman, swooning on her unnatural ebb of passion. He saw her thus, knew that she wanted no more of him than that kiss. And the heavy form of this woman hung upon him. His whole body ached like a swollen vein, with heavy intensity, while his heart grew dead with misery and despair. This woman gave him anguish and a cutting-short like death; to the other woman he was false. As he shivered with suffering, he opened his eyes again, and caught sight of the pure ivory of the lamp. His heart flashed with rage.

A sudden involuntary blow of his foot, and he sent the lamp-stand spinning. The lamp leaped off, fell with a smash on the fair, polished floor. Instantly a bluish hedge of flame quivered, leaped up before them. She had lightened her hold round his neck, and buried her face against his throat. The flame veered at her, blue, with a yellow tongue that licked her dress and her arm. Convulsive, she clutched him, almost strangled him, though she made no sound.

He gathered her up and bore her heavily out of the room. Slipping from her clasp, he brought his arms down her form, crushing the starting blaze of her dress. His face was singed. Staring at her, he could scarcely see her.

"I am not hurt," she cried. "But you?"

The housekeeper was coming; the flames were sinking and waving up in the drawing-room. He broke away from Winifred, threw one of the great woollen rugs on to the flame, then stood a moment looking at the darkness.

Winifred caught at him as he passed her.

"No, no," he answered, as he fumbled for the latch. "I'm not hurt. Clumsy fool I am-clumsy fool!"

In another instant he was gone, running with burning-red hands held out blindly, down the street.

192

THINGS

They were true idealists, from New England. But that is some time ago: before the War. Several years before the War they met and married; he a tall, keen-eyed young man from Connecticut, she a smallish, demure, Puritan-looking young woman from Massachusetts. They both had a little money. Not much, however. Even added together it didn't make three thousand dollars a year. Still-they were free. Free!

Ah!-freedom! To be free to live one's own life! To be twenty-five and twenty-seven, a pair of true idealists with a mutual love of beauty and an inclination towards "Indian thought"-meaning, alas! Mrs Besant-and an income a little under three thousand dollars a year! But what is money? All one wishes to do is to live a full and beautiful life. In Europe, of course, right at the fountain-head of tradition. It might possibly be done in America: in New England, for example. But at forfeiture of a certain amount of "beauty". True beauty takes a long time to mature. The baroque is only half-beautiful, half-matured. No, the real silver bloom, the real golden-sweet bouquet of beauty, had its roots in the Renaissance, not in any later or shallower period.

Therefore, the two idealists, who were married in New Haven, sailed at once to Paris: Paris of the old days. They had a studio apartment on the Boulevard Montparnasse, and they became real Parisians, in the old, delightful sense, not in the modern, vulgar. It was the shimmer of the pure impressionists, Monet and his followers, the world seen in terms of pure light, light broken and unbroken. How lovely! How lovely! how lovely the nights, the river, the mornings in the old streets and by the flower-stalls and the book-stalls, the afternoons up on Montmartre or in the Tuileries, the evenings on the boulevards!

They both painted, but not desperately. Art had not taken them by the throat, and they did not take Art by the throat. They painted: that's all. They knew people-nice people, if possible, though one had to take them mixed. And they were happy.

Yet it seems as if human beings must set their claws in something. To be "free", to be "living a full and beautiful life", you must, alas! be attached to something. A "full and beautiful life" means a tight attachment to something-at least, it is so for all idealists-or else a certain boredom supervenes; there is a certain waving of loose ends upon the air, like the waving, yearning tendrils of the vine that spread and rotate, seeking something to clutch, something up which to climb towards the necessary sun. Finding nothing, the vine can only trail, half-fulfilled, upon the ground. Such is freedom-a clutching of the right pole. And human beings are all vines. But especially the idealist. He is a vine, and he needs to clutch and climb. And he despises the man who is a mere potato, or turnip, or lump of wood.

Our idealists were frightfully happy, but they were all the time reaching out for something to cotton on to. At first, Paris was enough. They explored

193

Paris thoroughly. And they learned French till they almost felt like French people, they could speak it so glibly.

Still, you know, you never talk French with your soul. It can't be done. And though it's very thrilling, at first, talking in French to clever Frenchmen-they seem so much cleverer than oneself-still, in the long run, it is not satisfying. The endlessly clever materialism of the French leaves you cold, in the end, gives a sense of barrenness and incompatibility with true New England depth. So our two idealists felt.

They turned away from France-but ever so gently. France had disappointed them. "We've loved it, and we've got a great deal out of it. But after a while, a considerable while-several years, in fact-Paris leaves one feeling disappointed. It hasn't quite got what one wants."

"But Paris isn't France."

"No, perhaps not. France is quite different from Paris. And France is lovely-quite lovely. But to us, though we love it, it doesn't say a great deal."

So, when the War came, the idealists moved to Italy. And they loved Italy. They found it beautiful, and more poignant than France. It seemed much nearer to the New England conception of beauty: something pure, and full of sympathy, without the materialism and the cynicism of the French. The two idealists seemed to breathe their own true air in Italy.

And in Italy, much more than in Paris, they felt they could thrill to the teachings of the Buddha. They entered the swelling stream of modern Buddhistic emotion, and they read the books, and they practised meditation, and they deliberately set themselves to eliminate from their own souls greed, pain, and sorrow. They did not realise-yet-that Buddha's very eagerness to free himself from pain and sorrow is in itself a sort of greed. No, they dreamed of a perfect world, from which all greed, and nearly all pain, and a great deal of sorrow, were eliminated.

But America entered the War, so the two idealists had to help. They did hospital work. And though their experience made them realise more than ever that greed, pain, and sorrow should be eliminated from the world, nevertheless, the Buddhism, or the theosophy, didn't emerge very triumphant from the long crisis. Somehow, somewhere, in some part of themselves, they felt that greed, pain and sorrow would never be eliminated, because most people don't care about eliminating them, and never will care. Our idealists were far too Western to think of abandoning all the world to damnation while they saved their two selves. They were far too unselfish to sit tight under a bho-tree and reach Nirvana in a mere couple.

It was more than that, though. They simply hadn't enough Sitzfleisch to squat under a bho-tree and get to Nirvana by contemplating anything, least of all their own navel. If the whole wide world was not going to be saved, they, personally, were not so very keen on being saved just by themselves. No, it would be so lonesome. They were New Englanders, so it must be all or nothing. Greed, pain and sorrow must either be eliminated from all the world,or else what was the use of eliminating them from oneself? No use at all! One was just a victim.

And so-although they still loved "Indian thought", and felt very tender about it: well, to go back to our metaphor, the pole up which the green and anxious vines had clambered so far now proved dry-rotten. It snapped, and the vines came slowly subsiding to earth again. There was no crack and crash. The vines held themselves up by their own foliage, for a while. But they subsided. The beanstalk of "Indian thought" had given way before Jack had climbed off the tip of it to a further world.

They subsided with a slow rustle back to earth again. But they made no outcry. They were again "disappointed". But they never admitted it. "Indian thought" had let them down. But they never complained. Even to one another they never said a word. But they were disappointed, faintly but deeply disillusioned, and they both knew it. But the knowledge was tacit.

And they still had so much in their lives. They still had Italy-dear Italy. And they still had freedom, the priceless treasure. And they still had so much "beauty". About the fullness of their lives they were not quite so sure. They had one little boy, whom they loved as parents should love their children, but whom they wisely refrained from fastening upon, to build their lives on him. No, no, they must live their own lives! They still had strength of mind to know that.

But they were now no longer so very young. Twenty-five and twenty-seven had become thirty-five and thirty-seven. And though they had had a very wonderful time in Europe, and though they still loved Italy-dear Italy!-yet: they were disappointed. They had got a lot out of it: oh, a very great deal indeed! Still, it hadn't given them quite, not quite, what they had expected; Europe was lovely, but it was dead. Living in Europe, you were living on the past. And Europeans, with all their superficial charm, were not really charming. They were materialistic, they had no real soul. They just did not understand the inner urge of the spirit, because the inner urge was dead in them; they were all survivals. There, that was the truth about Europeans: they were survivals, with no more getting ahead in them.

It was another bean-pole, another vine-support crumbled under the green life of the vine. And very bitter it was, this time. For up the old tree-trunk of Europe the green vine had been clambering silently for more than ten years, ten hugely important years, the years of real living. The two idealists had lived in Europe, lived on Europe and on European life and European things as vines in an everlasting vineyard.

They had made their home here: a home such as you could never make in America. Their watchword had been "beauty". They had rented, the last four years, the second floor of an old Palazzo on the Arno, and here they had all their "things". And they derived a profound satisfaction from their apartment: the lofty, silent, ancient rooms with windows on the river, with glistening, dark-red floors, and the beautiful furniture that the idealists had "picked up".

Yes, unknown to themselves, the lives of the idealists had been running with a fierce swiftness horizontally, all the time. They had become tense, fierce hunters of "things" for their home. While their soul was climbing up to the sun of old European culture or old Indian thought, their passions were running horizontally, clutching at "things". Of course, they did not buy the things for the things' sakes, but for the sake of "beauty". They

195

looked upon their home as a place entirely furnished by loveliness, not by "things" at all. Valerie had some very lovely curtains at the windows of the long salotto, looking on the river: curtains of queer ancient material that looked like finely knitted silk, most beautifully faded down from vermilion and orange and gold and black, to a sheer soft glow. Valerie hardly ever came into the salotto without mentally falling on her knees before the curtains. "Chartres!" she said. "To me they are Chartres!" And Melville never turned and looked at his sixteenth-century Venetian book-case, with its two or three dozen of choice books, without feeling his marrow stir in his bones. The holy of holies!

The child silently, almost sinisterly, avoided any rude contact with these ancient monuments of furniture, as if they had been nests of sleeping cobras, or that "thing" most perilous to the touch-the Ark of the Covenant. His childish awe was silent, and cold, but final.

Still, a couple of New England idealists cannot live merely on the bygone glory of their furniture. At least, one couple could not. They got used to the marvellous Bologna cupboard, they got used to the wonderful Venetian book-case, and the books, and the Siena curtains and bronzes, and the lovely sofas and side-tables and chairs they had "picked up" in Paris. Oh, they had been picking things up since the first day they landed in Europe. And they were still at it. It is the last interest Europe can offer to an outsider: or to an insider either.

When people came, and were thrilled by the Melville interior, then Valerie and Erasmus felt they had not lived in vain: that they still were living. But in the long mornings, when Erasmus was desultorily working at Renaissance Florentine literature, and Valerie was attending to the apartment; and in the long hours after lunch; and in the long, usually very cold and oppressive evenings in the ancient palazzo: then the halo died from around the furniture, and the things became things, lumps of matter that just stood there or hung there, ad infinitum, and said nothing; and Valerie and Erasmus almost hated them. The glow of beauty, like every other glow, dies down unless it is fed. The idealists still dearly loved their things. But they had got them. And the sad fact is, things that glow vividly while you're getting them go almost quite cold after a year or two. Unless, of course, people envy you them very much, and the museums are pining for them. And the Melvilles' "things", though very good, were not quite as good as that.

So the glow gradually went out of everything, out of Europe, out of Italy-"the Italians are dears"-even out of that marvellous apartment on the Arno. "Why, if I had this apartment I'd never, never even want to go out of doors! It's too lovely and perfect." That was something, of course, to hear that.

And yet Valerie and Erasmus went out of doors; they even went out to get away from its ancient, cold-floored, stone-heavy silence and dead dignity. "We're living on the past, you know, Dick," said Valerie to her husband. She called him Dick.

They were grimly hanging on. They did not like to give in. They did not like to own up that they were through. For twelve years, now, they had

196

been "free" people, living a "full and beautiful life". And America for twelve years had been their anathema, the Sodom and Gomorrah of industrial materialism.

It wasn't easy to own that you were "through". They hated to admit that they wanted to go back. But at last, reluctantly, they decided to go, "for the boy's sake". "We can't bear to leave Europe. But Peter is an American, so he had better look at America while he's young." The Melvilles had an entirely English accent and manner-almost-a little Italian and French here and there.

They left Europe behind, but they took as much of it along with them as possible. Several van-loads, as a matter of fact. All those adorable and irreplaceable "things". And all arrived in New York, idealists, child, and the huge bulk of Europe they had lugged along.

Valerie had dreamed of a pleasant apartment, perhaps on Riverside Drive, where it was not so expensive as east of Fifth Avenue, and where all their wonderful things would look marvellous. She and Erasmus house-hunted. But, alas! their income was quite under three thousand dollars a year. They found-well, everybody knows what they found. Two small rooms and a kitchenette, and don't let us unpack a thing!

The chunk of Europe which they had bitten off went into a warehouse, at fifty dollars a month. And they sat in two small rooms and a kitchenette, and wondered why they'd done it.

Erasmus, of course, ought to get a job. This was what was written on the wall, and what they both pretended not to see. But it had been the strange, vague threat that the Statue of Liberty had always held over them: "Thou shalt get a job!" Erasmus had the tickets, as they say. A scholastic career was still possible for him. He had taken his exams, brilliantly at Yale, and had kept up his "researches" all the time he had been in Europe.

But both he and Valerie shuddered. A scholastic career! The scholastic world! The American scholastic world! Shudder upon shudder! Give up their freedom, their full and beautiful life? Never! Never! Erasmus would be forty next birthday.

The "things" remained in warehouse. Valerie went to look at them. It cost her a dollar an hour, and horrid pangs. The "things", poor things, looked a bit shabby and wretched in that warehouse.

However, New York was not all America. There was the great clean West. So the Melvilles went West, with Peter, but without the things. They tried living the simple life in the mountains. But doing their own chores became almost a nightmare. "Things" are all very well to look at, but it's awful handling them, even when they're beautiful. To be the slave of hideous things, to keep a stove going, cook meals, wash dishes, carry water, and clean floors: pure horror of sordid anti-life!

In the cabin on the mountains Valerie dreamed of Florence, the lost apartment; and her Bologna cupboard and Louis Quinze chairs, above all, her "Chartres" curtains, stored in New York-and costing fifty dollars a month.

A millionaire friend came to the rescue, offering them a cottage on the Californian coast-California! Where the new soul is to be born in man.

With joy the idealists moved a little farther west, catching at new vine-props of hope.

And finding them straws! The millionaire cottage was perfectly equipped. It was perhaps as labour-savingly perfect as is possible: electric heating and cooking, a white-and-pearl-enamelled kitchen, nothing to make dirt except the human being himself. In an hour or so the idealists had got through their chores. They were "free"-free to hear the great Pacific pounding the coast, and to feel a new soul filling their bodies.

Alas! the Pacific pounded the coast with hideous brutality, brute force itself! And the new soul, instead of sweetly stealing into their bodies, seemed only meanly to gnaw the old soul out of their bodies. To feel you are under the fist of the most blind and crunching brute force: to feel that your cherished idealist's soul is being gnawed out of you, and only irritation left in place of it: well, it isn't good enough.

After about nine months the idealists departed from the Californian west. It had been a great experience; they were glad to have had it. But, in the long run, the West was not the place for them, and they knew it. No, the people who wanted new souls had better get them. They, Valerie and Erasmus Melville, would like to develop the old soul a little further. Anyway, they had not felt any influx of new soul on the Californian coast. On the contrary.

So, with a slight hole in their material capital, they returned to Massachusetts and paid a visit to Valerie's parents, taking the boy along. The grandparents welcomed the child-poor expatriated boy-and were rather cold to Valerie, but really cold to Erasmus. Valerie's mother definitely said to Valerie one day that Erasmus ought to take a job, so that Valerie could live decently. Valerie haughtily reminded her mother of the beautiful apartment on the Arno, and the "wonderful" things in store in New York, and of the "marvellous and satisfying life" she and Erasmus had led. Valerie's mother said that she didn't think her daughter's life looked so very marvellous at present: homeless, with a husband idle at the age of forty, a child to educate, and a dwindling capital, looked the reverse of marvellous to her. Let Erasmus take some post in one of the universities.

"What post? What university?" interrupted Valerie.

"That could be found, considering your father's connections and Erasmus's qualifications," replied Valerie's mother. "And you could get all your valuable things out of store, and have a really lovely home, which everybody in America would be proud to visit. As it is, your furniture is eating up your income, and you are living like rats in a hole, with nowhere to go to."

This was very true. Valerie was beginning to pine for a home, with her "things". Of course, she could have sold her furniture for a substantial sum. But nothing would have induced her to. Whatever else passed away-religions, cultures, continents, and hopes-Valerie would never part from the "things" which she and Erasmus had collected with such passion. To these she was nailed.

But she and Erasmus still would not give up that freedom, that full and beautiful life they had so believed in. Erasmus cursed America. He did not want to earn a living. He panted for Europe.

Leaving the boy in charge of Valerie's parents, the two idealists once more set off for Europe. In New York they paid two dollars and looked for a brief, bitter hour at their "things". They sailed "student class"-that is, third. Their income now was less than two thousand dollars, instead of three. And they made straight for Paris-cheap Paris.

They found Europe, this time, a complete failure. "We have returned like dogs to our vomit," said Erasmus; "but the vomit has staled in the meantime." He found he couldn't stand Europe. It irritated every nerve in his body. He hated America, too. But America at least was a darn sight better than this miserable, dirt-eating continent; which was by no means cheap any more, either.

Valerie, with her heart on her things-she had really burned to get them out of that warehouse, where they had stood now for three years, eating up two thousand dollars-wrote to her mother she thought Erasmus would come back if he could get some suitable work in America. Erasmus, in a state of frustration bordering on rage and insanity, just went round Italy in a poverty-stricken fashion, his coat-cuffs frayed, hating everything with intensity. And when a post was found for him in Cleveland University, to teach French, Italian, and Spanish literature, his eyes grew more beady, and his long, queer face grew sharper and more rat-like with utter baffled fury. He was forty, and the job was upon him.

"I think you'd better accept, dear. You don't care for Europe any longer. As you say, it's dead and finished. They offer us a house on the College lot, and mother says there's room in it for all our things. I think we'd better cable 'Accept'."

He glowered at her like a cornered rat. One almost expected to see rat's whiskers twitching at the sides of the sharp nose.

"Shall I send the cablegram?" she asked.

"Send it!" he blurted.

And she went out and sent it.

He was a changed man, quieter, much less irritable. A load was off him. He was inside the cage.

But when he looked at the furnaces of Cleveland, vast and like the greatest of black forests, with red- and white-hot cascades of gushing metal, and tiny gnomes of men, and terrific noises, gigantic, he said to Valerie:

"Say what you like, Valerie, this is the biggest thing the modern world has to show."

And when they were in their up-to-date little house on the college lot of Cleveland University, and that woe-begone débris of Europe-Bologna cupboard, Venice book-shelves, Ravenna bishop's chair, Louis Quinze side-tables, "Chartres" curtains, Siena bronze lamps-all were arrayed, and all looked perfectly out of keeping, and therefore very impressive; and when the idealists had had a bunch of gaping people in, and Erasmus had showed off in his best European manner, but still quite cordial and American, and Valerie had been most ladylike, but for all that "we prefer

199

America"; then Erasmus said, looking at her with the queer sharp eyes of a rat:-

"Europe's the mayonnaise all right, but America supplies the good old lobster-what?"

"Every time!" she said, with satisfaction.

And he peered at her. He was in the cage: but it was safe inside. And she, evidently, was her real self at last. She had got the goods. Yet round his nose was a queer, evil, scholastic look, of pure scepticism. But he liked lobster.

THE END

www.ingramcontent.com/pod-product-compliance
Lightning Source LLC
Chambersburg PA
CBHW031959170626
46807CB00006B/2567